did I mention I MISS YOU?

ALSO BY ESTELLE MASKAME

Did I Mention I Love You?

Did I Mention I Need You?

did I mention I MISS YOU?

ESTELLE MASKAME

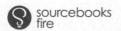

sourcebooks fire

Published by Sourcebooks Fire, an imprint of Sourcebooks, Inc.
P.O. Box 4410, Naperville, Illinois 60567-4410
(630) 961-3900
Fax: (630) 961-2168
www.sourcebooks.com

Originally published in 2016 in the United Kingdom by Black & White Publishing
Ltd.

Library of Congress Cataloging-in-Publication data is on file with the publisher.

Printed and bound in the United States of America.
VP 10 9 8 7 6 5 4 3 2

To all the Tyler and Edens out there. No te rindas.

chapter

1

The water is cold, yet that doesn't stop me from wading into it, up to my ankles. I have my Converse in my hands, the laces wrapped around my fingers, and the wind is picking up, like it always does. It's too dark to see far out over the low waves, but I can still hear the ocean crashing and rolling around me, and I almost forget that I'm not alone. There's also the sound of fireworks, of laughter and voices, celebration and joy. I almost forget, just for a second, that it's the Fourth of July.

A girl runs past me, through the water, disrupting the calm and gentle flow. A guy is chasing her. Boyfriend probably. He accidentally splashes water on me as he brushes past, laughing out loud before he grasps the girl and pulls her against him. I'm grinding my teeth together before I even realize it, my grip around my laces tightening. These people are around my age, but I've never seen them before. They've most likely come from out of town, from a neighboring city, to celebrate the good old Fourth of July in Santa Monica. I don't know why. The Fourth of July isn't anything spectacular here. Fireworks are illegal, which is the second-biggest bullshit law I've ever encountered in my entire life after it being illegal to pump your own gas back in Oregon. So there are no fireworks, only those from Marina del Rey to the south and Pacific Palisades to the north, which are visible from here. It's after 9:00 p.m., so both displays have just begun. The colors light up the sky far in the distance, small and out of focus, but they're enough to satisfy the tourists and the locals.

The couple is kissing in the water now, in the dark beneath the lights of Pacific Park. I turn my eyes away. I begin to walk away from the pier, wading slowly through the Pacific Ocean as I distance myself from all of the Fourth of July commotion. The crowds are much thicker up on the pier. Down here on the beach, it's not so busy, so I have room to breathe. This year, I'm just not feeling the whole Independence Day excitement. There are too many memories attached to this day that I don't want to remember, so I keep walking, farther and farther along the coast.

I only stop when Rachael calls my name. Until then, I'd forgotten that I'd been waiting for her to return. I turn around in the water to face my best friend as she half leaps, half jogs across the sand toward me. There's an American flag bandana wrapped around her head, and she comes bearing two sundaes. She disappeared to get them almost fifteen minutes ago from Soda Jerks, which, like most stores along the pier, is open later than usual tonight.

"I got there just as they were closing up," Rachael says, slightly breathless. Her ponytail swings around her shoulders as she comes to a stop and hands me the sundae, but not before she licks some of the overflowing ice cream from her index finger.

I edge out of the water to join her, thanking her with a smile. I've been quiet all night, and I still can't bring myself to pretend that I'm okay, that I'm happy just like everyone else. So I take my sundae in my free hand, my red Converse still in the other—red footwear is as patriotic as I'm going to be today—and quickly run my eyes over the ice cream. It's called the Toboggan Carousel, named after the Toboggan Carousel itself, which is inside the Looff Hippodrome up on the pier. Soda Jerks is on the corner. In the three weeks that I've been home, we've stopped by for sundaes more than once. In fact, I think we take an ice cream break more often than we take a coffee break these days. It's much more comforting.

"Everyone's up on the pier," Rachael reminds me. "Maybe we should head up." She sounds almost cautious as she makes the suggestion, like she's expecting me to immediately cut her off and say no. She drops her blue eyes to her ice cream and scoops up a quick mouthful.

As she swallows, my eyes drift over her shoulder to the pier. The Pacific Wheel is performing its annual Fourth of July show, where its thousands of LED lights are programmed to display transitioning sequences of red, blue, and white. It started just after eight, at sunset. The two of us watched it for a few minutes when it first began, but it got very boring very fast. Holding back a sigh, I shift my gaze to the boardwalk instead. It's way too overcrowded, yet I don't want to test Rachael's patience any more than I already have, so I say sure.

We turn back and head across the beach, weaving our way through the people spending their evening down on the sand and eating our sundaes in silence from our plastic to-go trays. After a few minutes, I stop to slip my Chucks back on.

"Did you find Meghan yet?"

I glance up at Rachael as I finish tucking my laces in. "Haven't seen her." In all honesty, I haven't been looking. Although Meghan is an old friend of ours, that's all she seems to be. Nothing more than that. But she's home for the summer too, so Rachael's making the effort to reunite our former trio.

"We'll find her eventually," she says, and then changes the subject almost immediately by adding, "Did you hear that the wheel is apparently programmed to the beat of a Daft Punk song this year?" She skips ahead of me, twirling on the sand and shimmying back over. She reaches for my free hand and pulls me toward her, her grin wide and dazzling as she spins me around. Unwillingly, I dance a little with her despite the fact that there's no music. "Another summer, another year."

I pull back from her, careful not to drop my sundae, and study her. She's still swaying, still dancing to whatever song is in her head. As she closes her eyes and twirls again, I think about her words. *Another summer, another year.* It's our fourth summer of being best friends, and despite a slight falling-out last year, we're as close as ever. I wasn't sure if she'd ever forgive me for the mistakes I made, but she did. She let it go because there were more important things to focus on. Like supplying me with ice cream and taking me on road trips around the state to distract me, to make me feel better. Desperate times call for best friends. Yet despite the fact that the time came for me to head off to Chicago, where I've spent the past year surviving my freshman year of college, we've still remained best friends. Now that I'm back in Santa Monica until September, we have months to hang out together.

"You're drawing a crowd," I tell her. The corners of my lips pull up into a smile as her eyes flash open, her cheeks flushing with color as she glances around. Several people nearby have been observing her silent dancing.

"Time to make our getaway," she whispers. She latches on to my wrist and starts to run. She yanks me across the beach, kicking up the sand beneath our feet, our laughter echoing around us as I'm given no option but to dash off with her. We don't run far: only a few yards, far enough to get her away from her spectators. "In my defense," she huffs, "you're allowed to look like an idiot on the Fourth of July. It's a rite of passage. It emphasizes the fact that we're a free nation. You know, 'cause we can do whatever the hell we want."

I wish that was the case. If there's anything I've learned in my nineteen years of breathing, it's that we most certainly *can't* do whatever the hell we want. We can't pump our own gas. We can't set off fireworks. We can't touch the Hollywood Sign. We can't trespass. We can't kiss our stepbrothers. Of course, we *can* do these things, but only if we're brave enough to face the consequences.

I roll my eyes at Rachael as we ascend the steps up to the pier, the music from Pacific Park gradually growing louder the nearer we get. The Ferris wheel is still flashing with red, blue, and white. The rest of the amusement park is also illuminated, albeit not so patriotically. We're weaving our way through the upper parking lot on the pier, squeezing between cars that are parked way too close to one another, when I spot Jamie. He's with his girlfriend, Jen. They've been dating for almost two years now. Over by the corner of the lot, he has her pressed against the passenger door of an old, beat-up Chevy. They're making out. Obviously.

Rachael must notice them too because she pauses alongside me and rests her eyes on the scene. "I've heard he's quite the troublemaker," she murmurs. "He's like a miniature blond version of his brother when he was that age."

I flash Rachael a warning glance almost automatically at the mention of Jamie's brother, who is also my stepbrother. We don't talk about him. We don't ever say his name. Not anymore. Rachael must notice the sudden tautness in my face and the sharpness in my expression because she mouths a quick apology, pressing a hand to her lips.

Relaxing only slightly, I look back at Jamie and Jen. Still kissing. Rolling my eyes, I toss the remainder of my ice cream into a nearby trash can and then clear my throat, yelling, "Don't forget to breathe, Jay!"

Rachael laughs under her breath and playfully swats my shoulder. When Jamie glances up, eyes glossy and hair ruffled, I lift my hand and wave. Unlike Jen, who almost collapses dead with embarrassment the second she spots me, my stepbrother only gets pissed off, the same way he always does whenever I try to say anything to him.

"Screw you, Eden!" he yells across the lot, his coarse voice echoing around the cars. Grabbing Jen's hand, he turns and yanks her away in the opposite direction. He's most likely been trying his best to avoid Ella the entire night, because when all you want to do is hook up with your girlfriend, the last person you want spotting you is your mom.

"He's still not talking to you?" Rachael asks once she stops snickering.

Shrugging, I start to walk again as I run my fingers through the ends of my hair. It's just below my shoulders now. I cut it back in the winter. "Last week he asked me to pass him the salt," I say. "Does that count?"

"No."

"Then I guess we're still not talking."

Jamie doesn't particularly like me. Not because he's seventeen with a serious attitude problem that came out of nowhere last year, but because he's still sickened by me. And his eldest brother. He can't stand either of us, and no matter how many times I've tried to convince him that there's nothing to worry about anymore, he refuses to believe me. He usually storms away and slams a door or two in the process. I sigh with frustration as Rachael and I head over onto the main boardwalk, which is still as busy as it was hours ago. There are a lot of parents with small kids and a lot of dogs dodging the mass of strollers. There are many young couples, like the pair back on the beach in the water. I can't bear to look at any of them. Their interlocked hands and exchanged smiles only make my stomach knot. And not in the way that creates butterflies, but in the way that physically hurts. Today of all days, here of all places, I despise each and every couple I see.

Rachael stops after a few minutes to talk to some girls she knows who were in her grade back in school. I remember them only vaguely from passing them years ago at school or at the promenade. I don't know them. They know me though. Everyone knows me now. I'm *her*. I'm *that* Eden. I'm the girl who gets disgusted glances cast over me, the girl who gets sneered and snickered at wherever I go. It's exactly what's happening now. No matter how hard I try to offer these girls a warm smile, it's not returned. Both of them fire me a sharp glare out of the corners of their eyes and then angle their bodies away from me, stepping closer to Rachael and cutting me out completely. I press my lips together and fold my arms across my chest, kicking at the wood beneath my feet as I wait for Rachael to finish.

This is exactly the kind of thing that happens every time I come home to Santa Monica. People don't like me here anymore. They think I'm crazy and weird. There are the few exceptions, like my mom and Rachael, but that's about it. Everyone else just judges, but they don't know the full story. I think the worst was when I came home for Thanksgiving last year. It was the first time I'd come home since I left for college in September, and word had gotten out and had spread like wildfire in the mere month that I'd been gone. So by Thanksgiving, everyone knew. At first, I didn't know what was going on and why things were suddenly different. I didn't know why Katy Vance, a girl I shared some classes with back in school, put her head down and turned in the opposite direction when I waved at her. I didn't know why the young girl ringing me up at the grocery store laughed to her coworker as I was leaving. I had no idea why these things were happening, not until I was at LAX on Sunday waiting to board my flight back to Chicago, when a girl I'd never seen before in my life quietly asked, "You're the girl that dated her stepbrother, right?"

Rachael doesn't talk for long. She glances warily over at me every few seconds, as though she's trying to gauge if I'm okay or not, and even though I shrug nonchalantly back at her in an attempt to reassure her that I'm fine, she still cuts the conversation short and tells the girls that we need to be somewhere, even when we don't. That's why I love Rachael.

"For that, I'm never talking to them ever again," she states once the girls walk off, her voice firm as she throws her sundae into the trash and hooks her arm around mine instead. She spins me around toward Pacific Park so fast that it almost gives me whiplash.

"Honestly, it really doesn't bother me anymore," I try to tell her. We're drifting through the crowd, which actually doesn't feel that thick once we're in the middle of it, and I let her pull me along the boardwalk.

"Uh-huh," Rachael says in a distant voice, like she doesn't believe me.

I'm about to argue my point even further, telling her that *no, really, it's fine, I'm fine, everything is fine* when Jake Maxwell comes barreling toward us out of nowhere, sliding in front of us and stopping us dead in our tracks. He's an even older friend of ours than Meghan is, and we've already spoken to him tonight. That was a couple of hours ago, when he was still mostly sober. The same can't be said now.

"There you guys are!" Reaching for our interlocked arms, he separates us and takes both our hands in his and places a sloppy kiss on our knuckles.

It's the first summer that Jake has come home from Ohio, and when we bumped into him earlier, for the first time in two years, I was surprised to discover that he's now sporting a beard, and he was even more surprised to discover that I still live in Santa Monica. He had somehow gotten the idea that I'd moved back to Portland like forever ago. But beard and assumptions aside, he hasn't changed. He's still a player, and he still doesn't try to deny it. When Rachael asked him how he was doing, he told us that it's not going too great because both of his two girlfriends have recently broken up with him and he still doesn't know why. I could guess.

"Where do you keep getting the beer from?" Rachael asks, wrinkling her nose as she pulls her hand back from him. She has to talk over the sound of the music from Pacific Park.

"TJ's," Jake says. And in case we don't know, he rolls his eyes over his shoulder and points his thumb behind him, off into the distance. TJ has a condo over on the beachfront. Like I could forget. My stomach flips at the thought of it. "He's sent me over here to round up the troops. Are you guys down for an after-party?" His eyes light up at the word, and I find it hard to take the tank top he's wearing seriously. It's got an eagle on it. Placed on top of the US flag. With "FREEDOM" written in block capitals across the eagle's feet. It looks totally ridiculous, yet not as crazy as the temporary eagle tattoo he's wearing proudly on his left cheek. I'm starting to wonder if he's buzzed from more than just beer.

"After-party?" Rachael echoes. We exchange glances, and I can tell immediately by the look in her eyes that she wants to go.

"Yeah, yeah," Jake says, his voice overflowing with enthusiasm as he grins down at us through that beard. "There are kegs and everything! C'mon, it's the Fourth of July. It's the weekend. You gotta come. Everyone's gonna be there."

I frown. "Everyone?"

"TJ and all the guys, Meghan and Jared are already there, Dean's coming by later, I think Austin Camer—"

"Pass."

Jake stops talking, and his grin twists into a frustrated scowl. He looks to Rachael, and for a brief second, I'm convinced he's just rolled his eyes. When his bloodshot gaze focuses back on me, he gently grabs my shoulders and shakes me around. "Helloooooo?" He dramatically widens his eyes and pretends to scour every inch of my face. "Where the hell is Eden? I know I haven't seen you in a hell of a long time, but surely you can't have gotten *this* boring in the space of two years."

Not amused, I shrug Jake's grip off me and take a step back. Because he isn't a close friend, or even a friend at all anymore, I don't find it necessary to explain myself to him. So I remain quiet, staring at my Chucks and hoping Rachael will step in and save me as usual, because that's all I've been depending on lately. I depend on Rachael to remind everyone that I never actually *dated* my stepbrother and that I never will. I depend on her to get me out of situations where I might bump into Dean. I'm still too ashamed to face him after everything that's happened, and I doubt he wants to deal with me either. No one wants to deal with their ex-girlfriend, especially one that cheated on them.

As always, I hear Rachael tell Jake, "She doesn't have to go if she doesn't want to." I continue to stare at my shoes, because every time Rachael comes to my rescue, I feel more weak and pathetic than I did before.

"You can't avoid him forever," Jake mutters. He suddenly sounds solemn, and when I glance up, I realize it's completely obvious to him that the reason I don't want to go to this party is because of Dean. I can't deny it, so I only shrug and rub at my temple. There's a second reason, of course. It's the same reason my stomach has tightened. I've only been to TJ's once before and that was three years ago. I was there with my stepbrother. Tonight of all nights, I really don't want to head over there again.

"You go," I tell Rachael after a moment of silence. I can see how desperately she wants to go to this party, yet I know she'll most likely turn down the offer so that she doesn't leave me alone. That's what best friends do. But best friends also compromise, and Rachael has already spent her evening making sure that I've been okay on this dreaded day, so I really do want her to go have some fun. After all, the Fourth has landed on a Friday this year, so many people are making the best of it. Rachael should too. "I'll go find Ella or something."

"I don't mind."

Even I can tell she's lying. "Rachael," I say firmly. I nod toward TJ's condo, off in the distance. "Go."

Apprehensive, she pinches her lower lip between her fingers and contemplates for a short while. She's hardly wearing any makeup tonight—she rarely does anymore—so she barely looks seventeen, let alone twenty. "Are you sure?"

"Positive."

"Then c'mon!" Jake explodes, his overbearing grin back on his eagle-tattooed face as he reaches for Rachael's hand, yanking her toward him. "We've got a party to get to!" He begins to pull my best friend away, hauling her down the boardwalk and away from the pier. She manages to wave good-bye just before they disappear through the crowd.

Once they're gone, I check my phone for the time. It's after nine thirty. Both the Marina del Rey and Pacific Palisades firework displays are over by now, so there are a lot of people beginning to head home. I pull up Ella's number and start to call her. Unfortunately, my mom and her boyfriend Jack are both working this evening, so only my dad and my stepmom are out here at the pier to celebrate the Fourth of July. They're my ride home, so I've got no choice but to hunt them down. But what's even more unfortunate is that it's Dad's turn to have me stay with him for the week. That's the worst part about having divorced parents: being thrown back and forth between different houses. I hate staying at Dad's place, and he loathes it even more than I do, mostly because it's unbearably tense and awkward. Like Jamie, Dad only talks to me if it's absolutely necessary.

Ella's phone is busy, so the call is directed straight to her voice mail. I don't leave a message, hanging up as quick as I can. I dread the idea of having to call Dad instead. I scroll through my contacts, pulling up his number and calling it. It starts to ring, and I feel myself frowning as I wait for his coarse voice to answer.

Yet as I'm standing on the boardwalk with people milling around me and with my phone pressed to my ear, something catches my attention. It's my youngest stepbrother, Chase. He's lingering over by the Bubba Gump restaurant, and he's alone when he shouldn't be. Despite this, he doesn't look too worried, mostly just bored as he paces slowly back and forth.

I hang up the call to my dad and head over toward Chase. He spots me as I approach, and instantly he stops pacing and looks sheepish.

"Where are your friends?" I ask once I reach him. I glance around, searching for a group of soon-to-be-freshmen boys, but I can't see them.

Chase twirls a thick lock of his blond hair around his index finger. "They took the bus to Venice, but I didn't go because—"

"Because your mom told you not to leave the pier," I finish, and he nods. Chase's friendship circle is prone to getting into trouble often, but he's smart enough to know when not to break the rules. I'm sure his friends' parents don't want their kids sneaking off to Venice on the Fourth of July. It'll be pretty rowdy over there right now, so I'm glad Chase has chosen to stay behind. "Wanna hang with me?"

"Sure."

Throwing my arm over his shoulders, I pull him away from the restaurant and head toward Pacific Park. Chase loves the arcade games, but before we've even gotten within a twenty-foot radius of the Playland Arcade, I have to stop when my phone starts to ring. Picking up the call, I have to take a second to prepare myself mentally before I can answer when I see that it is Dad calling me.

"What did you want?" is how he greets me, his tone gruff. That's all it ever is these days.

Angling my body slightly away from Chase, I press my phone closer against my ear and tell him, "Nothing. I was just wondering where you guys were."

"Well, we're at the car," Dad shoots back, as though he expects me to know that already. "Hurry up and meet us here unless you want to ask your brother to give you a ride home instead, which I'm sure he won't."

With that, I promptly hang up the call without saying anything more. Most of my phone calls with Dad usually end like this, with one of us hanging up midsentence, and most of our conversations face-to-face end with one of us storming off. Admittedly, I'm the one who hangs up the calls. Dad's the one who storms out.

"Who was that?" Chase asks when I turn back around.

"We're heading home," I answer, dodging the question. It's not that Chase is oblivious to the fact that my dad and I can't stand each other, it's just easier to keep the tension to a minimum when it comes to the rest of the family. Whatever our family is. I pull Chase even closer against me as I spin him around once again, this time away from Pacific Park and back toward the city. "No arcade games tonight."

Chase shrugs under my arm. "I already won a load of tickets earlier."

"How many?"

Slightly smug, he grins and pats the back pockets of his shorts. They're both bulging with yellow tickets. "Over seven hundred."

"No way. What are you saving them for?"

"I'm trying to reach two thousand."

We talk about the arcade games and the tickets and the Pacific Wheel and the fireworks and Venice as we make our way back down the boardwalk and out onto Ocean Avenue, tracing our steps back to the car. Parking on the Fourth is always incredibly hectic, and after spending a couple of minutes disagreeing with Chase over where Dad parked earlier in the evening, I realize I'm the one who's wrong. We're not parked north of the freeway like I'd thought, but south of it, down on Pico Boulevard and Third Street. It's a good half mile away, so we walk pretty damn fast. Dad doesn't like to be kept waiting. Ever.

The Lexus is wedged against the sidewalk between two other cars when we reach it ten minutes later, and to my surprise, Dad's standing outside the car. Arms folded across his chest, foot tapping the ground impatiently, same ugly expression as always.

"Oh, good, you found your brother," he says sharply, emphasizing that final word. Jamie and Chase are never simply just "Jamie and Chase" anymore. For the past year, Dad has always referred to them as my brothers as though to prove a point. Jamie hates it as much as I do, whereas I don't think Chase has picked up on it at all.

I keep my cool and instead of growing irritated at Dad's disdainful tone, I glance over his shoulder, resting my eyes on Ella. She's in the passenger seat of the car, her body turned away from the window, but I can still see her phone pressed to her ear. Most likely still the same call she was engaged in when I called earlier. I look back at Dad. "Business?"

"Uh-huh." He leans over and raps his knuckles harshly and quickly against the window, startling Ella to the point where her phone almost flies out of her hand. She spins around in the seat and looks back at Dad through the glass, only for him to nod his head toward Chase and me. Ella nods back, moves her device back to her ear, murmurs something, and then hangs up. That's when Dad finally tells us to get inside the car.

Chase and I clamber into the backseat, pulling on our seat belts as Dad slips into the driver's seat, fixing me with a firm glare in the rearview mirror, which I ignore. As he starts to drive, Ella cranes her neck over the back of the passenger seat.

"Don't you want to stay out a little later?" she asks me, blond hair framing her face. It's nearing ten by now, so I'm not sure what she was expecting me to stay out for. The last thing I wanted to do was go to that party at TJ's, so I'm happy to be going home.

"Not really," I tell her. I don't mention the party. Nor the fact that the entire night has sucked.

14

"What about you, buddy?" Dad cuts in, nodding to Chase in the rearview mirror. "I thought Gregg's mom was going to take you all home later."

Chase stops texting to glance up. He fires me a sideways glance, so I rack my brain for a second before telling Dad, "He didn't feel too good, so I told him to come home with us." To make it sound convincing, I look at Chase with fake concern and ask, "How are you feeling now?"

"Better," Chase says as he plays along, pressing the back of his hand to his forehead and rubbing it soothingly. "I think the Pacific Wheel was giving me a migraine, but I'm totally fine now. Can we stop for burgers? Please, Dad? I'm dying over here. You don't want me to pass out, do you?"

Ella rolls her eyes and turns back around in her seat. Dad only says, "Let me think about it."

With neither of them paying much attention to us, I curl my hand into a fist and rest it on the middle seat. He bumps his own fist against mine immediately, and we subtly smile at one another. If Dad knew about the trouble that Chase's friends often got themselves into, Chase would never be allowed to see them again. It's always better not to mention it, even when Chase always does the right thing.

We end up dropping by the Wendy's drive-through over on Lincoln Boulevard on the way home. Dad and Chase both get burgers. I get a vanilla Frosty. A large. I spend the rest of the car journey home eating it, staring out the window at the dark skies, listening to Dad and Ella talk over the eighties music they've put on in the background. They're wondering if Jamie will be home before his curfew at midnight. Dad reckons he'll be an hour late.

We're back on Deidre Avenue within ten minutes due to the traffic having eased slightly, where Dad parks up on the drive by Ella's Range Rover. With my empty cup in my hand, I push open the car door and step out once Dad switches the engine off. I'm about to make my way up to the front door when Ella catches my attention, calling my name over the roof of the Lexus.

"Can you help me get some groceries out of the trunk from earlier?" she asks in a firm voice and gives the Range Rover a clipped nod. Because I like Ella, I make my way over to her car without hesitation. She follows me as she fumbles in her purse for her keys, and once she finds them, she pops the trunk.

I glance down, ready to reach in to gather up a bunch of grocery bags, but I'm perplexed to discover that the trunk is empty. Wondering if Ella's having a moment of forgetfulness, I arch an eyebrow and look up at her. Her eyes are suddenly wide and wary, and she's surreptitiously peering around the car, watching Dad and Chase make their way into the house. Once they're inside, her eyes lock on mine.

"Tyler called," she says.

I take a step back, defensive. His name feels like a weapon. That's why I never say it anymore. That's why I never want to hear it. It always hurts far too much. Already my throat feels tight as I forget to keep breathing and a shiver runs throughout my body. The earlier call wasn't a business call at all. It was Tyler. He always calls Ella, once a week or so, and I'm perfectly aware of this. She desperately awaits his calls, but she never mentions them to the rest of us. Not until right now.

She swallows and glances back at the house before she talks again, fearful that Dad might hear her. No one is allowed to mention Tyler's name around me. Dad's strict orders, of course, and I think it's the only thing we've ever agreed on. Yet Ella continues, looking at me in a way that's both pitying and sad as she quietly says, "He asked me to wish you a happy Fourth."

The irony almost makes me laugh, but it angers me to the point where it's impossible to find it funny. The Fourth of July, three years ago, Tyler and I were in the hallways at Culver City High School during the firework display. That's where all of this mess really started. That's when I realized I was looking at my stepbrother in the way that I shouldn't have been. We got arrested for trespassing that night. The Fourth of July, last year, Tyler and I weren't at a firework display. We were in his apartment in New York City, alone in the dark as the rain drenched the city. He quoted a Bible verse. Wrote on my body, said that I was his. They were the other Fourth of Julys. Not this one. To wish me a happy Fourth tonight is almost like some sort of joke. I haven't seen him in a year. He walked out and left me when I needed him by my side the most. I'm not his anymore, so how dare he wish me a happy Fourth of July when he's not here to spend it with me?

As my mind tries to process everything, I feel my temper flaring up. Ella's waiting for me to say something back, so before I turn around and storm into the house, I reach up and slam the trunk shut.

"Tell Tyler it's been far from it."

♥

chapter

2

I get a call from Rachael just after midnight. I'm not quite asleep, but I'm getting there, so the interruption only annoys me. I reach out and answer my phone, rubbing my eyes and fighting the urge to roll them as the sound of music and yelling echoes through my device. "Let me guess," I say. "You need a ride?"

"Not me," Rachael says after a second, her voice loud and, surprisingly, not slurred. "Your brother."

It's the last thing I expect her to say. It takes me so much by surprise that I quickly sit up, already reaching for my car keys on my bedside table. "Jamie?"

"Yeah. TJ wants him out," she explains. She sounds almost sober, and I can sense her frowning. "He's playing with the set of knives in the kitchen, and he just threw up."

"What the hell is he doing there in the first place?"

"TJ's brother is here, and he invited a bunch of his friends over, so there are seniors running around all over the place and it's making me feel really old." Rachael pauses for a moment as someone in the background yells at her to shut up, most likely one of the aforementioned high school kids, and after cursing back at them, she moves her phone back to her ear. "Actually, can you come get me too? This whole thing is kinda lame."

"I'll be there in five." Once I've hung up, I sigh and swing my body out of my bed, flicking on the light and grabbing my same red Chucks from earlier. Keeping my pajamas on, I pull on a hoodie over the top and then leave my room.

The house is quiet. Not because Dad and Ella are asleep, but because they're not here. They're across the street at Dawn and Philip's house, Rachael's parents, who've been hosting some sort of Fourth of July get-together all night. Dad and Ella promised them they'd drop by later. I can imagine it already: all the middle-aged moms and dads drinking beer and cocktails, socializing to the crap music that they considered cool back when they were my age. I'm glad they're there, however, because it lets me make an easy getaway to rescue Rachael and Jamie without Dad interrogating me.

I make my way downstairs without having to tiptoe around the house, and I don't bother to tell Chase that I'm heading out because I don't want to wake him. Before I leave, I grab a bucket from the backyard and take it with me. The last thing I want is my stepbrother throwing up all over my seats. I lock up and make a quick dash for my car, just in case Dad or Ella happen to be standing near the front window of Rachael's living room. The lights are all on, and behind the closed blinds, I can see the shadows of everyone milling around. I don't dither. I just throw myself and the bucket into my car and get going.

The roads aren't busy at this time, so it's only a five-minute drive to TJ's place, straight down Deidre Avenue and onto Ocean Avenue, along the beachfront. The pier is closed by now, so everything feels too still compared with how it was a few hours ago. TJ's condo, on the other hand, is far from still. The streets are lined with cars, including Jamie's BMW, and it's impossible to pull up and park, so I wait in the middle of the road, ready to move if I cause a late-night obstacle. I text Rachael to let her know I'm here, and I also text Jamie and tell him that he needs to get his drunken ass outside within a minute.

While I wait, my eyes drift up to the condo on the second floor. It's the only one with all its lights on. The huge floor-to-ceiling windows allow me to see straight inside, but all I can make out is a mass of bodies. I don't remember the condo being all that huge from what I can recall from three years ago, but it seems TJ has ended up with too many guests on his hands. Jake's probably in there trying to entice some poor girl to go home with him. Dean's probably in there making sure no one does anything stupid. Meghan and her boyfriend Jared are probably in there doing whatever Meghan and Jared do. I wouldn't know.

It doesn't take long for both Rachael and Jamie to appear. Through the glass doors at the front of the building, I see them emerge from the elevator, Jamie stumbling all over the place as Rachael quite literally drags him outside. She throws me an exasperated look when she sees me, so I push open my car door and get out to help her.

"I hope you have a hangover straight from hell tomorrow," I tell Jamie as I reach for his arm and place it over the back of my shoulders to help steady him. His eyes are half-closed, his hair ruffled, his limbs immobile. He's so drunk that he can hardly move.

"I hope you *go* to hell," he somehow manages to shoot back at me. I'm not offended or deeply wounded by it though. Jamie often throws remarks like these at me, so, just like everything else, I've grown accustomed to his contemptuous attitude.

Over the back of his shoulders, Rachael furrows her eyebrows at me with deep concern but says nothing. Instead, she holds Jamie up as I reach for the car door, and together we shove him into the backseat, having to bend his legs and arms to get him inside. I fumble with the seat belt as I try to pull it around him, but he pushes me away, so I quickly give up and slam the door.

"He sure does hate you," Rachael murmurs as she walks around to the passenger side. Her hair is no longer in a ponytail but rather falling over her shoulders in long, tangled waves, and her bandana is wrapped around her wrist. She's also completely sober.

"He might hate me, but in the morning, he'll be glad it's me who took him home and not our parents," I say. "Talk about being grounded for life." Pulling open my car door, I slide back into the driver's seat at the same time as Rachael slips into the passenger side. She holds the bucket up to me with an eyebrow raised, and when I shrug, she laughs and passes it to the backseat. Jamie immediately takes it from her, but not without grumbling something under his breath.

"Did your parents go to my place?" Rachael asks once I start to drive, leaving the party and all its drunken commotion behind.

"Yeah." As I talk, I can't help but keep checking on Jamie in the rearview mirror. He's slumped across my backseat, the bucket resting on the floor behind the passenger seat as his head dangles over it. I frown, praying to God that he won't throw up, and then drop my eyes back to the road in front of me. "They're still there. Everyone is."

Rachael throws her head back against the headrest and groans, tilting her face to the window, allowing the glow from the streetlights to illuminate her skin. "I'm so sneaking in the back door," she says. "I wanna avoid all my parents' friends asking me what I'm doing with my life."

"What are you doing with your life?" Rachael looks back over at me and sharply narrows her eyes. I grin, but not for long, because my attention is drawn back to Jamie.

"Let me out," he mutters from the backseat. When I glance in the rearview mirror, I see him reaching for the door, so I quickly apply the locks. He tries the handle, pulling his body up into a seated position, hitting the window with his hand when he realizes he's locked in. "I don't wanna be in this car!"

"Too bad," I say nonchalantly, both hands on the wheel, my attention mostly on the road as we head back home.

"Rachael!" Jamie leans forward and stretches his arms around the passenger seat, grabbing at Rachael's shoulders and refusing to let go. "As my neighbor for as long as I can remember, can you *please* let me out of this car?"

Rachael manages to wrestle Jamie's grip off her, her body twisting around her seat belt as she dodges his desperate hands. Within seconds, she's turned around to face him and her back is pressed against my dashboard. She holds up a finger. "Don't touch me. Ever," she warns him through the gap in the headrest.

"But you gotta help me!"

Rachael lets out a deep sigh while she presses her index finger to her temple, her voice having adopted a condescending tone when she asks, "What do you need help with, Jamie?"

"Help me get away from *her*," he says, and when I steal a look over my shoulder, he's jabbing a finger in my direction, his bloodshot eyes narrowing in disgust when our gazes meet. "She's a freak."

"Get over it already," I snap back at him as my grip around the wheel tightens, accelerating even faster along Deidre Avenue and ignoring the way I can feel Rachael glancing between Jamie and me. She knows we don't get along anymore, but I don't quite think she's ever witnessed it like this.

It's almost impossible for her to remain quiet, for her to let an argument break out, so she peers around the headrest of the passenger seat to fix Jamie with a stern look that warns him not to say anything more. "Words of advice: you're drunk, and you're being an asshole, so shut up."

Almost indignantly, Jamie slumps against the backseat, staring at Rachael as he dares to muster up a reply. When it comes, he sounds almost nonchalant, his lips moving slowly as he says, "I'm drunk? Huh. I'm being an asshole? Even bigger huh. Sound familiar to anyone?" Slowly, he sits up again and leans toward me, a drunken, lopsided smile capturing his face. It's far from friendly, yet he places a hand on my shoulder as I drive, squeezing way too hard as his eyes flicker back to Rachael. "Throw in some weed and she'll be falling in love with me too."

Immediately, I shove his hand off my shoulder, elbowing his chest and pushing him away from me. The car swerves slightly, but I'm quick to move both hands back to the wheel, and then I flash my eyes back over my shoulder once more to fix him with the fiercest glare I can possibly pull off right now. It doesn't take much effort. "What the fuck is your problem?"

Out of the corner of my eye, I see Rachael slowly settling back against the passenger seat and throwing me a disapproving glance. At the same time, she slowly moves her hand to the wheel too, as though she's afraid I'll career the car off the road. "He's just drunk, Eden."

But I can't listen to her because I'm not referring to what's going on right now. I'm referring to everything from last summer until this exact moment. Jamie hasn't been able to accept the truth, despite having a year already to do so, and I'm starting to wonder if he's ever going to let it go. I'm starting to believe he'll forever hate Tyler and me. "Seriously," I snap, throwing a hand up in exasperation, "what is your damn problem? Spell it out for me."

Jamie swallows hard before leaning over the center console and setting his rolling eyes on me, slowly spitting out the words, "You. Are. Gross."

I'm quiet for a while. The only thing I can hear is my car engine as I drive and the grinding of my teeth. Part of me wants to kick Jamie out of the car. The other wants to cry. The truth is, I know Jamie feels that way. I *know* he thinks I'm crazy and gross and disgusting and out of my mind, yet he's never actually said it out loud until now, and for the smallest fraction of a second, I feel sick.

"I don't know what you expect me to say to you," I say quietly. "I really don't. There's nothing going on between…" I pause, clear my throat, and then try again. "There's nothing going on between Tyler and me anymore. He and I are long over. So *please*, Jamie. Please stop hating me."

Jamie stares at me blankly for a second and then flops back against the seat once again, but this time he reaches for the bucket and promptly throws up. Rachael squeals, pressing a hand to her mouth as she gags, and she backs up against the dashboard again, trying her best to stay as far away from Jamie as she can get. My nose wrinkles, and I roll down all four windows, allowing fresh air into the car.

"And yet he says *you're* the gross one," Rachael murmurs sideways to me through her hand.

Jamie continues to hurl and wheeze and groan and curse the rest of the way home, which is thankfully only a few minutes away. Neither Rachael nor I say anything. We only listen to the wind in silence as Jamie suffers. The second I see the house, however, he is no longer the only one who's cussing. I am too.

As if Satan himself had planned it, Dad and Ella are walking back from Rachael's house at the exact same time as I'm pulling up. They both pause on our front lawn when they notice my car approaching, and Dad's hands immediately go to his hips as he presses his lips into a firm line, his eyes narrowing in the sternest of ways.

"Shit," I say for the fifth time. "Shit, shit, shit." Slowly, I bring the car to a stop against the curb and roll all the windows back up before cutting off the engine. Through my windshield, I can see Ella frowning as she squints to see who I'm with. Unfortunately for her, I have her drunk son throwing up in my backseat.

Rachael shakes her head and throws a pointed glance back toward Jamie. "Someone is *so* dead."

"He sure is." Taking a deep breath, I yank my keys out of the ignition and kick open my car door, stepping out at the same time Rachael does. Slowly, I turn around to face Dad and Ella.

"Rachael, I believe your parents were wondering where you were," Dad says stiffly, with the smallest of nods in the direction of her house. All the lights are still on, and shadows are still moving around.

"Thanks, Mr. Munro. I'll go let them know," Rachael replies in as innocent a voice as she possibly can, but I can still hear the air of sarcasm in her words. Because Dad is in his forties with graying hair and without a single memory of what it's like to be a teenager, he doesn't pick up on it. He only gives her a tight-lipped smile and waits for her to leave. She spins around and heads for her house, but not without brushing past me and murmuring, "I can't wait to move out."

There's silence out on the street for a minute. I don't want to be the first to speak. Jamie is still in the back of my car, Ella's still squinting, and Dad is waiting for Rachael to disappear. The second she does, his eyes flash over to me and he asks, "Where the hell have you been?"

Not only is Dad the aforementioned aging asshole, he's also quick to make assumptions. Right now, it's clear by his expression and tone that he's already assuming my reasons for leaving the house are on the reckless side, like I can't possibly leave the house at twelve thirty at the age of nineteen without planning to cause trouble.

Trying my utmost hardest not to roll my eyes, I walk around my car and then motion down to my attire. It's difficult to hide the contempt in my voice when I bitterly point out, "I'm in my *pajamas*." Reaching for the car door, I pull it open and immediately Jamie and the gross bucket emerge from the backseat. "And for the record," I say, eyes on Dad as I close the door again, "I was picking him up. You know, since he got kicked out of a party for being way too drunk."

"God, Jamie!" Ella groans, burying her face into her hands before she comes rushing across the lawn to fetch him.

My eyes are still on Dad's, my glare even as I fold my arms across my chest. He's watching in extreme disapproval as Jamie trips all over the lawn while Ella tries to steady him. Once she has a firm hold on her son and is keeping him upright, his intoxicated mind decides to yell, "Eden was totally tryna kiss me!"

Taken aback, my eyes fly to Jamie and I scrunch my face up. Shaking my head in disbelief, I can't stop myself from raising my hand and flipping him off. "Seriously, fuck you, Jamie," I hiss back at him, and Ella fixes me with a twisted frown at the same time as Dad puffs out his chest and opens his mouth.

"Eden Olivia Munro," he says in low voice, and I know immediately by the use of my full name that he's preparing to rip me to shreds. "Give me your car keys. Right now." He doesn't move an inch, only extends his arm and holds up his hand, palm facing upward.

"Why?"

"Because you think it's acceptable to sneak out and curse like that. Keys," he says again, this time much firmer. I can see his glower deepening with each second that passes.

I glance down to the set of keys in my hand, and I tighten my grip around them even harder, and then I look back up and shake my head. "So he can stay out past curfew and come home drunk, and *I'm* the one who gets punished?" I look over at Jamie and Ella again, and although he may be excessively drunk, Jamie still manages to snicker. Gritting my teeth, I move my eyes back to Dad. "For *what*? For giving him a ride home?"

"Give me the damn keys," Dad orders once more through stiff lips, jaw clenched, and I laugh. I can't stop myself. It's so typical of him. Every single time I've come home to Santa Monica over the past year, Dad has always found a reason to be harsh. It's not difficult to guess why: he's still punishing me for getting involved with Tyler, for falling in love with my stepbrother.

"Dave," Ella murmurs, and I notice the way she gives Dad a small shake of her head as she's dragging Jamie over to the front door. "She hasn't done anything wrong."

Dad ignores her, like always, because Ella apparently no longer gets a say in how he parents his kid, yet he always has the final say in how she parents hers. Growing aggravated by my defiance, he starts to move, storming across the lawn toward me as though he's prepared to yank the keys straight out of my hands.

Before he has the chance to do so, I dart back around to the driver's side, pulling open my car door and stepping one foot inside. "Screw this," I say before I slide in. It may be Dad's turn to have me for the week, but there's absolutely no way in hell I'm staying here. "I'm going home."

"This *is* your home!" Dad pathetically tries to yell across the roof of the car to me, but even I can hear the strain in his voice as he says it. He knows it's a lie. He doesn't want this to be my home because, quite honestly, he's made it clear over the past year that he doesn't even want me in the family.

"Well," I mutter, "it sure as hell doesn't feel like it." Sliding behind the wheel, I slam the car door shut behind me and quickly start up the engine before Dad can attempt to stop me. But he doesn't. I think he's glad actually.

As I drive off, heading up Deidre Avenue toward my mom's house, I watch them all in my rearview mirror. Chase is at the front door, confused as always and half-asleep. Dad and Ella have started yelling at one another, their hands moving with angry gestures, and I realize then, as I'm driving off and leaving them all behind, that whatever our family is, it's far from perfect.

The truth is, it's been broken for a year.

chapter

3

On Thursday, I spend my morning the same way I usually start any other day: with a jog along the beachfront to Venice and back again, before stopping by the Refinery halfway back to the house. It's the routine I've gotten myself into ever since I got home for the summer. I've been slacking off on my running for the past year while eating whatever the hell I want to, gaining pounds here and there without caring about it for the first time in my life, but enough is enough, and now I'm desperately trying to lose the weight again before I head back to college in the fall. As for the trips to the Refinery, I've simply missed their to-die-for coffee.

I'm sipping on my vanilla latte by the glass windows, studying the people of Santa Monica Boulevard as they stream past endlessly. Sometimes Rachael meets me here, but she's already left for Glendale to visit her grandparents, so today I'm alone. I don't mind. To start with, that is.

It doesn't take long for someone to notice me huddled over in the corner, the girl who apparently dated her stepbrother. I've got one earphone in, so I don't know how I even manage to hear them, but I do. They're a group of four girls, younger than me, leaving the Refinery. One of them murmurs something, and the only reason my attention is drawn to them is because I faintly hear the word "stepbrother." When I glance up, I see that they're already looking at me, but they quickly stop snickering and glance away before they disappear through the door.

Taking a deep breath, I close my eyes and move my other earphone to my ear, blocking out everything else around me by listening to La Breve Vita on full volume. The band broke up last summer, so all I have left is the music they once made. I linger in the Refinery for another five minutes or so, finishing the remainder of my latte and enjoying being out of the sun for a while. When it's hot as hell outside and you throw running into the equation, it's enough to make you pass out, so I'm always grateful for a midrun break.

It's only when I'm getting to my feet and switching playlists before heading back out that my phone starts to ring in my hand. It's Ella, so I don't decline the call, like I would if it was Dad. Instead, I pull out my earphones and press my phone to my ear, asking her what's up.

"Where are you right now?" she immediately asks, unusually abrupt.

"Uh, the Refinery," I answer a little unsurely.

"Can you come over?" Quickly, she adds, "Don't worry, your father's at work."

I furrow my eyebrows as I twirl my earphones around my fingers, making for the door and slipping out onto the sidewalk. "Aren't *you* at work?"

"I'm working on a brief," she says and, without a moment's pause, asks, "How fast can you get here?"

"Like, twenty minutes." As I'm turning the corner onto Fifth Street, I end up frowning, confused. Ella usually calls me to ask what I want for dinner or if I need cash or to check up on how I'm doing. This time is different. She never usually calls like this, asking me over to the house that I hate going to, so I'm slightly concerned. "Is everything alright?"

"Everything's fine," she says, but something shaky in her voice tells me otherwise. "Just be quick."

When she ends the call, I immediately set off again, earphones in, music up, pace faster than usual. The house is over two miles away, so at best I'll get there in fifteen minutes. Ella really doesn't sound like she wants to be kept waiting, and as I carefully weave my way through the people on the sidewalks, I find myself mentally listing possible reasons for why she needs me so urgently. None of them seem probable though, so I give up trying to guess and focus instead on running even faster. The quicker I get there, the sooner I'll find out.

With that mentality, I end up back at the house in just over fifteen minutes. I wipe my brow with the back of my hand, breathing heavily as I approach the front door. It's the first time I've been here since I left on Friday night. I haven't spoken to Dad at all since then either.

The house is silent when I walk into the hall. No Jamie, no Chase, no Dad. Only Ella, dressed smartly in a fitted skirt and a blouse, who I only notice after I hear her faint footsteps at the top of the stairs. I gaze up at her and run a hand over my sweaty forehead as she peers down at me. My breathing is still a little uneven, and I try to bring it under control as I wait for her to tell me what it is that she so desperately needs me for.

However, there's no explaining, only an anxious frown as she nods behind her and quietly says, "Can you come up here for a second?"

If I wasn't worried before, then I certainly am now. I'm suddenly afraid that if I go upstairs, I'll find my bedroom empty and converted into a guest room with whatever belongings I'd left here packed into cardboard boxes. *That's it*, I think. *She's kicking me out.* Not that I actually mind that much.

Blowing out a breath, my entire body fatigued and aching, I force myself up the staircase, trying my best not to make too much eye contact with Ella. I'll bet it was Dad's idea to never let me stay here again, not hers. She's just the one who has to break the news to me. Like, *I'm sorry, Eden, but you're too despicable and disgusting and dangerously reckless to stay in this house for a second longer.*

"Where's Jamie? Chase?" I ask, glancing down the hall out of the corner of my eye to see if I can spot any boxes. There are none. I fix my full attention back on Ella, but she only turns around and walks through to her office, the room next door to mine. I follow.

"Jamie's taking Jen into the city for the day," Ella says nonchalantly over her shoulder as her heels click against the floor, "and Chase is at the beach."

I stop a few feet into the room, not because it's Ella's private workspace, which none of us are usually allowed in for confidentiality reasons, but because this room hasn't always been an office. It's only been this way for half a year. Although the walls have been repainted ivory, I can still see the navy shining through from Dad's crap painting skills. The old carpet was also pulled up and replaced with hardwood flooring. But other than a missing second coat of paint providing a reminder, it's sometimes easy to forget that once upon a time this was a bedroom.

"So Jamie isn't grounded?" I want to roll my eyes. Incredible, really, that Jamie can come home drunk, throwing up all over the lawn, and be let off the hook.

"He is," Ella says, then pauses as she turns around to look straight at me, her blue eyes intense yet soft at the exact same time. "But today I didn't want him in the house."

"Oh." I press my lips together and tuck some strands of hair that have strayed from my messy bun behind my ear. Curious, I cast a quick glance over Ella's desk and the stacks of paperwork that cover it. All cases she's working on, all client information. I glance back at her before she can notice me looking. "Why don't you want him here?"

"Because I haven't told him yet," she says slowly. It's not quite the answer I expected, and, in fact, it surprises me. She swallows and places a hand on the back of her chair, and as though she can see how puzzled I am, she adds, "I haven't told any of you yet. Especially not your dad."

31

Oh my God. The reason I'm here suddenly becomes so clear that I find myself blinking in disbelief, reaching for the door handle in order to support myself before I pass out or hurl or both.

"You're pregnant?" I splutter.

"God, Eden." Ella shakes her head fast, and her cheeks flush with color. She presses her hand to her chest, composes herself, and clears her throat before saying, "Definitely not." A little awkwardly, she gives me a small smile while she tries not to laugh.

My rapid heartbeat slows as my chest relaxes and my shoulders sink with relief. I couldn't imagine Dad doing the whole father thing again. He's yet to be good at it. Slightly embarrassed at myself for jumping to conclusions, I bite at my lower lip and shrug, still as confused and as worried as I was before. "Then what are you talking about?"

Ella takes a deep breath and exhales slowly, the entire house silent. My patience starts to wear thin. I don't like this. I hate not knowing what's really going on or why I'm here. Maybe she's about to tell us that they're moving across the country. Maybe she's quitting her job. Maybe she's planning to file for a divorce. But the latter is my wishful thinking, for her sake.

Yet she remains silent, her lips moving only slightly, as though she's trying to form words but doesn't know what to say. After a few seconds, she doesn't have to say anything at all. Her eyes say it for her.

They've drifted over my shoulder to something behind me, her gaze concentrated and calm, and then I hear the voice that has the power to completely paralyze me. It's impossible to mistake it for anyone else's, which is why my breathing stops and my stomach twists the moment the first word leaves his lips, and why everything, absolutely everything, stops when I hear him say, "She's talking about me."

Startled, I spin around. And he's there. Just like that, after an entire year, he's there in front of me, standing tall and broad, with his dark hair and emerald eyes, wearing black jeans and a white T-shirt—the person who I never realized was my everything until the moment he left and never came back.

That person just so happens to be my stepbrother, Tyler.

I retreat farther into the office, stepping back defensively. Disbelief and shock consume me as my throat tightens and I shake my head at him. He hasn't changed at all. He's exactly how I remember him from last summer, from our time together in New York, with that same stubble and sharp jaw and huge arms and bright eyes that are set on me and nothing else. The corners of his lips quirk up into a smile.

Yet in the tense silence that surrounds all three of us, I can't help but feel as though I've been ambushed and lured here for no logical reason whatsoever. Ella knows I can't bear to think about Tyler, let alone look at him, so I shift my glare to her. "What the hell is this?"

Ella looks like a nervous wreck. She's glancing rapidly between Tyler and me, her eyes wary and her forehead creased with worry. "I've got a meeting to get to," she manages to say, her voice wavering. She turns away from us, gathering up her jacket and a pile of binders before quickly brushing past me. As she passes Tyler, she reaches up to squeeze his shoulder, and then she simply leaves. Her heels click against the stairs until she reaches the front door, and after a small thud, there's nothing but complete and utter silence.

I'm blinking fast as I try to wrap my head around the fact that Tyler is standing three feet away from me, and eventually I'm forced to look up at him. My eyes meet his, but unlike his sparkling pair, mine are flaming with anger. He takes a bold step into the office, a foot closer to me, and he does the most incredible thing yet again. He smiles. A huge, beaming smile that displays his perfect row of teeth, and it stretches so far up his face that it reaches his eyes.

"Eden," he murmurs. His voice is quiet, almost as though my name is delicate, and a small breath of relief escapes his lips.

It infuriates me more than anything ever has before. For him to appear out of nowhere after a year, to smile at me as though everything is perfect, and for him to even dare say my name is all it takes for me to snap, for a year's worth of anger and hurt to explode all at once.

Fueled by rage, I can't stop myself from swinging, and before I even realize what I'm really doing, my hand has already collided harshly against Tyler's left cheek with a sickening slap. There's so much adrenaline flooding through my veins that I don't even notice that my palm stings until later.

Tyler's turned his face to one side, down to the ground, eyes tightly shut as he exhales a long breath. Slowly, he moves his hand to his cheek and rubs at his skin, as though to soothe away the pain I've inflicted—the pain I've yet to feel guilty about. I'm too furious right now, which is why when his eyes flicker back open and he stares at me in stunned silence, I find myself hissing, "What are you doing here?"

With no smile left, his shock turns to confusion and he furrows his eyebrows at me as his cheek glows a bright red. "I told you I'd come back," he says quietly. His voice is deep, with that same old husky undertone that I remember. That was back when I adored his voice and the way my name sounded on his lips. Now his voice only aggravates me.

"And I thought you meant you'd come back after a couple weeks, or a month at most." Swallowing hard, I take several more steps backward until I'm up against Ella's desk and there's nowhere else I can go. I can't bear to be anywhere near Tyler. Not now, not ever again. Filled with the hatred that stems from the fact that he walked out and left me behind, it's easy for the words to keep on spilling out of my mouth, and now I'm yelling, "Not an entire year!"

Tyler's perplexed stare falters, and his eyes fill instead with guilt and hurt. It's as though he hadn't ever thought there was a chance that I might be mad at him until now, and suddenly I can see the gears in his mind shifting as he looks across the room at me, wide-eyed and unsure of how to reply. He definitely doesn't want to smile anymore. I'm not sure how he was expecting me to greet him, if he thought I'd throw myself back into his arms and be overflowing with joy, or if he thought that perhaps I'd kiss him like I've never kissed him before and be eternally happy. But whatever he was expecting, it's clear he did not expect this—rage and contempt and a girl who is no longer in love with him.

But I don't want to stand here and yell at him. I don't want to argue and fight. I don't want him to try to explain or beg for forgiveness. I just don't want to deal with him in any way at all, so I decide to leave: calmly, despite the way my chest is burning, but quickly, because the longer I'm around him the more I feel like the anger might just turn to tears, the hot, burning kind. So I walk across the office without looking at Tyler, keeping my head up and my eyes ahead, and I head straight past him. I can sense his gaze following me as I descend the staircase, and when I pull open the front door, I hear his footsteps at the top of the landing.

"Eden," he says. "Wait."

But I don't want to wait. I spent months waiting, wondering and guessing and driving myself insane as the days rolled into months and the months rolled into a year. I gave up on waiting a long time ago. I gave up on *him* a long time ago.

I slam the front door shut behind me, and I run. I run as fast and as hard as I've ever run before, desperate to get as far away from Tyler and the house as I possibly can, my heart pounding and my ears ringing with each step I take. Yet the farther away I get, the more aware of the situation I become, and the more aware I become, the more my adrenaline fades and the more nauseous I feel. Now I finally feel the pain in my hand. My palm is burning, so I tightly curl my hand into a fist and try not to think about it.

I'm back at my mom's place in under five minutes, and I'm still running until the moment I'm over the threshold and inside. Panting, I shove the front door shut and lock it, squeezing my eyes shut for a moment as I try to catch my breath. I can hear a talk show on TV, and it doesn't take more than a few seconds for Gucci to appear and start nipping at my feet.

"Please don't tell me you're running from the cops," Mom says, and when I spin around to the sound of her voice, she's already approaching me while drying her hands with a small towel, an eyebrow raised suspiciously. The faucet in the kitchen sink is still running.

Keeping my dog entertained is the last thing on my mind right now, so I push her away from me and look back at Mom instead. She must gather immediately that something is seriously wrong because her small smile falters, the warmth in her brown eyes disappears, and concern dominates her features. The wrinkles around her forehead seem to deepen as she studies me, and all she can say is, "Eden?"

My lower lip quivers. I'm trying my hardest not to let my emotions overwhelm me, but it's becoming increasingly difficult. I didn't think Tyler would ever come back. After a while, I just came to believe he was happy wherever he was and that he didn't need any of us anymore. I never imagined that I'd be faced with this situation. I'm furious and confused and upset and frustrated, and my silence is only making Mom even more worried, so I swallow hard and murmur, "Tyler's back."

And the moment I say his name out loud, I burst into tears.

chapter

4

Mom lets me sleep for a while. But I'm not really sleeping, just laying in bed, wrapped up in my comforter, staring at my ceiling through swollen eyes. I cried for a while. Showered, pulled on a pair of sweats, climbed into bed. I haven't left my room since, even though it's long after noon by now and I'm wasting a whole lot of daylight. Honestly, I don't want to move for the rest of the day, or perhaps the rest of the week. My head hurts too much and feels too heavy and is on the verge of exploding. So I'll stick around in the comfort of my bed for as long as I can, even though I know Mom will never in a million years let me lock myself up in here for longer than a day, despite the fact that I so desperately wish I could.

The truth is, I don't think I can bring myself to face Tyler again. Whatever hope I had for us last summer is long gone. Maybe we had a real shot at being something back then. We were so close to finally being together, officially and openly, yet Tyler made the entire situation much more complicated than it ever needed to be. He didn't have to leave, especially not when I needed him the most and especially not for so long. I understood though. I got it. Eventually, after a few weeks, when the initial shock and pain of his abrupt departure finally eased off. I knew he was doing right by himself, but what I didn't know was why I had been completely thrown out of the picture. I tried to call him, but he never answered. I left endless messages, but I doubt he listened to them. I sent text after text, question after question, but I never received a single reply. Even when I simply asked if he was okay, he was silent. Soon I grew tired of trying, and my calls and messages and texts gradually began to decrease in number as day after day went by, and by November, I wasn't trying to contact him at all. I had college to focus on: new classes and new people and a new city.

And that was great for keeping my mind off him. For a while, at least. Abusing caffeine while studying in the library, making late-night trips to convenience stores with my roommate whenever we realized we'd run out of food, and sneaking home drunk across campus in the middle of the night after a dorm party can only distract a person for so long. Sure, I met new guys and even went on a couple of dates over the months, but every single one of those dates felt flat and far from special. By February, I was thinking about Tyler again. Only then, I wasn't upset. I was livid.

I simply couldn't understand it. I couldn't understand why Tyler spoke to Ella but not me, and I couldn't understand why he still hadn't come back to Santa Monica like he said he would. It'd been seven months. He should have come home forever ago, yet he hadn't, which angered me. It felt like he'd forgotten about me, packed up and moved on and left me to deal with the mess we made together. I'm the one who had to cope with all the sideways glances and murmured comments whenever I was back here in Santa Monica. Not him. I'm the one who had to deal with Dad and Jamie. Not him. I'm the one who got walked out on. Not him.

And that's why my fury continued to grow: because he left and never came back, because he couldn't even bring himself to call me, because he was happy wherever the hell he was. And wherever *he* was, *I* wasn't. Which meant he was happy and content without me, and that hurt a whole lot more than I ever thought it could.

The first time he ever called me back was during spring break. I was in San Francisco for the first time in my life, hiking my way up the streets with Rachael by my side whining about the steepness, when my phone rang. I stared at my screen, contemplating whether or not I should answer, before the call rang off and went to my voice mail. Tyler didn't leave a message, but after that he did start calling every day. I never answered a single one, because by then it was too late, and all I felt toward him was nothing but seething anger.

It's currently three weeks short of a year to the exact day he left, which is why I never expected him to come back *now* after so long. Even Ella gave up hope, back when she decided it was time to convert Tyler's old room into an office so she didn't have to keep working out of the kitchen. That's when it became clear to all of us that even she didn't think he'd come back. It's fair to say that Dad was rather pleased that day, and he was quick to rush off to the hardware store to buy that ivory paint that he later made a complete mess of applying. If there's anyone who's going to be more furious than me about Tyler being back, it'll be Dad when he finds out. That's if he doesn't know already, but I'm guessing by the way Ella was so secretive this morning that he doesn't. In fact, the more I think about it, the more I'm pissed off at her too. Ella purposely put me in that situation, face-to-face with Tyler again, without warning, even when I'd expressed multiple times to her that I never wanted to see him again and that I was glad he hadn't come back.

Now everything's a total mess again, and I'm not quite sure how to deal with it all and how I'm supposed to stay here while knowing that Tyler is back. Avoiding him forever is, sadly, not at all possible. Yet the saddest thing of all? A year ago I was completely and entirely and endlessly in love with him. Now I don't want to be anywhere near him, and that's the part that infuriates me the most.

I don't realize I'm crying again until my mom enters my room.

Quickly, I dab at my tears with my sheets and sniff a little. Mom heads straight for my blinds and opens them up, allowing the midafternoon sunlight to flood my room, to which I groan and bury my face into my pillows.

"Okay," I hear her say, and I don't even have to look at her to know that her arms are most likely folded across her chest. I can just tell by the tone of her voice. "Get up."

I pull my comforter completely over my head. "No."

"Yes," she says firmly. "You've had your four hours of crying. Time to get up and forget about him. Where do you want to go? Coffee? Late lunch? Spa? Your choice."

"Don't you start your shift soon?" My voice is muffled through my pillows and my comforter and my sheets. I've pretty much buried myself, and I don't plan to get up anytime soon.

"Not until eight." I vaguely hear her shuffling across my carpet, and then, moments later, she's pulling at my comforter, hauling it completely off me to greet me with a closed smile. "So get dressed and we'll head out, and we can bitch about the male species for as long as you so desire. Beats crying yourself to death. Trust me. Been there, done that."

As I unwillingly push myself up, I'm rolling my eyes. That's my favorite thing about Mom—she gets it. Dad walked out on her too, only that was six years ago. She's pretty much an expert when it comes to coping with a breakup. Rule number one? No more crying after four hours, apparently. I'm not so sure if this rule applies to a situation where the guy walks out and then *comes back*.

My eyes sting and my chest still aches, but I know Mom's right, as always. Staying in bed crying my heart out all day isn't going to do me any good. Mom learned that the hard way. I can remember. So, as much as I don't want to, I still manage to force myself up and onto my feet. My hair's still damp, and I run my fingers through it as I offer Mom a small smile of defeat. "Promenade. Twenty minutes?"

Her eyes are warm in the saddest of ways as her own smile grows. "That's my girl," she says, and then tosses a pillow toward me before she leaves the room.

While I try my best to look even half-acceptable, I play music, mostly bubbly pop music as a way to trick myself into believing that I'm totally happy. But I'm not, and the music only makes me even more pissed, so I shut it off after five minutes and dry my hair instead. I decide to leave it down. And I apply some makeup. And I pull on my newest shirt. And my best fitted jeans. And even that doesn't make me feel any better.

Mom and I head down to the promenade just after two. We do stroll around some stores for a half hour, but it isn't boosting my mood or anything, not even when I discover the cute skirt I've been eyeing up in Abercrombie & Fitch the past few weeks is now on sale. But when I buy it, I flash Mom a small smile, and that's enough to make her less concerned. Later, it doesn't take either of us much convincing to stop by Pinkberry for frozen yogurt.

"You know," Mom says, "I might talk to Ella about this."

We've managed to find ourselves a free bench outside, just opposite Forever 21, and although my mouth is on the verge of becoming numb, I still manage to ask, "Talk to Ella about what?"

Mom looks at me as though I'm being dumb on purpose or something, and then she shakes her head, scoops up another mouthful of her fro-yo, and continues anyway. "I'm not sure what she was thinking. It's unfair for her to throw Tyler at you like that. Is she insane?"

"She didn't exactly throw him at me," I murmur, giving a small shrug. My eyes drop back down to the cup in my hand, and I play around with my own frozen yogurt with my plastic spoon for a few seconds.

Original flavor, overflowing with fresh strawberries and blueberries, and most likely giving me back half the calories I burned off earlier. But today, I don't care. "She made it seem like there was a real emergency or something. I asked her if she was pregnant."

Mom almost chokes, and she looks at me, horrified for a second before she starts to laugh. Face-palming on my behalf, she presses her hand over her face to smother her childlike giggles. "You didn't."

"I did." My cheeks feel hot suddenly, so I toss a strawberry into my mouth and wait for Mom's laughter to die down. "I mean, it's not like it wasn't a possibility. She's still in her thirties."

"God, her thirties." Mom releases a low whistle, and then her features harden again when she realizes I've distracted her. "I'm still going to talk to her," she says.

"And say what?"

"Can you keep your kid away from my kid before the guy we both married kills them both?" Mom says, yet she's holding back even more laughter. However, she must immediately gather from the way that my eyes narrow that I'm not impressed, because she clears her throat and looks at me much more sincerely before giving me a real answer. "I'm just going to ask her to make sure Tyler leaves you alone." She holds up her cup of frozen yogurt and studies me intently from over the rim. "If that's really what you want, of course."

The way she says this, slow and almost suggestive, is enough to make me raise an eyebrow. "For starters, Mom, I don't need you to get involved. Second," I say, "what do you mean by that?"

"Well," she says, slowly lowering the cup again, "are you sure you—in your own words—never, ever, ever, ever, ever want to see Tyler again?"

I can see her searching my eyes, as though she'll discover some truth in them, but even though I have no hidden emotions, I still find myself blinking fast in a lame attempt to throw her off. I'm also confused as to why she's even saying such a thing, and as though I haven't been angered enough today as it is, my temper flares up again. "Of course I'm sure. Shouldn't you of all people understand how it feels to be walked out on?"

Mom momentarily looks hurt, and I realize immediately that my words haven't come out the way I meant them to. Mom can talk about Dad endlessly so long as his name is surrounded by a string of profanities, exactly like she has been doing for the past six years, but when it comes to the harsh truth that he walked out, that's something she never likes to talk about. It's clear when she turns away from me and gets to her feet that she's not happy with me bringing it up again. "I think we should head home. Like you said, I've got work soon."

When she tosses her empty cup into the trash can next to us and walks off without waiting for me, all I can do is groan. She's mad. After all these years, she still can't bear the fact that he left. I'm starting to understand why. It hurts like hell.

I feel guilty for the remark, so I slide off the bench and trail after her, drifting through people and trying to catch up. When I do, I hang back slightly and follow her in silence all the way back to the car. By the time we reach our level in the parking structure, my frozen yogurt has made me feel sick, so I dump it the first chance I get and then slide into the passenger seat of Mom's car without saying a word.

Mom doesn't say anything either. She drives with her eyes trained on the road, her lips occasionally twitching as she fights the urge to curse whenever another car pulls out a little too tightly in front of us, and only once every so often reaching over to increase the radio volume or the AC.

I still feel bad, and I hate when she doesn't talk to me, so, after fumbling with my hands in my lap for a few minutes, I lower the radio volume back down until the car is almost silent, and I look at her. "I didn't mean it the way I said it."

"You were right," Mom shoots back, her tone a little snarky. "I do know how it feels." When we stop at a red light, she leans back against her seat and folds her arms across her chest, but she doesn't look at me. "I know how it feels to be left behind and to spend every day wondering what you did wrong and if there was anything you could have done to stop them from leaving. I know how it feels to feel like you weren't good enough. I know how it feels to realize you weren't worth staying for." Finally, she glances sideways at me, and she looks incredibly angry. "You? You don't know how that feels."

I blink at her. I don't know whether to be furious, confused, or surprised. In fact, I'm all three. I'm furious at her for saying I don't know how it feels, confused at this aggression that has risen out of nowhere, and surprised at her for expressing herself the way she just has. She's never done that before. "What?" is all I can say at first, and then, gritting my teeth, I murmur, "I know exactly how that feels."

"No, Eden, you don't," she says, tone harsh and firm, as the light flashes to green and she reaches for the wheel again, driving off rapidly. "Tyler didn't leave because *you* were the problem. He left because *he* was. And me? *I* was the problem. So don't compare our situations, because I don't understand how you feel"—*I thought she did*—"likewise you don't understand how I feel"—*I thought I did*—"however much you think you do."

"Feel?"

She looks at me. "Felt."

Mom's never really been honest with me about what happened six years ago. I know the basics. I know that Mom was too laid-back for Dad. I know that Dad was too organized for Mom. I still don't know if it had always been that way. All I remember growing up were disagreements and arguments, so I'm guessing it had. When I was twelve, Dad spent a week at his cousin Tony's place. Mom never told me why, only smiled and told me he'd be back soon, but looking back, it's clear that she wasn't sure if he would be. Dad began to stay with his cousin more and more frequently that year. When I was thirteen, I hadn't seen him in a couple of days, and when I asked Mom if he was staying at Tony's again, she pulled me close, eyes brimming with tears, and said no. Tears were the only thing I saw for months after that. I knew Dad leaving really hurt her, I knew the divorce settlement was killing her, I knew she'd never be the same after that, but I've never known how she really felt. I didn't dare ask. She didn't dare tell me. Until now.

I'm quiet for a minute. "Do you still feel like you're not good enough?"

"How do you expect me to feel?" she snaps. She throws a hand up in frustration, and the car almost swerves, but she reaches back for the wheel and quickly steadies the vehicle. "When Ella's over there with that slim figure and perfectly blond hair that never seems to suffer from shitty gray roots and who doesn't have a single crow's-foot in sight and who drives a fucking Range Rover and is a damn lawyer. That's what your dad has now. What did he have before? Someone who can't cook a pot roast to save her life and someone who wears scrubs rather than suits and someone who once crashed that shitty Volvo we once owned because I rear-ended someone on the freeway. Of course I wasn't good enough for him. Your father's a perfectionist, and in case you hadn't noticed, I'm not perfect."

"And you think Ella is?" I yell at her, my cheeks burning. I feel like I have a responsibility to defend Ella. She welcomed me with open arms three years ago and has been there for me ever since, and hearing Mom talk about her in such a way angers me, so rather than taking my own mother's side, I take Ella's. "You don't think she's suffered through a divorce the same way you have? You don't think she had to go through weeks and weeks of court trials with Tyler? You don't think she has to live with the fact that her husband was beating the hell out of her kid and she didn't even notice? You don't think she blames herself every damn day for what happened? Because she does. She's not perfect and neither is her life, so just *shut up*."

What I really want to say is: *And you're the best mom I could have ever asked for. You might have to touch up your roots every few weeks, but your hair always looks great. You might have wrinkles, but you're so pretty that you can pull them off. You might not be the best driver, but you always get from A to B eventually. You might not be a lawyer, but you're an amazing nurse who always knows how to make people feel better, even outside the hospital. You might not be Ella, but I'm glad you're not.*

And I also want to say: *You're luckier anyway. You've got Jack, who's seriously great, and Ella has Dad, who's seriously an asshole. So who's really the winner here?*

But I don't because I'm furious.

"Oh, yeah. That's right," Mom says, rolling her eyes to the back of her head in annoyance as she scoffs. "She's your second mom. You'd know exactly, wouldn't you? Looks like you've replaced me with Ella the same way your father has."

I stare at her in disbelief. *Where is this coming from? Why are you so mad?* "What is wrong with you?"

Mom doesn't answer. She flicks the radio volume back up, louder than it was before, so that I can hardly hear myself think. She drives without looking at me or saying a word, her expression taut and her eyes narrowed. So I do the same. I angle my body away from her, fold my arms, and glare out of my window. I purposely kick my feet up onto the dash because she hates it when I do that, but she doesn't yell at me to take them down, so I don't.

The radio continues to blare all the way back to the house. Mom only turns it down when the car pulls up onto the driveway, and once we're stopped, she doesn't immediately cut the engine and jump out like she usually does, so I figure she wants to apologize. I look up from my sneakers, my arms still folded, and I wait. Her features have relaxed slightly, but now she looks confused. She looks at me and then over my shoulder.

I sit up and drop my arms, spinning my head around so fast that I'm surprised it doesn't snap off, and I see him. Sitting on the doormat outside the front door, anxiously picking at the hem of his white T-shirt, is none other than Tyler freaking Bruce. Again.

When my eyes meet his, he doesn't smile this time. He just pushes himself up and stands, waiting and waiting and waiting.

"The biggest difference between your dad and Tyler?" Mom says quietly. She hesitates for only a moment. "Your dad never came back."

chapter

5

No matter how much I plead with Mom to put the car in reverse and drive off, she won't do it. She turns off the engine completely and swings the keys around her index finger, tapping on the wheel with her free hand and refusing to say anything at all. No consolations, no reassurances. Just a stern expression as she forces me to get out of the car and face up to the one person I can't bear to look at.

It takes a lot of effort to walk over there. I'm quite literally dragging my feet, glancing over my shoulder one last time to throw Mom the biggest SOS I possibly can with my eyes, but she just shrugs and darts around the side of the house, opting to head inside through the back so as not to interrupt us out front. Tyler's still standing on the doormat, hands now stuffed into the front pockets of his black jeans, and he's anxiously chewing his lips.

I stop a few feet back from him and fold my arms. Up close, I can see the faintest blemish of red on his cheek, and I quickly feel guilty. So guilty, in fact, that I don't really want to meet his eyes, so I kick at the concrete path beneath my feet and let my eyes rest on a spot just below his shoulder. "Sorry for hitting you," I say.

Tyler shrugs slowly and reaches up to touch his cheek. "Don't worry about it."

Silence ensues. And it's so unbelievably awkward and uncomfortable that I think I could cry. *How did it end up like this? How did we get here?*

And then I remember the reason, and my urge to cry turns to the urge to lash out again, but this time I refrain. I keep kicking at the ground, scuffing the rubber around the front of my Converse. All I can hear are cars driving past.

"Can you come with me?"

I look up into Tyler's eyes now. "Where?"

"I don't know. I just want to talk for a while," he says, and I can hear the anxiety in his tone and see the worry in his eyes. "Can you at least give me that?"

"There's nothing to talk about," I say.

"There's everything to talk about."

No matter how much I'd rather avoid his gaze, his green eyes draw me in, like they always do. I used to love them, but right now I hate what they're doing to me. He's trying to gauge whether or not I'm going to argue against the idea, but I can't argue against something I agree with. He's right: there *is* everything to talk about. I just don't want to.

I think about it for a few long seconds, and as much as I want to run inside my house, I get the feeling that Tyler isn't going to let this go, so I figure it's best to at least get it over with now. That way he can leave me alone sooner rather than later. I don't answer him, but I nod once, and he immediately exhales in relief, as though he's been holding his breath the entire time.

Reaching into his back pocket, he pulls out his car keys, and at the same time, I catch Mom's eye. She's watching from the living room window, and when she realizes I've caught her, she ducks and disappears out of view. When I think about it, I would much rather talk to Tyler than her, so I turn and follow him across the lawn.

After a few steps, I realize something. His car isn't here. I even glance down the street twice, left and right, back and forth, and it's definitely not here. It's the kind of car that's hard to miss too, with its sleek design, gleaming bodywork and black rims, yet Tyler keeps walking, so I keep following. I arch my eyebrows when he leads me over to the vehicle parked across the street.

This isn't Tyler's car. This is black, and has four seats, and wheels covered in dry mud, and a couple of scratches along the passenger door, and is definitely not brand-new. It is, however, still an Audi. It's a model that's pretty popular, the type I see all over the city.

As Tyler heads around to the driver's side and unlocks the vehicle, I stare across the roof at him in confusion until he shrugs nonchalantly and says, "I downgraded." Then he slides into the driver's seat, so I get in the passenger side, pulling the door shut behind me.

"Why?"

He shoots me a sideways glance, his expression solemn. "I needed the cash."

I press my lips into a small line and look away as he starts up the engine. The car smells vaguely of an aftershave I don't recognize, and there's also a lingering scent of multiple air fresheners. There are three trees dangling from his rearview mirror. As he drives, my eyes continue to flit around the car so that I don't have to look at him. There are random brochures and shreds of paper at my feet, a trail of his T-shirts decorating the backseat, and some dust accumulating along the dashboard. The black leather seats are well worn, but it's still a pretty nice car.

We've been driving in silence for a few minutes, the radio off but the AC on full blast, when Tyler quietly says, "I like your hair like that."

Because I'm still slightly off-balance from being around him again after so long, I don't realize what he's talking about, so I reach up to pull down my sun visor. I slide open the tiny mirror and study my reflection. Right. My hair. The last time he saw me it was almost double the length. Now it only barely passes my shoulders.

I close the sun visor and pick at the threading around the tear in my jeans. "Mmm."

I think of all the other things about me that have changed too. Like the fact that I stopped applying mascara on a daily basis back in the fall because I grew tired of smearing it every time I teared up, and the way I sometimes take a minute to breathe before heading inside Dad and Ella's house. Like the gradual shift in my temperament, from being able to remain relatively cool and collected to losing it and snapping over the smallest of things because I am so filled with anger. Like the few extra pounds I have gained here, there, and everywhere.

A lot of things have changed.

Too much has changed.

My eyes fall to my lap, and I suck my stomach in so hard that breathing is difficult, but it's nothing I'm not used to. Back in sophomore year, I was an expert. I remain like this for a while. Occasionally, I relax for only a few seconds at a time when Tyler's attention is focused fully on the road. Even when my hips start to ache, all I can think about is that I don't want Tyler to notice my weight gain, so I keep on going, folding my arms across my stomach in an effort to hide myself and lifting my thighs slightly up off the leather passenger seat so that they don't appear so huge.

We drive for a while. We actually leave the city. Rush hour is upon us, so the traffic is already starting to build up, which makes the silence all the more painful. I don't make an attempt at starting up a conversation, because I don't have anything to say. Tyler is the one who has a lot of talking to do, not me, so we keep on driving for almost an hour despite how uncomfortable we both are, straight through Beverly Hills and West Hollywood until we pull onto North Beachwood Drive. I look up. And then I realize.

"Why are we here?"

Tyler doesn't cast a glance over at me. He only shrugs farther back against his seat and releases a small sigh. His eyes rest on the Hollywood Sign, perched high and far in the distance. "Because I don't know about you, but I haven't been here in a while. Up there *and* in this city."

Understatement of the year, I think. Rolling my eyes, I shake my head once and firmly say, "I'm not heading up there with you.

"You are," Tyler replies with an edge of confidence. "I've got some water in the back."

More silence, but only because this time I'm trying to string together a decent argument for why I can't fucking hike up Mount Lee right now, like: (1) because I'm wearing my best jeans and my new shirt, (2) because I really couldn't care less about heading up there, (3) because it's way too hot, and, finally, (4) because I really don't want to do this with Tyler. The effort of arguing my case, however, seems like more hassle than doing the hike itself. So I keep my thoughts to myself and frown instead.

We pass by the familiar sign for the Sunset Ranch and pull up a few moments later into the small parking area at the foot of the Hollyridge Trail. Like Tyler, I haven't been here in forever either. I've only ever done this once before, and that was three years ago, back when things were a whole lot different to how they are now.

When Tyler shuts off the engine, he doesn't hesitate. He pulls the keys from the ignition and pushes open his door, stepping out and glancing up at the sky. I get out too and walk around the car to meet him by the trunk.

"Just to be clear," I say as he opens it, "I really don't want to do this."

With one hand resting up on the lid of the trunk, Tyler looks at me from under his arm, and then looks away again. His trunk is full of all sorts of crap. Like more scraps of paper, a jacket, jumper cables, empty crushed cans of root beer, a small toolbox, and several bottles of water, which I doubt are fresh. He hands me one and shuts the lid.

"Let's get moving," he says.

In an act of defiance, I walk dramatically slowly while passing the warm bottle of water back and forth between my hands, humming. If it irritates Tyler at all, he certainly doesn't show it. I keep up the act for a few minutes before I realize I'm acting like a complete kid and he's way more mature than me. I quit it and catch up with him. And then we just walk, up and up, passing girls on horses and, later, a pair of middle-aged guys most likely on their way back down from the sign.

The entire time, there is silence. I'm starting to worry that it'll swallow us up soon. Somewhere between last July and now, we lost everything. We lost our inside jokes and our knowing glances, our special moments and our strongest promises, our courage and our secret. We lost the love and desire we shared.

I think silence is the only thing we have left.

We don't stop to catch our breaths as we continue to head up Mount Lee, following the Hollyridge Trail as it contours around the slopes, but I do start walking backward the majority of the time. I figure the view is prettier that way. There's something almost exhilarating about distancing yourself from the city and watching as it grows smaller and smaller beneath you. It's better than having to look at Tyler, that's for sure.

There's also something sad about being up here again, hiking over five hundred feet to see a bunch of letters perched on a mountain, winding around sharp turns under the burning sun. The first and last time I did this, I was with my friends. Or at least people I thought were my friends. Everything seemed a lot simpler back then and everyone seemed a lot nicer. I was friends with Tiffani. Rachael. Meghan. Jake. Dean. All of them. Or at least I thought I was. We were laughing and getting along and passing water around and jumping fences and being completely reckless together. But between then and now, over the space of three years, through arguments and fallings-out and breakups, I guess we all grew up.

What Tyler said in New York last summer was right—everyone does drift apart, everyone does stop talking, everyone does go their separate ways after high school. Our colleges are scattered across the country. Illinois, Ohio, Washington, and even here in California. I heard a few months ago from Rachael that Dean got into Berkeley. He'll be starting in the fall. Of course he didn't tell me himself—who would want to talk to their ex-girlfriend? Especially one who cheated on him with his best friend. But even though Dean hates me now, I still want the best for him and I'm sorry for how I hurt him. I almost find myself smiling as I think about him getting into Berkeley. I know just how badly he wanted to go there.

Tyler and I are on the paved road now, Mount Lee Drive, winding away from the sign only to curl back around toward it. I barely remember any of this. Along the ridgetop, I come to a stop and look out over the northern slope. I can see downtown Burbank. I don't remember this from the first time. Back then, I think my attention was focused on the Hollywood Sign and nothing else, so I take a minute to study Burbank while squinting through the harsh sunlight. I wish I'd remembered my sunglasses. Tyler has his.

"That's San Fernando Valley up there," he says quietly, and he nods off into the distance, way past Burbank.

"I know," I say dryly. "I do live here."

"Okay."

We walk again, passing some communications equipment, and shortly after that we round the turn back onto the southern slope. And there it is for the second time: the famous Hollywood Sign. Huge and bold as always, grasping the attention of millions of tourists each year, sitting proudly on its reserved spot on the steep south side of Mount Lee and protected by a fence and security cameras that crush thousands of dreams each year when people climb all the way up here only to realize that it is, in fact, illegal to touch this global icon.

There's no one here right now though, besides us. Tyler walks over to the fence, hooks his index finger around the metal, and then sighs.

"Are you gonna jump it?" I ask. Because I don't want to go through all of that again—touching the sign for a fraction of a second before making a beeline down Mount Lee and risking either a citation or death. I stay back and sit down on the dirt trail, crossing my legs. The ground is hot.

Tyler glances over his shoulder, and suddenly he looks way too old for his age. He's grown up so much. Maybe too much. "No."

He turns around and walks over to me, sitting down on the ground to my right. He doesn't come too close, but he doesn't leave a lot of space between us either. His legs are stretched out in front of him, and his palms are behind him, pressed flat on the dirt. Anxiety is radiating from him, and it feels almost contagious, because as I wait for how this conversation will start, I feel sweat on my forehead. I try to convince myself that it's just the heat.

It's incredible that despite how busy the city is, up here everything is completely calm and still. It reminds me of New York and how being up on the roof of Tyler's apartment building made it feel like we were cut off from the rest of the city for a while. Up here feels just like that.

Tyler still hasn't said anything. I shift my gaze from the fence, turning my head to look directly at him. He's staring ahead, his eyes narrowed softly, his lips pressed together, and for the first time since I saw him this morning, I take a few minutes to really look at him. His hair is longer, and so is his stubble, which I used to find incredibly attractive.

It traces his jaw almost carelessly now, messily making its way down his neck. My eyes trail from his lips to his arms, and finally I notice it.

I'm not sure if I wasn't paying attention or if I'd temporarily gone blind up till now, but I see my name. I'd forgotten all about it being there until right now. It's those four small letters that I thought were so stupid, even more so now, and they have faded slightly after a year. But they're no longer on their own. Around them, there are several new additions to his bicep, all connected and rolled into one huge tattoo, almost like half a sleeve. There's a clock face and a whole bunch of roses all wrapped up together, surrounding my name, with a lot of swirls and dark shading. It actually looks pretty good, but there's one question running through my mind.

Why didn't he cover up my name while he had the chance?

I swallow and look away before he can turn to meet my gaze. My hands are resting in my lap, so I tilt my wrist up toward me. There are no longer any words there, because they're covered up by a huge flying dove that I picked out of a book during spring break. It was when Rachael and I were in San Francisco. She got a string of flowers around her hip bone, and after she finally stopped crying with pain and after I stopped crying with laughter, she shoved a stack of the artist's books into my arms. I told her I didn't want another tattoo. She told me that wasn't what she was trying to say—she thought I needed a better one. And she was right. The artist told me that a dove symbolizes a new beginning, like in Noah's story in the Bible, and although I'm not particularly religious, I liked the idea of a fresh start.

That was the day I really gave up on Tyler, and the words *No te rindas*—Don't give up—were gone forever.

I bury my hand and my wrist back into my lap and bite at the corner of my lip. Part of me feels guilty for erasing the motto we lived by last summer, but I can't figure out why, because I have no reason to feel bad about it. I realize I'm shaking my head, but only at myself, and I try not to think about it. I look back to Tyler again instead.

His head is lowered now, his eyes boring intently into his jeans, and in the silence it's easy to hear his long, slow sigh. "You're mad at me," he says. It's a statement. A fact.

"And why are you surprised?"

Slowly, he lifts his head and fixes his soft eyes on mine. "I don't know. I guess I never thought about what to expect. I just thought—"

"That I'd be happy?" I finish for him. I'm much calmer now than I was earlier. Our voices are low and gentle, even though the atmosphere around us is growing tense. "That I'd be right where you left me? That I'd have spent a year waiting?"

"I mean," he murmurs, swallowing, "I guess so." His chest rises again as he releases another sigh, this one much heavier. "I thought you understood."

I take a long moment to play my next words through my head before I say them out loud. Then I take a deep breath and I begin to explain.

"I did at first. I got it. Everything that was going on was too much. Your dad, our parents, us." I hesitate on that final word for only a brief second, and then my eyes flicker away from Tyler again and toward the Hollywood Sign as I anxiously squeeze the bottle of water in my hand. I stare at the huge *H*. "But didn't you stop for a minute to think that maybe it was hard on me too? No, you didn't. You just ran away like a coward and left me to deal with all the shit we got ourselves into." I squeeze the bottle even harder, and I drop my eyes, staring at the cap instead. "I couldn't leave for Chicago until September, so I had to stick around here for two months. I wasn't even allowed in your house. My dad didn't talk to me, and the only times he did were when he was threatening to stop paying my tuition. Your mom couldn't look me in the eye, and don't even get me started on Jamie. You won't have a fucking clue, because you haven't been here, but he's kind of an asshole. He hates us both. Oh, and by the way, everyone knows about us. Absolutely everyone. But you wouldn't know that either. You wouldn't know the things people have said behind my back, and you wouldn't know how they look at me. You don't know anything because you didn't have to deal with any of it. *I* did, all on my own, and no matter how many times I called you just to hear your voice so that you could at least tell me it was going to be okay or something, you didn't even answer."

Tyler is silent, but I can feel him staring at me with that intense gaze of his. I breathe fast, and it's hard to stop my cheeks from burning up. *Don't cry*, I tell myself, over and over, until I'm mentally chanting it to myself like a mantra.

Don't cry. Don't cry. Don't cry.

You're mad at him. You're mad at him. You're mad at him.

Don't cry—you're mad at him.

"I don't know what to say," he finally admits. His voice is so shaky and so quiet that it's verging on a whisper, and he pulls his legs up toward him and leans forward, resting his arms over his knees.

"You can start by saying sorry."

A sideways glance again. A pained look in his eyes. A crease of worry on his forehead. He angles his body slightly to face me, and he reaches over to place his hand firmly on my knee, squeezing hard. "I'm sorry."

I stare at his hand on my body. It's been a while. His touch is almost uncomfortable, and I don't want it. I really don't. Pressing my lips together, I push his hand off my knee and look back out over the city. The afternoon is almost hazy, but Hollywood still looks beautiful, the way it always does. I can see downtown LA and its patch of skyscrapers, and my gaze lingers on them as I think about what sorry really means for Tyler.

Is he sorry for leaving in the first place? Sorry for our family turning against me? Sorry for being gone for so long? Sorry for ruining what we had?

For everything that he has done, sorry does not feel like enough.

"I am," Tyler says after I don't reply, and this time he doesn't reach for my knee, but my hand. He doesn't interlock our fingers, only grips my hand so tight that it almost hurts. "I really fucking am. I had no idea."

"Of course you didn't." I yank my hand free from his before pushing his chest back, shoving him away from me as my temper slowly flares up. "What did you expect? Did you think you'd just come home and everything would be fine? Did you think you'd just come back and I'd still be in love with you and our parents would accept us and everyone else would think we were super cute? Because it's nothing like that. My dad is *still* furious at me. Everyone thinks we're disgusting." I look at him straight in the eye, glaring as fiercely as I can without bursting into tears. "And I'm not in love with you."

Tyler physically recoils, as though I've just slapped him again, as if my words have physically hit him hard. His expression twists and his eyes pool with confusion. I can see a million questions running through his mind all at once, but he doesn't say any of them out loud. He only rests his elbows on his knees and presses his hands to his face before running them back through his hair. He pulls on the ends before dropping his hands again and tilting his head back. He's looking up to the sky, but his eyes are closed.

I kind of want to go home now. I don't want to be here with him. Chewing at the inside of my cheek, I reach for a couple of stones by my foot and gather them up into my hand. And then I throw them one by one toward the fence, toward the sign, toward the city. It distracts me from Tyler, because although I like to think that I don't care, I don't want to see how hurt he is.

"Why?"

My hand hovers in midair as I raise an eyebrow at him. "Why what?"

"Why aren't you…?" His voice tapers off into silence, and he simply can't force the words out of his mouth. He shakes his head fast instead. "What happened? What changed?"

"Are you kidding?" I lower my hand and quite literally laugh, but it's more out of contempt than humor. "Are you seriously fucking kidding?" I have to stop for a second to compose myself and control my anger before I explode like a grenade right there in front of him. Breathing in and out, I squeeze my eyes shut and count to three before I open them again to look back over at the complete moron by my side. "You disappear for a year, and you expect me to be that girl who sits around and dedicates her life to waiting for a guy? No. I've studied hard and I've met awesome people and I've loved living on my own and despite all the other bullshit that I've had to deal with, my year has been pretty damn good. So in case you weren't aware, I can live my life without you. I can survive without the mighty Tyler Bruce."

I run out of steam then, so I stop, even though there's so much more I could say. I don't want to admit the entire truth, however. I don't want to tell him how many tears were shed the first few days after he left, I don't want to tell him that the reason I've gained weight again is because eating junk food and ice cream with Rachael were the only things that comforted me, and I don't want to tell him that the longer he was gone the angrier I became.

The truth is, I have not been hopelessly in love for the past year.

I have been endlessly furious.

"Come home with me," Tyler says quickly, but his words are too fast and too urgent, and his voice is too cracked and too broken. "Come back with me, even for just a couple days, and let me show you. Let me show you what I've been doing and let me show you how much better I am and let me show you that I'm sorry and let me…let me…" He trails off to catch his breath before he lowers his voice to a mere whisper and says, "Let me fix this."

"You're already home," I blankly state. With both hands, I motion in front of me toward the sprawling city.

"No," he says, and he runs his bright eyes so intensely over my face that it makes me uncomfortable. "I don't live here anymore. I only came back for a couple days to…to see you. I got here last night and Mom's put me up in that swanky hotel by school that I can't even pronounce because she doesn't want your dad to know that I'm back, which I get. I go home on Monday."

I blink at him for a long while. "What?" My mind feels far too slow as I try to process what he's saying. There's information missing, yet I'm still pathetically trying to piece things together. Going home on Monday? He's already home. LA is his home. He's supposed to struggle to integrate back into the family and he's supposed to argue about his room being converted into an office and he's supposed to fight with Jamie the same way I do. That's what coming home means. "You're leaving again?"

He nods only once. "But this time I want you to come with me. My life's in Portland now and—"

"Portland?" I cut in so sharply that Tyler quite literally freezes, his lips still parted and his words caught in his mouth. "*Portland?*"

"It was the first place I thought of," he admits.

My blood immediately heats up with so much fury that my skin feels like it's on fire. My grip around the bottle of water in my lap tightens so hard that it almost explodes. I push myself up off the ground and get to my feet, taking up my stance directly in front of Tyler as I glare down at him. "You've been in *Portland?*"

I know I hate Portland. I know I shouldn't care where he's been because it shouldn't matter to me. No matter which city he's been in for the past year, it's the fact that he was gone that I found difficult. But there's something about the thought of him in Portland, in the city I was born in, walking the streets I once walked, that is really getting to me. I suddenly feel far too protective over Portland, like the city is *mine*. I don't want Tyler taking anything that's mine. Out of all the other cities in this damn country, why did he have to end up in the one I once called home? What's even more surprising to me is that I didn't know any of this until now. I've spent an entire year without knowing where the hell Tyler was. For a while, especially at first, I figured he most likely would have gone back to New York. But apparently not. Apparently, shitty Portland with its shitty rain and its shitty mountains was enough for him.

"Come back with me," he says again, only now his voice is pleading. He stands, takes a step toward me, and grasps my waist with both hands, his touch firm against my hips. "Please just come to Portland and give me a chance to fix this fucking mess, alright? Just for a few days, I swear, and if I'm not worth sticking around for any longer than a couple days, then you can go home. That's all I'm asking."

I stare straight back at him and I take a minute to really, really look at him up close. His eyes haven't changed at all. It's easy to search them for answers, for hidden truths and masked emotions. That's something I think I will always adore about him. And right now, he seems completely exposed. I can see absolutely everything in his eyes, from panic and worry to pain and anguish, all wrapped up as one powerfully intense gaze that is drawing me in. To think that I was once so utterly and entirely in love with this person is almost too hard to believe now. I have so much resentment toward him these days, so much contempt, that sometimes it hurts.

I do not want to go to Portland with him.

"We're done talking," I murmur, and then I press my hands to his chest and shove him a step back, breaking his hold on me once more. Pushing him away is what I'm best at now.

If I thought he couldn't look more pained than he already did, then I was wrong. His lips form a bold line as he stuffs his hands back into the front pockets of his jeans, and his eyes never leave mine. He has nothing else left to say. Watching me is all he can do.

I glance over my shoulder at the city one last time. And then I begin to retreat, slowly backing away from my stepbrother until I'm several feet away from him. For the first time, my words seem to catch in my throat and it proves difficult to get them out, but when I finally do, it's such a relief to hear my own voice say, "We're done, Tyler."

chapter

6

The ride home is even more awkward and unbearable than the ride here. Tyler and I haven't said a word to each other in over an hour. I didn't even walk back down Mount Lee alongside him; I walked ahead, and he kept some distance between us, lingering about fifty feet back. But only until we reached his car, and we're now trapped in a confined space with one another and have nothing to talk about. We've said everything we needed to. Yet although the atmosphere is tense, I feel content because I am consumed by relief. Talking to Tyler turned out to be a good idea. It was like I finally got some closure.

Rush hour is over by now, so the traffic isn't so bad on the route back to Santa Monica. We've been gone for almost four hours, so while Tyler focuses on his driving, I type out a text to my mom, letting her know where I've been and that I'm on my way home, but then I remember that I'm still mad at her, so I delete the message rather than sending it. I glance at Tyler out of the corner of my eye. He's driving with both hands under the bottom of the wheel, his eyes empty and his stare never leaving the road, his jaw clenched tight. I decide to text Rachael instead, and she's grateful for my information overload because apparently her grandparents are driving her insane as per usual.

So I tell her everything. I tell her about the way Tyler ambushed me this morning. I tell her about the argument with my mom. I tell her about Tyler waiting outside my house and demanding we talk. I tell her about the Hollywood Sign and the conversation that unfolded. And I tell her about Tyler living in Portland the entire time he's been gone and his insane request for me to go back there with him.

Her replies come fast.

WHAT DO U MEAN TYLERS BACK??
OMG you seriously hit him?
why would he live in portland? no offense or anything
he took you up to the sign????
I hope you didnt forgive him

Talking to Rachael makes the journey home that slightest bit more bearable.

It's almost 7:00 p.m. by the time we get back. The sun is already beginning to dip toward the horizon, even though it won't completely set until an hour from now, and I keep my eyes trained on it with such extreme concentration that I don't even realize Tyler has pulled up on Deidre Avenue, right against the curb outside Dad and Ella's place.

I push the sun visor up and angle my body to look at him. "I'm staying at my mom's place," I blankly point out, then cough, because my throat feels dry from being so quiet for so long.

"I know," Tyler says. He isn't looking at me; he's cutting the engine and releasing his seat belt. "But my mom wants us both here." It's only when he's pushing open his car door that he seems to hesitate, and I watch the way his eyes narrow at something through his windshield. I realize after a second that he's staring at Dad's Lexus parked up on the drive.

He's home from work. Of course he is. Dad usually gets home most days just after six unless he gets held up. I tend to like it when that happens. Today that isn't the case though, and it appears Jamie is home now too. His BMW is parked carelessly out on the street just ahead of us, and his wheels are pressed against the curb, most likely adding even more scratches to his already-wrecked alloys. Ella's been telling him for months now to be more careful, but he doesn't listen because he's Jamie, and Jamie never fucking listens.

I glance over at Tyler again. "I hope you know that if you step one foot over that threshold right now my dad will probably have you arrested or something. If there's anyone he hates more than me, it's you."

Tyler pulls the car door shut again, and just when I think he's about to finally take me home, he takes out his phone and calls Ella instead, pressing the device to his ear. He still hasn't looked at me. I don't think he has since we left the Hollywood Sign and made our way back down from the top of Mount Lee. I'm finding it difficult to gauge how he's feeling because for once his eyes aren't providing me with the answers. I can't tell if he's upset or furious or if he simply couldn't care less.

But his nonchalance doesn't last for too long, because as soon as Ella picks up the call, he becomes incredibly tense. "Yeah, hey, we're outside." He pauses. "I thought you weren't going to tell him." He's quiet again as he listens, and finally his eyes flicker toward me for a second before he lowers his voice and murmurs into his phone, "Mom, you know he's gonna kick my ass if I walk through the door with her." Another pause. I'm so curious, and the fact that I can't hear what Ella's saying is driving me insane. "Alright, but I can bet that this will backfire," Tyler says, and then hangs up.

I raise my eyebrows at him, my expression one huge question mark.

"We need to go in the back," he tells me, and then he promptly opens his car door again and steps out, slamming it behind him. So much for an explanation as to why the hell Ella wants us both here.

Sighing, I follow suit and step out onto the parking strip. The grass is bone dry and patches are fading to brown in places, but, like everyone else across the state, we just have to deal with it. If we turn on the sprinklers, we'll most likely be hit with a fine for wasting water during such an exceptional drought. It hasn't rained since April.

Tyler heads straight up the driveway, and he seems light on his feet and his movements are fast, like he's on a secret mission or something and he's trying not to get caught. In a way, I guess that's true. He's trying to avoid Dad. I am too, so I trail on his heels, following him through the gate and into the backyard. The pool is drained and several of Chase's soccer balls are lying at the bottom.

As we head across the dry, patchy brown lawn toward the patio doors, Ella scares the hell out of both of us when she appears out of nowhere on the other side of the glass. Frantically, she slides open the doors and ushers us in, telling us to shush and remain quiet, and then grasps my wrist.

"Stay in the hall until I tell you otherwise," she hisses to Tyler, her hold on me tightening as she begins to pull me across the kitchen. She's still in her suit, although now she's a few inches shorter without the heels and her steps are silent.

I still have no idea what's going on or why I'm here or why Ella isn't uncomfortable with Tyler and me turning up together. Explaining that doesn't seem to be her priority right now. Pulling me into the hall is.

"Can I ask you something?" I murmur, keeping my voice low.

Ella stops tugging and glances over her shoulder at me, and then at Tyler, who is following behind, before she rests her gaze back on me and raises an eyebrow as though to say, *Well?*

"What's going on?"

"Family meeting," she says without missing a beat. She fixes Tyler with a firm look, and he seems just as perplexed as I am. "Now wait here."

He does as she asks, and he leans against the wall, hands in his pockets, watching us both closely. At the other end of the hall I can hear voices, muffled slightly by the sound of the TV, but Dad's voice is impossible to ignore no matter how loud the TV is. Ella's still pulling me toward the living room, closer and closer, until she whispers, "I'm sorry," and then leads me into the room, leaving Tyler behind in the hall.

I'm not sure what she's apologizing for, but it immediately makes me anxious and unsettled. Why is she insisting on putting me through hell? First she ambushes me with Tyler and now Dad. But maybe this time it's the other way around. Maybe she's ambushing Dad with me. He's slumped back against the couch, his tie resting over the arm of it, with a cup of coffee in one hand and his feet up on the coffee table. He doesn't bother to lower the volume of the TV. "Look who decided to show up," he remarks, and then nonchalantly takes a sip of his coffee as though he couldn't care less. This is the first time he's seen me in almost a week.

"I told you she'd come back," I hear Jamie mutter from the floor. My eyes flicker down to him, but he hasn't even glanced up. He's sitting with his back pressed against the other couch, and his eyes are focused rather lazily on his laptop, which is resting on his knees. He's scrolling endlessly through a forum.

Chase is sprawled out on the couch, his phone in his hand and his earphones in. I don't think he's even realized that Ella and me have entered the room.

"How long will you be staying this time?" Dad asks, but he's verging on laughter as he sits up. Leaning forward, he takes down his feet from the coffee table and places his coffee there instead, and then he looks at me the way he always does, with contempt and disgust and a sense of sadness because he's unfortunate enough to have a daughter like me.

"The full week? A few days? A couple hours? Let me know, Eden, just how long you'll stick around this time before you drive off like a brat again."

I look back across the room at him the same exact way, with that same contempt and disgust and sense of sadness because I'm unfortunate enough to have a father like him. I can sense Ella rubbing her temples beside me. "Don't start sweating, Dad. I'm not staying."

"Alright," he says with relief. "Then what are you doing here?" He's deadly serious as he asks this, and his expression is blank despite the fact that I'm almost certain I can see dread in his eyes. It's like it's impossible for him to fathom the idea of a relationship between a father and his daughter where they actually *want* to see each other. But, luckily for both of us, I'd rather be anywhere else than here right now, so he doesn't have to worry about me dropping by to ask if we can spend a good old father-daughter day together. The thought almost makes me want to laugh.

"I don't know why I'm here," I say, and then I fold my arms across my chest and turn to Ella with a glare, my eyebrows knitting together while I wait for an explanation. "Maybe you can help me out."

Ella looks anxious again, even more so than she was earlier, right before she decided to throw Tyler back at me, and I'm not surprised. If there's anyone who's going to take the news of Tyler's reappearance any worse than I did, it's going to be Dad. Ella has every reason to be nervous, yet she builds up the confidence to walk into the center of the room, yanking Chase's earphone out of his ear as she passes. "Turn it off," she says to Dad once she's standing before us all in front of the TV.

"I'm waiting for the weather report," says Dad.

"Blue skies and still no sign of rain. There's your weather report," she says, and then places her hands on her hips. "Now turn it off."

Dad doesn't look too pleased, and as he reaches for the remote and finally switches off the TV, he's scowling as though he's a kid who's just been scolded. He's not exactly the kind of person who likes to be told what to do; he's more the kind of person who likes to do the telling.

"Jay," Ella says, but he doesn't look up from his laptop despite hearing her perfectly clearly. He purposely ignores her and switches tabs on his screen, pulling up Twitter and typing so fast that his fingers hitting his keyboard is the only thing we can all hear. He's most likely complaining about his dysfunctional family again. Ella clears her throat and swaps her firm voice for her stern voice, which you'd think are similar but are surprisingly easy to differentiate. Her stern voice is so sharp that the second you hear it, you know not to challenge her. "Jamie."

He looks up, dramatically sighs, and then shuts his laptop. He folds his arms across his chest and presses his lips together. "Tell me why we all have to stop what we're doing just because Eden decides to show up."

"That's not what this is about," Ella says. The stern voice is gone. The anxious one is back.

But Jamie's constant digs always aggravate me, so I end up talking over the top of Ella, saying, "Will you ever just cut it out?"

"Will you?" Jamie fires back. Ella lowers her head, presses her fingertips to her temples again, and exhales a long sigh.

"What's that supposed to mean?" I drop my hands to my hips and glare down at him on the floor. I'm used to Dad throwing remarks at me these days, mostly because he's been doing it for years now, but I'm still not accustomed to Jamie muttering under his breath and complaining every time I'm around, so it's much easier to snap at him than it is to snap at Dad. I think Dad likes it when Jamie and I fight. If I'm a troublesome kid, it makes his loathing for me seem more valid.

"Both of you stop," Ella orders, her voice so loud and clear that we immediately do. Jamie and I glance over to her.

"Are we moving or something?" Chase asks quietly, removing

his other earphone and twirling the wires around his index finger. "Because if we are, can we move to Florida?" Ella only shakes her head back at him.

These so-called family meetings are very unusual for us all—so unusual, in fact, that we've never had one before. I guess it's because we're not a real family. Real families don't hate one another like we do. Real families aren't as strained as we are. Real families don't have to deal with the stepkids falling in love like Tyler and I did.

Since the moment last summer when Dad and Ella found out the truth about Tyler and me, everything has changed. They argue more. They have fights that don't get resolved for days. Dad only lets me stay in the house every second week when I'm home for the holidays because he has to, because that's what fathers do. But he hates it. He absolutely hates it, and he doesn't hide it. If it weren't for Ella and Chase, I doubt I'd agree to it.

Jamie's turned to rebellion, fighting back against our messed-up family. He doesn't want to be associated with us, because we're an embarrassment, something to be ashamed of. Tyler hasn't even been here, so I'm not sure if he even counts as a member anymore. I think Chase is the only one holding us all together. He's the only one who remains accepting and innocent and happy.

I guess in a way we're all just broken pieces, hoping somehow to fit together to become a perfect picture, a real family. But that will never happen. We will never, ever fit.

"We aren't moving anywhere," Dad clarifies for Chase, but his words are gruff and he quickly shoots Ella a questioning glance, as though he's checking this is true. She nods. "So what is this all about?"

"I need you all to keep your cool," she begins. Her eyes flicker around the room as she rests her gaze briefly on all of us, even me: as though I don't already know what the big news is, as though I have no idea that

Tyler is standing in the hall. She looks at Dad a little longer than she looks at the rest of us and she says, "Especially you."

"I hope you're not quitting your job," Dad mumbles, but at least now he's giving her his full, undivided attention. I think he's even starting to worry slightly. Ella's usually not one for dramatic announcements like this.

"New car?" Jamie guesses.

"Are you being sued?" Dad asks after clearing his throat. He sounds much clearer now, and I can see the brief panic in his eyes.

Chase sits up. "Wait. Lawyers can be sued?"

Ella loudly exhales and throws her hands up in frustration. "Can you all stop jumping to conclusions just for one second?"

They all shut up. The room goes silent. All four of us look at her. We wait for her to say something, but she doesn't. At least I know what's going on. I'd be going insane if I didn't because all Ella is doing now is pacing the living room back and forth. She ends up nervously circling the coffee table while murmuring under her breath, most likely testing the truth on her lips before she reveals it out loud. In a way, it saddens me that she's so anxious about her own son being home. I might not be able to bear Tyler anymore, but it's still uncomfortable to see how fearful she is of the rest of the family knowing the truth. It shouldn't be like this.

"Maybe we wouldn't jump to conclusions if you would tell us what this is all about," Dad remarks dryly after Ella's been pacing for a good minute. He's leaning forward now, sitting on the edge of the couch, his hands interlinked between his knees.

Ella stops walking. She glances over at me, presumably for some kind of reassurance or encouragement, but she gets neither. I only fold my arms across my chest again and sit down on the arm of the couch next to Chase. He offers me a small smile before focusing his attention back on his mom. We're all still waiting. It feels like this morning all over again, with Ella unnecessarily dragging out the all-important fact that Tyler is back and he's here and he's in the hall and there's about to be a riot in this house.

"Now listen," she finally says, but we already are. We've been listening for several minutes now. "This shouldn't come as a surprise to any of you because we all knew this was going to happen eventually. And you need to keep in mind that things have changed and certain situations aren't the same, so there's no need to cause a scene." She catches my eye only briefly, and I realize exactly what she means about things having changed. She means: *It's okay, there's nothing to be worried about now, Tyler and Eden aren't like that anymore, they're not crazy, they're normal again.* I like to think we've always been normal.

"Ella…" Dad straightens up on the couch and then pauses for a moment. "Don't tell me…I swear to God. Do not tell me that that damn kid is moving back in."

She looks at Dad and only at Dad. "And what if I did tell you that? He has every right to move back in. He's my son."

"Wait," Jamie interjects. He pushes his laptop off his thighs and gets to his feet. "Tyler's moving back in?"

"That kid is *not* moving back in here," Dad answers stiffly, but his eyes are trained on Ella rather than Jamie. He stands, leaning over her by several inches, as he fixes her with a fierce look that only the bravest of people would challenge. "I will not have him here, and that's final, so if that's the big news you're about to tell us, don't."

"If he wanted to move back in, then I'd let him," Ella says, and her voice is strong and clear, all signs of nervousness long gone. She's one of those brave people. "But he doesn't. He's just visiting for a few days and that's all."

"When?"

"He's already here," she says a little more quietly. Spinning around, she walks toward the door with her head held high, refusing to back down when it comes to defending Tyler. I think I'll always admire her for that.

"Here?" Dad echoes, staring after her in disbelief. "He's *here?*"

Ella doesn't answer. She only glances at me as she passes. She swings open the door into the hall and disappears for a second. All I can think is that I would not like to be Tyler right now. The thought of him walking into this room makes me nervous because it's clear that it is not going to go down well with either Dad or Jamie.

"Don't you dare get any ideas," Dad hisses at me while Ella's gone, like he honestly believes I'd throw myself at Tyler and kiss him right there and then in front of them all. *News flash, Dad: I already know he's here, I've already set things straight with him, and I've already gotten over him.*

"I couldn't care less about Tyler," I say. Although I could. Tyler being back is still uncomfortable, still awkward, and still painful. But trying to tell Dad this would only be a waste of time, as always. Like Jamie, no matter how many times I have tried to emphasize the fact to Dad that there's nothing between Tyler and me anymore, he still doesn't believe me. Dad once told me that if we were able to lie about our relationship before, then we'd be able to lie about it again. I remember thinking at the time, *There's no relationship to lie about.*

Ella reappears by the door, but, of course, this time Tyler is with her. He walks into the room first, brushing past me and Chase, and then through the middle of Dad and Jamie before heading around the coffee table and stopping in front of the large bay windows. Ella doesn't follow him but instead lingers by the door, standing right by my side.

"Mom's right," Tyler says, and his voice is tight and clear. He looks at everyone but me. "I'm not moving back in. I'm only back in town to see how everyone is doing. I'm leaving on Monday." Unbelievably, the corners of his lips pull up into a soft smile. "Surely you guys can put up with me until then, right?"

But the joke doesn't go down well at all, and it becomes immediately obvious that Tyler has underestimated just how strained our family really is. No one laughs or heaves a sigh or rolls their eyes as though to say, *Well, whatever. You angered us all, but that was a year ago, so I guess we're over it now*, because no one is thinking that. No one wants him here, besides Ella and possibly Chase. Tyler standing over there in front of us all makes him look isolated, and there's this sense of sadness somewhere inside of me again. I know how much it hurts to feel like the rest of your family is against you.

"Are you kidding me right now?" Dad spits, his voice sounding guttural as he flashes his eyes to Ella in complete disbelief. She rushes over to him while stammering a series of useless pleas.

"Why wait until Monday?" Jamie says casually at the same time as he takes a threatening step toward Tyler, like he's gearing up for a fight. They're both pretty much the same height now, and they're eye level with one another. "Why not leave now? No one here wants to talk to you, except—I don't know—Mom? And your *girlfriend*, I guess." He throws a disgusted glance over his shoulder in my direction.

The confusion and surprise is evident on Tyler's face, and his expression contorts, his eyebrows drawn together and his jaw clenched. It's hard to believe that once upon a time, he and Jamie actually got along. "What the hell, man?" He looks over at me on the arm of the couch, almost like he's begging for an explanation as to why his brother is suddenly against him.

"I did warn you," I say loudly over the sound of Dad and Ella arguing, but then I remember the "girlfriend" reference, so I turn to glare at Jamie instead. "And damn it, Jay. Does it look like I'm totally damn thrilled that he's here? Because I'm not. I'm just as pissed off at him as you are."

Jamie only grinds his teeth together and fixes his eyes back on Tyler. "Isn't that another reason for you to get the hell out of here? We don't need you here, and we're all better off when you're gone."

"Why are you so mad?" Tyler asks, and he is so lost and unsure of what's going on that it makes him appear vulnerable and young. He's struggling to comprehend why things are so drastically different to how he remembers them, but that's because he hasn't been around to witness them changing. "I mean, I get why Dave is…" He frowns at Dad and Ella, who are still arguing. "But why are you? I haven't done shit to you, man."

"Except make school hell. I'm *your* brother. That's all I am. Tyler Bruce's brother." Jamie hesitates for a second to keep his temper, blowing out a long breath. "You know what people are saying now?" he asks. "They're saying that insanity runs in our fucking genes, man. That we've got no morals. First Dad, then you, and guess what? Apparently it's my turn to do something sick and twisted next. A couple months ago, some kid I don't even know asked if I was already hiding something, because apparently we're all infamous for keeping secrets in this damn house."

Dad and Ella's raised voices seem to fade out, because all I can hear over and over are the words Jamie has just spoken. I stare at him with wide eyes, the same way Tyler is staring at him. I had no idea that Jamie felt that way. He has never expressed himself so openly before, but now that he has, his attitude finally makes sense. He isn't just disgusted by the thought of Tyler and me together; he is being tormented over it the same way I have been. And I understand that now. I understand that the kids his age, that the people he faces every day, must think that we're a joke of a family. I'll bet they laugh about it. I'll bet they snicker about the guy whose siblings apparently dated one another. I never thought about the way the truth about our relationship would impact everyone else until now. I can't blame Jamie for being hostile and distant, because it's *our fault*, and now the truth about his dad's violent nature and his brother's inappropriate love interest are being used to taunt him.

And for all the time I have thought that Jamie and I are nothing alike, maybe we aren't so different after all. Maybe we lash out because it's the easiest way to cope.

I rise to my feet and warily steal a look at Tyler to determine whether or not the reference to their father has triggered a nerve, but it appears it hasn't. He would be furious right now if it had, because as long as I've known Tyler, he's never been able to handle the sensitive topic of his father. And I can't blame him for that. I can't blame him for hating his dad after the abuse he put him through. I can't blame him for the way he flipped out last summer when he heard about his dad being released from prison.

But today, for some reason, all Tyler has done is take a step back from Jamie, who is much more enraged than he is. Jamie's cheeks are flaming such a vibrant red that I fear he might just burst a blood vessel any second now. Tyler looks relatively still in comparison, but I've known him for years now, and I have a pretty good idea of just how easily his temper can snap. I scamper over to the two of them.

I want to tell Jamie that I'm sorry. That I didn't understand until now. That I didn't mean for any of this to become such a mess, so damaged and so broken. I want to tell Ella that I'm sorry for ruining her relationship with Dad. I want to tell Dad that I'm sorry for disappointing him. I want to tell Chase that I'm sorry about all the arguments he has to witness. I want to tell Tyler I'm sorry that this is the family he has come home to. *I'm sorry, I'm sorry, I'm sorry.*

"People are acting like that?" Tyler finally says, but his voice is low, like he's not really registering how serious all of this is. I think he's possibly still in shock over just how much of a war zone this house has become. Jamie nods once, so Tyler moves his attention back to me. There are thousands upon thousands of questions in his eyes, but I don't have the energy left to keep giving him answer after answer. I've already done that today.

"I did warn you," is all I can say again. Maybe back at the sign he thought I was exaggerating. Maybe he thought I was just being dramatic when I told him everyone knows about us, that Dad's an even bigger asshole than he's ever been before, that Jamie can't stand us. Maybe if he had believed me, this wouldn't have come as such a surprise to him. Maybe then he wouldn't be at a loss for words right now.

I hear Chase quietly ask, "Why do you guys have to fight? Why are you guys fighting in the first place?"

I hadn't even noticed Chase edging himself between me and Jamie until he spoke. We're in a circle now, the four of us, and our eyes scour each other as we wait for someone else to answer, because none of us know what to say. It's not that Chase is clueless—he knows about Tyler and me; he watched the fallout last summer, and he didn't say much for a few days after—but the unspoken rule in this house is that we keep him out of all of the drama.

"I don't want you to leave," he says. He's looking up at Tyler. "You just got back. And hey, I like those." Lifting a finger, he points toward Tyler's bicep and the design that will forever remain there. He doesn't appear to notice my name amid the roses and the swirls and the clock face, and if he does, he certainly doesn't point it out. "Did it hurt?"

Tyler's eyes fall to his arm as he angles his bicep toward him, like he's forgotten that the tattoos are even there, and he pulls up the short sleeve of his T-shirt to reveal even more of the picture. "Like a bitch," he says in such a low voice that it's almost a whisper, and then he smirks and holds out his hand, palm up. Chase low-fives him, and then, as though the atmosphere in here isn't toxic and suffocating, Tyler steps forward and pulls him into a hug, wrapping his arm around the back of his brother's neck and holding him tightly. "Missed you, kid. You keep getting taller. Last time I saw you, you were—what?—maybe this high?" He holds his hand out flat against Chase's shoulder, laughs in a way that is genuine, and then releases his grip on him. Chase is sheepish as he backs away, and Tyler's playful expression falters back to a solemn gaze that ends up resting on Jamie. "You too," he says. "Seriously, I have."

"Don't even try it," Jamie warns him.

I'm about to say something at this point, but Ella grasps my shoulder and pulls me out of the sibling-rivalry circle. I hadn't even noticed that the arguing with Dad had ceased until now, when an uncomfortable silence falls upon the living room and Ella spins me around to face her. It's like she's suddenly developed years' worth of wrinkles in the space of a few minutes just from the stress of the situation that she's in, because her taut, worn-out expression suddenly makes her seem much older than she really is.

"God, everyone just stop!" she yells in exasperation, but her throat is dry and her voice is croaky. Squeezing her eyes shut, she concentrates on slowing her heavy breathing before she talks again, and, like before, we all wait.

Dad's standing at the opposite side of the room, his hands on his hips, his wide stance intimidating. He's shaking his head as though he's still refusing to accept any of this. Like Jamie, the anger in his eyes is impossible to ignore.

"There's something else," Ella says.

Now she's got my attention. Something else? I knew about Tyler being back, but I didn't know about this. I didn't know that there even could be anything else. What is there left to tell? What can she possibly throw at us now? Tyler and I exchange a sideways glance, but it seems he's searching my expression for answers the same way I'm searching his, and neither of us have them.

"What now?" Dad quite literally groans. His voice is still strident and hard, but that's nothing unusual. "Has he brought a criminal record home with him? A probation order? Do we need to pay for a damn lawyer next?"

I wrinkle my nose at Dad in disgust. If I were Tyler, I'd have thrown a punch by now, and I'm kind of hoping that he will. He doesn't. Actually, he hardly even flinches at the remark, and the fact that there is no reaction whatsoever makes me question if he's even heard Dad's snide words. He just keeps his eyes fixed on Ella, his jaw tight.

Ella exhales, and then, ever so slowly, she announces, "We're going out of town for the weekend. All of us."

And I think, *What?* Out of town? All six of us? This pathetic excuse of a family? It's quite possibly the most dangerous idea I've ever heard. I do not want to be stuck with Dad, and I do not want to be stuck with Tyler. *No, no, no, no, no.* I am not going. I will refuse to.

"Excuse me?" Dad stammers.

"Look at us and try to tell me that everything is fine," Ella says sharply, motioning all around the room with both hands, to all the broken pieces standing in front of her. "We all need to spend some time together for *once*."

"We don't need to be taking trips out of town together."

"Oh, please, David," she snaps, her patience wearing far too thin. "I refuse to put up with comments like yours, so we are fixing this and we are fixing it *now*. Have you even heard the way you talk to Eden lately? Don't you think there's something wrong here?" By the way Dad blankly stares at me, it is obvious that he does not. "The weekend will do us all some good. We're going to Sacramento, and we leave tomorrow, so all five of you get packing."

And then there is a total uproar.

Jamie is whining, "I'm not going to Sacramento! What the hell, Mom? I'm taking Jen out for dinner on Saturday."

And Ella is saying, "You're grounded, so that definitely won't be happening. And I'm sure Jennifer can survive a weekend without you."

And then Dad is barking, "Have you no consideration at all for the fact that I have work?"

And Ella is saying, "Yes, and I spoke to Russell, and you've been granted absence on exceptional circumstances. Family emergency."

And then Tyler is murmuring, "Mom, I gotta leave on Monday."

And Ella is saying, "You can head home on Monday evening after we get back."

And now I'm arguing, "Do we have to? Don't you think it'll make all of this even worse than it already is? Sorry, but I'm out."

And Ella is saying, "I don't think this can get any worse."

And I guess she's right.

Dad's the first to storm out of the room, muttering and cursing under his breath, his hands moving rapidly in sync with his words as he swings open the living room door so hard that I'm surprised it doesn't snap off its hinges.

Jamie is the next to leave, and Chase follows him out. I hear their footsteps on the stairs, pounding as they jog up them, and then the slamming of a bedroom door, which can only be Jamie's.

Ella's hands are pressed against her forehead as she rubs her temples with her thumbs, trying to soothe away the headache this evening has caused her. She doesn't look at us before she leaves the room, and I wonder if it's because she's thinking, once again, that Tyler and I are the reason this family turned against one another.

And then we're the only two left. Tyler and me.

The house is entirely silent now. No more yelling or arguing, because no one is talking anymore. Tyler looks at me and I look at him, but we have nothing left to say either. I glance away after a few seconds.

I'm the first to leave, and, for once, he is the last.

chapter

7

The next morning, I'm at Rachael's house by ten. Mom got off her shift at six, so by the time I woke, she was already home and asleep. I was glad about that in a way, because I'm still pretty mad at her. I was able to leave the house without having to face her, but at the same time, I still haven't got a chance yet to tell her that later I'll be leaving for Sacramento. I did tell Jack, and he promised he'd let Mom know as soon as she wakes.

"Isn't it considered kidnapping? Forcing you to go against your will?" Rachael queries. She's sprawled out across her bed, her head resting over the edge to allow her to look down at me on the floor. The remnants of yesterday's makeup are visible on her face.

I'm laying on my back, repeatedly tossing my phone into the air and catching it again, staring at the ceiling and wondering why half the things in my life have to suck so much. "It wouldn't be so bad if it was only for one night, but it's not. It's three," I murmur.

Rachael frowns down at me. She's currently on a *Desperate Housewives* marathon, so there's an episode playing in the background that neither of us have really been paying any attention to. "And I thought being stuck with my grandparents for a day was bad. You're stuck with your dad *and* your ex-boyfriend for three days."

I roll my eyes sideways at her. "He's not my ex-boyfriend. We were never official."

"Ex-lover then." She props herself up onto her elbows and rests her head in her hands, rubbing at her eyes, smudging her mascara even more than it already is. "I still can't believe he was in Portland, literally in the state next door, and he still didn't come and see you. Isn't it only a few hours' drive?"

"More like fourteen." I drop my phone on my face, almost cracking a tooth, so I throw it across the carpet in aggravation and then sit up. "But I know, right? And the weird part is that he's calling Portland his home. Like, how did that happen? How did my home become his and how did his become mine?"

Rachael blinks. "What?"

"Never mind." Heaving a sigh, I draw my knees up to my chest and run my hands back through my hair, fighting the urge to scream Rachael's house down. *I do not want to go to Sacramento.* I lift my head and look at her, my expression solemn and my tone flat as I say, "Let's run away."

Rachael grins. "I've always wanted to go to Vegas."

"Then Vegas it is."

She tosses a pillow at me, so I hurl it back at her, only for her to tuck it under her chest to prop herself up. "So is there anything different about him?"

"What?"

"Tyler," she says. "Has he grown his hair down to his shoulders? Pierced his lip? Shaved a slit into his eyebrow? Discovered a religion? Preaches about saving the planet? Anything?"

I shake my head. "Just more tattoos."

"More? Did he have tattoos before?"

"Just one." I don't want to tell her about that tattoo, about my name being forever etched into his skin, so before she can ask, I add, "And he's a lot calmer, I guess."

"Calmer? Are we talking about the same guy here?"

"You're doing it again," I say, and my lips form a bold line as she looks at me with an eyebrow arched questioningly. "You're so adamant about believing that he's an asshole, but you *know* he's changed since high school, Rach. You saw the difference last summer."

"Last summer I remember Dean coming back to our hotel with his face all busted up, and we both know who did that," she mutters, and then rolls over to the opposite side of the bed.

"Oh my God. *Please* don't bring that up."

"But it's true!" she groans, shooting upright on the bed and glaring down at me on the floor. "Why do you keep acting like Tyler is some magically reformed guy who's a total saint or something? Seriously, Eden? He left you because he's a total coward, he screwed Dean over the same way you did, and he'll throw a punch at anyone who says anything that pisses him off, yet you're still sitting here defending him right now? Are you still in love with him or something?"

I narrow my eyes and push myself up off the floor, getting to my feet so that I'm the one now glowering down at her. "I'm far from in love with him, and you know that. But I can't deny the fact that he's changed. Do you wanna know what happened last night? Jamie made a reference about their dad right in front of his face, and Tyler didn't even flinch. Dad said something about criminal records and probation orders, and he *still* didn't flinch." I pause. "A year ago I would have been the one having to stop him from kicking both of their asses right there and then."

Rachael stretches up on her knees and folds her arms across her chest. "What's your point?"

"My point is that he's changed," I say again, much slower this time, as though it'll help to make that fact sink in. "And I don't know how many times I'll have to tell you that before you stop being so judgmental of him."

"Fine. Whatever," Rachael says nonchalantly, sighing as she flops back down onto her bed, turning to look at her TV. The episode has ended, so she reaches for the remote on the bedside table and flicks to the next one.

At the same time, I can't help but realize that I keep finding myself in arguments recently, and each one of them seems to have centered around Tyler. Constantly with Dad. Constantly with Jamie. Yesterday with Mom. Right now with Rachael. Even though Tyler hasn't been in my life for the past year, he has still managed to find a way to come back and ruin it. I blame him for all of this, for making every single part of my life a mess, and I feel as though I loathe him now more than I did before, although I'm not sure if that's even possible. And for the following three nights, I will be forced to be around him.

Biting at my lower lip, I make my way over to Rachael's window to look out over Deidre Avenue. Like mine, her bedroom is front and center, and sometimes we'll wave across the street to one another from our rooms. It's quite lame, really, but it makes us feel connected even when we aren't together.

Thinking of my room, I frown through the glass at Dad and Ella's house. All of the cars are there, except mine and Tyler's. As pathetic as it sounds, I parked mine a couple of houses down so that neither Dad nor Ella figure out I'm here. I'm trying to avoid them, but I still find myself wondering what they're doing right now. Will they still be arguing? Packing in silence and refusing to make eye contact with one another? Will Jamie be making a last-ditch attempt to worm his way out of the trip? Will Chase be the only one who is actually excited to go? I don't know, but I'm glad I'm not there.

"Do you think he's still in love with you?" Rachael asks over the sound of the episode's intro, reducing the volume at the same time. I'm not sure where her sudden change of subject has come from, but I do know that it takes me by complete surprise.

When I turn around to look at her, she's already staring back at me, her gaze soft. She is totally calm and relaxed again, as though we didn't just lose our cool with one another. "I don't want him to be," I say, my voice slightly raspy. I clear my throat and straighten up, padding across the carpet to retrieve my phone from the floor. I check the time and find that it's after eleven. "I should go. We're leaving at around one, and I haven't packed yet."

Rachael pauses the TV and heaves herself up off the bed, ready to lead me downstairs. Both her parents are at work, so we've had the house to ourselves, which I've been grateful for. Ella would not be happy if Dawn and Philip had heard me venting about our private drama. She prefers it when the cracks in our family aren't visible, although they're becoming increasingly hard to hide.

"Pack the ugliest panties you can find," Rachael says.

My eyes narrow, and I glance at her, mystified. "What?"

"It'll keep Tyler away."

"You're gross," I say, shaking my head and pulling a face, but she only sticks her tongue out at me. I purposely nudge her out of the way, but it's only playful. "I'll let myself out."

"Enjoy the trip," she tells me, but she's fighting the urge to laugh. "I can see it going one of two ways: you all bond exceptionally well and come home as one big old family of best friends. Or," she says, "you all end up killing each other by tomorrow morning."

"Probably the latter," I deadpan. "I'll end up calling you every half hour to rant, so I hope you won't mind."

"Never."

I tell her I'll see her next week, and she promises to pray for my sanity over the next few days, and then I head downstairs and leave her to finish her *Desperate Housewives* marathon in peace. I make a dash from Rachael's front door, and I'm careful to keep my head down. I'm satisfied when I make it back to my car without anyone noticing, and it makes me think about how tragic it is that I am now at the point where I am sneaking down the street in order to avoid Dad or Ella spotting me. As I'm driving home to Mom's place, all I can think about is turning the car around and driving the hell out of this city. Maybe to San Diego or Riverside, where I could hide out until Dad and Ella are forced to leave without me. That's how much I am dreading this trip to Sacramento.

But I don't have the courage to pull that off, so I end up back on my own driveway, back at my own house, and prepared to pack a suitcase for a trip that I do not want to take. Thinking about it has put me in a foul mood, so I enter the house looking much more disgruntled than usual. Surprisingly, Mom is awake and already stacking cutlery into the dishwasher. She pauses and straightens up when she hears me, pulling her robe even tighter around her.

"Oh," I say. I close the door behind me and hesitate in the middle of the living room, looking back at her in the kitchen. We haven't spoken since our argument yesterday. "Why are you up so early?" When she does night shift, she's never usually awake before one, so this is unusual.

"Jack told me you're going to Sacramento with your dad," she says very slowly, not quite answering my question.

I run the tips of my fingers over my eyebrow and then rub at my temples. "Yeah. I don't really have a choice."

"It's very last minute." She leans back against the kitchen countertop and studies me with great intensity.

"I know. Ella thinks it'll bring us all back together or something." I shrug and look around the house. Usually Gucci has knocked me to the floor by now. "Where's the dog?"

"Jack's taken her for a walk," she says. She pushes herself away from the countertop and approaches me with her arms folded across her chest and her slippers scuffing against the tiled kitchen flooring. There are still a few feet between us when she stops. "Do you want to go to Sacramento?"

"Does it look like I want to go to Sacramento?" I point at my own face with both index fingers to emphasize my pissed expression, sharpening my glare. "Ella's not giving me a choice."

"And is Ella your mother? No." Mom cocks her head to one side. "If you don't want to go, I can talk to her."

"What's the point? She's not going to back down." I groan out loud and run my fingers through the ends of my hair, dragging my feet across the living room toward the hall and my bedroom door. As I'm pushing it open, I throw a glance back over my shoulder at Mom, who's frowning at me. "So yeah, I'll be out of town from now until Monday. I gotta pack."

I head into my room and close the door behind me, hoping that Mom won't follow, and thankfully she doesn't. Maybe we'll do that thing where we don't talk about what happened yesterday and, instead, move on like nothing ever happened. I'm not sure which I'd prefer, but I don't have time to think about it because Dad and Ella are coming by to pick me up in just under two hours. I've left packing and showering and getting ready until the last minute, so now I'm rushing.

I drag out my suitcases from under my bed, tossing the smallest onto my bed and flipping it open. The flight labels from when I flew home last month are still attached, so I tear them off and then shred them up into as many pieces as I possibly can. Maybe this summer would have been better if I'd stayed in Chicago. I would have never had to deal with Tyler or Dad. I would be in Illinois, totally oblivious of the drama back home, heading out on road trips with my roommate and traveling around the Midwest. We'd stay up way too late, and we'd sleep all day. We'd go to parties and concerts and festivals. But that didn't happen because my roommate headed home to Kansas City while I came home to Santa Monica, and it is quickly proving to be one of the worst decisions I have ever made. The only thing that is keeping me going is the hope that when Tyler leaves for Portland again, things won't be so bad. Maybe this weekend will be the last I'll ever see of him.

Dad's Lexus pulls up outside the house fifteen minutes early. He keeps on honking the car horn, and Mom keeps on yelling from the living room that he's outside, and Gucci keeps on barking, but I'm not exactly ready. My hair is still damp after jumping in the shower, and I'm trying to throw last-minute essentials into my backpack, like my phone charger and the perfume Mom gave me for Christmas and my earphones and the February edition of *Cosmopolitan* with Ariana Grande on the cover that I found in my closet, all while yelling, "Yeah, I know! I can hear it, Mom!" and pulling on my Converse at the same time. I've almost broken a hip by the time I scramble into the living room, wheeling my suitcase behind me and wringing the ends of my hair with my free hand, my backpack slung over one shoulder.

Mom's dressed by now, and she's standing by the window, surreptitiously peering through the blinds, but as I near her, she suddenly darts away and says, "Here he comes."

A split second later, the doorbell rings, and then Dad's rapping his hand against the door. Mom is literally rolling her eyes straight to the back of her head while tutting, and as Gucci paws at the door, she steps forward and pulls it open.

Dad's outside, dramatically holding his wrist up to his face to make a point of looking at his watch, and Gucci makes a lunge for him, which I am so, so pleased about until Mom latches on to her collar and holds her back.

Dad immediately retreats a few steps while pulling a face, fixing Gucci with a dirty look, as though she'd been planning on tearing him to shreds or something. All the while, I'm lingering over to the side, slightly out of view.

"Yes, David?" Mom says nonchalantly, but with an air of sweet sarcasm as she rubs Gucci's ears.

Dad's lips form a tight line. "Has Eden gone deaf overnight? Where the hell is she? We have a six-hour drive ahead of us, and we need to leave now."

"Oh, I did hear about that," Mom says, and her voice has that bitter-sweet tone to it, which I'm sure Dad is picking up on. She pinches her lower lip with her free hand and adds, "Sacramento, isn't it? How fantastic. Eden's dreading it, so just know that you're forcing her to do this against her will, and I swear to God, Dave, if you make this weekend hell for her then I will drive up there myself and take her home."

"Oh, just stop it." He narrows his eyes at her with such rebuke that I can't wrap my head around the fact that, once upon a time, they were meant to be in love. "The last thing I want to do is take this trip. It's all Ella's doing."

"Clearly," Mom remarks dryly. "It'd be unlike you to plan some quality time with your family."

"For God's sake, Karen."

I don't want to see Mom's temper flare up, so I quickly slide into Dad's view before they erupt into an unnecessary argument. He spots me within a heartbeat, and his glare only sharpens further.

"What are you standing right there for?" he asks, but, of course, his tone is far from pleasant. As usual, it's gruff and strident and laced with resentment. "Get in the car."

Mom's quick to defend me: as soon as the words have left his lips, she's already raising her voice and saying, "Stop talking to her like that."

"It's fine, Mom," I say, although I know it's not, and I quickly rush over to draw her into a hug before she can start tossing death threats at him.

With one hand still holding back Gucci, she wraps one arm around me and whispers, "He's such an asshole," into my ear. When I pull away, I smile at her in agreement.

"Hurry up," Dad mutters, and my smile quickly falters as I wheel my suitcase outside, purposely elbowing him out of the way and avoiding eye contact. *I hate him.*

"Eden," Mom calls after me. "Remember I'm just a call away."

I look back over my shoulder at her, nod, and then continue to the car. The engine is still running and Ella's peering at me through the window of the passenger door, offering me a small wave. I sigh, but thankfully, she can't hear it. Mom and Dad are exchanging some final words of loathing back at the front door, so I open up the trunk and quite literally have to ram my suitcase inside, spending a good minute rearranging everyone else's in order for mine to fit. I slam the trunk shut and slide into the backseat with my backpack.

"Hi, Eden," Ella says, angling her body around to look at me over the back of the passenger seat. "Ready to go?"

"No," I say, blunt as ever, and then I glance to my left as I pull on my seat belt.

Chase is in the middle seat next to me, playing on his phone with a set of headphones over his ears. He looks up and smiles at me only briefly, and then returns to the app that he seems to be invested in. I lean forward to look past him and see that Jamie has his arms folded tightly over his chest, his head turned to the window and his earphones in. I take a deep breath and sit back, pulling a hair tie off my wrist and quickly stacking my hair haphazardly into a small messy bun, out of my face. It's a long drive to Sacramento.

Dad finally returns to the car, aggressively pulling the door shut behind him as he mutters something under his breath. It's most likely something about Mom, an insult that would probably shatter her if she'd heard. He and Ella exchange a look, communicating through only their eyes, and then Dad adjusts his seat and pulls away from the house. I cast a glance out the window, ready to throw Mom a final good-bye wave, but the front door is already closed.

And as Dad starts to drive, it only occurs to me then that something is missing. The car is full and we're one family member short, and the thought of him managing to get out of this lame-ass trip is enough to make me mad. If I have to suffer through this, then so should he. "So," I say, breaking the silence, "where's Tyler?"

"Wouldn't *you* like to know?" Dad mutters back, but I feel as though he didn't intend for me to hear it. So I pretend that I haven't, and instead I keep my eyes trained on the back of Ella's head through the gap in the headrest in front of me.

"He's driving up on his own," she says, and then turns on the radio and says nothing more.

And that's enough family communication for me for one day. I fumble around inside my backpack for my earphones, placing them in my ears and then pulling the hood of my hoodie up over my head. As I slump down in the seat, I tighten the drawstrings and turn to look out the window, turning up the volume of my music as loud as it can possibly go. It seems that the three of us stuck in the backseat prefer it when we're all blocking each other out. That way none of us have to say anything, and that's great, because none of us want to.

chapter

8

I've never been to Sacramento. I mean, sure, I've been around LA and I've been to San Francisco, but I have never visited the state capital until now.

It's just after 6:30 p.m. when we finally arrive, and my legs are numb and my back is stiff. By the time Dad finally pulls up at the lavish hotel Ella has booked for us, I couldn't be more desperate to get out of the car. It's been a long drive, and a dreadfully uncomfortable one at that.

For the entire weekend we're staying at the Hyatt Regency in downtown Sacramento, directly opposite the California State Capitol, as Ella informs us all, yet I can't even see the damn landmark because it's surrounded by so many trees. Once Dad has cut the engine and handed over the keys to the valet parking attendant just outside the main entrance to the hotel lobby, we all lethargically climb out of the car. To the attendant, we must appear to be the most sullen family to ever exist.

The early evening sun is still pretty hot, so I pull down my hood and fan my face while hauling my suitcase out of the trunk, accidentally pulling Jamie's with it. His tumbles to the ground, and of course, he's far from pleased, which earns me another of his infamous glares I've grown used to ignoring. I'm getting pretty good at ignoring things these days.

"Do you think this is gonna work?" Chase's voice comes from

behind me as I'm trailing along behind Dad, Ella and Jamie toward the entrance.

I slow down, drawing my suitcase to a stop and glancing over my shoulder to look at him. He jogs to catch up. "Do I think what is going to work?"

"This," he says, and then nods to the hotel, and then to everyone else, and then to the streets around us. "Do you think it's going to stop everyone fighting?"

"I don't know," I admit. Honestly, I doubt that all six of us being forced to spend time together will make a difference when it comes to changing our perspectives. I strongly believe we're past the point of no return. "But I guess we'll find out."

We head into the main lobby, all of us appearing surly apart from Ella, and she deserves some credit for somehow maintaining a positive outlook despite how glum the rest of us have been during the entire drive up here. She and Dad head over to check-in, while the rest of us hang back, sprawled out along the plush couches decorating the huge lobby.

"I hope Tyler runs out of gas," Jamie mutters. He's kicking at his suitcase, that same old scowl upon his face. "To be honest, I doubt that he'll even show up."

"Why wouldn't he?" Chase asks.

"The better question is: why *would* he?"

And I get Jamie's point. If I were Tyler, I wouldn't show up either. I'd keep on driving. Who knows? Maybe that's exactly what he's doing. Maybe he's heading straight for Portland and I'll never, ever see him again.

For some odd reason, my stomach tightens.

"Eden," Ella says as she approaches us, "you're with me." She holds up a key card while Dad rolls up behind her with their huge suitcase. "Jamie, you're with Dave. Chase, you'll be with Tyler."

"Sweet," Chase says. He pushes himself up off the couch just as the bellhop arrives to take our luggage.

I'm still finding this entire experience foreign. We have never done this before. I have never sat through a six-hour drive with my dad. I have never shared a hotel room with my stepmom before. I have never sat in a hotel lobby alongside my stepbrothers. And the more I think about it, the more surprised I am that we *haven't* ever been on vacation together. We have been a family for three years. Or at least we have tried to be.

We make for the elevators and head for our rooms, all three of them next door to one another on the seventh floor, facing the capitol building. We've all agreed to take a good half hour to ourselves to settle in before we go out for dinner, and although we're all pretty hungry, we're twice as tired. Traveling has done that to us, and it's only just turned seven.

The room Ella and I are sharing is huge, with two large double beds, and I make straight for the one nearest the window, sitting myself down on the edge of the soft mattress to claim it as mine. I cast a glance out of the window, and I see those trees again and the tip of the white capitol building. It's not that exciting, so I look away, to find Ella watching me from the other side of the room.

"I know you're mad," she says after a minute. Slowly, she moves across the carpet and sits down on a corner of the other bed, her eyes still locked on mine. "But I didn't have a choice, Eden. We're falling to pieces here."

I can't hold her gaze because she's right. I *am* mad, and I even feel guilty about it, so I look down at my feet. "I'm not mad about this."

"Oh." A moment of silence, except for the faint sound of traffic outside and a TV playing in the room next door. "Then what are you mad about?"

I shrug at first. I don't want to tell her because I don't want to talk to her about it. But then she says my name firmly, and my attention is forced back to her. I swallow and then I say it. "I'm mad about Tyler."

"I understand," she says softly, crossing one leg over the other and offering me a sympathetic smile, as though she's a goddamn therapist.

I narrow my gaze and stand. How can she possibly understand? "No, you don't," I argue sharply, and I believe it's the first time I've ever used such an aggressive tone with her. And once I start, I simply can't stop. "Because if you did, you wouldn't have thrown him at me the way you did. You *know* I didn't want to see him. Didn't I make that clear enough?"

"I'm sorry," she says, but she's blinking up at me with wide eyes, as though she's surprised, either because of the words I'm saying or the tone I'm using. I don't know which. "He was dying to see you."

"You know, that's what I don't get," I admit, shaking my head. "Why did you go out of your way to bring the two of us together? Are you *crazy*? Did you forget what went on last summer? Did you forget about him and me?"

"Eden…" She goes quiet.

Yet I'm doing that thing again, that thing where I can't stop yelling and my temper won't stop flaring up and I just want to scream. "I'm mad at everything. I'm mad at him for walking out. I'm mad at him for completely cutting me off. I'm mad at him for going to Portland. I'm mad at him for turning up again as though nothing has happened and everything is fine." And suddenly I've reached the point of fury that crosses the line from hot anger to pained anger, and now I'm crying yet hardly even realizing it at first. My eyes are burning and Ella is turning blurry in front of me and yet I'm still going on and on. "I'm mad at him for being half the reason this family is so messed up, yet I'm the one who's getting all the blame. I'm mad at him for being the reason I keep arguing with everyone around me. I'm mad at him for being the reason Dad hates me. And I know this sounds awful, but I'm mad at him for existing and I'm mad at you and Dad for ever meeting and I'm mad at myself for ever agreeing to come and stay with you guys that summer."

"Oh, Eden," I hear her murmur gently, both her voice and her touch tender and warm as she gets to her feet and pulls me into her arms.

I'm shaking hard and I'm sobbing uncontrollably and I feel pathetic for getting so worked up again. I'm nineteen, yet I'm crying against my stepmom's shoulder because of her son, and it's awkward and embarrassing and it shouldn't be happening, but it's too late now.

"Listen," she says by my ear as she rubs soft circles on my back, which makes me feel around ten years old, but it's comforting and I couldn't care less, "your father doesn't hate you, so please don't think that."

"He does." I force out the words through my blubbering, taking a short step back from Ella and looking at her with tears streaming down my cheeks. "And he can't stand me."

"That's not true. It's just…" Her words trail off as she thinks about the right thing to say, and her hands are now on my arms. "It's just difficult. We both know he's never been Tyler's biggest fan, and when you pair Tyler with you… It's just that… Well, your dad doesn't like it."

"But there's nothing even going on between us anymore, and yet he *still* won't let it go." I sniff. Reaching up, I dab at my eyes with my thumb. I don't even have to look in the mirror to know that I'm a mess right now.

"There's nothing going on?" Ella echoes, raising an eyebrow. "Does Tyler know that?"

"I straightened everything out between us yesterday."

Just as she's parting her lips to say something, her phone starts to ring. I recognize her generic ringtone immediately as it blares from inside her purse, and she lets go of me and fumbles around for the device for a few seconds before answering. She says hi. And then she says she'll be right down.

"He's here," she tells me once she's hung up, stating the obvious. "Dry your eyes and freshen up, okay? We'll go for dinner and we'll all talk. I'll be back in five."

The second she's gone, I sit back down on my bed, and I breathe. No more tears, no more anger, no more anything. My eyes rest on the carpet and my body is still, and the only thought running through my mind right now is that I'm tired of feeling this way. I'm tired of feeling guilty and tired of feeling hurt and tired of feeling alone. I am just so tired.

When Ella returns to our room, fifteen minutes later rather than five, we don't talk. I might have recovered and calmed down, but there's a sense of discomfort between us, most likely because I broke down over her son right in front of her. We brush past each other and make minor eye contact, but that's all. I have changed my clothes and applied some blush to give myself some color, and now we are leaving our room in silence to meet up with everyone else.

But none of them are waiting out in the hallway like they are supposed to be, so Ella starts knocking on their doors, telling them to "c'mon" and "hurry up." At almost the exact same time, both doors swing open and our four male counterparts join us in the hall. But I'm only looking at one of them, and that's Tyler.

I haven't seen him since last night, when I left Dad's house and walked all the way home. I'm not sure how he's feeling about all of this because he looks pretty nonchalant, especially when he notices my gaze lingering on him. I don't look away, and as Ella and Dad exchange suggestions about where we should head for dinner, we all start to make our way down the hallway toward the elevators. Tyler ends up trailing at the back by my side, and although there's a safe distance of several inches between us, I find myself wishing there wasn't. It's a strange feeling, and I feel so drawn to him because he's so familiar to me that I end up having to say something to him. I can't bring myself not to.

"How was the drive?"

He looks sideways at me as we walk, and he seems a little taken aback at first. It seems he wasn't expecting me to talk to him, and especially not so casually. But he's still my stepbrother at the end of the day, so I have to treat him that way. "It was alright," he says.

"Count yourself lucky you weren't stuck with the rest of us," I tell him. Out of the corner of my eye, I'm checking that Dad hasn't noticed us talking, and so I'm keeping my voice low. Talking to Tyler in front of Dad, no matter how innocently, will always be something that he won't like.

"You could have driven up with me," Tyler says, but then immediately he bites down on his lower lip and adds, "Sorry. Forget I said that."

We stop talking once we're shuffling into the elevator, and Dad eyeballs me suspiciously the entire way down to the lobby. He makes me feel forever guilty, even though I'm not doing anything wrong. He frowns and glances away once the doors ping open. We actually end up making for Dawson's, the hotel's own steakhouse, and Tyler sighs but doesn't comment on it. It seems he's still maintaining his vegetarian lifestyle.

Despite turning up without a reservation at 7:30 p.m. on a Friday, the restaurant manages to squeeze us in at a table over by the back corner. I can tell without even picking up the menu that the prices will be extortionate. There's a very sophisticated feel to the place, and it's extremely formal, which makes me feel underdressed despite having already changed my outfit. It's dark but cozy, and the six of us get comfortable, musing as we scour the menu and then appearing totally normal as we all order.

But then the silence comes again.

Dad taps the table with his fingertips. Jamie starts twisting his knife around his hands. Chase pulls out his phone and discreetly uses it beneath the table. Tyler's sitting opposite me, so it's easy to see the way he's looking at his hands in his lap, interlocking his fingers over and over. Ella and I are the only two glancing around at everyone, and she shakes her head at me, as though to say, *Can you believe this?*

I *can* believe it, so I just shrug.

"Put the phone away," she orders Chase, and just by the sound of her voice, firm and stern, we can all tell she's got something to say. One by one, we all look up at her and we wait, just like we did yesterday. "Let's talk," she says.

It feels like she's about to break up with us all because I get that sick feeling in my gut that only comes with hearing those words. Jamie groans and places his knife back down, dramatically leaning back in his chair and folding his arms across his chest.

"Here?" Dad asks. Unsurely, he furrows his eyebrows as his eyes glance around the restaurant. Everyone else is chatting and laughing and smiling and having a good time: everything we're not.

"Right here," Ella confirms. "None of you are going to make a scene in front of *all* these people, are you?" She arches an eyebrow, and it reminds me once again that she is incredibly clever when it comes to dealing with tricky dilemmas. It's her job, after all, only this weekend her line of work has shifted from settling civil matters to easing the tension running throughout this family. "Exactly," she says when no one replies. "So let's finally talk in a civilized manner."

"And what exactly is there to talk about?" Dad challenges her. Sometimes I wonder if he does it just to purposely irritate her. He knows that there is *everything* to talk about.

Ella ignores him. Instead, she rests her interlocked hands on the table and glances at each of us individually. "Who wants to start?"

No one says anything. Tyler's eyes fall back to his lap, and Dad only stares back at Ella with an unpleasant frown plastered upon his face. Jamie reaches for his drink and sips at it with great concentration. Chase looks at me, but I don't know what he expects from me, so I shift my gaze back to Ella.

"Eden?" she urges. But I don't want to go first. In fact, I don't want to talk at all, so I shake my head and pray that she'll drop it. She does, but not without pressing her hand over her eyes and sighing. "Someone please just tell me when all of this started."

"When what started?" Jamie asks. He places his glass back down and angles his chair toward her.

"When did we all stop talking? When did we all start arguing so much?"

Jamie swallows. "Um, you know when." He looks at Tyler. And then he looks at me.

"Someone just say it out loud already," Ella says, but her frustration is evident in her tone. "Why can't we just talk about it instead of tiptoeing around the subject like we've been doing for the past year?"

"Is this a joke?" Dad cuts in, blinking at her.

She narrows her eyes straight back at him. "Does it look like I'm holding back a punch line?" He doesn't reply.

My eyes find their way to Tyler, and he glances up at me immediately, as though he can sense my gaze on him. His stubble is a little neater today, like he finally decided to tidy it up a little, but his eyebrows are thick and pulled together. We both know Ella is referring to us, to last summer, to the moment the truth about our relationship came out. It is not difficult to pinpoint that moment as the day that we cracked. We all know it.

Slowly, he exhales, and I watch his lips as he says, "All of this is because of Eden and me." And with each word he murmurs, his eyes remain locked on mine until eventually he has to tear them away. He looks at Ella.

"Right," she says. "We'll start with that."

Dad almost gags. He reaches for his beer and takes a long chug while angling his body away from us all, clearly wishing not to take part in the conversation. I understand because the last thing *I* want to do right now is talk about my previous relationship with Tyler, especially in front of them all. But it seems that's exactly what Ella wants us to do.

"Jamie," she says calmly. "You're first. Say what you want to say."

"Anything?"

"Anything," she confirms.

Jamie thinks for a moment, glancing back and forth between Tyler and me, like he's trying to remind himself of everything he feels toward us. I'm expecting him to explode with a similar rant to yesterday's, but he doesn't. All he says is, "It's embarrassing."

Ella nods and then shifts her intense stare. "Chase?"

"It's just *whatever*," Chase says. "I mean, is it really that big of a deal?"

"Of course it's a big deal," Jamie mutters, and Chase flinches, which leads me to believe that Jamie has just kicked him beneath the table. "Do you even get it? It's like you kissing Eden. How gross is that?"

My lips form a firm line, and I glare at him. "You know, Jamie, acting like a dick doesn't help the situation."

"Eden," Dad hisses. I hear the clink of his beer as he slams it back down onto the table, and my attention is immediately reeled in toward him. "Cut it out with that attitude of yours."

"*My* attitude?" My eyes widen, and I quite literally laugh in disbelief before the aggression sets in. "What about Jamie's attitude? What about yours?"

Dad shakes his head endlessly and takes another swig of his beer, his eyes boring into a random spot on the restaurant wall. He doesn't reply because that's what Dad does when he doesn't have a logical thing to say. He knows I've got a point, no matter how badly he doesn't want to admit it.

So I keep pushing, and, out of the corner of my eye, I can see Tyler watching me closely. "Ella's right, Dad. Let's finally talk. Why don't you like me? Go on," I demand. "Tell me. Tell me why I'm such a pathetic daughter to you." I want to hear him say it. I want to hear him *admit* it.

Ella exchanges a wary glance with me, but at the same time, she seems almost relieved, like she wanted me to say that all along. When her eyes flicker away, she leans across the table and pulls Dad's beer out of his hand. "Answer her," she says. "Nothing is ever going to get resolved unless you do."

"You want an answer?" Dad spits, snatching the beer back. The couple at the table next to ours cast a concerned glance toward us all. "Alright," Dad says. "You've been nothing but a disgrace since the moment you arrived in Santa Monica. I wish I'd never asked you to come and visit. You snuck around and didn't come home half the time, and just when I thought you were finally becoming bearable, you arrive home from New York and I find out that you've got some sort of disgusting fling going on. God, I can't even *think* about how stupid I was to agree to letting you spend the summer over there." He glances at Tyler and his expression twists. "I don't understand what you can possibly see in him. All I know is that the two of you together is wrong. But that makes sense, doesn't it? Neither of you are all that great when it comes to doing things right."

I can't stay at the table any longer.

There's a tremendous screech as I push my chair back and get to my feet. Ella's burying her head in her hands and Jamie's murmuring, "Well, I agree with the last part," and Chase is blinking frantically with wide eyes and Tyler is still staring at me and Dad is chugging the remainder of his beer and *I am done.*

I know the purpose of talking here in the middle of such a classy restaurant was to prevent any of us from getting too riled up and causing a scene, but I just have to leave. If I don't, I'll end up yelling something equally harsh back at him, and there's a lot I could say about Dad right now. And if I stay and bite my tongue and keep quiet, I'll surely burst into tears because these days I seem to only have two moods: burning rage and unending sorrow. So no, I am leaving while I still have my dignity.

As I'm squeezing by Jamie though, I hear another chair scratching the floor, and when I glance quickly over my shoulder, Tyler's standing too. Still watching me, his eyes still intense. And I think for a moment that he's coming after me, that he's about to run out of this restaurant with me and tell me that my dad's an asshole and that it's okay and that's he's sorry for leaving me to deal with all of this on my own for a year. I need that right now.

I weave through tables and waitstaff as swiftly as I can, and I head straight for the door, back into the hotel. But I pause when I get there, waiting for Tyler to catch up with me.

Only he's not coming. He's seated back down at our table off in the far corner, but his eyes are still on me. It seems either Dad and Ella have stopped him or he has changed his mind. Maybe now, after everything I told him yesterday, he thinks I'm no longer a girl worth running after.

And the only thing worse than that is the fact that I wanted him to.

chapter

9

Ella has the key card to our room, so I can't go back there, which sucks, because all I want to do is crawl into that large double bed of mine and sink into the soft mattress and never wake up again. Instead, I linger in the lobby at first, pacing back and forth until my breathing has calmed, and then for a good half hour I slump down against one of the plush couches again to watch the people around me, guests dressed to the nines constantly coming and going, heading out to enjoy their Friday night. I wish I could enjoy mine.

By the time it's eight fifteen, I grow tired of observing everyone else, so I decide to get up and follow a young couple into the hotel's bar and lounge. I ditched my salad back in the restaurant before it even arrived, so I'm still hungry and I'm at the point now where I don't care *what* I eat.

The atmosphere in the lounge feels elegant, bright, and chic, and although I look as though I could be sixteen, no one immediately approaches me to kick me out. Maybe it's because there's no one manning the doors and maybe it's also because I've bypassed the bar completely, searching for somewhere to sit where I won't draw any attention to myself. That's when I spot the outdoor patio.

The sun has set and it's twilight by now. Outside on the patio it's not so busy. The tables are more scattered out here, with umbrella shades over each. And there's something I've never seen before: outdoor fireplaces too, all lit up and bright, surrounded by wicker couches and armchairs. One of the fireplaces is free, so I make straight for it and settle into the couch, my body sinking back against the cushions. I close my eyes and feel the heat of the fire against my face.

Then my phone vibrates in the back pocket of my jeans.

I sit up and reach for it, expecting it to most likely be a text from Rachael, but an entirely different name is on my screen. Tyler's.

Are you ok?

My stomach tightens. I begin to write back, telling him that I'm fine, but then I frown and end up deleting it.

not really, I type instead.

Where are you? he replies within a split second.

I could lie and tell him I'm in bed trying to get an early night's sleep so that he'll leave me alone. But the truth is, I could do with some company right now. I don't want to lie. I want to talk to him, and I want to tell him everything.

in the lounge, I tell him. can you come? im outside on the patio

I wont be long.

I stare at his message for a minute before placing my phone down on the table in front of me and sinking back against the couch. A server approaches me, and I order the first thing I notice on the menu: parmesan wedge fries. I don't even consider how many calories there are; I just order them and wait. The waiting and the loneliness and the warmth from the fire must make me tired because I'm almost asleep by the time my food arrives ten minutes later, but then I perk up a little. I still feel deflated though, like I have no energy left to deal with Dad or Jamie or Ella, so I pick at my fries so slowly and numbly that I don't even enjoy them that much.

"Everyone's wondering where you are."

I look up, half a fry in my mouth, and find Tyler standing there. He's a safe distance away, a distance that says *we used to be a lot more than this*, and his hands are in the front pockets of his jeans. Half his face is lit up orange from the fire and the other half is dark and shadowed, and his expression is completely gentle, his gaze delicate.

I swallow. "Did you tell them?"

"No," he says. "Did you want me to?"

"No."

He sits down. Not beside me on the couch, but across from me on the wicker armchair, and he doesn't exactly lean back and get comfortable, just interlocks his hands between his knees and looks into the fire for a while. "I'm sorry about your dad," he says quietly, not looking over.

"Yeah," I say. "Me too." There's no awkwardness. No tension. I kind of like it this way, being wrapped up in a warm silence that's almost comfortable. I pull my legs up onto the couch and cross them, my eyes resting on Tyler's stubble-lined jaw. "Didn't it get to you too?"

"Didn't what get to me?" He tilts his face toward me and our eyes lock.

"What my dad said."

He shakes his head no. "Not really. I mean, it sucked, but I'm getting better when it comes to ignoring shit like that." He squints. "Why? Did you expect me to react?"

I reach forward to grab another fry, and then I toss it into my mouth and shrug. "A little. The old you would have pummeled him, I bet."

Slowly, the corner of Tyler's lips pull up into a tiny smile, and he raises an eyebrow. "The old me?"

"The you that hit him last summer."

"So there's a new me?" His eyebrow arches even higher.

I nod because I can't deny it. There's something different about him, and it's as though every summer he becomes a more advanced, improved, polished version of his former self. I thought he was at his prime last summer, but it turned out he wasn't. He had a positive outlook, sure, but he still snapped incredibly easily. He lost his cool a lot last year.

"It seems so," I murmur, and I narrow my eyes back at him as I study him intently. I'm trying to search his eyes for some truths, but the glow from the fire is reflected in them and making it difficult.

"Good," he says slowly, and his lips twitch. "If there wasn't, then I'll have spent an entire year without you for nothing. I'll have messed everything up for *nothing*." He breaks the gaze we're sharing and looks back at the fire for a moment before dropping his eyes down to his interlocked hands.

My throat tightens.

I was so in love with you.

I don't hate Tyler. I might have told Rachael that over the past year, but it's a lie. I might have told Ella that I never wanted to see him again, but I've realized that's a lie too. I could never hate him. I'm just…mad. I am mad at the fact that I no longer feel the way I used to, and I am mad at him for making me feel this way.

I want to rewind to last summer. I want to be back in New York, up on the roof of Tyler's apartment building while he murmurs in Spanish to me. I want Dean to have never gotten hurt, and I want Dad and Ella and Jamie and everyone to have understood. I want Tyler to have stayed.

I want everything to be different because I really do not want this.

I want to be in love with you.

My eyes are still fixed on him, my face warm, and I do the only thing I can think of to keep the conversation going: I offer him a fry and push the dish toward him. But he declines, shaking his head gently and holding up his hand, so I pull it back.

"Lame family trip, huh?" he jokes, cracking the silence.

I laugh and lean back. "Sure is. It wouldn't be so bad if my dad and you weren't…" Quickly, I stop myself and my voice tapers off into silence. I bite down on my lower lip and pray that he doesn't pick up on my words, but he does, of course, because he's listening to everything I say with great concentration.

"Here?" he finishes.

I purse my lips and shrug, finally tearing my eyes away from him and looking at the group of friends sprawled over the couches around the fireplace next to ours, sipping on cocktails and laughing loudly. I wish I were as happy as them. "Yeah," I admit. I shrug once more, and then I look at him again. It's easy to look at him tonight. Somehow, it doesn't hurt. "But I take it back."

"You take it back?" His eyebrow quirks upward again.

"Yeah. I'm glad you're here," I say, but my voice has gone quiet, and I swallow hard. "I'm glad you're right here right now." Without thinking over my actions too much, I shift over a couple of inches and then nod at the empty spot next to me on the couch. "Sit with me," I whisper.

Tyler analyzes my expression at first, as though he's unsure if I'm being serious or not, because he studies me long and hard before he finally gets up. His movements are slow, cautious, like he's afraid of accidentally brushing up against me. When he finally sits back down by my side, there are still several inches between us. "Eden," he says, and then he looks sideways at me, pausing for only a moment. "What is it that you want?"

"What?"

"What is it that you want from me?" he asks quietly, but not in a passive-aggressive way, more with genuine concern than anything else. He presses his lips together while he waits for an answer, but his head is lowered, his face tilted down, his eyes gazing softly back at me from beneath his eyelashes.

I release the breath I'm holding, and then, without hesitation, I tell him exactly what it is that I want. "Truthfully? I want everything to be the way it used to be. I don't want anyone to know about us. I want everything to be a secret again. It was easier that way."

"You know it couldn't stay that way," he says. He's frowning, but his eyes are still bright, reflecting the warmth from the fire.

"I know," I murmur, my gaze never leaving his. "But I keep thinking that maybe if it had, you would've stayed too."

He shakes his head and glances away, running a hand through his hair and leaning farther back against the couch. After a minute, he sighs and fixes his eyes back on me. "I didn't leave because of that, Eden."

"Then why did you?"

"I told you," he says.

I think I am only now realizing that my anger doesn't stem from the fact that Tyler left, but rather from the fact that I don't really know why he did. Not fully understanding why he left for so long is what really hurts. "Tell me again."

Tyler rubs at both his eyes as he sits back up, straightening up next to me and angling his body to directly face me. By moving, he seems to have reduced the distance between us.

"Here's the full story," he says, but his voice is low and husky, which sharpens my attention even more than it already is, and I latch on to every single word he says. "I needed the space, and I needed the time to figure things out. We both know that I didn't really know what I was doing or where I was going. Sure, I was done with New York, but *then* what? That's what I didn't know. I didn't know where I wanted to go next, and I needed to figure that out, but at the same time, I still wasn't okay, and you know that, right? You know that now?"

He moves his face toward me, his eyebrows pulled together, and he lifts his hand as though he's about to reach over to touch me, but he doesn't, and I nod once. That's when he continues.

"I shouldn't have started smoking weed again. I shouldn't have hit your dad. I shouldn't have tried to beat the hell out of mine. And the only thing that got me out of those situations was you because I didn't want to…I don't know. I didn't want to let you down. That's the only reason."

He pauses for a minute, maybe because he's done talking, and I keep thinking that he's already told me this. He told me all of this last summer, right before he left, only then I was too numb to really listen, too heartbroken to let it sink in. But he's not done yet, because he parts his lips and exhales a long breath, and then goes on.

"I know I've messed up before and I've made some fucked-up decisions, and I know I've blamed all my actions on my dad, but the truth is, I've always had a choice. I *chose* to throw my life away when I could have chosen to do something positive about it instead. New York and the tour were a start—you know, talking about what I went through with my dad definitely helped, and all—but that wasn't enough, which is why I had to leave, Eden. I didn't want to keep making mistakes. I wanted to be a better person, not because I owed it to you, but because I owed it to myself." He goes silent, tilting his face down to his lap, and then quietly he murmurs under his breath again, "I owed it to myself."

My chest feels so heavy that I think it might just split open. My throat feels dry with guilt, although I can't pinpoint why. I shouldn't feel guilty, but I do. I feel guilty for hitting him yesterday morning. I feel guilty for yelling at him up at the Hollywood Sign last night. I feel guilty for never understanding, for hating him rather than supporting him this entire time. In that exact moment, my head floods with the thought that perhaps I have been the selfish one. The one who has complained and wept and moped for the past year, all because he wasn't with me, because I was alone. As I think about it now, it hits me that if Tyler had stayed, then perhaps he wouldn't be as okay as he seems to be now. Dad would have put him through hell. So would Jamie. He'd have had to deal with his dad walking the same streets again, the twisted expressions of those we once went to school with, the fallout. It would have been too toxic to stay in Santa Monica.

"Tyler," I whisper, shaking my head slowly. *Where do I start? How do I even begin to apologize?*

"Let me say this," he cuts in, and he lifts his head again, sincere eyes piercing mine. After all these years, I have become an expert at reading his expression. "I'm *sorry,*" he says. "I'm sorry for leaving. I was thinking about myself, and I should have thought more about you. You're right—I left you to deal with all of our shit on your own, and I know now that I messed up. I shouldn't have cut you off. I should have told you that I was in Portland. I should have come back earlier. I shouldn't have ruined all of this, and do you know what the worst part is? I don't know if I can fix it, and I don't think you want me to."

I part my lips to speak, but words fail me. I don't know what to say or how to feel. But my heart is beating painfully with a sense of longing. For all that I have convinced myself that I hate Tyler, the truth is that I have just missed him. I've missed hearing his voice and seeing him smirk and feeling his touch. I've missed Tyler, and there's no denying it now, but things are complicated. He lives in Portland. I live in Chicago. Dad and Ella don't accept us. Jamie despises us. Our friends are uncomfortable.

Maybe Tyler and I are done, not because we're not in love with one another, but because we are an impossible pair.

He's still watching me, and I'm still watching him, and I want nothing more than to touch him right now. But I know that I can't, so I place both my hands in between my crossed legs in an effort to restrain myself.

"We were never going to work," I say, and immediately he frowns. "It's been three years, and all we've done is spend most of them apart. Is that how it would work? We spend the summer together and then end up separated for the rest of the year? Is that all it was ever going to be?"

"No," he says, and then when he lifts his hand again, he really does touch me this time. He squeezes my knee and I don't push him away. "Please just come to Portland with me. We can go right now, just you and me. Let's forget about everyone and everything else while we figure this out. I'm not going back without you because I don't care what you say; I need to fix this." His hand falls away from my knee as he stands up, tall and broad and towering over me, and he reaches into the pocket of his jeans and pulls out his car keys. His expression suddenly screams desperation, the same way it did yesterday up at the sign. "Please."

He's never going to let this go, but, truthfully, I don't know if I can go back to Portland. I've only been back twice since Mom and I moved down to Santa Monica, and that was to pack and to visit Mom's extended family. Both times, being back in the city reminded me of nothing but bad memories. I used to hate the life I had back in Portland. Not that my life in Santa Monica is any better. In fact, it's worse.

And why would I go to Portland with Tyler? Why would I let myself get involved with him again? Why would I go back to him after spending so long trying to move on? Maybe I don't want to start over or fix whatever there is between us now. Maybe I've accepted the fact that it's time to just give up.

"We can't just leave, Tyler," I mumble, tilting my head back to look up at him. With the fire glowing behind him, his entire face is shadowed and dark. My thoughts are all over the place. "Leaving when things are a mess will never resolve anything, and you should know that by now.

So why don't you stick around for once? And maybe *then* I'll consider Portland." I extend my hand, offering a deal, and he contemplates it for a few seconds. Finally, he places his hand in mine, and we shake on the possibility that I might just go with him.

"We should probably head back," he says. His eyes scour the patio, which is growing busier and more raucous as the night wears on, and then he slips his car keys back into his pocket.

Uncrossing my legs and stretching them, I slowly rise to my feet. "Do they know you were coming to find me?" He knows who I'm talking about.

"Do you think your dad would have let me come if he did?" he asks, but he's smiling a little as a low laugh escapes his lips. "Only Chase. Everyone's in the rooms. Early night, apparently, but Mom said she's not going to sleep until you show up."

"Did my dad say anything after I left?"

Tyler scratches the back of his neck and doesn't reply, which makes it pretty clear that Dad *did* say something, and, judging by Tyler's silence, it seems it wasn't anything nice. "C'mon," he murmurs, and he steps back to allow me out first.

We make our way back inside to the bar, weaving through the people and the noise and the laughter until we've reached the lobby. It's just after 9:00 p.m., so it's not even late, yet I feel so tired. The six-hour drive has knocked all the energy out of me, so I find myself yawning as we head for the elevator. We're not talking, but we're not ignoring each other either, more basking in a comfortable silence while trying not to get caught looking at each other for too long.

By the time we're back up on the seventh floor, we're merely strolling toward our rooms. I run my fingertips along the wall, my steps slow, and Tyler's pace has matched mine. We're in no rush to get back, but inevitably we end up outside the doors to our rooms. Dad and Jamie are in the center room, with mine and Ella's on the left, and Tyler and Chase's on the right, so there are several feet separating us as we pause outside our doors.

Tyler stands with his key card in one hand and his other on the door. "So," he says quietly, as though our family will hear our voices through the walls if we speak any louder. His eyes are smoldering back at me.

I was so in love with you.

"So," I say. I reach for the handle of my own door, ready to knock for Ella to let me in. Part of me doesn't want her to. Part of me wants to stay out here.

I want to be so in love with you.

"I guess it's good night then," he murmurs. And then he smiles, so huge and so wide that it reaches his eyes, making them crinkle at the corners and making my heart hurt even more than it already is. "*Buenas noches.*"

It's impossible not to mirror his smile. "*Bonne nuit.*"

"I thought it was *bonsoir*," he says, raising an eyebrow, and I'm surprised he can even remember what it was that I said all those years ago when we murmured good night to each other before separating into our own rooms. My French has never been up to scratch, which is embarrassing, because his Spanish has always been pretty flawless.

"Yeah, well, it should really be *bonne nuit*," I say a little sheepishly. "I told you I wasn't fluent."

Tyler nods once and slides his key card into the slot in the door. "Then *bonne nuit.*"

"*Buenas noches,*" I say.

Somehow, his smile grows even bigger, and his door clicks as it unlocks. He turns away from me, as slowly as he possibly can, and then pushes open the door and heads into his room. The door clicks back shut again, and just like that, he is gone and I am alone.

I am so in love with you.

For the first time in a while, waking up and getting out of bed is easy. No roommate telling me I've missed my first class, no Mom telling me I need to wake up and live my life, no conscience forcing me to get up and run. For the first time in a while, I am not dreading the day. For the first time in a while, I am looking forward to it.

Even with my stepmom next to me, smoothing moisturizer onto her face in front of the hotel-room mirror while eyeing me with concern. Even with my dad in the room next door, most likely waking up to the sad realization that he has to deal with this family for another long day.

None of that can ruin my mood.

"I'm starting to think you're right," Ella says. We have been silent for a while, pivoting around one another as we've been getting ready. I look up from tying my laces. She stares back at me in the reflection of the mirror. "Maybe all of this *is* making everything worse."

I straighten up on the edge of my bed and fix her with a stern look, which I've grown all too used to giving her over the past year, like whenever she insisted I spend time with Dad or whenever she mentioned Tyler's name. "Please don't start saying sorry again for what happened last night."

She heaves a drastic sigh and turns her body around in the chair, her hands resting over the back of it as she looks straight at me. "But I really am. It was a bad idea. Your dad was completely out of line, and, trust me, I've told him that."

"And I bet he didn't care," I say, and I'm completely nonchalant because I am long past the point of worrying about my dad. I couldn't care less that he can't stand Mom or me, or that we both infuriate him, or that, in his opinion, Mom wasn't the best wife and I'm not the best daughter. Not one single fiber of my being even remotely cares. These days, his loathing for us has become almost funny.

Getting to my feet, I ignore Ella's growing frown as I near her, reaching for my phone on the dressing table. I grab the key card too, and a complimentary map of Sacramento provided by the reception staff, then change the subject while I have the chance to. "Where are we heading?"

"I'm not sure yet, but we'll find somewhere." She stands up, so I take a few steps back to give her some space as she picks up her bottle of perfume from the dresser, spraying a spritz of the Chanel fragrance on her wrists before placing it back. "Let's hope your dad's awake."

It's impossible for him not to be. The first thing Ella did this morning when she climbed out of bed was knock sharply on the wall, several times too. It's also after 9:00 a.m., and I bet the guys are starving.

Ella and I leave our room then, leaving the map behind and slipping out into the hallway of the eighth floor, ready to draw the family back together once more. Ella knocks on the door of Dad and Jamie's room. I knock on Tyler and Chase's, and it immediately swings open. Chase holds the door open with only his foot and stuffs his hands into the front pouch of his hoodie as he rolls his eyes over his shoulder and pointedly says, "Someone slept in."

I look past him, straight across the room to Tyler. He's in the process of slipping on a shirt while at the same time trying to pull on his other boot, and his eyes flicker over to meet mine only briefly. While he's hunched over, drops of water fall from the ends of his hair to the carpet, and when he straightens up, he grabs a towel from the floor and runs it over his hair to quickly dry it. I don't realize I'm staring until I hear him murmur, "Yeah, yeah, I'm coming. I only woke up ten minutes ago."

I shift my attention back to Chase while Tyler starts fumbling around in the pockets of another pair of jeans, fetching his phone and his wallet and his keys. "You didn't wake him?"

"No," Chase says, his hood pulled up over his head, "I was watching TV."

Ella must pick up on our words because she quits knocking at the room next door and walks over, peering around the doorframe and shaking her head at Tyler, who simply shrugs. "Don't you guys know that alarms exist?"

"Alarms don't exist when you're on vacation," Chase answers.

"This isn't a vacation." She steps forward and pushes his hood down, moving her hands to his hair as she attempts to tame it, but Chase only ducks and steps away. He promptly pulls his hood back up as he steps out into the hall to join us.

I hear the click of Dad and Jamie's door, and Dad's the first to drift out to meet us, muttering over his shoulder for Jamie to hurry up. Ella turns back around to talk to him, but I tune out from their murmured good mornings and focus instead on brushing past Chase, taking a cautious step into his and Tyler's room. I lean back against the door and hold it open.

"Tired?" I tease, my gaze resting on Tyler.

He runs his hand back through his damp hair and rolls his eyes at me as he darts around the room, turning off the TV and grabbing his jacket, which is resting over the back of the small armchair in the corner. He doesn't need it though, because according to Ella the weather is supposed to remain in the high nineties the entire weekend.

"I didn't sleep much," Tyler says, but he doesn't offer much of an explanation as to why. Instead, he quickly approaches and nudges me back out into the hallway while he pulls the door shut behind us.

Dad glances up from his conversation with Ella. "Morning, Chase," he says with a clipped nod. No "Morning, Tyler." No "Morning, Eden."

Chase half smiles. "Do they have IHOP up here, Dad?"

Out of the corner of my eye, I notice Tyler's body stiffen and his jaw tighten. At first, I don't understand why there's a sudden shift in the atmosphere, because Dad's asshole behavior is nothing out of the usual, but then it abruptly occurs to me why Tyler is so tense. I was taken aback the first time I heard Chase say it too.

"Of course they do," Dad tells Chase. "But it's not on the cards for today, buddy."

Finally, Jamie emerges from his and Dad's room, his permanent scowl plastered across his face. He makes a point of pulling the door shut way too hard, slamming it, and then shrugging when Ella flashes him a warning glance that means *Don't piss me off.* Recently, she's started looking at Dad that way too.

"So," she says now that we're all here, "is everyone hungry?"

Jamie groans and pulls out his earphones from his back pocket. He hooks them up to his phone and walks off toward the elevator without the rest of us, but I've grown all too used to his tantrums, the same way I've grown used to Dad's harsh remarks, so I barely even bat an eyelid.

"Well then," Ella murmurs under her breath. "Let's get going."

We're quick to follow Jamie, the five of us trailing down the long hallway after him and into the elevator. The entire time, there's silence, because no one in this family wants to talk unless they absolutely have to. It's past the point of being awkward and is now verging on becoming normal. How tragic that it's more unusual for us to talk to one another than it is for us not to.

Because none of us know the area, we make a stop in the lobby so Ella and Dad can ask the concierge for recommendations on where a dysfunctional family like ours can find breakfast nearby. He recommends Ambrosia, a café only a couple of blocks north, so we head off looking for it.

It's already hot out, despite the fact that it's not even nine thirty, and within seconds of leaving the hotel, Chase is already pulling off his hoodie. He ties it around his waist, only for Jamie to pull out his earphones and tell him that he looks stupid. That earns him a kick in the shin.

"Nice one," I tell Chase, and promptly high-five him. Dad and Ella are too busy leading the way to even notice.

"Shut up," Jamie hisses, casting a sharp glare over his shoulder at me. At the same time, he shoves his earphones back into his ears and speeds up.

"*Shut up*," I echo, my voice high-pitched as I imitate him in a voice that is the exact opposite of his. Chase grins.

"Eden," Tyler says, and I stop smiling and twist my head around to look at him. His lips are pressed together in a firm line, his eyes hidden behind his shades, and he's shaking his head at me in disapproval, rather condescendingly. "Don't make it worse than it already it."

"Okay," I say.

Our steps are slower, like we have nowhere to be and nowhere to go, and we walk side by side for several minutes in silence before my eyes are drawn back to his. His stare is intense.

"When did he start calling him *Dad*?" he asks quietly, and then nods ahead to Chase.

"No idea," I admit with a shrug. I keep my voice low because I don't want Chase to hear us talking about him. He'd get embarrassed. "But it was Thanksgiving the first time I heard him say it."

"Does Jamie call him that too?"

"No. Just Chase." I pause for a second, smiling as I add, "And me, unfortunately. But I didn't get a choice."

Tyler doesn't laugh. Instead, he's frowning as he studies Chase, like he can't fathom the idea of him viewing my dad, the moron that is David Munro, as a father figure. He's not much of a role model.

"I spoke to your mom about it, like, forever ago," I whisper. I take a step closer to Tyler, and I mentally convince myself that it's only so he can hear me better. "She told me that Chase doesn't remember your dad much, you know, because he was so young when your dad got…yeah." I swallow, glancing sideways up at Tyler to ensure I'm not making him uncomfortable, but he's only looking back down at me with keen interest as he listens, so I continue. "She said that it makes sense for Chase to latch on to my dad. I don't know. I guess she's right."

"I guess," he agrees.

Ahead of us, Dad sharply clears his throat. He's stopped walking, has turned around, and is fixing me with another of his infamous glares. "Eden," he says. "A word."

Ella pauses too, trying to catch Dad's eye, as though she's wondering what the hell this is about. I don't know either, but I do know that it's better to keep the peace, so I walk over to him.

"What?"

He doesn't answer. He only nods at Ella, communicating with her via strained looks and tight-lipped smiles that mean: *Don't wait up.* So she doesn't, and everyone else takes the hint, even Tyler, and they start to walk off again in search of Ambrosia. Dad's attention focuses mostly on Tyler as he brushes past us, and Tyler's lingers mostly on the sidewalk, as though if he were to even so much as to glance up at me out of the corner of his eye, Dad would charge him.

It's not until the four of them are several yards ahead of us that it occurs to me that maybe this is Dad's attempt at apologizing for last night, or maybe for everything. This could finally be it, the moment I hear him say: "Hey, Eden, I've been a pretty shitty father, but I'm sorry."

I look up at him. He hasn't shaved this morning because he never shaves on weekends. His hair is becoming predominantly gray, with very few dark patches remaining. I can't remember how old he is. "What?" I ask again.

"Nothing," Dad says. *Nothing.* "Let's go."

I sigh so loudly that the woman walking by glances at me with concern. I feel disappointed. I don't desperately want an apology from Dad, but it would be nice to have one, to know that he realizes where he's gone wrong. But that'll never happen because Dad's too stubborn to admit that he's not exactly the father of the year. "Are you kidding me?" I splutter, my mouth agape. "*Nothing?*"

Dad stops walking off and turns back around, narrowing his hazel eyes down at me. "What were you doing?"

"What?" My shoulders sink, and I take a minute to breathe deeply as I stare at him, confused.

"Why were you talking to him?"

"Tyler?" His silence is agreement. "Are you seriously kidding me, Dad?"

He folds his arms across his chest and waits, tapping his foot against the sidewalk. "Well?"

Now he's just being ridiculous, and it's completely unnecessary. I could laugh at how ridiculous he is, but I keep my cool and act nonchalant instead. "I was talking to him because he's my stepbrother," I state in monotone. "You know, *family.* And I know it's a bizarre custom to you, but these days people actually talk to their family."

I walk straight past him, fighting the urge to shove him out of the way with my shoulder, and keep a safe distance between us as I speed-walk to catch up with Ella and the guys. In an effort to defy Dad, I fall into step right by Tyler's side. I keep quiet though, and Tyler doesn't ask any questions, and soon Dad has joined us all again, and then that same old silence is back again until Ella says, "I think the concierge said it was this way."

We turn onto K Street, which is beautiful under the morning sun and lined with trees. Tracks for a light-rail system decorate the road, and the sidewalks aren't flooded with tourists the way they are in LA, maybe because it's early Saturday morning or maybe because Sacramento is boring as hell.

Ambrosia is only a minute or so down the street, right on the corner of the block, with huge windows that face out over an outdoor patio area and the cathedral on the opposite side of the street. Ella approves, so we head inside.

It's already busy, with a line that extends almost straight back to the door, so once they've memorized the order for us all, Dad and Ella send us off to claim a couple of tables that are free over by the windows. Chase has insisted that he gets three chocolate croissants.

The four of us settle down. Jamie still has his earphones in. His music is so loud that I can make out which band he's listening to. Tyler has pulled the two tables together, joining them up, making room for all six of us. I'm drumming my fingers along my thigh.

"Do you really think they're gonna get me three?" Chase asks after a minute. He's staring longingly over his shoulder to the counter, where Dad and Ella are talking to each other in hushed voices, leaning in close to one another while they wait in line. I bet they're arguing, but because they have the common decency not to create a scene, they're keeping their voices low and discreet.

"I doubt it," Tyler says.

Jamie abruptly stands then, his chair screeching against the floor as he pushes himself away from the table. He yanks his earphones out and turns for the door.

"Where are you going?" Tyler asks, raising his voice. He sounds authoritative, which is weird, because Tyler's usually the one challenging authority around here.

"Jen's calling," Jamie mutters, glaring back at him over his shoulder, and then he presses his phone to his ear and disappears outside. I watch him through the windows. Jamie never seems to talk these days without being aggressive. He never seems to smile without it being sarcastic. He never seems happy.

I divert my eyes back to Tyler. He has a dumbfounded look on his face as he glances between Jamie outside on the patio and Dad and Ella over by the counter, still presumably arguing. He looks at me for an explanation. "What the hell happened?"

"We happened," I say. My voice is flat and emotionless.

I've had an entire year to accept it, to understand that the reason this family is so shattered is because of us. Tyler's had only a couple of days, and it seems he's stuck in the denial stage. He's trying so desperately to convince himself that none of this is *really* because of us, when the harsh reality is that this is *entirely* because of us.

"I'm gonna talk to your dad," he says. It's the last thing I expected to hear him say.

"What?"

"To clear the air," he says. Chase is listening, and Tyler notices, so he says nothing more and smiles at Chase instead. "So," Tyler says, "eighth grade. Ready for it?"

Chase's face falls. "I'm gonna be a freshman."

"Shit, already?" Tyler blinks. In the two years that he's been gone, a year in New York and a year in Portland, it's clear that he's lost track of time.

Chase doesn't appreciate the mistake. He folds his arms dramatically across his chest and angles his body away from Tyler, apparently too deeply wounded to look at him.

"C'mon, Tyler," I say teasingly, tilting my head down and looking up at him in a patronizing manner from beneath my eyelashes. "You should really keep up to date. I'm nineteen, by the way." Slowly, my lips curve into a smile. "Just in case you forgot."

"Alright, alright," he says, shaking his head, but he's trying not to laugh. He sits up in his chair and reaches across the table, pulling a petal from the flower centerpiece and flicking it toward me.

When he sinks back against his chair, he's looking back across the table at me the way he used to: eyes smoldering so intensely that they could bring me to my knees, smile so natural that it's hard to believe he once faked it.

I enclose my fist around the petal before anyone notices. I mouth *Shh* to Chase, but it's not the flower I'm telling him to keep quiet about.

chapter
11

Surprisingly, no one tries to kill each other over breakfast.

Dad and Ella quit their arguing and act normal, as though they're as happy as they've ever been, like their lives are absolutely perfect. Chase fills the dull conversation with witty remarks while devouring all three of his croissants. Jamie doesn't sit with his earphones in. I'm even the first to finish eating for once, mostly because I'm still pretty hungry after missing out on dinner last night, but also because I don't feel so self-conscious today. I feel fine.

So, while everyone else finishes up, I pull out my phone. Dad shoots me a disapproving look before I've even typed in my pass code. He hates having phones at the table, but I hate *him*, so I give him a tight-lipped smile and then return to my screen.

I text both Mom and Rachael a summary of the last twenty-four hours. I even send my roommate from college a text asking how her summer's going. Most likely much better than mine is. And after that, it slowly dawns on me that I've got zero people left to message. My contact list is full of names, yet I don't feel close to any of them. I scroll up and down, back and forth, up and down, back and forth. I eventually send Emily a text because I'm pretty sure she's the only person left on my list who doesn't hate me. I spent an entire month in New York with her last summer, and occasionally we check in with one another to see how we're doing.

what's up stranger? i hope england isnt so bad these days

No one is replying. I lock my phone and unlock it again. Still no new messages. I switch to Twitter instead, and after only a minute, I'm wondering why I follow so many people that I've never said a single word to in my life. Yet I slowly come across recent updates from those I know all too well, and I feel a strange sense of longing for them all, despite all of the bad things that have happened over the past few years.

@dean_carter1: last couple months at the garage and then im off to Berkeley. Crazy!!

Attached is a picture of Dean in his jumpsuit, covered in grease, his dad by his side as they lean against a beat-up Porsche. I favorite it.

@x_tifff: thinking of getting my hair restyled… what do u guys think?

I haven't seen Tiffani in forever. I favorite it.

@x_rachael94: why is desperate housewives so addictive?

She's *still* watching it? I favorite it.

@meghan_94_x: friday night dates with jared are the best

I'm jealous of how easy it is for them. I favorite it.

@jakemaxwell94: I AM SO DRUNK!!!!!1!

It was posted at 3:21 a.m. I favorite it.

I search for Tyler and pull up his account. I've done this far too often, and still nothing has changed. His last update was June last year.

I glance up from my screen. Tyler's sitting directly across from me, silently eating the rest of his granola and listening to Ella as she suggests that we visit the capitol building. He pauses when he notices me watching, raising an eyebrow questioningly.

Zero updates. Not a single post. Complete silence.

I wonder how he's spent the past year. What he's thought about. How he's spent his days. Who he's spoken to. I wonder if he ever felt alone.

I gently shake my head back at him as though to say *Nothing*, and then I drop my eyes back down to my phone. I hate the way things are.

Tyler clears his throat, and when I don't look back up, I feel him nudge my foot under the table. My eyes flicker up to meet his. He's pushed his food away, and now he's resting his elbows on the table, his hands interlocked. Slowly, he smiles, but it's so gradual that I hardly even notice at first. And then he turns toward my dad.

"Dave," he says.

Dad's eyes flash over immediately. The conversation about him upgrading to a new car is cut short, and everyone is quiet, surprised at not only the fact that Tyler has suddenly spoken, but also that he has spoken to Dad, of all people. And, of course, Dad can't bring himself to reply, so all Tyler receives is a strong look of disdain.

That doesn't throw him off. He swallows, and I put away my phone to concentrate because I'm curious as to how exactly Tyler is planning to "clear the air." The first words to leave his lips are, "Can we talk outside for a second?" He nods to the door and stands.

"We can talk right here," Dad says. He doesn't move an inch, only remains in his chair, and his eyebrows pull together in the ugliest of ways. There's caution written all over his face because, knowing Dad, right now he'll be assuming that Tyler's intentions are malicious.

"Okay," says Tyler. He grabs his chair and moves around the table, placing it back down in between Ella and Dad, all eyes on him as he does so. It's extremely rare for Tyler and Dad to talk, and especially rare for either of them to *want* to.

Tyler straddles the chair and keeps his eyes trained on Dad in a way that is friendly yet firm. "So," he says, and then pauses for a second as though he's mentally stringing together the words he wants to say, all while we watch him closely, Ella more so than the rest of us. "So," he says again, "I just wanted to apologize."

"Apologize?" Dad repeats. The word sounds foreign on his tongue because he never, ever apologizes for anything. His eyes slowly drift to Ella, as though this is her doing, but she widens her eyes and shrugs back at him, although her face has lit up with relief. He looks at Tyler again.

"Yeah, apologize," Tyler says, and then he grips the back of the chair and leans back a little, sighing. I'm listening while holding my breath because an apology is the last thing I expected Tyler to be giving Dad. It should be the other way around. "I know I wasn't the easiest kid to deal with," he starts, "and I know I put you through hell with the constant arguing and all the sneaking out and all the drinking. I was a total jerk, so I get why you weren't exactly my biggest fan. But you've got to give me some credit. I graduated. I moved across the country. I did the tour. I got my shit together. I'm nothing like the kid you first met five years ago." He hesitates, as though he's nervous, his eyes catching mine for a split second. "And about Eden," he murmurs, and Dad almost chokes. "I get it. I seriously fucking do, but there's nothing I can do now to change the fact that it happened. It's just the way it was, and you can call us crazy, and maybe we were, but, Dave, you've seriously got to drop it. It's over, and you're going to drive yourself insane if you stay pissed like this." I hear Ella exhale each time Tyler curses. "So how about a fresh start?" Leaning over the back of the chair, he extends his hand to Dad. "What do you say?"

Ella looks elated. *Finally*, she's most likely thinking. *Finally we are on the road to recovery.* I disagree because I know for a fact that Tyler isn't telling Dad the entire truth. Just yesterday he was asking me again to go to Portland with him, to fix things between us, to give him a second chance, to get wrapped up in this mess all over again. And as badly as I have longed for closure this past year, suddenly I find myself liking the idea of unfinished business and the hope of possibility.

It's over, Tyler's telling Dad.

We're done, I've told Tyler.

But maybe it's not.

Maybe *we're* not.

My heart lunges halfway down my rib cage at the thought of it, and it quickly brings me back to reality. I blink a couple of times, slightly dazed, and try to focus on Dad.

He's staring at Tyler's outstretched hand as though he's never seen flesh before. His glare is contemptuous, and when he exchanges glances with Ella, she's desperately urging him on with a nod of encouragement. This is what she wanted this weekend to be about—apologies and forgiveness and the rekindling of relationships.

But Dad isn't on the same page, because rather than manning up and shaking Tyler's hand, he leans back in his chair and folds his arms tightly across his chest before angling his body slightly away. "If we're all done here, we should make a move."

You asshole, I think. The words are on the tip of my tongue, and I am so close to screaming them in the middle of this café. I have to grip the base of my chair with one hand and cover my lips with the other in order to restrain myself.

"*David*," Ella hisses. She looks absolutely stunned and undeniably furious. The hope of mending things has quickly disappeared, because not only is Dad too stubborn to give out apologies, but also to accept them. Nothing around here is ever going to change unless he changes first.

"I'll be outside," Dad says, voice gruff. He pushes his chair back from the table, his eyes never quite meeting Tyler's, and strides toward the door. We watch him through the huge windows as he drops down into a chair out on the patio, slumping back against it and facing the cathedral.

Inside, none of us say anything. Tyler slowly drops his hand and turns around toward us all, giving us a minute shrug. He's definitely the bigger person, and Dad is definitely the moron. Even Jamie is quiet, although I can't tell whose side he's on. He's usually on Dad's, but I get the feeling that today that isn't the case.

"Unbelievable," Ella murmurs, shaking her head in disbelief. She's staring out the windows at Dad, her lips forming a perfect frown, and when she glances back over to the rest of us, it's clear she's more pissed off than upset. "Stay here," she says. Now her voice is stern, and none of us say a word as she stands. There's a moment of hesitation before she leaves, when she clasps Tyler's face in both her hands and plants a quick kiss against his hair. "Proud of you," she whispers, and then squeezes his shoulder and makes for the door.

The four of us are silent as we watch her through the windows. She stands in front of Dad, glaring down at him, her hands on her hips as she no doubt asks what the hell he's playing at. Dad gets to his feet, and the aggressive hand gestures begin, the frustrated head-shaking and the angry eye-rolls, and it doesn't take long for Ella to catch us all watching very closely. She reaches for Dad's elbow and tugs him away, around the corner, out of view. It's as if they believe that if they don't argue in front of us, then it's as though the argument hasn't happened at all. Yet we all know it has, each and every time.

That's when Chase turns to Tyler and asks, "Why didn't he shake your hand?"

I don't think Tyler even knows himself because he looks at me as though I'll be able to offer an explanation for my dad's behavior, which I can't. I shrug and sink down farther into my chair, so all Tyler can say is, "It's complicated."

"Not really," Jamie says. His expression is blank, and he leans forward and crosses his arms on the table, his eyes trained on Tyler. "Dave doesn't like you. He never has and he never will. It's as simple as that." He's not saying this to be cruel. He's saying this because it's the truth, and we all know it.

Except maybe Chase because he raises his eyebrows and asks, "But why?"

"It's complicated," Tyler says again.

This time, Jamie doesn't try to explain it. Chase has always been kept in the dark about the truth surrounding Tyler's life. He doesn't know the truth about their dad. He doesn't know about Tyler's drug-taking. He doesn't know the real reason Tyler was in New York—Ella told him that Tyler was there as an events promoter, and he didn't question it. Sometimes I feel sorry for him, but most of the time I'm glad he doesn't know.

Out of the corner of my eye, I notice Dad and Ella. They're walking back toward the door, past the large windows, but they're not talking and they're not in line with one another. Dad is trailing behind, and of course, he's scowling. Ella doesn't look too happy either, but Dad waits out on the sidewalk as she makes her way back inside the café.

And the second she pushes open the door, a wide smile immediately spreads across her face. It's so forced that I think it might just be hurting her. But she maintains it nonetheless, beaming down at the four of us as she approaches, creating the illusion that everything is fine, she and Dad are fine, we're all fine.

"Let's go see the Capitol," she says, and we all rise from the table without hesitation.

By the time we're making our way to our rooms at 10:00 p.m., I have never felt so glad to be back at the hotel. It's been a long day, full of tangible tension between Dad and Ella, boring museums, malls, more awkward meals, and a stroll through the International World Peace Rose Gardens that didn't bring us any peace whatsoever. Tyler has been incredibly quiet and has barely said a single word since we left Ambrosia this morning, and he remained a good five feet away from me at all times, but this could be because Dad has been firing him death glares every thirty seconds. And Dad looks like he's in hell. He's hardly said anything since breakfast either, and he looks far too disgruntled for his age, like a kid sulking because no one wants to talk to him. Jamie has kept his head in his phone the entire day.

Although I woke up in a good mood, the day has been disappointing. We're all feeling pretty lethargic and deflated as we reach the doors to our rooms, lingering for a second as we wait to see who'll break the silence first.

As always, it's Ella. "Remember to set your alarms," she murmurs, tucking a stray strand of hair behind her ear. She glances around us all. We're standing in a perfect semicircle. "Actually, don't. It's Sunday tomorrow. No alarms."

"Hell yes," Chase says under his breath.

Dad is the first to pull out the key card for his room, and the first to unlock the door, and the first to disappear. He doesn't say anything to Ella. He doesn't say good night. They're still not talking because Ella is still livid. I can just tell, even though she's trying so hard not to let it show.

"Night," Jamie mutters. He follows Dad inside their room and pushes the door shut.

Immediately, Ella lets out a heavy sigh that she's been holding back the entire day. She tilts her face down and presses her hands to her temples, her eyes closed, as though she's on the verge of having a complete breakdown. I can't blame her. She's been trying to hold this family together for a year now, and it never seems to be getting any better.

"Hey," Tyler says, turning to Chase. He reaches into the back pocket of his jeans and pulls out the key card for their room. He hands it to Chase and nudges him toward the door. "Why don't you see if there's anything good on TV? I'll be in in a sec."

Chase knows not to say no. He nods and swipes the card through the slot, glancing back at us over his shoulder as he heads inside, and the second the door is closed, Tyler takes a step toward Ella.

"I'm so sorry," she blurts, her eyes crinkling at the corners as she looks up at him. He's much taller than she is. "I can't believe he did that."

"Don't stress out over it," Tyler orders, his voice firm but also low because Dad is only on the other side of the wall. Gently, he reaches for her wrists and moves her hands away from her face. He doesn't let go. "Seriously, Mom. Don't. It's not like I didn't expect it, and it isn't the end of the world. We can't expect him to like me overnight. It's gonna take time."

"But we don't *have* time, Tyler," she groans, her words a whisper as she pulls her wrists away from him. "Don't you get that? You leave on Monday, and nothing is going to have changed. Everything is going to be the exact same. And, Eden"—she turns to me—"you're leaving again in September, and there's been absolutely no improvement whatsoever with you and your dad."

"I don't mind," I say with a shrug. "You've probably already noticed, but I'm done trying."

She looks pale as she slowly shakes her head back and forth. "Do you have any idea how awful that is to hear? That you're at the point now where you don't even *mind* that you don't have a relationship with your father?"

I shrug again. "He doesn't want one. He never did, and especially not now, after everything." I can't help my eyes wandering to Tyler. Both he and Ella know exactly what I'm referring to.

"I don't know what to do," Ella admits.

"Sleep on it," Tyler says. "It's really not that bad."

She narrows her eyes at him. "I disagree."

"Trust me, Mom, it's not," he insists. His voice is husky as a result of how quietly he's talking. "Dave's going to lighten up eventually. So will Jamie, and once they do, I'm pretty sure everything will be fine. Because, c'mon, let's not kid ourselves here. None of this would be happening if it weren't for us." He glances sideways at me for a split second, but then his gaze returns to Ella. "So once they accept that it happened, then the arguments are gonna stop. You and Dave are gonna be fine."

When did he become so mature? When did he become the reassurer?

Ella still doesn't look convinced, so I tear my eyes away from Tyler and say, "He's right. They'll get over it," even though I don't entirely believe it myself.

"I can only hope," she murmurs. There's a brief silence as she stares down at the carpet, like there are a million worries and doubts running through her mind. When she looks up, she smiles: a sad one. "Right, time to turn in for the night." She slides her purse off her shoulder and begins to search inside it for the key card. "Try to actually get some sleep tonight, Tyler."

"Actually," he says, "can I borrow Eden for a sec?"

Ella stops fumbling around, and her eyes flicker up. She looks at

Tyler for a moment before she glances at me, and I have no idea what Tyler needs me for, but I do know that I'm fighting the urge to laugh. I can't believe he just asked her that. Never in a million years is she going to leave us alone together. That would be insane.

"Whatever you do or wherever you go, don't stay up too late," she says. Pulling the key card from her purse, she turns for the door to our room and inserts it into the slot.

"Wait," I say, blinking in disbelief. "What?"

"Don't stay up too late," she repeats as she pushes open the door. She holds it open and looks over at us with an eyebrow arched, as though she's just waiting for me to question her again.

Which I absolutely do. "I know, but I mean…*what?*" I stare at her with my mouth slightly open. "Why aren't you saying no? Have you forgotten about Tyler and me?"

"Oh, Eden," she murmurs, and for the first time today, she actually laughs a little under her breath. "Here." She extends her hand and passes me the key card. "Behave yourselves. I know it's a Saturday night, but please don't attempt to sneak into any clubs or anything of the sort."

"It's not worth the effort," Tyler tells her, but he's grinning. "Night, Mom."

"Good night, both of you." Blowing us a kiss, she makes her way into our room, and the door clicks shut behind her, leaving us in silence.

For a second, I'm utterly dumbfounded as to why Ella is allowing us to be alone together, just Tyler and me. It's like throwing a gas can toward a fire—you are not supposed to do it. It slowly becomes less surprising when it occurs to me that she did the exact same on Thursday morning after she ambushed me with Tyler. She left us alone. It's like she *wants* us to talk to each other.

I turn to him, my gaze quizzical. "What exactly do you need to borrow me for?"

He mouths *Shhh* and presses his index finger to his lips. He points to the door of Dad and Jamie's room with his opposite hand, and then nods his head sideways toward the elevators. As he makes a move, I follow. And when we reach the elevators, I immediately reach over to press the button, but he catches my hand and stops me.

His grip is firm but gentle, and my eyebrows knit together as I look at his hand around mine. When I glance up at his face, he's already staring back down at me with his forever warm gaze. My heart beats too fast at his touch, and I almost feel disappointed when he lets go and takes a step back.

For a moment, he studies my expression in the middle of the hallway, his intense eyes searching my features for an answer that I don't know the question to. "Portland," he states. "You, me. Let's go."

"Tyler..." My shoulders sink as I sigh. If I hear him mention Portland one more time, I think I might just flip. "Not this again."

"You said you'd consider it if I stuck around," he tells me, and already he sounds persistent, like he's prepared to plead with me. "I could have left last night, but I didn't. I stayed, and I made a damn fool of myself in front of your dad, and I know we've only got one more day left here, but I doubt we'll miss much. We don't even have to mention it. We'll be gone before morning."

"We can't just leave," I murmur. The elevator doors ping open and a semidrunk couple clings on to each other as they escort one another toward their room. Tyler and I shift over to the soda machine to let them by, keeping quiet until they're out of earshot.

That's when Tyler turns back to me, his words laced with more urgency than before. "Why can't we? Give me one good reason."

"It'll make the situation worse," I say without having to even think about it. "I don't think my dad will be exactly thrilled if he wakes up and finds out I've run off in the night with you, especially after you just told him that all of this was over."

"For someone who doesn't mind not having a relationship with him, you sure do worry a lot about what he thinks," Tyler points out. He raises one eyebrow and presses his lips together, but he doesn't give me the time to muster up a comeback. "Do you honestly care what your dad is going to think? You're an adult. He doesn't have a say in your decisions."

"What about your mom?" I ask quickly. I want to change the subject because I know Tyler has a point. I just don't want to admit it. "You're just going to leave her to deal with all this shit on her own?"

"If we're gone, there won't be anything left to deal with." He leans back against the soda machine and stuffs both hands into the front pockets of his jeans. "We're the problem here, remember?"

"Oh, yeah," I say dryly. "Nothing to deal with except for the fact that *we are gone*. If you think they won't care, then you're deluded. My dad will never let me step foot in the house ever again if I leave with you."

"I never said they wouldn't care. I just think that *we* shouldn't care." He tilts his head back against the machine, his eyes on the ceiling, and he removes his hands from his pockets and runs them back through his hair instead. "For once, Eden," he says quietly, voice breathy. "Just once."

I try to recall everything from the past three days, from the moment Tyler showed up until right now. I try to piece together every emotion I have felt, from fury to love. I try to pinpoint exactly what it is that I want, from closure to unfinished business.

But the truth is, my head has never been more all over the place. My thoughts are a mess, all entwined, making it difficult to figure out how I really feel. For the past few days, I seem to have been jumping back and forth between wishing that nothing would happen with

Tyler and wishing that something would. After last night, I'm leaning more toward the latter, but it's still tough to know for sure. Having our family surrounding us the entire time seems to be clouding my opinion because all I can think about is how impossible it all seems, Tyler and me. How unfair it is on them. How wrong it is. It's starting to take over my mind, and it's holding me back. The only way I will be able to decide how I feel is to spend some time alone with Tyler, with enough space and enough time to figure out if the two of us are still worth fighting for.

I need to go to Portland with him.

My head feels heavy as my gaze snaps back into focus. Tyler's chest is rising and falling as he breathes heavily, deeply, his face still tilted back toward the ceiling. I don't know what comes over me, but I just can't stop myself from taking a step toward him and pressing my hand to his chest, just to feel the sensation. It startles him, and he immediately looks down at my hand atop his shirt. I can feel his heartbeat as it speeds up.

"When do we leave?"

♥
chapter
12

It's 5:00 a.m.

I'm meeting Tyler out in the hallway in fifteen minutes.

I haven't slept yet. I *can't* sleep. It's not just because I'm worried that I won't wake back up again, but because I'm abuzz with nervous excitement. I've showered and dried my hair as best I can with a towel. I've tiptoed around the room in the dark, gathering up my belongings and packing them carefully into my suitcase. I've charged my phone and applied makeup. I've even watched some TV—on mute, of course. Ella is sleeping.

We could have left hours ago. We could have driven through the night and been in Portland before noon. Being in Sacramento, we're already almost halfway there. But Tyler wanted to get some sleep first. It would be unsafe for him to drive for so long otherwise. So although I may not have slept, I'm hoping he has.

I'm sitting in the chair in front of the dressing table, picking up my phone every few minutes to check the time, but it only seems to be going slower and slower. I release a slow sigh into the darkness around me and then quickly glance over my shoulder to check that Ella hasn't stirred. She hasn't, but the feeling of guilt is quick to diminish the excitement that's been flowing through me.

I think about how furious she'll be when she wakes up and discovers I'm not here, and how that fury will grow when she finds that Tyler isn't either. How she'll confer with Dad and piece together the obvious realization that Tyler and I have left together. How they'll never trust us ever again because once again we have caused trouble.

My eyes fall to the complimentary hotel notepad at the edge of the dresser. There's a fountain pen to match. Dad may not deserve an explanation, but Ella certainly does. I reach for the notepad and pen, chewing my lower lip as I toss sentences back and forth in my head, considering the best thing to say. Using the light from my phone to guide my hand, I scribble the first words that seem to make sense.

I can explain. Call me. Or call Tyler. It doesn't matter who—we'll be together.

I stare at it for a while. And then I add: *Sorry.*

I pull the page from the pad and get to my feet, turning back around toward Ella. She still hasn't moved. My steps are slow, careful, as I edge my way around the bed and place the paper down on the bedside table, right by her phone so that it's impossible for her to miss it in the morning. At least when she calls, I'll be able to explain myself without having to look her in the eye. It's easier that way.

I shift back around the room and turn off the TV. I tuck the chair back under the dresser. I smooth out the wrinkles in the comforter of the bed I haven't slept in. I even fluff up the pillows, and after all of that is done, I check my phone to find that it is 5:13 a.m. Time to go. Time to leave. Time to, essentially, run away.

Yanking out the handle of my suitcase, I wheel it across the carpet, my footsteps inaudible, my heartbeat thumping in my chest. I don't look back. I reach for the handle of the door, and slowly, so, so slowly, I pull it open. It does creak a little, but I slip out into the hallway and carefully click the door shut again. I breathe a sigh of relief and step back.

To my right, Tyler is leaning against the wall, the strap of his duffel bag resting over his shoulder, one hand in the front pocket of his jeans, the other toying with his car keys. He smiles when my eyes meet his. "We've got a long drive ahead of us."

All of a sudden, I'm numb. My legs feel as though they're buckling beneath me and my head feels weightless above my shoulders. I can't believe I'm really doing this. I'm really going to Portland. I'm really going with Tyler. It freaks me out and excites me all at once. I try my best to swallow back the nerves, and my voice is a whisper when I say, "Then let's go."

His smile stretches, and he nods down the hallway toward the elevators. The hotel is quiet, asleep. It won't stay this way for long. Very soon, everyone will be waking, just not Tyler and me. We'll be gone by then.

Our steps are light as we sneak our way down the hall.

Until we hear a door creak open.

Until we hear Ella's voice.

Until we stop dead in our tracks and spin back around.

Ella's peering around the frame of the door of our room. There's a jacket wrapped around her shoulders, which she holds together in front of her chest, and her eyes are sensitive to the sudden light as she squints down the hallway at us. "Would either of you like to explain?"

A sickening feeling washes over me, and my heart drops into my stomach. My lips are parted in disbelief as I blink back at her, and all I can process right now is the hard-hitting reality that *Shit, we're about to be placed on death row.* Portland is now officially off the table, and the possibility of any hope whatsoever for Tyler and me is now gone.

"Mom," Tyler says, voice low, and then he begins to stammer, "I—I mean, we—" until Ella interrupts him.

"Where are the two of you going?" she asks. She raises an eyebrow and glances suspiciously at my suitcase, and then at Tyler's duffel bag, and then she steps out into the hallway, but not too far. She has to hold the door open with her heel to prevent it from locking her out. "Please just tell me. Back home or Portland. Which is it?"

Slowly, Tyler exhales through the stillness of the hallway. His entire body seems to deflate next to me. "Portland," he says quietly.

"Okay," Ella whispers after a moment of silence. She's watching us both intently, her eyes a mixture of fatigue and warmth. She pulls her jacket tighter around her. "Please drive slow."

Now I'm staring at her the same way I stared at her last night, with the same expression that says: *What the hell?* There must be something wrong with her. There has to be. After all these months of it being drilled into my head that Tyler and I are wrong for each other, *now* Ella is telling us it's okay? It's okay to leave us alone to talk to one another? It's okay to send us off to a different state together?

Tyler must be taken aback too, because when I glance sideways at him to gauge if his reaction is as stunned as mine, he's widening his eyes and cocking his head to one side. "Drive slow?" he repeats.

"To Portland, of course," Ella clarifies without missing a beat. She tilts her head to mimic him. "Don't do anything stupid on the roads. I swear, Tyler. No speeding on the interstate."

"You're not going to stop us?" I ask. I must surely sound like a broken record to her by now, constantly questioning her decisions, but it's only because I can't wrap my head around it.

"Why would I? What reason do I have to stop you?" she shoots back, but in the softest and gentlest of ways. We're all talking in mere whispers, and the hallway is cold. "You're allowed to make your own decisions. And besides," she murmurs, "I highly doubt there's going to be a miraculous turnaround on this front tomorrow."

"But…*why?*" That's all I really want to know. *Why* she's passed on Tyler's messages to me over the past year, like the way she had on the

Fourth of July. *Why* she called me over to the house on Thursday morning to see him. *Why* she didn't grow tense last night at the thought of us being alone together. *Why* she isn't stopping us from heading off to Portland. Why, why, why? "I don't think my dad'll be happy when he finds out you didn't stop us while you had the chance."

"He doesn't have to know that I had the chance in the first place," she says, the corners of her lips slowly curving into a smile. It may even be on the verge of a smirk. "And, Eden, I can deal with your father. I may be married to him, but that doesn't mean I have to share the same opinions as him."

I realize what she's hinting at as soon as she says it. "As in…as in your opinion of us?" I glance at Tyler again.

Ella nods only once, but it's enough to tell me everything I need to know. It has taken me a year to realize it because I have never considered it even remotely possible. The thought never once crossed my mind. I have to say it out loud. I have to ask, just to be absolutely certain that I'm absorbing this correctly.

"You're not against us?"

Ella laughs under her breath the same way she did last night, like the answers to my questions are obvious, like this isn't a big deal when, in fact, it is. "When did I ever say that I was?" she says, still whispering. Not only is it ridiculously early, Dad is also ridiculously close. "It was a surprise, yes," she continues, "of course it was, but I care a lot more about the two of you than I do about some stigma. And I understand, I really do. The circumstances are unfortunate, and sometimes I feel I owe you both an apology. I'm not sure how to handle the situation either, but if you want to go to Portland, then go to Portland. If you want to stick around, then stick around. If you want to go home, then go home. It's your choice, and I'm not going to stand in your way."

I could throw up. *How is this possible?* Dad would probably file for divorce if he knew how different their views are. All this time I believed Ella was on his side.

When I look at Tyler again, he's smiling and it's reaching his eyes. "You know, Mom," he says, "I always had a feeling you were way cooler than I ever gave you credit for."

"You're right. I am," she agrees, but her smile quickly falters and she takes a deep breath. "But tell me, how long are you planning to stay up in Portland for? Because, Eden, you'll need to come home and then head back to Chicago eventually." She fixes me with a stern look, but it's kind and gentle, and I don't know how Ella manages to be strict in such a soft way, but somehow she does. Then she looks at Tyler with that exact same expression. "And I need *you* to come home more often these days," she says. "Not once a year. Once a month. I'll even pay for your flights to save you from driving."

"We can work on it," Tyler says with a nod. He's still smiling, and as he shifts from one foot to the other, he moves the strap of his duffel bag farther up his shoulder. He looks down at me. "Ready to get out of here?"

I can't even muster the ability to say yes. I'm still shocked, and my eyes keep finding their way back to Ella. "Are you sure?" My voice is riddled with doubt. I'm waiting for her to deliver the punch line of the joke.

"Absolutely sure," she says. "And if you're going to head off, then make your move so that I can catch a couple more hours of sleep. Also, this never happened. I never saw either of you." Slowly, she backs her way into our room again, but not without peering around the doorframe one last time. "Drive safely."

The door clicks shut as she disappears. We're left in silence. I turn to face Tyler. He's grinning so wide, with bright eyes and his perfect teeth on full display.

"You heard her," he says, but his voice has shot back to normal, and he winces when he realizes how loud he's spoken. He pulls the hood of his navy hoodie over his hair, and the next words to escape his lips are hissed whispers, full of adrenaline and euphoria, mischief and exhilaration. "Let's get the hell out of here."

He reaches for my hand. Our fingers intertwine, locking into place, the warmth from his skin radiating against mine, and I tighten my hand around his and squeeze so hard that my knuckles ache. I can't stop myself. I don't want to let go, and I don't want him to either. It's a much more thrilling sensation than I ever believed it could be, and for how simple it is, it still gets my pulse racing. Maybe it's the nerves that come with not knowing what I'm really letting myself in for. Maybe it's the excitement that, just maybe, I'm letting myself in for all of this; for Tyler's hand in mine, for the goose bumps that cover my skin, for the pain in my chest as my heart thumps frantically against my rib cage.

Hand in hand, we finally make our getaway. Our steps are quicker than before and my heart beats even faster as Tyler leads me down the hall to the elevator, my suitcase trailing along the carpet behind me. Even in the first elevator ride down to the second floor, my chest won't stop contracting. I pin it down to the fact that I am undeniably going crazy with a range of emotions. Anxiety and relief, trepidation and elation. Going to Portland is either going to be the best or the worst decision I've ever made, and only time will tell which.

It's not until we're in the second elevator on the way up to the parking area that Tyler asks, "Did you get some sleep?"

"No," I admit. Our hands are still interlocked like it's the most natural thing in the world. "Did you?"

"Yeah. I accidentally woke Chase up though," he says. With a shrug, he lets out a small laugh.

"Did you tell him?"

"No. He literally fell back asleep within a minute."

The elevator doors ping open to reveal the fourth floor of the parking structure. It's still pretty dark out even though it's dawn, and the air feels cool from the moment Tyler pulls me out of the elevator and across the concrete. His car is up by the back corner, and at first I don't recognize it because I'm still getting used to the change. It certainly doesn't draw attention to itself the way his old car did. Maybe he prefers it that way.

When we reach it, Tyler's firm grasp on my hand disappears, and immediately I begin to crave his touch again. My hand feels cold without it.

"You know, Eden," he murmurs as he unlocks the car, turning to face me, "I'm really, really fucking glad you decided to come up to Portland."

"Why?"

"Because otherwise," he says, "I would have had to give you this back."

He pops the trunk, and as it rises, I shift my gaze to what's inside. It's the matching counterpart to my suitcase, the larger one, the one I travel back and forth to Chicago with. There's a new label attached to it. I point to it and then fire Tyler a questioning glance, but he shakes his head and takes a step back.

I look back at the label and reach for it, flipping it over as I squint through the dark at the handwriting that is all too familiar to me. It's my mom's.

I'm sorry about the other day. Fix things before it's too late. Some of us don't get the chance to. And tell Tyler his mother is great.

—Your mom, who had every right to be walked out on. (I once burned your father's shirts in the backyard.)

Love you. X

"She packed it for you," Tyler says when he notices how confused I am. "Just in case you end up wanting to stay with me for more than a couple days."

"When did…when did you talk to her?"

"Friday, after you guys left to drive up here." He still has his hood up, and his face is shadowed. "So you don't have to worry about breaking the news to her. She liked the idea of you coming to Portland with me."

I'm rolling my eyes as a smile spreads across my face. "Of course she did."

Laughing, Tyler nudges me gently out of the way. He places my other suitcase into the trunk, along with his duffel bag, and then slams it shut as I make my way around to the passenger side. We slide inside the car, and I notice that he's cleared all the trash out of it.

The engine purrs gently to life. Tyler takes a few moments to adjust his seat, the climate control, and the radio, and then he swallows and places his hand on the gearshift. "Last chance to back out," he says, but he's smiling because he knows I won't. I believe I'm past the point of no return.

"Tyler," I reply, pursing my lips. I fix him with a firm look and gently place my hand over his on the gearshift. "Just drive."

chapter

13

When I wake to the bright sun shining through the windshield, I immediately regret not sleeping when I had the chance. My seat belt is twisted around the curves of my body, and my face is propped against the door. On my left shoulder, I feel the gentle, slow drumming of fingertips. In a way, it's almost soothing, and I force my eyes open as I raise my head, lazily glancing sideways to look at Tyler. He drops his hand from my shoulder and shifts back from me, one arm resting over the steering wheel.

"Sorry for waking you," he murmurs. His voice is soft, quiet, like he's afraid that he'll startle me if he speaks any louder.

"That's okay." I unbuckle my seat belt and push myself up, rubbing my eyes. I feel a little hazy, and a little stiff, and a little hot, so it takes me a while to notice that we're parked on a long, curving street. I look back at Tyler for an explanation. "Where are we? Portland?"

We're parked outside of a bungalow with white walls, a starved lawn, and a silver pickup truck up in the driveway. Thick trees line the street in a pretty way that must have been carefully designed. This street almost seems too nice to belong in Portland.

"Redding," says Tyler, and I blink in surprise. We're still in California. "We've only been driving for a couple hours." With a nod, he taps his knuckles against the clock on the dashboard. It's only 8:09 a.m.

"Why are we here?"

"I thought we'd make a pit stop. Get some breakfast and then hit the road again," he tells me, pushing open his door. He swings one foot out of the car before glancing over his shoulder and adding, "Besides, I promised them I'd stop by again on the way back up."

"Promised who?" I ask, but he's already shut the door. His words have fully woken me, and I make a good attempt at scrambling out of the car after him. Even though my legs are still pretty dead, I force them to move, following him up the driveway. "Promised *who*, Tyler?"

He's smiling as though it's funny, and by the time we're both standing on the front step, he's rolling his eyes at my dumbfounded expression. But then the humor of the mystery seems to vanish because he clears his throat and fixes his eyes on me. "My grandparents," he says.

I stare at him. This is the first time I'm ever hearing about him having grandparents in Redding. Even more surprising is the fact that he talks to them. "Your grandparents?" I repeat.

"Uh-huh."

I shade my face with my hand and squint up at him through the morning sunlight. "I thought none of you spoke with your mom's family."

"We don't," he says. Turning toward the door, he gently raps his hand against the wood a couple of times, and then reaches for the door handle and pushes it open. He looks back at me, his smile crooked. "But I never said they were my mom's parents."

He nudges the door open wider and motions for me to come inside. I follow him, albeit hesitantly at first, and I am both nervous and uncomfortable. Nervous because I'm inevitably about to meet some of Tyler's extended family for the first time. Uncomfortable because the only thing I find myself focusing on is that these people are Tyler's *dad's* parents, and the last thing I want to think about right now is his dad. Even at the best of times, it riles me.

The house smells of freshly brewed coffee and cough drops, mixed with

the vague aroma of sweet perfume and boiled cabbage. A wooden staircase leads upstairs, and the walls in the hall are covered with photographs
in slanted frames. I steal quick glances at the pictures as we pass, of faces
I've never seen. They seem to be from a long time ago, like the sixties or
even the fifties. I can hear the steaming of a coffee machine in the kitchen.

Tyler glances over his shoulder, and when he notices me anxiously
looking around, it's almost as though he wants to laugh. "Don't worry,"
he whispers. "They know all about you."

That doesn't make me feel relaxed. In fact, now I'm wondering just
what exactly Tyler has told them. The full truth? The bare minimum?
A slightly twisted version of the truth?

We reach the kitchen, and I follow Tyler inside. It's bright as the
morning sun floods in through the windows, with a patio door leading
out to the small backyard, and there's a woman huddled over the coffee
machine, her back to us.

Tyler loudly clears his throat. "You should really keep the door locked
while you're back here."

Startled, the woman almost knocks the coffeepot off the machine as
she spins around. She looks to be in her early sixties, short, her dark
hair scraped into an updo, her bronzed skin displaying several signs of
aging. "Tyler!" she gasps. She comes rushing across the kitchen floor,
arms extended, and wraps him up in a tight hug. "Why are you here?"
she asks once she pulls away, and there it is: a thick Spanish accent. "It's
only Sunday. I thought not until tomorrow?"

"We left early," Tyler says, and that's when she notices me standing
by his side. Her entire face lights up. "Yeah, this is Eden. Eden"—he
glances at me—"this is my *abuelita*. Or, you know, my grandma.
Abuelita Maria."

"Ah, Eden!" Maria says, my name slow and thick on her lips. She
nudges Tyler aside as she embraces me entirely, wrapping her frail arms

tight around my shoulders. She smells of the perfume in the hall, of roses and sweetness and love. "So nice to meet you." When she finally steps back, she takes both my hands in hers and squeezes her bony fingers around mine. "So, so nice." That grin of hers has yet to falter. In fact, I think it may just be contagious because I realize I'm smiling back at her equally as wide as I part my lips to say, "It's nice to meet you too."

"Sit, sit," she urges, motioning toward the table and directing me over to it. There're six seats, but only two place mats. "We have pancakes on Sunday. Every week," she says, and promptly ushers me into a chair opposite one of the place mats, her hands now on my shoulders.

I glance over at Tyler, surprised and searching for help, but he's watching in amusement with his arms folded loosely across his chest. Then he asks, "Where's Grampa?"

Maria releases her grip on me. "Garage. Car stopped working again."

Tyler chuckles and rolls his eyes. "I should introduce Eden to him," he says. Almost cautiously, he extends his hand, and I take it, allowing him to pull me back to my feet. "If you don't mind me borrowing her, of course."

Maria quickly retreats backward across the kitchen floor, holding her hands up, palms facing us. "No, no. Of course not. Go introduce her to Peter. And then the pancakes." She moves her hands to her hips, flashing her eyes over to the stack of pancakes on the countertop, still in their packaging. "They're only from the store. I'm no good."

"Pancakes are pancakes," Tyler says with a warm, reassuring smile.

His hand is still around mine, and Maria is still grinning at us, and so it quickly becomes obvious that Tyler has told his grandparents the full truth, that I'm more than just his stepsister. Like, a *hell of a lot* more. It's a strange feeling being so open, being like this, but I can only hope that it's a taste of what things *could* be like between us. We could be honest and accepted, content and in love. One day, that is.

Tyler leads me over to the garage door, while Maria returns to brewing some more coffee for the extra company. Before I know it, we're standing out in the garage, the door shut behind us, and our hands are suddenly no longer interlocked. I don't know if Tyler even realizes, but once again I do. Because the moment his touch is gone, I want it back.

The garage is cluttered, from stacks of boxes in the corners, to tools spread over makeshift countertops, to a rusty lawn mower leaning unsteadily against the wall. Right in the center, the unmistakable feature of the garage: a car. It's polished, shining red, with not a single scratch to be seen anywhere on the bodywork, and it's definitely several decades old.

"Is that the coffee ready?" a deep voice echoes from the other end of the garage, behind the propped-up hood of the car.

"Not exactly," Tyler says.

There's a pause, and then a thud as his grandfather knocks his head against the hood. At first, Tyler lets out a laugh, then he quickly shows concern. "You alright there, Gramps?"

The man curses under his breath, spluttering a cough, and then peers around the vehicle. He's rubbing the exposed skin on the top of his head, where his white hair is slowly disappearing. Thick wrinkles are carved into his round face and around his features, but his full set of teeth immediately forms a pleasantly surprised smile.

"The hell are you doing here, kid?" he asks, his voice not yet croaky, but getting there. He wipes his hands, smothered in black grease, on his jeans and then slowly tucks in his shirt. He isn't Hispanic. "Did I skip a day? Is it Monday already?"

"I left earlier than planned," Tyler tells him. He takes a few cautious steps around the tools scattered on the ground before throwing his arm over his grandfather's shoulders and gently patting his arm. "And in case you haven't figured it out already, *this* is Eden." The two of them look back at me, their gazes causing me to blush.

"My, my, my. Aren't you a pretty young thing?" Tyler's grandfather nods in what I can only assume is approval. He pulls his glasses from his face and elbows Tyler in the ribs. "Now I get it. No blaming you." Tyler cringes, covering his face with a hand, but his grandfather only chuckles and props his glasses back on the bridge of his nose, saying, "I'm Peter, but I go by Pete. It's wonderful to discover that Tyler wasn't bullshitting us. I must admit, I did have my doubts that you were real."

I laugh then, only because Tyler is shaking his head now, his eyes hidden behind his hand, his lips pressed into a firm line. I'm growing to like the thought of Tyler talking about me to his grandparents. I like the thought of my name on his lips, the thought of him smiling as he says it.

Pete chuckles again, and Tyler gently pushes him away before finally cracking a smile too.

"Grandma's probably got the coffee ready now. And the pancakes," he says, quickly changing the subject. "So how about a break, and then I can help you out with that battery again?"

Pete agrees, and he leads Tyler and me back into the kitchen, where Maria greets us with a warm smile. She's prepared multiple cups of steaming black coffee and added an extra two place mats to the table. The pancakes are stacked on a plate, surrounded by all sorts of spreads and fresh fruit, neatly aligned.

"Good thing you made me buy more than we needed," Maria tells Pete, and she rushes around the table, pulling out four chairs.

"Well," Pete says, "you never know when we might have guests." He sinks into a chair at the far end of the table as Maria hands him some coffee, which he promptly takes a sip of. Seemingly content, he watches us over the rim of the mug from behind the steamed-up lenses of his glasses.

"Please," Maria says, shifting her attention to Tyler and me, "sit." She directs me back into the same chair she ushered me down into earlier and sets some coffee in front of me. "Is this okay? Or do you drink tea? I can make you tea."

"Coffee is perfect," I say quickly, almost cutting her off to save her the hassle of ensuring that everything is perfect. Besides, coffee *is* perfect.

Maria is relieved to hear that I'm satisfied, so she grasps Tyler's shoulders and pushes him down into the seat next to mine. I don't think the rose hue has left his cheeks since the moment we walked through the front door, and seeing him so embarrassed is, surprisingly, enjoyable.

"Have you been driving all night?" Maria asks as she brings him a cup of coffee. She thrusts it carefully into his hand and then places her palm flat against his forehead, furrowing her eyebrows as though she's expecting a fever.

"Only a few hours," Tyler says. Quickly, he moves her hand away, and her expression is not only confused, but also slightly horrified. Tyler takes a quick sip of his coffee before adding, "And no, I didn't floor it along the interstate. We actually left from Sacramento, not LA."

"Of all the cities here in California," Pete murmurs under his breath, croaking his words, "why in the hell were you in Sacramento? I've never stepped foot in a city more ridiculously boring than that damn place."

"Long story," Tyler says. Even though it's not, really.

"Hm." Maria slides into the empty chair at the opposite end of the table, but I can tell by the curious glint in her eyes that she's thinking something. And that something is in Spanish. "*¿Fue duro convencerla?*"

Tyler glances sideways at me. It's only brief, and then he clears his throat and looks back at his grandmother. "*Sí. No pensé que ella vendría.*"

"*¿Le has hablado de tu padre?*"

"*Aún no,*" he says.

"I hate when they do this," Pete hisses to me. It draws my attention to him instead as Tyler and Maria continue, their conversation impossible to understand. "Very frustrating."

"You don't speak it?" I ask.

"Only the basics." He stretches across the table, stabbing at the pile of pancakes with his fork, his eyes not exactly trained on me. "Do you?"

I shake my head. "I wish."

Both Tyler and Maria seem to revert back to English then, exchanging firm glances with one another before Maria starts to pass the pancakes around. She's grinning from ear to ear.

"Tyler says you study in Chicago," she muses, arching a brow in interest as she slips a pancake onto my plate. Back home, I'd reject it. Here, I don't want to seem rude, so I quietly murmur *thanks*.

"And yeah," I add. "I'm majoring in psychology."

"Psychology," Pete echoes. "So, like brains and interactions?"

"Explaining the reasons behind certain human behavior," I rephrase. Reaching for my coffee, I take a long sip. I'm not the biggest fan of basic black coffee, but it serves its purpose of helping to wake me up. "I'd like to have a focus in criminal psychology one day."

Tyler's head snaps around the moment these words leave my lips. "I didn't know that."

"That's because you haven't been—" I bite my tongue to stop myself from saying *you haven't been around*. It's so easy to throw remarks at Tyler without thinking. Controlling my words is difficult.

I try my best to backpedal, taking a few seconds to gather my thoughts while sipping on my coffee again. "I just find it interesting," I say finally.

"Criminal psychology…" Maria murmurs. "What exactly is that?"

"Examining the possible reasons and triggers that lead a person to commit a crime."

There's an uncomfortable silence around the table, so tense that it's tangible. Pete shovels half a pancake into his mouth. Maria traces the rim of her mug with her fingertip. Tyler scratches the back of his neck, dropping his gaze to his lap. Only then do I realize what I'm saying, and who exactly I'm saying it to.

"I mean, every aspect of psychology is just so interesting," I blurt, attempting to steer the conversation in a different direction. I opt for the humorous route. "Like figuring out why people do irrational things, such as travel to Portland with their stepbrother."

It's a relief to see Tyler roll his eyes, watch Maria exhale, and hear Pete chuckle. It's a relief just to see *them* relieved.

The rest of the conversation over breakfast flows, which is nice. It would be unbearably awkward if it didn't. Maria asks a lot of questions. Pete does a lot of nodding in agreement. Tyler and I do a lot of answering. Tyler ends up explaining why we were in Sacramento, and Maria's expression floods with sympathy when she discovers the sad excuse behind the trip. Even sadder is that the trip didn't make the slightest difference to the state of our family. Except for Tyler and me, which definitely wasn't the intention. But I'm glad it's the outcome.

I tune out for a while, cutting my pancake into a handful of smaller pieces so that it doesn't seem like so much, and I wonder if Dad and Ella are awake yet. It's almost nine. They are most likely awake and arguing. Ella could be fighting our side on her own, defending us against Dad, stuck in the middle yet again. It makes me feel so guilty, so selfish. It makes me want to turn around and go back.

But I shake that thought by the time breakfast is over because Ella knows how to handle herself. She's a damn lawyer, after all, and Tyler doesn't seem worried, so I shouldn't be either. In fact, he appears to be more focused on helping Pete out with the car because they both immediately head back to the garage the second Maria stands to clear the table.

"We can get back on the road before ten. We'll be in Portland long before it even gets dark," Tyler tells me, hesitating at the door to the garage. I hate how effortlessly attractive he is. He glances over his shoulder, and I hear Pete asking him to grab a flashlight. When he looks back at me, his smile seems apologetic. "Do you mind?"

"Go ahead," I say, because I really don't mind hanging around here for an hour. I don't want to be the one to drag him away, and Maria looks like she could use a hand cleaning up, so once Tyler disappears, I join her at the table.

"So have you always lived here?" I ask because I'm curious, as per damn usual. And I don't exactly know what else to talk to her about. "In Redding?"

"No," Maria says with the shake of her head. She carries the empty plates over to the dishwasher, her back to me. "Just over seven years. We lived in Santa Monica too."

As I gather up the cutlery scattered over the table, I find myself raising my eyebrows. "Really?"

"*Sí,*" she says.

I join her over by the dishwasher, placing the forks and knives inside, watching her out of the corner of my eye. "Why move up here?"

"Ah." She gives me a closed smile and leans back against the countertop. "With everything that was going on at the time, we didn't wish to stay. It was very hard. So we came up here to Redding because we wanted somewhere peaceful, but we also loved living in the city. It's nice here."

I think about the time frame for a second. "Everything going on… with Tyler's dad?" I question, my tone soft, my voice cautious. Maybe I shouldn't press such a delicate subject, but I just can't help it. I hate not knowing. "With your son?"

"Ah," Maria says again. "Tyler did mention that you know the full story." She bends down to shut the dishwasher, and when she straightens up again, she heads over to the sink to wash her hands under the faucet. I worry that I may have upset her, so I remain quiet.

"But yes," she finally says, eyes trained on the stream of water, "it was a very difficult time for us. Very hard to deal with. Very hard to accept."

I can imagine, I think. I glance around the kitchen, feeling suddenly out of place, like I'm intruding. "Do you mind if I head to the bathroom?"

Maria looks at me, slightly confused at the quick change in subject, yet she also has that look of relief in her eyes again. "Upstairs. Second door. On left."

I waste no time in getting out of the kitchen. I feel uncomfortable, so I make my way up the stairs as quickly as possible. And at first, the walls seem like nothing more than a replica of the walls in the hall downstairs, with old frames holding even older photos. It's on the excessive side, and it's also creeping me out having so many faces looking back at me, up until I spot Tyler among them.

My heart does a little jump, and I have to squint at the photo first, stepping back to examine it from afar before I move closer again. It's taken on a beach, and it's a beach I recognize all too well. It's Santa Monica's beach, with the pier far in the background, but I'm more focused on the three people on the sand. Maria on the left, Tyler in the middle, Pete on the right. All huddled close together, arms thrown around each other's shoulders.

Only Maria is much younger, with a slimmer figure but the same round face. And Pete has hair. Thick, dark hair. But he still has his glasses, and both of them are definitely not in their sixties. Their early forties, more like.

Yet Tyler's there, maybe sixteen, maybe seventeen, with hair that's much longer and much more wild than I ever recall it being, and I don't understand how such an old photograph is even possible for him to be in.

And that's when it hits me.

Holy shit.

It's not Tyler at all. *It's not Tyler at all.*

"I bet I know what photo you're looking at right now."

My heart stops as I physically jump back a step, startled. Leaning against the wall halfway up the stairs, arms folded across his chest, is Tyler. And for real this time.

"You scared me," I whisper, my voice almost inaudible. I'm breathing so heavily and so deeply that it makes talking difficult.

"The one on the beach, right?" Tyler asks, continuing. He drops his arms and approaches me, climbing the remaining few stairs and falling into place by my side. "Everyone always said I was his double. They said I should have been his brother rather than his kid. Personally," he says, tilting his head as he studies the photo, "I don't see it. That hair? So not cool. What the hell was he thinking?"

I twist my face to look at him. "Your dad," I say. It's not a question because I know the answer. I know that's his dad in that photograph, and I realize that for the first time, I can actually put a face to the man I've developed such strong contempt for. Even if it is only a young, innocent face.

"Mm," Tyler says. Slowly, he leans back against the wall again, so casually and so nonchalantly and so calmly that I begin to wonder if Portland really *has* changed his entire mind-set. "His name is Peter, by the way."

"Peter? As in…your grandpa?"

"As in Peter Junior," he says. "And Peter Senior. And luckily, Mom refused to follow the tradition."

My eyebrows knit together as I analyze him closely. A year ago, I

ESTELLE MASKAME

had to stop him from kicking his dad's ass. Now, he's talking as though he couldn't care less about his dad. It's a huge contrast, a big change. When I run my eyes over the walls again, I realize there're a lot of photographs of his dad. "These don't bother you?" I ask.

"A year ago they did," he admits. "I actually stayed here for a couple days last year after I left. I didn't know where to head at first, so I came here, and trust me, I tried to tear every single one of those frames off the wall. But Gramps made me leave." He laughs, but I don't. "And then I dropped by again on Wednesday on my way back down to LA, and none of these photos bothered me anymore. They really don't."

I'm squinting at him even more now, but it's impossible to deny that there's sincerity in his eyes, honesty in his smile. There's nothing less these days. I suddenly have an overwhelming desire to hug him.

"And in case you couldn't already tell, my grandma's kind of a hoarder," he tells me, taking a step closer to the wall, to the photos and the faces. "She never wants to let go. Even of the things that everyone else has already let go of." He reaches up then, tapping his knuckle against a particular photograph in a gold frame, and he rolls his eyes and says, "Like marriages that ended eight years ago."

It's a wedding photo. His parents' wedding. Ella and Peter, both so young, not much older than we are now, with Tyler grinning in the middle of them. He's just a kid, adorable in a tiny tux, with the same huge grin that hasn't changed at all and the bright round eyes that I later fell in love with. Ella once told me that he walked her down the aisle, even showed me a similar picture, and it's such an awful thought to realize that he walked her down that aisle and handed her over to the man who would later shatter their lives.

I almost feel sick.

"Why do they..." My throat feels too dry, like my words are stuck, so I swallow hard and take a deep breath. "Why do they have all these

162

photos of your dad up? Aren't they mad at him? I know that it's not my place to say anything, but it seems a little...I don't know. Too forgiving, I guess."

"Of course they're mad, Eden," Tyler says, shaking his head at me. "But at the end of the day, he's still their kid." That's when he shifts, slowly stepping between the wall and me, blocking the photos from my view. The expression in his eyes seems to soften, and the emerald seems to brighten. "So we got the car started a lot quicker than I thought we would," he informs me. The subject change is sudden. "Turns out Gramps left the headlights on all night. Totally drained the battery. So," he says, "we can get going again."

"Okay. Give me a minute." Slowly, I back away from him and push open the door to the bathroom, suddenly acutely aware of his presence.

"Wait," he says. "Can I ask you something?"

I lean my weight against the bathroom door and watch him closely, trying my best to mirror his relaxed expression. "Sure."

"Did you figure it out yet, why people do irrational things such as running off to Portland with their stepbrother?" The corner of his lip quirks upward to create a cunning smirk, his eyes smoldering teasingly as he waits for an answer. He moves closer within the small confinement of the hall and presses his palm flat against the wall by my shoulder, the warmth of him making me shiver.

"Of course, I'm not exactly qualified to say," I murmur as fast as I can, trying my best to get my words out before they catch in my throat. I have to swallow and take a second to catch my breath because it's so surreal having Tyler not only back in the picture, but having him within such close proximity. Last summer, I was desperate to have him this close. Now I have to adjust to how it feels again because I have lacked his presence and I have lacked his touch for far too long. But I've also missed it.

When I do finally find my voice again, I continue with honesty, my words reduced to a mere whisper as I tell him, "But I'm pretty sure people only do such a thing when they have some hope left."

♥

chapter

14

It's a seven-hour drive to Portland. Seven hours confined in a car alongside Tyler, who I just so happen to have completely mixed feelings for right now. My thoughts have never been more all over the place. Between the anger at him for leaving that's slowly diminishing, the thrill from running off to Portland with him, and the amazement at how calm and relaxed and different he seems, I'm really struggling to pinpoint exactly how I feel at the moment.

What I do know is that he is ridiculously terrible at singing. I know this because he has been singing along to the radio for the past fifteen minutes, messing up on half the lyrics, yelling the choruses, tapping his fingertips against the wheel, and nodding his head in sync with the beats. Three years ago, I don't think Tyler would have ever been caught dead doing such a thing, because it's lame and definitely not cool. He's trying to make me laugh to make the journey go by quicker.

And I have been laughing. I've been laughing for each of those fifteen minutes that have passed, my stomach cramping each time he reaches for a high note, burying my head into my hands, embarrassed on his behalf. I'm slumped down in the passenger seat, the air conditioning directed straight at my face, my Chucks on the floor, and my feet up on the dash. It's painful to laugh, so I signal for a time-out and pull myself upright. I reach for the controls and reduce the volume of the radio, and at the same time, Tyler's awful singing trails off, and his sincere laughter fills the car.

"Okay," I say, grinning. It's almost four, and we passed through Salem a little while ago. We'll be in Portland soon, maybe thirty minutes from now. Finally, the scenery is beginning to seem familiar. "Are there any talent shows coming up soon? I'm signing you up for an audition."

Tyler glances at me, his huge grin mirroring mine. "You're my first groupie."

Just then, his phone rings. It's lying in the cup holder in the center console, vibrating profusely, the screen glowing, his ringtone bouncing around the car. He reaches for it, glancing down at the screen for a second, and then passes the device to me.

"It's my mom," he tells me. "Put it on speaker."

So I do just that.

"Hey, Mom," Tyler says.

"Hi, Ella," I say, holding the phone between us. "You're on speaker. Tyler's driving."

"Hey, you two," Ella murmurs across the line, almost like she's sighing. I have yet to figure out how it's possible for her to somehow sound cheerful yet sad all at the same time. "I'm just calling to check up on you. Shouldn't you be there by now?"

"We're about a half hour away," I inform her. "We stopped for an hour at—"

"At some diner for breakfast," Tyler cuts in. He fixes me with a sharp look, and very slowly, he shakes his head. I stare questioningly back at him. "And we've stopped for gas a couple times, but yeah, almost there. Where are you?"

"Up in the room," Ella says. The connection isn't the best, so her voice is crackling a little. "Chase is down at the pool, and Jamie's been talking to Jen on the phone for at least two hours now."

Neither Tyler nor I say anything at first. We exchange a concerned glance because we're both wondering the same thing. I'm the one who ends up asking the question we both want an answer to. "And my dad?"

Now it's Ella's turn to be quiet. We listen to her breathe across the line. "I'd be lying if I told you I knew where he was," she says finally.

Softly, my eyes close, and I throw my head back against the headrest of the passenger seat in disappointment. Tyler's doing a good job of frowning while keeping his attention on the road, and when I sit up again, I prop my elbow against the window and rest my forehead against the palm of my hand.

"So he knows the truth," I mutter. That'll explain why Dad's disappeared. He'll be off somewhere trying to get his anger to subside, I bet. I'm staring out of the window, my lips pressed firmly together as we head across a bridge that runs over the Willamette River which traces its way through Oregon. "What happened when he found out?"

"I had to tell him," Ella says. "As soon as I woke up, I went next door and just told him the truth. That you left for Portland together, and that you're both old enough now to make your own decisions, and that it's not up to me or him to stop you." She releases a frustrated laugh. "And the first thing I thought about were the charges the hotel would press against us if he punched a hole through the door. Thankfully, all he did was leave, and I haven't seen him since. The car's still here though, so he can't have gone far. I went out and checked."

"Did he say anything?" Tyler asks.

"It's probably best if I don't repeat it," Ella says quietly. The apprehension in her voice is palpable. "He's not all that impressed with me either."

I glance over to Tyler. He's shaking his head as he pushes his shades down over his eyes, his grip on the steering wheel tightening. "We should have waited until morning," he murmurs, almost as though he's talking just to himself. "We should have told Dave ourselves before we left."

"Trust me, Tyler, if you'd told him yourself, you wouldn't be anywhere near Portland right now," Ella says. "At least not with Eden. I hate to say it, but I bet he would have been thrilled to see you leave."

"That's true," Tyler agrees. "What about Jamie? Chase? Do they know we're gone?"

"Of course they do," Ella states matter-of-factly. I can just *sense* her rubbing her temples right now as she ponders the situation. "It's impossible to hide the fact that you're not here. And as usual, Jamie's being incredibly difficult. Chase only wants to know when you're both coming back."

"It's Eden's decision," Tyler says. Although he's focused on the road ahead, I can see the small smirk on his lips. I wish he'd take the sunglasses off again so that I could see the expression in his eyes.

"Hmm." I sit up and tap my index finger against my lips as I feign deep consideration. "I'm not sure yet, but I do know that if Tyler keeps on singing, I'll be back by tomorrow."

Ella laughs, and then Tyler does, and then I do, and for a moment, I forget just how risky all of this really is. By doing this, by coming up here to Portland with Tyler, I may have just ruined whatever chance I had left at salvaging a relationship with my dad. There's absolutely no chance in hell of him ever forgiving me after this.

"Right," Ella says. "I'll stop distracting you. Drive carefully, and text me when you get there."

Tyler nods even though she can't see him. "Will do."

She hangs up the call, so I lock Tyler's phone and drop it back into the cup holder. I pull my legs up onto my seat and cross them, trying to get comfortable for the remainder of the journey. *We're so close*, I think. And I don't know how I feel about it yet, about Portland. I like to think of Santa Monica as my home these days, but there's no denying the fact that I'll forever be a Portland girl. I was born and raised here. Admittedly, I adored Portland when I was younger, when things were the way they were supposed to be. Then my parents began to fight, and my friends turned cruel, and the bad memories have always seemed to outweigh the good ones. Maybe I just need some time to make some more memories here. Good ones, that is.

Cautiously, Tyler turns the volume of the radio back up, and I can sense him glancing at me through his sunglasses. He's biting back a smile, but he refrains from singing, all the way through Wilsonville and straight up to Portland.

And by the time we're within the city's boundaries, everything is so, so familiar. So *Portland-y*, if that's even a thing. You can just tell when you're in Portland. The interstate is lined by trees, covered by low clouds and the slightest breakthrough of sun. It's a short drive to downtown Portland, and it's not until the Willamette River appears alongside us that I remember just how beautiful the city actually is. In a natural, urban sort of way. There's nothing glamorous about Portland. No gorgeous promenades, no photogenic piers, no stunning beaches. But I think that's why it's such a unique city. The nature, the diversity. How liberal, green, and wet it is. For what it's worth, the majority of the people in Portland are pretty unique too, and it's a much friendlier city than Seattle, that's for sure. We Portlanders are pretty laid-back.

"I just remembered," Tyler says, finally taking his sunglasses off again and placing them into the cup holder alongside his phone, "I should probably stop and get groceries. I cleared out my refrigerator before I left, so my place is pretty bare right now."

I look at him. "Your place?"

"Yeah."

"You have a place?"

He directs his eyes away from the road for a second, over to me instead. "What? Did you think I've been staying in a hotel or something all this time? Living out of my car?" He has to laugh, but now that I think about it, I've never actually thought any of it through. "We'll head over, right after we stop by Freddy's."

I blink, holding back laughter. "Oh my God."

"What?" He seems genuinely confused, and creases appear on his forehead, right between his eyebrows.

"Nothing," I say, and finally I laugh. I have to. I can't help it. "It's just really weird hearing you talk like a native. You're from out of town, so you should only know it as Fred Meyer."

"You make it sound like it's difficult to learn how Portland works," he shoots back teasingly, a challenging smile playing on his lips. "I hate to break it to you, but it's not that hard. Go Timbers, go Blazers."

I raise my eyebrows suspiciously back at him. "Anyone can say that," I say defensively.

"But can anyone say that the Blazers won the NBA championship in 1977?"

My eyebrows arch even higher. "Okay, I'll give you that one. But still. It's kind of freaking me out having you know all this stuff about Portland. Call me crazy, but it's like you're invading my personal space."

"Kind of like how you invaded mine when you moved to Santa Monica?" He's grinning now, glancing rapidly between the road and me as though not to miss my expression, and I roll my eyes and playfully push his arm.

"Whatever."

It takes a good fifteen minutes to reach downtown, and with it being a Sunday, the traffic isn't bad. But we don't pull off the interstate. Instead, Tyler continues to follow it, straight onto the Marquam Bridge, one of many bridges that cross the Willamette. If there's one thing Portland is known for besides our overwhelming amount of trees, then it's our bridges.

I lean forward, looking past Tyler to the Hawthorne Bridge on our left, where I can just about see the Waterfront Park. It's where I used to spend the Fourth of July, sprawled out on the grass with Amelia, listening to music and bands we didn't even like at the Blues Festival. And over on our right again, way in the distance, is the faint tip of Mount Hood.

We're over into east Portland now, advancing along the Banfield Expressway, which I'm all too familiar with. It's the route I used to take with my friends downtown because Mom hated me taking the MAX when I was younger, especially because the line that runs through our old neighborhood starts over in Gresham, which doesn't exactly have the best reputation. According to Mom, I was likely to be assaulted by a gang member if I got on that train.

"So." I glance over at Tyler. "Which neighborhood then?"

"Irvington," he says.

I have to think about it for a second because Portland is a huge city with a hell of a lot of different neighborhoods, and after three years of being gone, my geographic knowledge isn't up to scratch. "Irvington… as in, Broadway Street? As in, over there?" I point over his chest, out of his window to the left of the expressway. There's nothing but thick trees, as with everything else in this city, but I'm pretty sure that Irvington is on the other side.

"Yeah," Tyler says with a small shrug. Even though it's just after four now, he's beginning to seem tired. It's been a long drive. "I'm renting an apartment up on the corner of Brazee and Ninth," he tells me. "And even though it doesn't exactly have a view like my apartment in New York did, I think you'll like it."

"Haven't you been lonely?" I blurt out, and he looks at me a little funny. I felt that way in Chicago at first. Settling into a new city, knowing absolutely no one, being thousands of miles away from everyone you *do* know. It kinda sucks, and I realize now that Tyler had to go through the exact same thing. "You know, like, living up here on your own? And I know you did the same in New York, but that was different. You had Snake. You had Emily. You had the tour. You were talking to people."

"And you think I don't talk to people here?" Now he just looks perplexed, and he hasn't glanced back at the road yet, so I can't help myself from reaching over and pressing my hand to his cheek, directing his eyes back to the expressway. "Trust me, Eden," he says, his gaze already finding its way back to me, "I've kept myself busy."

Again, I gently push his jaw so that he's facing the road. "Doing what?"

"I'll tell you later," he says quickly. "But for now, it's time to stock up on food."

He takes the next exit off the Banfield Expressway, and shortly after we head left into the Irvington neighborhood. Broadway Street is extremely familiar because a lot of the time Amelia and I would come here instead of heading downtown. It's dominated by stores, breweries and restaurants, but I hardly have time to look around, as Tyler is already pulling around the corner into the Fred Meyer parking lot, which is packed, because it's fucking Fred Meyer. And in Portland, Freddy's could seriously be a religion. I kind of miss it.

We pull into a spot and make for the entrance after taking a few seconds to stretch out the stiffness in our legs. It feels odd walking on Portland soil again, but luckily, the city seems to be experiencing its usual high summer temperatures. It's definitely hotter than eighty out right now, and definitely hotter than Santa Monica has been lately.

We head inside, and Tyler grabs a cart, heading straight for the aisles like a seasoned Fred Meyer shopper. He spends a good amount of time around the fruit and vegetable sections. I've never gone grocery shopping with a vegetarian before. It's an interesting experience watching all the food he's tossing into the cart, and even more interesting is the fact that most of it actually looks appealing. Still, I manage to slip two boxes of Lucky Charms into the cart when he isn't looking, only because it's a guilty pleasure of mine.

We head for the checkout lanes after strolling up and down the aisles for over half an hour, and I help Tyler stack the entire contents of the cart up onto the conveyor belt, all the while thinking about how mature I feel—which is weird, because I have gone grocery shopping in Chicago like a million times, but it's different with Tyler. It feels like we're a couple, carrying out our weekly grocery restock before heading home and ramming it all into our refrigerator and cabinets, then collapsing in front of the TV. That's how it should be. Only it's Tyler's refrigerator, not mine, and we're certainly not a couple. But it's a nice feeling, nonetheless. It makes me think about what our life could be like if we *were* a couple, and all the daily, mundane tasks we would have to do that would only be enjoyable because we were doing them together.

We're overloaded with bags by the time we get back to the car, and we have no choice but to stuff them all into the backseat. Our luggage is already taking up all the space in the trunk, and when we actually get moving and pull out of the lot, we can quite literally feel just how weighed down the car is. But thankfully, Tyler lets me know that his apartment is only five minutes away.

So we head farther into the neighborhood of Irvington, straight over to the corner of Brazee and Ninth, where Tyler pulls over by the curb. The street is lined with trees, obviously, and it has a mixture of two-story houses and bungalows. Except to our right. To our right is an apartment complex.

"Is this it?" I ask, although the answer is pretty obvious.

"Yeah," says Tyler, already slipping off his seat belt. I follow him out of the car and around to the trunk, where he collects our luggage. "It's a nice place, just the rent's a little pricey. That's why I sold my car."

"Priorities," I say, echoing his own words from several days ago.

Slowly, he smiles as he slams the trunk shut. "Exactly."

He leads the way into the complex, through the entrance in the wooden fence, right into a gorgeous courtyard. The apartments are all identical in design, with some being two-story houses, and they all curve around the communal courtyard like a giant C. Footpaths weave through the well-maintained lawn, where plants and trees and benches are dotted around. It's nice, especially with the sun out, but I can't imagine it looking as pretty as it does now during the fall when drizzle is hanging over the city.

"I'm just over here," Tyler says, slipping his hand into the back pocket of his jeans and pulling out a set of keys. I follow the direction of his gaze, which leads to a door that's named Unit 3. By the time we reach it, Tyler's cheeks are flushed. "It's a little, uh, bare," he warns me, and turns the key in the lock. "I'm not much of a decorator."

Pushing open the door, he steps back to allow me in first. And the first thing I realize when I take a few steps over the hardwood flooring of the living room is that he wasn't kidding. It *is* bare. The walls are white and empty besides a TV that's mounted. The rest of the living room consists of nothing but a single black leather couch and a fluffy beige rug in the center of the floor.

"In my defense," Tyler says quickly as he wheels my two suitcases toward me, "I didn't want to blow half my cash on shit I don't really need. And besides, I'm not even here half the time." He slides his duffel bag off his shoulder and throws it onto the couch, then moves toward the far corner of the room, where there're two doorways: one leading into a small hallway, one leading into a small dining room.

Tyler shows me the dining room first, which is simply a black table with two matching chairs, and then we're through another doorway and into the kitchen, which is a small cube in comparison to Dad and Ella's kitchen back home. But it has everything a kitchen needs, and I figure Tyler does have a point about not spending money on huge apartments and furniture just for the sake of it.

I follow him back through the dining room and into the small hallway now. There are two bedrooms, with the bathroom in the middle of the two. The bedroom on the left appears to be Tyler's, even though there's nothing exactly personal about it. Again, the walls are empty, and the only furniture in this room is the double bed pressed against the wall. The closet is built-in. And the only reason I figure this room is his is because the other room is entirely empty.

"I probably should have got around to setting this room up," Tyler says, his voice echoing. I look at him sideways, and he's rubbing at the back of his neck a little awkwardly.

"Mmm." We're both thinking the same thing: *Where the hell am I going to sleep?* The last thing I want is for Tyler to suggest that we bunk together because that's definitely not happening, so I quickly say, "I can take the couch. I don't mind."

He steps in front of me so that he can see my expression. "I can't let you sleep on the couch, Eden," he states, voice firm and strict, as though he's my parent. "My mom would kill me for the shitty hospitality."

"Seriously, I don't mind," I try more convincingly. "I live in a dorm, remember? So believe me, I've crashed on more couches than I can count."

He studies me, frowning. "Are you sure? I feel pretty bad."

"Positive," I say. "We should go get those groceries."

And that's what we do. It doesn't take us long to unpack it all, with me removing everything from the bags and Tyler placing them into the cabinets. By 5:30 p.m., we're settled in and hungry. It's been a long day.

So Tyler starts preparing some sort of pasta dish for himself, and I fetch myself a bowl of those Lucky Charms I picked up earlier. It's all I'm craving, and I pull myself up onto the countertop, crossing my legs, and eat slowly while I watch Tyler cook.

"You should text your mom," I say, my voice muffled and my mouth full. Quickly, I swallow. "Let her know that we're here."

"Shit, yeah." Tyler stops dicing tomatoes and wipes his hands on his jeans, fishing his phone out of his pocket. I scoop up another spoonful of cereal as he types, his eyes glancing constantly between his screen and the pasta that's cooking in the saucepan on the stove. I'm staring at his shoulders because I've never truly appreciated how broad they are before. Then my eyes trace a path down to his bicep, where his tattoos are peeking out from under the sleeve of his T-shirt, and I quickly blink when I realize I'm staring.

"Can I ask you something?"

Having sent the message, Tyler places his phone down on the countertop and picks up the knife again, turning his back to me. "Sure."

"Why didn't you want her to know that we stopped by your grandparents' place?"

As soon as I say it, he's sighing. He looks down, places the knife back, then slowly turns around to look at me. "Because she doesn't know I've been talking to them again. We didn't exactly keep in contact with them after Dad got locked up. They moved away, and we never visited—people don't typically travel nine hours to see the parents of their ex-husband, you know? And besides, anything relating to or about Dad, Mom hates. So there's no point in telling her."

I nod, and there's a brief moment of silence where I twirl my spoon around my bowl and where Tyler turns back to the saucepan, adjusting the heat. "She's a really great mom," I finally mumble. I've already told Ella this before because it's true. I just wonder if Tyler knows it too. "I'm just saying it in case you weren't already aware."

"No, I know," he says, turning back around to face me. "She's always been great, even though it wasn't easy for her after the truth came out about Dad. She was pretty much in pieces back then. So different from what she's like now."

I place my bowl down on the countertop and then wait for Tyler to hopefully expand. I like knowing about their lives because I'm part of them now. I'll never know exactly what Tyler's family went through, but I can at least try to understand it as best I can. Over the past three years, I've learned a lot.

Tyler runs a hand through his hair as though he's contemplating whether or not he's going to give in and open up to me, his gaze narrowing on the small window beside me. After a few moments, he turns to the stove and switches off the heat.

"She really fucking loved my dad, you know," he starts, gripping the edge of the countertop. "And he felt the exact same way about her, because seriously, when I think back to when I was a kid, all I remember is the two of them being totally obsessed with each other. So you know, when she found out about Dad and he got arrested, it shattered her. And it didn't matter how much she loved him because she couldn't bear to look at him anymore, so she filed for divorce as soon as he was sentenced."

He stops, looks at the ground for a moment, then back up. "She stopped working, and for like the first year after it all happened, she could hardly look at me either. She felt so guilty for not noticing what was going on before, and this one time when I got into a fight at school, I came home with my face all busted up, and she seriously burst into tears the second I walked through the front door. Her parents always said she'd never be a good mom, so I think she believed that for a while.

And obviously I wasn't making it any easier for her with all the sneaking out and the drinking and the smoking."

He pauses again, but this time he straightens up and takes a step toward me, coming to stand right in front of me. He has that gentle, sincere tone to his voice that was once rare but is now increasingly common. "But then she met your dad, and she stopped sitting in front of the TV all day with five cups of coffee. She started going out more, and as lame as it sounds, she seemed happy again because she was. I knew she'd met someone before she even told us. It was so obvious, and when she did finally tell us, it didn't really freak me out or anything like she thought it would. I was glad your dad came into the picture because that's when Mom started being herself again." Slowly, he runs his eyes over my legs, still crossed over the countertop, and he moves against me, placing both his hands on my knees. He hesitates before saying anything else, like he's waiting for me to push him back, but all I can think about is how quickly my chest has tightened. I couldn't push him away even if I wanted to because I feel frozen in place, paralyzed by the mere touch of his fingertips. He is the only person I have ever met who has such an effect on me. The only person who I *want* to have this effect.

"So," he says, smiling a little as he glances back up at me from beneath his eyelashes, "I actually met your dad for the first time when I was fifteen. Mom told us all to be on our best behavior, but you know, I was going through my I-don't-give-a-fuck phase, so I'd been out drinking with some guys a whole lot older than me, and when I got home, I was pretty paralytic. As soon as Mom walked into the kitchen with your dad, he'd barely even introduced himself before I threw up on the floor. Gross, I know. Talk about bad first impressions. So Mom was mortified, and your dad was horrified, and to this day I'm still surprised he stuck around after that. And I know I've gone way off subject, but the point is, your dad didn't like me straight from the get-go."

I sense him swallow, and the kitchen is silent. His voice is almost a whisper when he speaks again. "And I can't help but think that if I hadn't acted the way I did when I was younger, then maybe your dad wouldn't be so against..." His words taper off, and his breathing is slow, deep. I can't see his eyes because I'm staring at his lips, at the way they're edging toward me. My legs almost feel numb as he runs his hands from my knees to my thighs, and his lips are so close now that his forehead is against mine, both our eyes closed. "This," he whispers.

But I can't do it. Not yet. There's too much left to figure out, too many things to fix. Kissing him now is the easy way out.

Carefully, I cup his jaw in my hands and shake my head no against his. I keep my eyes closed, and the small smile on my lips is almost apologetic as his touch slowly disappears. First from my face, then my legs. I interlock my hands and place them in my lap.

Tyler takes a step back, and when my eyelids flutter open, he's staring at me. I can tell by his eyes alone that he's not angry at being rejected. More disappointed than anything else. He nods once and gives me a warm, understanding smile, then turns away, back to the stove where he turns the heat back on.

My body feels strange, different. I reach for my cereal, but it's turned to mush, so all I can do is twirl the spoon around and around in the bowl again. But the entire time that I do, my eyes aren't on the Lucky Charms that I wanted so badly.

They're on Tyler, who I might just want even more.

chapter

15

It feels like I've slept for no more than an hour when I wake. I feel so groggy, and my head is heavy. It's almost impossible to open my eyes, so I squeeze them shut and pull the blanket closer to my chest. I'm starting to regret not sleeping on Saturday night, because now the mere two hours of sleep I had are catching up with me. Yet the hand that's massaging my shoulder is persistent. It feels nice, but it's pulling me out of my slumber, so I quickly nudge the hand away by jerking my body to one side. And if that isn't enough to display my irritation, I also release a quiet groan.

And then there's that familiar laugh, and I don't even have to look to know that it belongs to Tyler. A brief wave of excitement surges through my body at the thought of him next to me, at the simple fact that he's here, and my eyelids ping open, suddenly startled.

For the briefest of seconds, I have no idea where I am or why I'm even with Tyler, alone, until I blink a few times to wake myself up fully. That's when everything comes back to me, and I think: *Oh, Portland.* It's a rather sobering thought to wake up to.

Tyler's crouching down by the couch, fully dressed and smelling of cologne, and he's looking directly back at me. My face is level with his, his eyes bright.

"I'm sorry for waking you," Tyler says. His arms rest along the edge of the couch, his hands interlocked, thumbs twiddling.

Despite the fact that it feels like it's the middle of the night, daylight is streaming through the large windows. My eyes are too sensitive, so I narrow them into slits and push myself up into a seated position. I can feel the heat on the back of my neck and the way my hair is stuck to my skin.

"What time is it?" I ask. Even my voice croaks, and I'm completely exhausted. I idly wonder if it's possible to feel hungover without having even touched alcohol. Like a different type of hangover, like a travel hangover, or a stepbrother hangover. I feel lousy.

"Just after eight," Tyler says slowly, and he smiles, small and crooked.

"Eight in the morning?" I blink some more, and I don't even care that I probably look like a ferret on steroids. "On a Monday? In the summer?"

"I hate to break it you," he says, laughing, "but the rest of us don't get summer vacation. The rest of us have work to do." He presses his hands against the leather of the couch and pushes himself to his feet.

"Work?"

"Of some sort." He tilts the watch on his wrist toward him, frowning slightly. Then he looks back down at me. "What are the chances of you being ready to go within the next half hour?"

"What sort of work?" I ask. It's not quite the reply he's looking for because he heaves a sigh. I'm a little taken aback, because although it makes complete sense for him to have spent his time doing *something* this past year, I've never once considered what exactly that could be.

"It's…" He pulls a face and shrugs. "It's complicated. And because I wasn't supposed to leave Santa Monica until today, I still have the day off. So I don't *really* go back to work until tomorrow. But yesterday you asked me how I've spent the past year," he says, that incredible, raw smile of his capturing his lips once again, "so today I'm showing you."

And that alone is enough to get me out of bed. Or off the couch. Whatever. Quickly, I'm on my feet and making a beeline for my suitcases in the spare bedroom. I don't even care that I have knots in my back or that my neck is stiff because I'm too busy throwing myself into the bathroom to shower. I'm too eager to get ready, too desperate for Tyler to give me insight into the life he's been living for the past year. That's why he wanted me to come back to Portland with him in the first place. He wants to show me what exactly it is that he left for.

He's definitely impressed when I drift back into the living room twenty minutes later, dressed and ready to go, my hair already dry. I've pulled on my burgundy U of C sweatshirt even though it'll probably hit eighty out at some point today, and on my feet I'm wearing my white Converse.

Tyler turns off the TV and stands up, pausing and angling his head to one side, looking curiously down at my Chucks. I know exactly what he's wondering: if it's the pair he bought me in New York, the pair that has his handwriting scribbled along the rubber.

"They're new," I inform him, my voice blunt. I even lift up my foot to show him that there's no writing. The pair he gave me last summer has been in the back of my closet for a year now. I couldn't bring myself to wear them any longer, so I bought a new pair. But even though Rachael urged me to throw the old ones in the trash or drop them off at a thrift store or burn them, I couldn't do it.

"Okay," Tyler says quietly. It's slightly awkward, and judging by how uncomfortable he looks, there's no doubt that he's not exactly thrilled. But he understands because he adds, "I get it," and then immediately changes the subject as he grabs his car keys from the arm of the couch. "First things first, we gotta stop for coffee."

"I can't object to that," I say, and just like that, we're back in neutral territory.

Portland has some of the best coffee around, even if I do say so myself. We're kind of famous for it, and I firmly believe that no one can be a true Portlander unless they crave it first thing in the morning, like I do now.

We lock up and head outside, and it's nice to actually see a lawn that's green for once. It isn't even nine yet, so the sun is still relatively low but bright, and the air is clean and fresh. I may not like early mornings, but I like mornings like these.

"Before we get going," I say once we're inside Tyler's car, "please tell me you don't buy your coffee from Starbucks." As I'm pulling on my seat belt, I lock my solemn gaze on him, never blinking. I wonder if he thinks I'm kidding because at first he laughs while starting up the engine.

"I don't."

I relax my features and lean back against the seat. "Good. So," I say, "where are we headed?"

"Downtown."

"Yes," I say, "but *where?*"

Tyler turns to face me, his small smile spreading into a wide grin that makes me wonder if he's okay. He's shaking his head slowly, grinning like he's won the lottery, and I'm pulling a face back at him as though to say: *What the hell?*

Tyler has an extremely clever way of avoiding giving answers to questions he doesn't want to answer. He always has.

"I've missed your questioning," he says instead. Still wearing that huge grin, his perfect teeth shining back at me, he continues, "And how opinionated you are. And how persistent. And how you jump to the dumbest of conclusions. And how you never fucking back down."

"Do you want me to get out of the car or something?" I ask, reaching for the door handle and pushing open the car door a few inches. "Because you're really making it sound like you don't want to be around me."

"I said I've missed those things. Not that I hated them." He leans across my body, reaching for the car door and pulling it shut again with a small thud. His arm brushes against my chest, and I have to bite down on my lower lip and hold my breath to stop myself from reacting. Then he sets his hands back on the wheel and smirks.

We make for downtown Portland, and the good thing about Portland, unlike LA, is that the morning traffic isn't horrific. Sure, it takes a little longer, but the traffic never really comes to a standstill, because if people aren't using the MAX to commute, then they're taking their bike. Which means less traffic on the roads.

The journey takes just under twenty minutes. It's a refreshing start to the day, and being back in the vibrant and diverse downtown region of the city makes me feel even better.

I think I took living in Portland for granted because I don't recall ever appreciating its weirdness as much as I do right now. This city has its pros and its cons, and this is obvious as we're navigating the city blocks that are home to hundreds of independent stores, breweries, movie theaters that actually sell beer, and an endless array of strip clubs. The city blocks where you won't find a fast-food joint for miles, where the restaurants don't believe in gluten, where the homeless population is spiraling out of control, where driving a car isn't considered cool, and where people walk wherever the hell they want. We even pass Powell's, the largest independent bookstore in the world. Long gone are the days where I would spend hours there, searching through their millions of books for the correct textbooks back in sophomore year.

Back then, Portland was lame and boring and really fucking indie.

It still is indie. It just doesn't seem that lame anymore. It actually seems cool.

By nine thirty, we're parked and making our way down the street. My bearings are a little off at first despite how familiar everything is, but having Tyler lead the way doesn't quite feel right. It should really be the other way around.

"You know," he says, "Portland isn't as bad as you made it out to be."

I don't want to admit that he's right, that I was wrong to portray it as the worst city in the world, so I just shrug and keep on walking. We've walked only two blocks when I suddenly know exactly where in downtown I am. Pioneer Square.

When Tyler tries to turn left around the corner, I reach out for him and yank him back. "Portland's living room," I murmur, although I don't mean to say it out loud.

"Yeah," he says, "I know."

I throw him a dirty look. Even though I'm kidding, I can't help but also feel irritated. Maybe it's selfish of me to be so protective of Portland, but I'm still getting used to the fact that he's now calling it his home when really it's mine.

We're standing on the corner of the block, right next to Nordstrom. Tyler remains quiet while I take a few moments to study the square. It's meant to be one of the best in the world, and I couldn't agree more. Pioneer Square takes up an entire city block, with the center shaped like an amphitheater. The bricks used to pave the ground are inscribed with thousands of names. Unlike Hollywood, you don't have to be famous in Portland to have your name on the ground. You just have to pay.

I used to adore coming here before I moved. There's always something going on, like the lighting of the huge Christmas tree the week after Thanksgiving, which Mom and Dad took me to every single year without fail, and the Flicks on the Bricks events during the summer, where a giant screen is rolled out and hundreds gather around the steps, pulling out deck chairs and picnic mats, all to spend the evening together watching a movie.

Santa Monica may have its beach and it may have its pier and it may have Third Street Promenade, but Portland has the Willamette and Mount Hood and Pioneer Square. They seem a million worlds away from each other, two entirely different cities that are unique in their own way.

"Cool, huh?" Tyler says. He has his sunglasses down over his eyes again, so I can't read his expression fully as I fire him a look of disdain. I think sometimes he forgets that I did live here for sixteen years. "We can come back later if you want to. Maybe later in the week, when we're free."

I step around him so that I'm directly opposite him, my chin tilted up. "When we're free?" I echo.

"When *I'm* free," he corrects, adjusting his shades until they're resting snugly against the bridge of his nose. "Like I said, not all of us are on vacation. Now can we please just get some coffee?"

"Yeah, yeah." I shake my head quickly and glance one last time over my shoulder. "Sure."

We round the corner and not long after come to a stop almost immediately at the end of the block. Before us is the door of a small indie coffee shop. It's one I've never actually tested out before, because although us Portlanders live for coffee, there's just too many places to try and not enough time to do so.

"Forget about the Refinery back home," Tyler says. "This place blows it out of the water. But maybe I'm biased." He chuckles and reaches for the door, pulling off his sunglasses. I can't help but grin, noticing the way he holds the door open for me and lets me enter first. It's something he's done for as long as I can remember, and never once has he forgotten.

Inside, it's nice and small and cozy, just as all coffee shops should be. It's busy too, with a line snaking all the way back to the door. No doubt it's full of those dropping by for a coffee to go during their morning commute.

Tyler slips his sunglasses off and hangs them over his flannel shirt, reaching for his wallet. "Extra hot vanilla latte with an extra shot of caramel, right?" He glances at me in that subtle, smoldering way of his, and he's trying his damned hardest to suppress his smug smile.

I stare back at him and hope that the thrill this gives me isn't noticeable in my expression. "You remember my order?"

"It's not exactly what I would call complicated."

"Yeah, I guess." I run my eyes over the line of customers, over the employees behind the counter, over my body. Even though I'm wearing a sweatshirt, I still feel self-conscious. "I'll skip out on the caramel for today," I tell Tyler. I doubt it'll make a difference, but at least I feel less guilty about taking the latte.

"No problem," he says, and then he scours the small shop and nods to a table over by the large windows that face out onto the street. "Save us those seats? I'll get the drinks."

I make a beeline for the table and plunk myself down on the chair. Usually, I like to angle myself toward windows whenever I can because I like to people-watch, but today I want to look at Tyler.

The odd thing is that he blends right in, which he shouldn't because he's from LA. But Tyler seems so ordinary here, so normal. It could be the shirt. It could be the stubble. It could be the tattoos on his arm. It could be the fact that he's standing in a coffee shop. It could be the laid-back, easygoing attitude. I just don't know why he seems to fit in so well, like he belongs here.

He starts up a conversation with the guy standing in front of him, the pair of them chatting a lot more than what is considered small talk. There must be a few jokes thrown in there too, because Tyler laughs a couple of times. When he reaches the counter, he's talking to the barista too, a young guy with multiple piercings on his face. They greet each other with fist bumps and grins, like how you'd greet a best friend, and I realize then that perhaps Tyler is one of their best customers. Maybe he comes here every single day, because they talk nonstop over the top of the coffee machines as the guy makes our drinks. Once he hands the two to-go cups over to Tyler, Tyler turns around and points one toward me. The barista raises his eyebrows, smiling widely at me and lifting his hand to wave.

I panic and quickly offer him a small wave back in the I-don't-know-who-you-are-or-why-you're-waving-but-it-would-be-rude-to-ignore-you sort of way. And luckily, Tyler laughs and makes his way over to me, placing my latte on the table and sitting down on the opposite chair.

"Who was that?" I ask.

"That's Mikey," Tyler says, nodding toward the register. "He knows all about you. He wants me to let you know that he's glad to finally see you."

I look over at the counter again, and although Mikey is working away behind the espresso machine, he still manages to throw me a thumbs-up. As fast as I can, I glance away, my eyes back on Tyler. It's a little weird that he talks about me to one of the baristas here, but I decide not to question it. Instead, I nod to the guy who was standing in front of him in the line, the guy who's now sat at a table on his own at the other corner of the shop. "And that guy? Who was he?"

Tyler has to follow my gaze, smiling. "His name is Roger. He comes here every morning, and it's always before nine. He takes a medium, half-shot decaf latte with no foam, and he likes it in a large cup."

I blink at him as my eyebrows knit together. "What the hell, Tyler?"

"And that lady right there"—he nods to the one that's at the counter, with her hair in a ponytail and a backpack slung over one shoulder—"is Heather. And she's most likely just ordered a large two-shot white mocha with no foam, but with one shot of strawberry, one shot of vanilla, cream, and cinnamon dust on the top. Super light on the cinnamon."

It only takes me a fraction of a second to piece together the obvious. "You work here?"

Tyler just smiles and leans back in his chair, his coffee in hand, dangling from the tips of his fingers. "Yep. I'm usually the one serving them."

"Really?"

He laughs at first, then takes a sip of his coffee and leans forward again, resting his elbows on the table as he sets his cup down. "Sure do," he says.

I study him because my first instinct is to think he may just be messing around. The thought of Tyler serving up coffee doesn't fit with my image of him. But it actually makes sense. Tyler loves coffee as much as I do. He has the friendly smile for it. It doesn't require a degree. It's easy to get a job as a barista here in Portland. Hell, half the college students work in Starbucks. "This is where you've been working for the past year? You're a barista?" My eyes drift toward the counter again, where Mikey and a girl are navigating swiftly around each other as they alternate between brewing coffee and serving customers. I try my best to picture Tyler doing the same. And in all honesty, I *can* imagine him there behind the counter.

"Yeah," Tyler says. He traces a pattern on the table with his index finger, his eyes never leaving mine. "Every single morning, from six until noon. Gotta earn some money on the side."

Now he has me confused again. "On the side of what?"

"The other thing I do," he says cryptically. He knows that I don't have any idea what he's even talking about, and I think he likes it because there goes that smug glint in his eyes again that he's trying so hard not to show. "I have to balance both."

I haven't even had a sip of my latte yet because I'm too focused on hearing what Tyler has to say. "The other thing?"

"Yeah," he says, "and it's where we're headed now." He gets to his feet, pushing his chair back and reaching for his coffee. "It's not far from here," he tells me as I stand too. "Only a couple blocks away. Usually when my shifts are over, I just head straight over."

"Are you working two jobs?" I question.

"Not exactly." When I open my mouth to take another guess, he holds up his free hand. "Don't ask. Just wait. You'll see."

So I shut up from there on out, brimming with curiosity. There is nothing I hate more in this world than not knowing something I am desperate to know. And it's like Tyler wants to make me wait as long as possible because he heads back over to the counter one last time to tell Mikey that he'll see him tomorrow when he's back at work. Which makes me think: *Shit, what the hell am I supposed to do tomorrow and every single day after that while Tyler's here doing his shift?* But I decide that I'll think about it later because right now I can't focus on anything other than where Tyler is taking me.

We head outside, coffees in hand, sun beating down on us. For a second, it almost feels like we're back on the streets of New York, thousands of miles away from anyone we know, free to act and feel however the hell we want to. I miss those days of being carefree together. Even being in Portland is risky, despite the fact that the odds of anyone recognizing me after all these years is low. I just can't bring myself to brush my hand against his. And I hate feeling like that, like it's wrong. I absolutely hate it.

We head east, toward the Willamette, which splits the city in two, the east and the west, and I find myself actually enjoying the walk around downtown Portland again. It's refreshing to see something other than just chain stores and restaurants. We've only walked a couple of blocks—just like Tyler said—when his pace slows to a halt. He points in front of us, to a large black door wedged between a tattoo studio and a clothes boutique. And that's all it seems to be: just a door.

"Come on in," Tyler says. As he takes another gulp of his coffee, he pushes open the door. Holding it open with his shoulder, he lets me step over the threshold. I am greeted by a small entryway with nothing but a set of stairs. I guess they lead up to the second floor above the tattoo studio and the boutique. The fluorescent lighting is extremely bright.

And if I wasn't already confused before, then I am absolutely clueless now. Even slightly worried. "Where the hell are we?"

Tyler takes a few steps up the stairs, then stops to look back at me. He's smirking as he says, "Come upstairs and you'll find out."

I follow him, anxiously biting my lower lip. I'm not sure what I'm expecting there to be up here, but knowing Portland, it could be anything.

I am completely relieved and surprised when we reach the top of the stairs and Tyler pulls open a second door to reveal something I never expected to see.

Music immediately sweeps over us, loud but not *too* loud. As Tyler reaches for my wrist and pulls me a few feet into the open space, I'm gawking. We're in a large area with vibrant red walls and a soft black carpet. There are a lot of people here too. It's all teenagers, both guys and girls. Some are slung over the bright, plush chairs in the far corner. Some are competitively hunched over the handful of foosball and air hockey tables that are in the center of the room. Some are lingering around the multiple vending machines against the walls. Some are glued to the row of laptops propped up on a long, low shelf that runs along the length of the far wall. There are even a couple of plasma-screen TVs mounted up there, and when I look at the ceiling, I notice it is covered in words. Quotes and phrases. Mottos and mantras. Inspirational and hopeful.

"What is this, Tyler?" My eyes focus back on him.

His gaze is intense as he takes in everything that's going on, a small smile on his face as he watches, but he seems to snap out of it when he hears my voice. Slowly, his eyes meet mine, his look serious. "A youth group."

"A youth group?" I echo. "You work here too?"

"For starters, it's a nonprofit organization," he says matter-of-factly, like I should know, although he's being gentle about it. "So I don't work here; I run it. Voluntarily, hence the job on the side."

I cross my arms as I try to process his words, to actually make sense of them. "This place is yours?"

"Sure is," he says with a beaming grin. The pride in his voice and in his smile and in his eyes is impossible not to notice.

"And you run it all on your own?"

Just then, a voice yells Tyler's name. A female British voice, followed by footsteps jogging across the carpet. And I know it's her before I've even turned around because there's no other person that voice could possibly belong to. Yet at the same time, there's so much new information to absorb that I'm beginning to feel disoriented, so when I do eventually spin around, the sight of Emily rushing toward us is enough to make me dizzy.

chapter

16

I haven't seen Emily in a year. Not since last summer in New York.
Tyler and I left for LA. She left for London. And I never really expected
to see her again, but apparently I was wrong to assume that, because
here she is now, pulling Tyler into a brief hug.

"You're back early!" she says as she steps away from him, her eyes wide
with surprise. "I thought you weren't supposed to be back until tomorrow."

"It didn't take as long as I thought it would to convince someone
to come with me," he says, the corner of his lips curling as he gives a
pointed glance in my direction.

"Ah, Eden! You're actually here!" she exclaims, almost leaping into
my arms at the same time. The perfume she's wearing smells amazing,
and her hair is soft against my face as she wraps her arms around me.
It's darker than I remember it being, and she notices the difference in
mine too, because when she stands back to examine me, she asks, "Did
you cut your hair?"

"A long time ago," I murmur, glancing down at the tips of my hair
and running my hands through the ends. When I glance back, I have
to shake my head at her. "What are you doing here?"

"I'm volunteering here," she says. "I'm helping Tyler out for a few
months."

Tyler's sheepish now, and he anxiously touches his sunglasses as he
steps in front of me, side by side with Emily. It's unlike Tyler to be shy.

"I eventually got to a point where I realized I couldn't do all of this on my own, so I called Emily up and said, '*Hey, want to come back to the states and live in Portland?*'"

"And of course I said yes," she finishes, flashing Tyler a dazzling grin. I can't seem to fathom just how proud they both look in the humblest of ways. "Best decision I've ever made, besides the tour, obviously."

"Both of you have been here in Portland?" I ask. It's Emily I'm looking at. Not only did Tyler keep me in the dark about this, but apparently she did too. Neither of them ever thought to tell me, and it makes me feel as though they didn't trust me enough to keep me in the loop. "And you didn't mention it to me?" A pang of hurt jabs at my heart, but I try to push it away.

Emily's smile slants into an apologetic expression, her eyes dimming as though asking for forgiveness. Then suddenly she throws her head back and covers her face with her hands. "Ah, I know. I'm sorry. Tyler didn't want me to bring it up because then you'd ask what I was here for, and then I'd have to lie."

I think about this for a second, and I understand it. I get the whole thing about Tyler needing space. I get the part that he didn't want anyone to know where he was. What I don't understand is what stopped Tyler from telling me about this, about what he was doing. He could have sent one text. One damn text, telling me that things were fine and everything was going well for him, because for the past year, the only news I ever got was from Ella, when she'd find ways of slipping small pieces of information into daily conversations when Dad wasn't around. She never appeared to be worried about him, so I guess I always knew that he must have been okay. By the time he did start calling, it was far too late. My contempt for him was overbearing, and I could never bring myself to answer. Maybe if I *had* answered, he would have told me everything he is telling me now. Just maybe.

I only realize I haven't replied when Tyler steps toward me and asks, "Are you okay?"

"It's just…" I shake my head and press my hand to my cheek. "This is crazy, Tyler."

Emily glances between Tyler and me a few times, then slowly backs away. "I'll let you guys talk," she mumbles in that accent of hers, her features gentle. "I'm really glad you actually came, Eden. I'll catch up with you later, yeah?"

I nod, and she wanders off across the room. I watch her closely as she throws herself into conversation with a group of young girls in the corner by the vending machines, laughing and smiling as though they're her best friends, despite the fact that they look to be freshmen in high school.

I turn back to Tyler and ask, "What exactly is it that you do here?"

"C'mon." He nods at a door in the opposite corner. With our coffees still in tow, he reaches for my hand and gently leads me across the carpet.

As we're making our move, a young guy cautiously approaches. He can't be much older than sixteen. Anxiously, he pulls the sleeves of his hoodie over his hands as he says, "Hey, Tyler. Emily said you weren't gonna be here again until tomorrow."

"Yeah, I know," Tyler answers. We stop just outside the door, yet he doesn't immediately let go of my hand like he would have done a year ago the second anyone came near us. It's an odd feeling standing here, surrounded by people with our hands tightly interlocked. It's a feeling I could grow used to. A feeling that one day I just might not feel guilty about. "I got back into town yesterday. Any news about your mom yet?"

"Nothing yet." The kid drops his eyes to the floor and shrugs. "My dad's gonna call me later once she gets out of surgery."

"That's good," says Tyler. "I'll come talk to you in a sec, okay? This is Eden, by the way." He lets go of my hand at this point and throws his arm over my shoulders instead, so casually and so easily. It's difficult to focus on anything else besides his constant touch, but I force myself to keep my eyes trained on the kid opposite us.

"Hi," I say, offering the gentlest of smiles my features can possibly allow.

But he doesn't say anything back, only nods at the ground and turns around, shuffling toward the laptops.

"That's Bryce," Tyler explains, pressing his back against the door and pushing it open. "His mom's been in the hospital for the past couple weeks, so he hangs out here to keep himself occupied. He's super reserved."

I follow Tyler through the door and into a smaller room. It's an office. In the center sits a huge oak desk with a black leather adjustable chair behind it. The floor is hardwood, the walls red to match the room we just came from. Lining one wall are filing cabinets with folders piled on top of them.

Tyler clicks the door shut and takes my coffee from me, placing it down on the desk and urging me to sit.

I shoot him a look. "Huh?"

"Sit down so I can talk to you," he says, laughing softly.

Slightly hesitant, I seat myself in the chair. It's extremely comfy. I spin around once or twice, then I rock back and forth, nodding with approval. "Nice," I say.

Tyler chuckles and slides some of the sheets of paper out of the way so that he can perch himself on the corner of the desk. It makes him look so professional, like a lawyer or a principal who's getting ready to bombard me with information.

He flips off the lid of his coffee and places it on the desk, then takes a long sip. "So," he begins. "Welcome to my nonprofit. We're open every day from eight until ten in the summer. Emily's here from eight until five. I turn up at noon after my shift at the coffee shop and stay until ten, so there's always one of us here, if not both of us, plus a small group of extra volunteers to help out. As for what we do?" His smile widens, and his eyes grow bright. "We're just here to talk, to provide someplace where people can come if they need to. All sorts of kids turn up—from sixth grade to seniors. They come for all different reasons. Some come to make friends. Some come if their parents have argued and they want to get out of the house. Some come just so they have someone to talk to. And I think it works that we're only twenty ourselves, you know? We're not some fifty-year-old parents trying to tell them what's wrong or what's right. I think they find it easier to talk to us because we're more on their level."

I nod, taking his words in, but before I can ask more about what he does here, Tyler continues.

"You know what was crazy?" He glances down, picking the lid of his cup up and turning it over in his hands. "There's a sophomore called Alex who's here all the time, and a couple months back, I got a text from him late one Friday night just as I was packing up to leave here. He was at some house with a group of guys he didn't really know all that well, and he was supposed to be staying over, but they started pulling out acid tabs, and Alex is a good kid. He didn't want to stick around, but he doesn't have his license and he didn't want to have to call his dad, so he called me. I drove all the way over there and picked him up, yet he didn't want to go home because then his parents would wonder why he'd come home and he didn't want them questioning him. So he stayed at my place." He stops playing with the lid and glances at me, and it only occurs to me then that for once, he's actually stopped smiling. His lips are pressed together, and his gaze is soft yet almost pained in a way that I don't think I've ever seen before. "I think that's when I realized that *Hey, I'm actually doing something good here.*" He tilts his face down, his eyes trained on his lap, and I stare numbly back at him, wondering just how exactly it's possible for someone to grow as much as he has, to make such a drastic turnaround, to become so…so *inspiring*. In that instant, I realize there isn't a better person to run this group than Tyler. He's been through a lot, from abuse to addiction, from the breakdown of his family to manipulative relationships, from feeling alone to having to act like everything is fine. He understands the struggle that some of these kids may be facing. He knows how they feel.

"It's supposed to be a positive environment," he says as he gets to his feet. "Somewhere people can come to distract themselves, to get advice, to have fun. Emily likes to call it a safe haven."

"I think this is amazing," I say honestly. Yet I can't help but think that perhaps things may have been different if he had just told me long before now. Maybe I wouldn't have been so mad, maybe I would have understood more. Maybe I wouldn't have spent twelve months wondering what was really going on. "Does your mom know about all of this?"

"For the most part, yeah." Tyler turns around, his back to me. Slowly, he moves to a filing cabinet in the corner of the room, opening the first drawer. He spends a good few seconds rummaging through files before pulling out a folder, which he opens briefly to skim, then he looks back at me over his shoulder. "I don't tell her everything, you know? There are a couple things I've never mentioned."

"Like what?"

"Like the same things I haven't mentioned to you." He gives me a small smile and slams the cabinet drawer shut, reaching for his coffee and turning to face me. "But I'm getting to it. I just have to think of the right words first."

I roll the chair back across the carpet and stand, joining Tyler. "When you say shit like that, you stress me out," I tell him. "Did you know that?"

He grins. "My bad."

There's a soft knock on the door, and then it opens up a crack. Emily peers around the frame. "Am I interrupting?"

Even though I'm nowhere near what is considered close proximity to Tyler, I still take a subconscious step back. "No," I say.

Emily pushes the door open fully and moves into the room, her hair now scraped back into a high ponytail that swings around her shoulders. Her gaze settles on Tyler. "Bryce is waiting for you. He's been asking for you all weekend, and I know it's your day off, but would you go talk to him?"

"Yeah, I'll go catch up with him right now." He makes a start for the door, but then he seems to remember that, unlike usual, I'm here too, because he pauses and glances back at me. "Eden?"

I wave my hands toward the door. "Go."

There's gratitude in the smile he gives me before he leaves. Then it's just Emily and me. Alone, Emily crosses the room toward me, her eyes lit up in the most content and happiest of ways, and I wonder then just what exactly that must feel like.

"I'm seriously so happy that you're here," she says, reaching for my arm and gently tugging me through the door and out into the main room. "It's been so bloody long."

"And *I'm* seriously so confused that *you're* here," I reply. I still can't get over the fact that Emily is by my side right now. "This entire time, I thought you were back home, suffering at the hands of the British weather you used to complain so much about."

Emily laughs uneasily as she leads me over to the windows that allow the morning sunlight to stream into the property, keeping it bright. "Honestly," she says, sighing, "being back home was the worst, so I couldn't say no when Tyler called me up and asked if I would consider coming over here to help him out over the summer. It took a few months, but eventually I was on a flight over."

"You came back just like that?"

She shrugs and then pulls herself onto the window ledge, crossing her legs. I mirror her actions so that I'm up there next to her, with the sun beating down on us. "I wasn't really doing anything productive anyway," she admits, tucking some loose strands of hair behind her ears. "I was in the same position as Tyler. It's like you come home from the tour and reality hits you, and you have to think, *Shit, what now?* When Tyler rang, I was so bloody bored working checkouts at Tesco that it wasn't exactly a hard choice to pack up and give him a hand. So far, I think I actually like it here better than New York."

"Seriously?"

"It's a big city with a small-town vibe," she says. "That's rare to find." I nod in agreement before turning my attention to the teenagers around us. A couple of them are watching us out of the corner of their eye, most likely wondering who the hell I am. A few others are just starting to arrive.

I can't help but marvel at the space, at all the technology in it, and the way these kids gravitate toward it. It's a weird feeling knowing that this is what Tyler has been doing for the past year, but at the same time, it's satisfying. A good feeling. It's nice to know that he's been doing something good, something productive and worthwhile, something meaningful.

Observing all the activity, I voice my thoughts. "How are these kids even awake? It's summer. And it's not even ten yet."

"Trust me, this is when it's quiet." She laughs. "Wait until after noon. That's when it gets busy."

My eyes find their way to Tyler. He's at the opposite end of the room with the kid from before, Bryce. He's relaxed, his shoulders low and his expression warm and inviting. He nods each time Bryce finishes talking. Watching him, I can tell he really does belong here. This place has changed him in ways I never thought possible.

"I should introduce you to everyone," Emily says out of nowhere, and my eyes immediately snap back over to her. "Most of them know about you, anyway. They know that the reason Tyler took a few days off was to go see you." She slides off the window ledge, landing softly on her feet. "But tell me," she continues, hands on her hips, eyes studying me, "how would you prefer to be introduced? As Tyler's stepsister, or as his..." Her voice tapers off, and she gives me an anxious smile as though she's afraid she may have hit a nerve.

"Stepsister," I say. Whatever the hell Tyler and I are, I am definitely not *that* word. I never have been. And given our circumstances, I'm still not sure if I ever will be. Even if Dad and Jamie do eventually come around and accept us, I still have to go back to Chicago in the fall, over two thousand miles away from here, from Tyler. It just seems so impossible.

Emily nods in understanding, then leads me over to the nearest group of teens, a small huddle of girls stretched over the chairs in the corner. She introduces me as Eden, Tyler's stepsister from LA, who is actually from here, from Portland. And there's some *ohh*ing and some quiet *hey*s, and then they turn back to what they were doing and we move on, repeating the process over and over again until every single person knows my name.

By that time, Tyler is free again, and he pads his way across the carpet toward us with his never-ending smile still dominating his features. Seeing him smile like that really does hurt, and I don't know why. "What's up?"

"I've introduced Eden to everyone," Emily tells him, then she glances quickly between us. "But seriously, guys, you don't need to stick around here. Go and spend the day together, and Tyler, don't come back until tomorrow like you were supposed to."

My gaze finds Tyler's, and I wait for him to say something, secretly hoping that he'll agree with her. I wouldn't mind spending the day with him, just the two of us. That's why I came back to Portland with him in the first place. I came to find out if we had anything left, and with each day that has passed since Thursday, with each hour, each minute, it is becoming increasingly obvious that we do. I came to find out if we're worth saving. And just maybe we are.

"You're right," Tyler says. I bite the inside of my cheek to stop myself from smiling like a fool. Luckily, he doesn't notice because he's taunting Emily by asking, "Are you sure you can handle it?"

"Please," she says with a scoff, "I've been handling it all weekend."

All three of us laugh, but it's brief, and then we say our good-byes until tomorrow. Emily heads off while Tyler and I turn for the main door. He walks slowly, with his arms swinging by his hips, and it's so, so tempting. So fucking tempting.

"Anywhere specific you want to go?" he asks, and I tear my eyes away from the veins in his hands and pray he doesn't notice the color rising to my cheeks.

"Not particularly," I murmur. Tilting my head down, I allow my hair to fall over my face, hiding my expression so Tyler can't read it.

"I've got an idea," he says quickly, his voice light and enthusiastic.

I turn around then to face him, expression curious. "Which is?"

"I'll show you." His eyes bright with mischief, he reaches for the door and pulls it open, and I spin back around, ready to descend the stairs back to the street.

But I don't get very far, not even one step, because I've already collided into something before I even get the chance to make a move. It's something hard, a person, a kid running up the stairs too fast, most probably.

In the instant that it all happens, I find myself retreating back while mumbling, "I'm sorry," as fast as I can.

And then Tyler reaches for my arm and moves me to the side as he steps forward, and that's when I finally look up at the poor kid I've most likely tumbled halfway back down the stairs. However, I'm entirely perplexed to find that it's not a kid at all.

In fact, it's an adult, a man. He's standing there near the top of the stairs, mere inches in front of us, eyebrows arched so high in surprise that they may just disappear into his dark hairline. There's a folder clutched tightly in his hand, a shining gold watch on his wrist, and his shirt is tucked neatly into his pants, a tie loose around the collar. At first, I think he's in the wrong building. This is a youth group, not a conference center or an office complex, and I continue to think that until Tyler talks, making it clear that this is no stranger.

"What are you doing here?" he asks. There's some urgency in his tone, but for the most part, he just sounds confused. "You weren't supposed to fly in until next Friday."

The man, who still appears relatively young, maybe nearing forty, glances at the folder in his hand and then raises it. "The accountant finished that forecast we wanted earlier than planned, so I thought I'd come drop it off." He's surprisingly soft-spoken for such a strong-looking man, and there's something about his features that draws my eyes to his clean-shaven face. "And I should ask what *you're* doing here. Weren't you heading home for a few days?"

"Yeah, but I got back last night." Tyler shifts his footing, uncomfortable, both hands stuffed anxiously into the front pockets of his jeans. The man gives a pointed look in my direction, and I notice the way Tyler swallows the lump in his throat before forcing himself to say, "This is Eden."

"Ah," the man says. He studies me, analyzing my expression as he gives me a tight, tense smile. I'm staring back, not because I'm curious, but because I cannot tear my eyes away. I'm so drawn in by him, and my stomach slowly starts to twist as I take in his tanned complexion and the dark hair and the bright eyes that I'm slowly realizing are much more emerald than they first appeared. He's familiar, and the resemblance to the person standing opposite him is impossible to deny.

"And, Eden, this is…" Tyler's voice catches, and he swallows once more, exhaling shakily. He takes a second to compose himself and control the sudden anxiety that seems to have hit him. When he speaks again, I've already realized what he has to say before he's even opened his mouth. "This is my dad."

chapter

17

I say it out loud. I literally splutter, "What the fuck?" Almost defensively, I find myself shifting backward, closer to Tyler, away from the man standing opposite me. The man I've grown to loathe over the past few years. I feel sick to my stomach. So sick, actually, that I have to hold my breath to stop myself from throwing up. My thoughts are all over the place, and I can't focus on a single one. I am so confused, so taken aback, and so shocked.

Eventually, the only thing running through my head is still, *What the fuck? What the fuck? What the fuck?* Because I don't know why he's here. I don't know why he's in Portland, why he's here in this building, why he's standing here in front of us.

"I can explain," Tyler says quickly, turning to face me directly. It's like he can *see* the growing list of questions in my head, the panic and bewilderment in my eyes, the same way I can see the stress and anxiety in his. *More explanations*, I think. Just when I believe I finally know everything, it turns out there are still some things he hasn't thought to mention.

"You haven't told her yet?" his dad asks. Again, I think, *What the fuck?* He sounds surprised, and when I glance over in contempt at every single fiber of his being, his green eyes read disbelief. He doesn't look like how I imagined him to, like a criminal. He presents himself well. I never expected to ever lay eyes on him, but if I did, I never expected him to look so average. I expected harsh glares and grazed knuckles and lips set in a permanent scowl. I expected him to *look* like someone who's capable of inflicting abuse. But he doesn't. He looks respectable, and that's even worse.

"I was getting to it," Tyler mumbles in reply. He closes his eyes and presses a hand over his face, rubbing his right temple. Then he adds, "I thought I had until next week."

"Well," the asshole across from me says, "I'm sorry for dropping by so unexpectedly." He tucks the folder under his arm and switches his gaze back to me, his lips boasting a warm, friendly smile. It's the most infuriating thing in the world. "Peter," he says, giving me a clipped nod.

"I know who you are," I snap back at him. My voice is seething with disgust, my glare fierce. I can't suppress it. I hate this man, and I just can't bring myself to tolerate him, to be nice to him. He doesn't deserve my respect, and never will he gain it.

"What the hell is going on, Tyler?" When I flash my eyes back to him, he looks as though he's desperate to disappear. The discomfort is evident across his features.

"I can come back later…" Peter offers, holding a hand up as though in surrender as he backs away. He's frowning now, seemingly unsettled by the tense atmosphere. That, or my fueled temper. Perhaps his first impression of me isn't a good one, but right now, I really don't care.

"No," Tyler says. He drops his hand from his face, straightening up and releasing a long breath, shoulders broad, chest out. "Give those files to Emily," he orders, fixing his dad with a firm look, which is the strangest yet most satisfying thing I believe I've ever seen him do. The control in his voice and in his eyes and in his stance is comforting, because surprisingly, that power isn't Peter's. "Eden, let's go."

Urgently, he reaches for my hand, his fingers automatically intertwining around mine, like they simply belong there. Tugging me desperately down the stairs, we leave his dad behind, and I throw one final glance over my shoulder only to find that he's staring down at us, running a hand through his hair the *exact* same way that Tyler does. I grit my teeth as Tyler pulls me outside onto the sidewalk, the door slamming shut behind us.

We hesitate there on the street, looking at each other as strangers stroll past us. Tyler breathes heavily as he squeezes his hand even tighter around mine. Then he leans back against the window of the tattoo studio, perching himself on the window's ledge, and he draws me closer toward him. When he looks at me, his gaze is a mixture of a hundred and one different emotions, like he can't decide how exactly he feels.

"That's what I needed to tell my mom," he murmurs, and then even quieter, he adds, "It's what I needed to tell you."

"What is?" I ask, retracting my hand from his and folding my arms across my chest instead. "I have no idea what's going on right now. Please can you just tell me what the hell your dad is doing here."

"The short version?" He swallows hard. "He's been back in my life since September."

I draw in a sharp breath as deep creases of surprise develop across my forehead. Slowly, I relax my arms and drop them to my sides. It takes a great amount of effort just to remain calm. "Why…?" I ask. I don't understand, and it's making me feel exasperated. I simply can't fathom why Tyler would even let this happen. It makes my head feel heavy, like I'm drowning in questions that desperately require answers. "How?"

Tyler straightens up, and his eyes dart from left to right as he warily scans the people milling around. Then he reaches into the back pocket of his jeans for his car keys and clenches his fist around them, his lips forming a tight frown. "Come back to the car," he tells me, starting to walk. His steps are quick, and his free hand finds mine again. Because I'm in a total state of shock and disbelief, I am numb to the feeling of his skin against mine. "What I need to tell you," he explains, "I can't say out here."

I don't know what to think as we trace our way back to the parking garage. My eyes aren't focused on anything in particular, and I'm entirely zoned out as Tyler leads me back past the coffee shop on the corner where he works, past Pioneer Square. I hardly take notice of them. All I can do is blink, my mind elsewhere. Questions and questions and questions, all of which I need answers to in order to understand what's going on—but the most important question cannot wait until we get back to the car.

Glancing sideways up at Tyler, I simply ask, "Are you…are you okay?"

Immediately, he looks down at me. He doesn't seem to be freaked out about his dad turning up, so clearly, this isn't the first time they have come face-to-face, but yet Tyler is still incredibly unsettled. "Yes," he says. "I just wasn't…ready."

He looks away again as he begins to rub soft circles over the back of my hand with his thumb. At first, I think it's to reassure me that all of this isn't as crazy as it appears, but then I realize he's doing it because he's nervous. Over and over again, he bites down on his lip before slowly releasing it, his eyes in a distant trance, as though he's in deep thought. A mental list of explanations and possibilities of what he could possibly be about to tell me grows longer with each second that passes.

We get to the parking structure and climb the stairs, his hand still so tight around mine that my fingers are growing stiff. For all of the confidence that Tyler has, he has double the anxiety. I fear he might pass out from the nerves he seems to be battling right now. Somehow, he manages not to, and once his car is in sight, he lets go of my hand. He unlocks the vehicle and slides behind the wheel the slowest I've ever seen him do, throwing his keys into one of the cup holders by the center console. I join him inside the car as I slip into the passenger seat. When I shut the door gently behind me, silence falls over us. The strangers on the street are gone. The parking garage is empty and quiet. It's just us. I gaze at him impatiently. "What the hell is going on?"

Tyler's lower lip is, surprisingly, still intact after all the gnawing he's done. He stares at the dashboard for a long moment before leaning forward and slumping himself over the steering wheel. He presses his forehead against the wheel and wraps his arms around his face so that I can't see his expression. "I hadn't figured out how I was gonna say this yet," he admits, voice muffled, "so bear with me."

"Just tell me why your dad is in Portland, Tyler." That's all I need to know. That's why we're here right now: because of his asshole of a father. I can't comprehend it, and the lack of information from Tyler isn't doing much to justify the reason why his dad is within a fifty-mile radius of him.

"Because he funds the youth group," Tyler says quickly, loudly, as he lifts his head. He's still hunched over the wheel, but he tilts his face toward me, his eyes crinkled at their corners. "He pays the insurance," he explains. "He pays the rent. He takes care of the legalities. He takes care of everything that I can't afford to."

"That's it?" I shake my head, pulling my legs up onto the seat and crossing them. His words don't exactly offer me the answers I'm looking for. At least not all of them. "How did this even happen? When did you start talking to him again? *How* did you start talking again?"

Tyler winces with each question I throw at him. At the same time, a man walks past the car, making his way back to his vehicle, and Tyler shifts his eyes over to him, watching. He waits until the man has disappeared out of sight, as though he would have been able to hear us from outside the car, before he looks back at me. "It's not easy to tell you," Tyler admits.

"It wasn't easy for you to tell me the truth about him in the first place," I remind him as gently as I can. Sometimes Tyler just needs a little pressure before he opens up, a small nudge. "But you still did it. I'm listening, okay?" My mouth forms a small smile. One that's tight and reassuring, a smile that lets him know I care. I've always cared. I think sometimes he forgets that.

He swallows hard and nods once. Then he shifts back from the wheel, leaning against the driver's seat with his shoulders slouched. It's almost like he's physically deflating right in front me. He touches the bottom of the steering wheel with the tips of his fingers, his eyes studying his hands. His veins are bold and blue. "The night that I left…" he starts, and immediately I prepare myself for a long story, for the full story. Tyler never delivers anything less. It's either nothing or everything.

His voice is low, and he continues to anxiously run his fingertips along the lower rim of the wheel. "I didn't know where to go," he admits. "So I just kept driving, and when I was driving through Redding, I stopped by my grandparents' place. I'd been driving all through the night, and I was exhausted. I think the last person they ever expected to knock on their door was me." He finally glances up, and his hands tighten around the wheel. The corners of his lips curve into a small smile, but that's all. I'm glad when his gaze remains on me. "I actually spent a couple days there while I figured out what the hell I was actually doing and where I was going to go. But those photos all over the walls? The ones with my dad? I couldn't cope with them." Slowly, he exhales, pursing his lips. "I tried to take them all down, but Gramps told me to leave. I was so pissed. I started yelling at them, and they told me I was out of control." He pauses once more as hurt flashes across his face. It's as though the mere thought of his grandparents saying such a thing is too much to bear. "And the worst part was that I knew I was. That's why I left Santa Monica in the first place, and I knew I had to do something about it as soon as possible. I didn't want to be that angry."

I'm frowning. There's always something so heartbreaking about the way Tyler opens up. Something so honest, so sincere, and so raw that I get this sinking feeling in my stomach. I think it's because his past is so tragic. So unsettling and so unfair, so upsetting and uncomfortable. Everything about Tyler's life seems that way. "No one can blame you for feeling that way about your dad," I say, having to force myself not to reach out and wrap my arms around him the way I always used to whenever he needed some comfort and reassurance that everything was going to be okay.

"But they can blame me for not controlling it." His tone is harder now as he turns his eyes back to the windshield. The parking garage may be packed with cars, but there's not a single person in sight. "I wanted to see you."

"What?"

"When I was mad about those photos," he murmurs, "I wanted to see you." He runs his fingers around the full circumference of the wheel. Once, twice, three times. He's staring blankly at the old Ford parked in the spot opposite us. "I already knew it wasn't healthy for me to depend on you so much. I couldn't live my life depending on you to tell me to calm down, or to tell me that everything was okay, or that I should just breathe for a second. That's why I didn't turn back after that. I could have. I fucking wanted to. But turning back would have been the easy way out." He stops tracing his fingers around the wheel. His eyes have flickered back to me, and for a moment, he is completely still. "I was halfway between Portland and you," he states. "And I knew I had to choose Portland, because if I couldn't have you, then I could at least have a *part* of you."

There are goose bumps along my arms now, and my throat feels parched. I focus on my breathing because I'm afraid that I may forget to do it unless I think about it. Inhale, exhale. "Did Portland lead you to your dad?" I ask. "Is that where this is going?"

Tyler shakes his head. "Just listen," he says. It's forceful and abrupt, like he doesn't want me to interrupt. So I gaze apologetically back at him as I hold up my hands in surrender. No more questions. Just listening.

"I got all the way up here," he continues, "and for the first couple of weeks, I seriously did nothing. I was just pissed off every day, and I didn't know how to make myself feel better without, you know, hitting something." He curls his left hand into a fist and holds it up as a tiny smirk tugs at the corners of his lips. Then he drops both his hands into his lap and his frown returns. "I just couldn't wrap my head around the fact that my dad was out, and I needed a way to release all that anger I'd been holding on to for years. I didn't know how to do that until I really started thinking about my options." His voice keeps getting quieter with each word that leaves his mouth. He's swallowing between each sentence, and he's staring at his hands in his lap, interlocking his fingers. "And I finally realized what I needed to do, even though I hated the thought of it. It was…it's embarrassing." Another pause. He takes a deep breath as his hands freeze. "At the end of August, I gave in and booked an appointment with a…" He can't say it because he heavily exhales again. Then he squeezes his eyes shut, and through stiff lips, he whispers, "I booked an appointment with a therapist."

Silence.

I don't know what I expected Tyler to tell me, but it certainly wasn't that. The word carries with it a weight that immediately thickens the atmosphere surrounding us. All three syllables are ringing in my ears. Tyler hasn't opened his eyes again. In fact, I think he's squeezing them closed even tighter.

I'm blinking, partially in surprise and partially in disbelief. Even my lips have formed a round *O*. "Therapy?"

He nods once, and his hands fly up to his face, covering it. I've never seen him look so humiliated in all of the three years I've known him.

"Mom always wanted me to talk to someone," he murmurs. His voice is muffled behind his hands. That word still echoes around my head, bouncing back and forth. "Back when it all happened. When Dad got locked up. She always wanted to get me a therapist so that I had someone neutral to the situation who I could vent to. But I refused." Slowly, he drops one hand away from his face. He rubs at his eyes with the other. They're still closed. "I was thirteen then. I was starting eighth grade that fall. I didn't want to be that kid who needed help. I wanted to be normal.

"I wish I'd gone back then," he says. "I kept thinking that maybe things would have been different, and that's when I realized that they still could be. So I looked into it, booked an appointment, and regretted it the second I walked through the door. The first session had me feeling like the biggest moron in the world. I felt so stupid sitting there on that couch with some plant towering over me, and a woman double my age asking me how I was. Her name is Brooke. She wanted me to tell her why I was there, so I blurted out my speech that I used on the tour last year. I have it memorized, so now it's nothing but a script to me. It's easier to talk about things if I feel disconnected from it all."

I know Tyler doesn't want me to interrupt. I know he doesn't want me to keep asking questions. But I just can't fight that urge to react, to say something. I extend my hand toward his almost subconsciously, and carefully, I lace our fingers together. I like it better this way. His skin against mine; my skin against his. I keep our hands there, squeezed tight together and resting against his thigh. My gaze has yet to leave his face. "Like what you're doing now?" I ask.

Almost immediately, he pulls the hand down from his face and his eyes flutter open. It's slow, and there's no energy in his movements as he angles his head to look at me. It's like he's numb, forcing himself to blink, because his eyes are wide and the expression within them is empty. "I'm sorry," he mumbles. He looks at our hands, radiating warmth between us. He doesn't glance back up, but he does release another long breath of air. "It's hard to look at you."

"That's okay." Tyler may be getting better over the years when it comes to opening up, but that doesn't mean it's any less uncomfortable for him. I know he hates doing this, yet he always pushes through and does it anyway. He's a lot better at it than I'll ever be, so I remain patient. "So then what happened?"

He shrugs and keeps his eyes trained on our hands. "We just… talked. I was seeing her twice a week. It turned out not to be that bad until three weeks down the line, when she asked if I'd ever considered talking with my dad. You know, like confronting him in a controlled environment. She said it'd help. I thought she was insane." He moves his free hand to my wrist, where he traces soft circles around the bracelet I'm wearing. "But when I went back a couple days later, I told her I wanted to do it. It made sense, and I'd always wanted Dad to have to look at me. I didn't want him to get it easy, so I called up Uncle Wes and hung up the second he answered. Then I called back and asked him to tell Dad to be in Portland the following Monday. Passed over the address of the office and said it was the only chance I was ever going to give him. Then I hung up again before I could regret it."

"And he came?"

"He came," Tyler confirms. "I felt so sick waiting that morning, I seriously thought I was going to pass out on Brooke's floor. I had a feeling he would bail, and honestly, I was kind of hoping that he would. Brooke was a little more optimistic, and she was right to be, because he actually turned up right on time." His eyes drift to meet mine now, and he gives me a closed-mouthed, tight-lipped smile. It's another one of those sad smiles that I will never believe in. "It was the weirdest fucking thing. He walked in and sort of just froze, and he just stared straight at me, even while Brooke was introducing herself and shaking his hand. He didn't say a word, and I was glaring at him, wondering why he still looked the exact same as how I remembered him. I wanted him to look different so that he'd seem like a different person."

I don't think Tyler cares that I'm asking questions again, so I quietly cut in and ask, "How long had it been?"

"Eight years," he tells me, then shakes his head as though in disbelief. "He hadn't seen me since I was twelve. Twelve...like, that's crazy. I'm twenty, and I think he was seriously stunned for a good ten minutes. He missed my entire teen years, and I bet that was weird for him, seeing some guy standing across from him rather than some kid."

"Were you...angry?" My voice is quiet as I ask this, my tone gentle.

"No," Tyler says, and he seems pleased to be able to say that. "I don't even know what I was feeling. Kind of empty, like there's just nothing there. So I sat down, and then Dad did too, and there was nothing but silence for at least five minutes." His fingers move from my wrist and back to my hand, where he taps each of my knuckles one by one, softly and slowly. It almost seems like he needs to keep his mind half-concentrated on something other than the words he's stringing together. Like touching my wrist and tapping my knuckles and squeezing my hand tighter are all just ways to distract himself. "Brooke made me tell him everything."

I raise a brow. "Everything?"

"Everything from the moment he got locked up to right now," he says. Deep breath, brief close of his eyes, the tightening of his hand around mine. It's always the same whenever Tyler's about to say something he doesn't want to. "I told him about the three times I got suspended from school. I told him that I was fourteen the first time I got high. Sixteen the first time I tried coke. I told him that my grades sucked because I didn't care about anything, that I treated Mom like dirt, that I actually liked getting drunk. I told him about the times I was sitting in the back of a cop car, and I told him about the kid's nose I fractured back in tenth grade. I told him about New York, and I told him about you. I told him why I was in Portland. I said I was here because of him, because I needed to fix the mess *he* made of me."

I don't realize I'm crying until I blink and the first tear escapes. My chest feels blocked, my head heavy with the weight of his words. I already know all of these things, but hearing the pain in Tyler's voice as he says them is what really hits me. I don't think his father will ever truly know just how much damage he's caused. The abuse may have been physical, but the damage is psychological.

"And I think that was the biggest relief, Eden," he says, loud and clear, like that same relief is flowing through him again. When I blink away the tears gathering at the corners of my eyes, I realize his gaze has found mine once more. He bears yet again an expression laced with nothing but sincerity. "Getting to look straight at him and *blame* him for everything he'd done…it was kind of satisfying, and he broke down right in front of me. My dad was never one for crying—trust me on that. So I was surprised because it was so unlike him, and then it slowly dawned on me that maybe he did regret it all. Maybe he hated himself for it. Maybe he really was sorry. It's all he kept saying, that he was sorry, sorry, sorry. And so I calmly stood up and walked out of the office, leaving him there, babbling like a fucking idiot. And honestly?" He smiles. "I did feel better."

With our hands still interlocked, I wrap my free arm around his and lean in close to him across the center console, pressing my cheek to his bicep. The soft material of his shirt catches my tears as they cascade down my cheeks, and I can't bring myself to reply because I'm too busy squeezing my eyes shut. I hate crying, and the only time I ever do is because of Tyler. Always fucking Tyler.

And he himself finally notices. "What are you crying for?" he asks, surprised. With one hand he moves my chin to face him, sweeping his thumb under my eyes. Then he squeezes our interlocked hands even tighter. Any second now, one of us is going to burst a blood vessel from the pressure, I'm sure of it.

"You're not a mess," I say. If anything, I am. I'm the one crying on his shoulder. I'm the one who can't fix things with my dad. I'm the one who can't say no to ice cream at the pier. I'm the one who's counting the days as they go by, relieved that they're over, rather than doing something to make them better. That's why I admire Tyler so much. He had that determination to change things. He moved to a new city, he went into therapy, he's spoken to his dad, he's set up a youth group, he's working, he has his own place. That didn't happen because he spent his time moping around.

Back when I first met Tyler, I never thought that one day I'd be so desperate to be just like him.

"Not anymore," he says. "Having Brooke has really helped. That's why I kept going back. I just didn't expect Dad to be there at the next session. I was so confused when I first walked in, and then Brooke told me that Dad was sticking around for a while. She said we still had a lot of fixing to do, so Dad stayed in Portland and came to every single session, three times a week for the following three weeks. It got easier to talk to him each time, so I eventually told him that I was on the fence about starting a youth group. He liked the idea and offered to help. He can't work with minors directly, so he said he'd handle the costs. Apparently, it's the least he owes me." I glance up, and Tyler's grinning, trying not to laugh at the understatement. "But he kept his word," he continues, pulling me closer against him, "and he pays the bills, and he comes back to Portland every month to check up on how things are going. He actually lives in Huntington Beach now. He's been investing in companies for the past year and trying to build himself back up. I hate to say it, but he's doing alright. I can't blame him for trying to make things right because I'm doing the exact same thing."

I rub at my eyes and lean away from him, sitting up. Our hands are still intertwined. "Why was it so hard to tell me this?"

Tyler groans and glances away, suddenly going quiet and nervous again. "It's just…" His words taper off, and he heaves a drastic sigh. "It's just the therapy," he says. "I wanted to tell you, but it's hard to admit it."

"Why?"

"Because when was therapy ever considered cool, Eden?" He flashes his eyes to me, and for a second, I think he's about to lash out at me for questioning him, but there's no anger in his expression nor in his tone. Long gone are the days when his temper was hot. "Therapy isn't something you should be proud of."

"Isn't it though?"

His eyebrows furrow. "What?"

"You *should* be proud, Tyler," I say, fixing him with a firm look through my damp eyes, then I release our hands. "Therapy doesn't mean that you're weak, you know. It means that you're strong, and you should be proud that you made that decision. Just look at how much happier you seem."

"Why do you always do this?"

"Do what?" I ask.

Slowly, a smile spreads across his face, lighting up his eyes. "Make me feel better with all your wise words."

I grin at him, as wide as I possibly can, because his smile is just that contagious. He may not be proud of himself, but *I'm* proud of him. I don't think he'll ever stop surprising me when it comes to discovering how incredible he is. "Because when you really care about someone," I tell him, "you *want* to make them feel better. That's just what you do when you love someone."

Something flashes in his expression, but it's so quick that I hardly have time to recognize it. He angles his body slightly toward me as his lips curve into a playful grin, one that's full of both relief and joy. "Love, huh?"

I feel the color rise to my cheeks from the intense pressure of his stare. His glossy eyes are watching me as he waits for confirmation, but I feel so sheepish that I can't bring myself to look him in the eye as I say it.

I lean over the center console toward him, quietly murmuring, "Always have," while wrapping my arms around his bicep and burying my face into his shirt before I get a chance to even see his expression. He throws an arm around me and pulls me in even closer, the two of us holding on to one another so tight it's as though our lives depend on it. I like having his body against mine like this. Not just sensing his touch, but actually feeling it.

Now I want to kiss him. I really, really want to kiss him because I'm in love with him. I can feel it in every inch of my being, in every cell of my body, in my absolute entirety. It's always been there, and no matter how hard I've tried to convince myself this past year that there has been nothing left, the truth is that it never went away in the first place. I've been in love with him ever since I was sixteen.

I'm so ready to kiss him. But now isn't the right time again. This is Tyler's moment, and my body against his already feels like enough. He rests his chin atop my head, and I can feel his breath against my forehead, warm and slow. It's a gentle rhythm that's the most relaxing thing in the world, and we remain like that for a short while, our arms around one another, tangled up in the front seats of Tyler's car in the middle of this parking garage in downtown Portland. A year ago, I never imagined my life could be like this again, but now that this *is* my reality, I wouldn't dream of changing it.

Next time, I think.

Next time I'm kissing him.

chapter

18

It doesn't take long for the idea to hit me.

I'm sitting there, my breathing in sync with Tyler's, our eyes half-closed as we rest our gazes lazily on the windshield, when suddenly my body shoots upright. I lean away and straighten in the passenger seat. The abruptness of the movement startles Tyler because he flinches and then fires me a questioning glance.

It's not even eleven, so we have the entire day ahead of us. A full day that Tyler's free before he returns to work tomorrow. Emily said to go have fun, and that's exactly what we're going to do. Portland style.

"Change of plans. Pass me the keys," I say. I'm biting back the smile that's threatening to spread across my face because I'm trying my hardest to maintain a look of mischief. I want to surprise him for once. Usually, it's the other way around. Usually, Tyler is the one who comes up with the great ideas, like taking me to the pier for the first time and making reservations in advance at Italian restaurants, like teaching me to play baseball and buying us tickets to the Yankees game, like letting me drive his freaking supercar in the middle of the night in a parking lot in New Jersey and buying me new Converse that he later wrote on. In Spanish. Tyler always has exciting ideas that make my day. Now it's my turn to make his.

"Huh?"

"The keys," I repeat. "I need them to drive."

Tyler glances at his car keys that are in the cup holder in the center console, then at me, then at the keys again. He seems wary, as though he honestly believes that whatever I have in mind could be dangerous. It's not. Just adventurous. Eventually, he reaches for the keys and slips them into my hand.

"But I thought we could—"

"Just switch," I order. "And trust me."

Tyler doesn't linger. He opens the door and steps outside, and as he makes his way around to the passenger side, I climb over the center console and get settled in the driver's seat. I've never driven this car before. The old one, yes. This one, no. It's nowhere near as powerful as the former, so I feel pretty at ease as I start the engine and pull on my seat belt. Thank God it's an automatic.

By the time Tyler joins me back inside the car, he's smiling in such a way that tells me he's confused but intrigued. He adjusts the seat, clicks his seat belt into place, and then leans back and gets comfy. "Is your idea legal? No trespassing? No reckless driving?"

I cast him a glance. "Of course it's legal. Why would I do anything that wasn't?"

"Well, we *are* pretty bad at breaking the law," he says, and we laugh as though our previous conversation didn't even happen. His anxiety is gone, replaced with humor and a sparkling glint in his eyes that's only there whenever he's truly at ease. I think he's glad that conversation is over, and I think he's even happier that I'm not saying anything more on the issue. Life isn't always about dealing with the bad stuff. Sometimes enjoying ourselves has to come first.

I set the car in drive and navigate my way out of the parking structure, back out onto the warm streets of Portland. I don't want Tyler to know where we're going, so having him drive isn't entirely an option. And where we're going is outside the city boundaries.

"So," Tyler says when we're stopped at a red light, "is this an abduction? I know you haven't seen me in a year, but there's no reason to resort to this. Car theft and kidnapping."

I roll my eyes, and then I finally allow that smile I've been holding back to spread over my face. "I'm taking you on an adventure," I announce. "We've got a couple of stops to make. The first is a forty-minute drive away, and I really hope you haven't already visited it."

Tyler releases a hearty laugh, then he goes quiet and does nothing but stare at me with a smile on his lips. There's something in his expression that I don't think I've seen before. It's not gratitude. It's not relief. It's appreciation.

The atmosphere in the car is so different now. It's shifted from tense to electric, fueled by good vibes and laughter and constant smiling. The radio is back on, echoing the latest mainstream chart singles while the sun beats down on us through the car's windshield. For the first time, it actually feels like summer. This is what summer is made for—days of sunshine filled with adventures with the people you love most right by your side.

The traffic is still light, so getting out of downtown and across the Willamette isn't a nightmare. It's actually easy, and soon we've merged onto the highway. This highway has some amazing scenery, and it's hard to believe that my dad actually took me on long drives across this route when I was younger. We'd take road trips every Saturday morning, but that weekly norm stopped the moment his relationship with Mom began to break down. These days, we can barely even look at each other without feeling aggravated, let alone spend some quality time together. It's sad how different things can become over time.

The drive doesn't feel like forty minutes. We head east, leaving Portland behind and enjoying the view of the river as it glistens in the sunlight. This drive is never as nice when the weather is bad. The time also passes much quicker because I don't think Tyler and I have stopped talking for even a matter of seconds. He keeps trying to guess where I'm taking him, and he keeps guessing wrong. No, I'm not taking him across the river to Washington. No, I'm not taking him up to the peak of Mount Hood. And no, I'm definitely not taking him Jet-Skiing, which I think he's secretly hoping for. When we're a couple of minutes away from my brilliant destination, his expression changes. His face brightens, and he reaches to shut off the radio before turning to me, a lopsided smile plastered across his face. "Multnomah Falls," he says.

I almost slam on the brakes out of frustration. "Oh, c'mon!" I throw one hand up from the wheel in agitation at my surprise no longer being a surprise, narrowing my eyes at him. "How'd you know?"

He laughs and sits up, pointing back over his shoulder. "The road sign back there? Yeah, it said Multnomah Falls."

Multnomah Falls is Oregon's tallest waterfall, a prime attraction in this region of the state. I haven't been in years, but it was one of my favorite places to visit, especially with Dad. We used to hike straight to the top together, ask a stranger to take our picture, then send it to Mom, who would reply saying she wished she was there with us. "Please tell me you haven't already been. I want to show you it."

"I haven't," Tyler says, and I breathe a sigh of relief.

The thing about Multnomah Falls is that it's special. That's why it's our first stop, because today feels special. There's something in the air, lingering around us. I can feel it, and I like it.

We pull into the parking lot just opposite the Multnomah Falls Lodge. Tyler seems on edge as I maneuver his car into a tight spot between two others. Thankfully, I do it without losing both his side mirrors. I yank the keys from the ignition and squeeze my way out of the car.

"I'm guessing that's it?" Tyler asks, joining me and nodding over my shoulder as I roll the sleeves of my sweatshirt up to my elbows.

I don't even have to glance behind me to know that yes, he's looking at the falls. It's so noticeable that you can even see it from the highway, on your right as you pass by, and right now, we're really not that far away from it. "Yeah."

"Alright. Lead the way," he says.

Immediately, I reach for his elbow, pulling his arm back so that I can slide my hand into his, intertwining our fingers once more. Over the past hour, everything seems to have just clicked. I don't need to hesitate anymore when it comes to deciding how I feel about Tyler because there is *nothing* holding me back anymore from accepting the fact that I'm still in love with him. I understand now. I understand why Tyler had to leave. I understand why he came here to Portland. I understand why he's made the decisions he's made, and I understand why he needed to make them on his own, for no one else but himself. I understand, and now that I have answers and explanations to all of the questions and doubts I have had over the past year, there is no anger left toward him, no mixed feelings. Only love and forgiveness. Lacking his touch for so long has driven me insane, and now that I have finally pinpointed exactly how I feel, I'm desperate to feel his skin against mine. I'll take advantage of any opportunity that arises, like right now, as I'm leading him across the road with our hands bonded together like glue. Luckily, Tyler doesn't seem to mind.

There's already several other people around us, a group of young girls and an elderly couple, and they all make their way toward the beginning of the paved trail. We follow behind them.

I love that the falls is so accessible. It's only a five-minute walk to the base. For those who want to go higher, it's possible to hike straight to the top.

So there we are, Tyler and I again, hand in hand, normal. The truth is, no one even knows we're stepsiblings. It's impossible for them to, and as I'm glancing at the people around us now, I wonder why I've been so scared of how strangers would react if somehow they discovered that Tyler is my stepbrother. That's all they are; just strangers. Their opinions don't matter to us, and they most definitely shouldn't affect us. The way I feel right now, happy and content with Tyler right by my side, is what really matters.

The walk is so short that before I even realize it, we're at the viewing area at the base of the falls. It's here where its sheer height can really be appreciated, all six hundred feet of it. People are already merging into one large group as they snap pictures and pull their ponchos out of their backpacks. No matter how hot Portland can get in the summer, Multnomah Falls will always be colder with a layer of mist covering it, the ground always damp.

"Pretty sweet," he says loudly over the sound of the falls. The water tends to spray all over the place, and it keeps on sparking toward us.

"We're going up there," I say, then point a finger up to the Benson Bridge, a footbridge that spans the base of the first tier. I do firmly believe that it must be one of the most exhilarating views in the world.

Again, hand in hand, we move on. It's not too far of a walk up to the bridge, only several hundred feet or so, but we have to fight against the current of people who have the same idea as us. Sometimes I wish Multnomah Falls wasn't as well-known as it is, because when we do get to the bridge, it's already flocked by fellow spectators. Tyler moves his hands to my shoulders, brushing his body against mine from behind as he directs me forward, squeezing along the bridge until we find a spot to stop. And finally, *finally*, I feel like I'm really home.

Being up here, with the sheer height of the first tier of the falls above me and the drop of the second below me, I feel a million miles away from California. The smell of wet moss. The freshness in the air. The trees that are green and alive and not suffering from the effects of a drought. *This* is Oregon.

"Photos are mandatory," I tell Tyler as I turn to look at him. He has his head tilted straight back, his face up to the very top of the falls. He blinks a couple of times, then looks at me, a warm smile on his face. He doesn't even hesitate to fish his phone out of the back pocket of his jeans.

"If they're so mandatory," he murmurs, "then start smiling." He moves back a few steps and holds up his phone, a huge grin on his face as he laughs and tells me to say cheese.

With the waterfall as my backdrop, I lean back against the bridge in the midst of everyone else and I smile. It comes so naturally that I can feel it lighting up my entire face. I'm so happy in that moment that I forget I'm posing for a picture, and I end up laughing, at myself and at Tyler, at the giddy grins we can't seem to suppress today.

And when he's done taking the picture, we switch. It's Tyler's turn to stand with his back to the waterfall. He shows another wide grin, holding up two thumbs to the camera while I snap some shots of him. Then I leap over to join him, pressing my body against his and holding his phone in front of our faces. He tilts his head against mine and rests his jaw against my temple, and we smile one more time into the small camera of his phone, just like we did a year ago in New York. Only this time, our background isn't Times Square.

I take the picture then lower my arm, stepping around and in front of him and passing the phone back into his hand. But the smile on Tyler's face has suddenly faltered into a frown, which is enough to cause mine to do the same. His gaze rests on my wrist for an increasingly long moment, and I don't understand why he's furrowing his eyebrows until he delicately reaches for my arm and turns my wrist toward him. That's when I remember my tattoo, and I think Tyler is only noticing it for the first time. It's not the same one he remembers me having. He remembers three words. Now there's a dove that has one wing bigger than the other because I'm pretty sure the artist in San Francisco was just a trainee.

Tyler grasps my other arm, checks that wrist. Nothing. He looks at that horrible bird with disdain, then slowly lets go of my arm and looks up to meet my anxious eyes. "Where's…?" I know exactly what it is he's desperate to ask. Where's *No te rindas*, where's his handwriting, where's last summer's memory, where's my hope? "Did you cover it?"

That disappointed look on his face is enough to make me want to disappear over the edge of this bridge. I'm too embarrassed even to meet his eyes, so I quickly roll the sleeves of my sweatshirt back down and kick at the ground with my Chucks. All I can do is shrug. "During spring break," I tell him.

"Why?"

My eyes slowly meet his, surprised that he even has to ask. Tyler, I've realized, is incredibly awful at understanding the most obvious of things. I don't want to lie to him, so I tell him the truth without so much as blinking. "Because I'd given up by then, Tyler."

"I get it." He turns away and folds his arms against the bridge's barrier, looking at the water below. I'm not sure what I'm supposed to say, and I fear the incredible atmosphere around us is now ruined. I'm not expecting him to say anything for a while, so it takes me slightly aback when he straightens up and faces me with a devious smirk on his lips. "Have you still given up?"

There he is again, asking another question to which the answer is obvious. "You know I haven't," I say.

"Prove it," he says. That smirk grows even more crooked as he raises his eyebrows and nods to my wrist. He waits for me to realize what he's suggesting.

"You want me to get it again?" I ask, my tone blank, my expression blanker. I'm not quite sure if he's kidding or if he's serious. The thought of getting that tattoo all over again has never once crossed my mind.

"I think you should," he states, then adds, "Maybe I'll get it too."

Within a heartbeat, I'm sticking out my hand. *He's said it now*, I think. *Don't let him change his mind.* "Sounds like a deal."

"Eden," he says as his features relax. "I was kidding."

Now I'm the one who's smirking. "I wasn't."

Tyler studies me, taking in my challenging gaze and my hand that's still extended to him. Then he rolls his eyes, heaves a sigh of defeat, and shakes on the deal. "I'll call my artist tomorrow," he tells me as he slips his phone back into the pocket of his jeans. "Ask if he can fit us in at some point."

"No," I cut in. "We need to go right now. Today is all about being impulsive."

Again Tyler hesitates, deciding if I'm still being serious, and when he realizes that I am, his smile returns. Exhaling, he holds up his hand, ready to grasp mine. "Then let's go."

chapter

19

Tyler's preferred tattoo artist is a guy named Liam. He works in a small studio in the downtown area of Portland. He's the same guy who did all the work on Tyler's left bicep, the same guy who carefully kept my name visible.

It's late afternoon by now, and we've been sitting in Liam's waiting room for a good two hours, waiting until 5:00 p.m. because it's the only spare time he has today. He's fully booked otherwise, and an entire array of people have been coming and going in the time that Tyler and I have been here, paying and filling out our disclaimer forms and trying to decide where exactly we're going to place our newest tattoos. We've also strolled around the block four times, but we're so filled with adrenaline that we can't force ourselves to stay away for too long.

There's a girl who works here too, only she does piercings rather than tattoos. She leans across the small desk in the waiting area and raps her knuckles against it in order to get my attention. "You sure you don't want that piercing?" she asks when my eyes flicker toward her. She nods to the huge clock hanging above my head. "Still got ten minutes. We've got time to do a quick pierce of the good old helix. What'd you say?"

"I'm good," I reply for what seems like the ninetieth time now. Tyler finds it hilarious each time she asks to pierce a body part of mine, and I think all the caffeine he's consumed while we've been here is really starting to spike his energy. He's been back and forth to the coffee shop next door multiple times. Either that or the overwhelming smell of green soap here is starting to have an effect on him. It's starting to get to me too.

"Okay," he says. "I've decided."

"Well?"

He gets to his feet, still holding an empty to-go cup in his hand, then points to the right side of his chest, right on his pec. "I'm thinking here. I'm not too sure I want to start adding any more words to my arms," he muses, glancing down at the artwork on his left bicep that he's been working on over the past year. My name is currently the only piece of writing there, hardly noticeable amid the rest of the dark ink that covers his skin. "And I've already got *guerrero* on my back, so chest it is."

We may be getting matching tattoos, but we definitely aren't going for matching placements. Tyler wants his fresh ink to be on his chest, whereas I wish for mine to be on my inner right forearm. The best part? Our new tattoos are going to be in each other's handwriting.

The door to the actual studio swings open, and a burly man saunters out boasting a bandage on the back of his leg. He already has numerous tattoos all over his body, and when he first turned up forty minutes ago, he'd told Tyler and me that he was adding a tattoo of the boat his father used to own as something to remember him by.

Liam strolls out behind him, and no matter how many times I've seen him drift between the studio and the waiting room, I still find myself staring at him in surprise. He just doesn't look like a tattoo artist. For starters, he seems about my age, maybe a few years older than me. Second, the only tattoo that I can spot is a compass on his neck, just behind his ear. Third, he's not very intimidating, which is good. He looks like the guy from the dorm next door who you'd ask to borrow instant noodles from because you know he's too nice to tell you to fuck off.

Liam sees the man out then turns to us, an apologetic smile on his face. He knows how long we've been waiting here, the two of us so desperate to get these tattoos done today that we were willing to wait around and be harassed by his fellow coworker for the better part of two hours.

"Right, guys," he says, ducking down behind the desk as the girl scoots out of the way. He pops back up with a thick wad of paper, which he proceeds to place on the small table in the center of the waiting room. "You want to draw it up yourselves, right? Don't worry about making it the correct size that you're looking for yet. I can do all of that on the computer. Just get the words down." He passes us some pens, then tells us he'll be back soon, after he's done setting up the studio for us.

The second Liam leaves, Tyler stands and grabs a pen, pulling a sheet of paper from the stack and placing it smoothly back down against the wood of the table. He gets started without hesitation, and I watch in extreme satisfaction as the pen glides across the paper, as the letters appear one by one. *No te rindas.* I never thought I'd be seeing Tyler write these words again, and I fall in love with even the way he flicks his wrist in between each of them. Once finished, he straightens up and frowns down at the paper, examining it. The letters are slightly misaligned, some thicker than others, some taller. I think it looks adorably childlike, but Tyler seems to loathe it, because he shakes his head and then crushes the sheet of paper into a ball. He throws it in the trash and takes another sheet of paper, then tries again. This time he tries block capitals, but he hates it all the same, and once more, he throws it in the trash.

Running a hand through his hair, he heaves a frustrated sigh as he sets a new sheet of paper in place. "So much pressure," he murmurs, then drastically exhales before biting down on his lower lip with extreme concentration. His hand hovers over the paper, the pen gripped tight. "It's gotta look good if it's going to be permanent."

"I don't want it to be perfect, Tyler," I remind him, and I place a hand on his shoulder, glancing at him from beneath my eyelashes as our gazes lock. "I just want it to be yours."

He appears to relax at my words because he nods and averts his eyes to the paper, where he promptly scribbles those three words all over again without overthinking it. It's still a little crooked, but it's simple and it's real, which is exactly how I want it.

"How's that?" Tyler asks, handing me the sheet.

"Hmm." I cock my head to one side and feign deep contemplation, even tapping my index finger repeatedly against my lips for added affect. I glance between the scrawled words and my inner forearm, trying to imagine them there, but even just thinking about it is enough to make me grin and snap out of my charade. "I love it," I finally reply.

It's so impromptu, but I stretch up on my feet and plant a kiss right bang on the center of Tyler's cheek. Apparently, today is all about being spontaneous.

Just as I'm finishing my own piece for Tyler's chest, trying my best to make my handwriting appear slightly more masculine than my usual cursive style, Liam comes strolling back into the waiting area, rubbing his hands together. "Right. Who's first? I'm guessing you, Tyler," he says, then rolls his eyes. "The girls *never* want to go first."

Immediately, I step forward. Partly because I'm anxious as hell and want Tyler to think I'm tough, and partly because Liam's sexist remark needs challenging. "I'll happily go first," I say, loud and clear. Really, I feel sick with nervous anticipation.

Both Liam and Tyler look over at me, their expressions full of surprise.

"Really?" Tyler asks.

"Yep." I reach over and take the sheet of paper from his hand, then pass him mine in exchange.

"Alrighty then," Liam says. "Come on through." He holds open the door to the small studio in the back, and I waltz through with an air of confidence while Tyler follows close behind me.

The studio, like most, is small. The walls display a selection of framed pieces of artwork, from huge tigers to small roses, and there's a bed pressed against the wall, which Tyler plunks himself down on the edge of. He appears quite smug, and he's smiling at me as though he's just waiting for me to change my mind and ask him to go first instead.

"Take a seat," Liam tells me, so I do exactly that. I settle down into the leather chair as he sits himself opposite me on another. "So, placement?"

"Right here." I hold out my right arm and run my index finger along the skin of my inner forearm. That shitty dove I have is on my left. I wish Rachael had never convinced me to get a cover-up.

Liam nods and takes Tyler's sheet of paper from me, twirling his chair around to face a computer that's set up along the countertops. He spends a few minutes scanning the paper, then blowing it up on the screen, then printing it back off again, then tracing it onto transfer paper, which he then presses onto my inner forearm. "How's that looking?"

The words are a stencil on my skin. It's not too small, but not too large either. It's around three inches in length, and it runs down my arm just the way I pictured it. Only it's not quite permanent yet. "Go for it," I say.

I exhale and lean back in the chair, trying to get as comfortable as I can in such a situation. The tattoo artist in San Francisco seemed to have a heavy hand back during spring break, and I suffered in agony for a good fifteen minutes. The wait for the pain to begin is always the worst part. I don't know how Tyler can do this so often.

Liam snaps on a pair of latex gloves as he gets to work on prepping both me and the ink. It takes only a few minutes, from setting up the machine to cleaning my arm and running a razor across my skin before cleaning it once again. Then he tells me to relax, which is impossible after he switches on the machine and the loud buzzing begins. *Shit.*

I have no idea why I'm so nervous. I've done this before. Twice, and I was never as anxious as I am right now. I think it's the fact that I'm making such a huge commitment. The first time I got this tattoo, I never thought I'd end up regretting it. I thought Tyler and I would be together, like, forever. Maybe I was deluded in thinking that back then, because a couple of weeks later, he left and never came back. Yet here I am again, perhaps deluded once more. Things could go wrong in a couple of months.

But when I cast a glance at Tyler and I see his gentle gaze watching me with an expression filled with so much love and warmth, I realize I'm prepared to give it my all to make us work whether or not we have our family's acceptance, whether or not we have our friends' approval. I'm ready to make that commitment now, ready to do it once and for all without letting anyone else get in the way. Getting this tattoo represents that. *I'm ready.*

"Would you like to hold my hand?" Tyler teases, offering it to me.

"Yes," I say, "but simply because I want to. Not because of the pain. My tolerance is pretty high." *Bullshit*, I'm thinking. *Such bullshit.* I may not feel so nervous anymore, but that doesn't mean I'm not dreading it.

He releases another of his genuine laughs, and I grasp his hand in mine and almost yank him off the bed. He rests his elbows on his knees and leans forward to reach me more comfortably, then he begins to rub his thumb in soft circles over the back of my hand.

Liam reaches for my right arm and gently places it down on a propped-up padded stand. He wheels his chair right up next to me, then hovers over my skin. "Ready?"

"Mmm," is all I can say because I'm already biting down far too hard on the inside of my cheek, and then I nod once.

Immediately, it starts. I grit my teeth and squeeze my eyes shut, my grip on Tyler's hand clamping down even tighter. *It's worth it*, I remind myself. It's hard to believe it when my skin is on fire, when it feels like my flesh is being burned by hot scratches. I hear Tyler biting back laughter, and when I peel open one eye to glare at him, I discover that he's pressing the back of his free hand to his mouth to stop himself.

"I'm sorry," he says when he notices me watching. "It's just—it's just your face, Eden. High pain tolerance, huh?"

"Distract me," I order. *Fuck, it hurts.*

"Uh." He glances quickly around the small room, searching for something to talk about. I'm holding his hand so tight that I'm surprised I haven't given him a cramp. "What'd you think of that one?"

I follow his gaze to some artwork on the wall. It's a ridiculous portrait of a clown with a full set of pointed teeth. "Awful," I answer.

"Hey," Liam says. He stops working to shoot me a stern look, but he's kidding because he laughs before returning to finish the second word. Two down, one to go. Thank God it's only a small tattoo.

In the final few minutes it takes for Liam to finish up the entire quote, going back over it to fill in any faint spots, I can't help but wonder how everyone is going to react to the new addition to my skin. Dad hated this tattoo the first time around, and that was without him even knowing that it was associated with Tyler, so I doubt he'll be impressed when he eventually finds out that it's made a reappearance. Mom, on the other hand, loved it once I told her the real meaning behind it. She liked that it was in Tyler's handwriting. *Very personal and very cute*, she said. I think she'll be pleased when she discovers it's been restored.

"And you're done," Liam announces, wheeling back his chair. "What do you think?"

My eyes flicker open as I sit up, releasing my firm hold on Tyler's hand. Tilting my arm toward my face, I run my gaze over the fresh ink, and it fills me with such satisfaction that, inevitably, I'm grinning like a damn idiot. There's some blood trickling over my skin, but that's okay. "I love it."

"Looks sick," Tyler says. He's leaning over my shoulder, peering at my arm with an approving nod. Our eyes meet, and immediately a grin that mirrors mine captures his lips.

Liam smothers my skin in ointment before wrapping a bandage around the fresh tattoo. Then I swiftly twirl out of the chair, beaming from ear to ear, relieved that it's over and that now it's Tyler's turn.

While Liam is getting set up for him, he asks over his shoulder, "So how long have you guys been together for?"

I glance sideways at Tyler, and I can't help but roll my eyes. I even press my lips firmly together and take a step back, leaving it up to him to be the one who has to explain that we're not actually together, that we're really stepsiblings.

"Something like three years," he tells Liam. My eyebrows knit together, and I shoot him a questioning glance, but all he does is smirk while offering me no explanation besides a shrug.

"Nice," says Liam. He spins around in the chair and points to the piece of paper in Tyler's hand, the one with my handwriting. "Can I get that?"

Tyler hands it to him, and then he gets to work again, doing the exact same thing all over again. Scanning, editing, printing, tracing, transferring. Soon Tyler's in the chair with his shirt off and the stencil on the right side of his chest, prepped and ready. He's extremely easy on the eyes as I watch from the bed with my legs dangling lazily over the edge. I can see *guerrero* on the back of his shoulder.

"Would you like to hold my hand?" I ask once the buzzing begins, batting my eyelids at him.

"Sure," he says, chuckling, "but because I want to. Not because I can't handle the pain. My tolerance is *so* high." I swat his arm, and he laughs, right before slipping his hand into mine and rubbing those soft circles on my skin again.

When Liam begins, I'm paying more attention to Tyler's body than I am to the development of the tattoo. I'm holding his hand, my lips parted as I fall into a trance at the mere sight of the defined contours of his abs. I blink after a few minutes, snapping out of it and praying he hasn't noticed. He hasn't flinched, hasn't even tensed up, only pulls his phone out and nonchalantly scrolls through his texts. I'm not trying to pry, but I do happen to catch him send Ella a message. Emily gets one too, and within the space of ten minutes, his new tattoo is finished, cleaned, and wrapped. Of course I'm biased, but I think my handwriting looks pretty damn awesome on his chest.

"I like the concept of having it in each other's handwriting," Liam comments as Tyler pulls on his shirt. He's moving around the small studio, rearranging things and tossing stuff into a trash can. "Send me over some pictures later of them both when you take those bandages off."

"Sure," Tyler says.

Liam leads us out of the studio and back into the main waiting area, where there's already a girl in her early twenties waiting with a pair of headphones on, and we thank him for fitting us in. Tyler lets him know that he'll be back in a few weeks to get some touch-ups to his existing tattoos. At that, Liam looks at me, as though expecting me to say that I'll be back too, but honestly, I don't think I want any more tattoos for a while. So I tell him, "Maybe."

On the short walk back to the car, I think both Tyler and I are running on nothing but adrenaline. We're on a total high, laughing every time we so much as glance at one another, and I can't stop staring at my arm, wishing I could tear off the bandage and show my new ink to the world. Even my heart is beating abnormally fast against my chest, and I have to accept the fact that it's down to the thrill of getting not only a new tattoo, but a matching tattoo with Tyler, of all people. In theory, it's undeniably clichéd and statistics could probably tell us that we'll regret it three months from now, but in practice, it's perfect and it's right and it's the best thing we could have possibly done today. I don't think Tyler is even thinking about what went down this morning.

We clamber into his car, and I get back in the passenger seat. Tyler has been back in the driver's seat since we left Multnomah Falls, so he looks at me expectantly as he awaits my next plan of action.

But the thing is, I don't have a plan. I've been making decisions as I go all day, so I quickly rack my brain for what we could do next on this spur-of-the-moment adventure. It's just after 5:30 p.m., and although sunset isn't for another few hours, the sun is already beginning to dip, creating an early evening glow that's hazy. Pretty summer skies call for pretty sights.

I pull on my seat belt and then look to Tyler. Suddenly, I know exactly where I want to go next. "You know where Voodoo Doughnut is? Third Avenue?"

"Ah," Tyler says. His smile grows wider as he turns to face the wheel and puts the car in reverse, glancing over his shoulder as he backs out of our spot. "I think I know exactly where we're headed."

"Surprise ruined," I joke. The truth is, where I want to go, I don't care if it's a surprise or not. Tyler is bound to have already seen it. You can't live in Portland and not know about *the* mural. It's smack-dab in the middle of downtown too.

And because we're already downtown, it doesn't take us too long to get there. The flow of traffic is a little thicker at this time, with everyone heading home after their day at work, so we do get stuck in a couple of traffic jams on route, but we hardly even notice. Tyler's too busy singing along to the radio again, and I'm too busy laughing out loud as I film him with my phone. He was never this easygoing, never as carefree as he is now. And I can't get enough of it. I can't get enough of *him*.

Over on Third Avenue, the line for Voodoo Doughnut is out the door. I always remember it being like that during the summer. Mom would drive past, and there'd be flocks of people lining the sidewalk, desperate to grab a misshapen doughnut with bacon on it. But it's not the doughnuts we're here for. It's for the iconic sign on the opposite side of the street that I haven't seen in years.

I don't even have to tell Tyler to pull into the tiny parking lot because he's already doing that after having figured out where we were going. The parking lot really is small, with limited spaces, and he reverses into a spot that faces the mural we're here to see.

On the wall of the back of a building, there're three huge words, painted in block capitals and in yellow graffiti. They have been the slogan of this city for the past ten years. A slogan we're proud of, a slogan that we live by: *KEEP PORTLAND WEIRD*.

Portland's always been weird and unusual, quirky and eccentric. In any other city, a guy riding a unicycle while dressed in a Santa suit and playing a set of bagpipes that are on fire would be considered bizarre. In Portland, it's acceptable and almost normal. People can do whatever they want in this city without being judged for it, and that's something I've missed. In LA, the pressure to live the perfect life is growing unbearable because it's impossible. People only want to fit in. Here, people want to stand out.

"C'mon," Tyler says. He shuts off the engine and steps out of the car, and I watch from inside as he makes his way around the front of the vehicle, appearing at the passenger door and smiling through the window at me. He opens up the door and reaches for my hands, pulling me up and out.

It's still so hot outside even though it's getting later. I wish I hadn't worn jeans today, and I'm starting to become aware that I look like a complete idiot with this huge bandage covering my right arm, the sleeve of my sweatshirt rolled straight up past my elbow. Quickly, I roll up the other sleeve so that they match.

Out of nowhere, Tyler slides himself onto the hood of the car, then immediately flinches and pulls his hands away from the metal. "Alright, it's a lot hotter than I expected it to be," he admits. "Come on up."

I'm not sure what the point of this is, but I like that we're continuing the theme of doing whatever the hell pops into our heads first. So I attempt to join him, but the slope of the hood and the heat of the metal makes it difficult, so eventually Tyler has to grab on to my wrist and yank me up himself. We settle down and get comfortable, with him leaning back against his windshield, legs outstretched in front of him, and me sitting with my legs crossed and my hands in my lap. The mural is directly in front of us, with only a row of cars separating us from it, and the sun is still relentlessly beating down over the city. It's nice sitting here, basking in the warmth of the summer air with Tyler right next to me. I never want to take these moments for granted.

"Not quite the Hollywood Sign, huh?" Tyler comments. I cast a glance at him. He's analyzing *KEEP PORTLAND WEIRD* with great intensity, the same smile he's had on his face all day still there upon his lips. He's right. The Hollywood Sign is much more glamorous, calling for attention, visible for miles over the LA basin yet so far away. Here, this mural feels a lot more humble, more down-to-earth, more like the people of Portland. A simple mural in graffiti on the wall of an old building in the middle of a tiny parking lot in the busy downtown area, accessible and viewable by everyone and anyone. I think having it so close to us makes it feel like it's ours, and for that reason alone, I think I prefer it over those dumb letters up on Mount Lee that take an hour alone just to get to. The Hollywood Sign feels so disconnected from everything else.

And the more I think about this, the more I realize that actually, I prefer Portland as a whole to Santa Monica. I never thought I would, but I do. I seriously miss this city and everything it stands for.

"I think we fit in better here," I muse, my own gaze resting on the wall, on those words. Weird is all Tyler and I have ever known because it'll *always* be weird to fall for your stepsibling. People will always be taken aback at first. People will always take a minute to understand. But weirdness is embraced in Portland, and I'm starting to believe we'd gain a lot more acceptance here than we would back home. People here would think we were awesome and edgy for doing something different and risky.

"That's because we do," Tyler says.

I look at him. My smile is gone now for the first time in hours, and I have no choice but to ask the question that's repeating itself over and over again in my head. "So you're really staying here?" I murmur. "You're never coming back to Santa Monica?"

Tyler heaves a sigh, and his smile disappears too, because both of us know exactly how this will all eventually end: he will stay here, and I'll go back to Chicago for my sophomore year of college. We'll be apart, which is what we're all too well accustomed to. It's starting to feel extremely unfair.

"I did plan to come home, Eden," he says, sitting forward. "I'd always planned to come back. You know that. But I don't think I can now, and honestly, I'm not sure if I want to. My entire life is in Portland, except for the part that involves you." He pulls his knees up to his chest and rests his arms over them, pressing his lips together and locking his eyes on nothing in particular. "And I know that makes everything so much more complicated than it already is, me being here and you being halfway across the country for another three years, but it's just the way things are right now."

Carefully, I shift closer to him, so that my hip is against his. Everything around me goes quiet, even though there's traffic and voices from across the street and the sound of birds echoing from the trees. All of that seems to tune out, and the only sound I'm left with is that of my heartbeat, pumping in anticipation of what I'm desperate to do next. "I think we're used to complicated by now," I say, but my voice comes out as a breathy whisper. "We could make it work."

Tyler lifts his head and turns to face me, a sparkling glint in his eyes. I see the way the left corner of his lips starts to quirk up, forming the faintest of smirks. "Make what work, Eden?" he whispers in a challeng-ing, teasing tone while leaning in as close as ever, his nearness making me lightheaded and giddy. He knows exactly what I'm talking about, but it's like he wants to *hear* me say it.

And it's so, so easy to say it, because for once, the thought of it doesn't make me nervous nor does it scare the hell out of me. Actually, it excites me.

"Us," I say.

Right now. Right now is the perfect moment I've been waiting for. The perfect situation, the right mood, the correct timing. This is my chance. This is my *next time*.

Pressing my hand to the soft stubble along Tyler's jaw, I tilt his face closer toward mine, and I go for it. I don't even think about it—I just do it. Closing my eyes, I capture his lips with mine, and at first, it's so soft and so gentle. Nothing but our lips together at last, after so long sincerely believing it would never happen again. I'm so relieved to be kissing him, to be the one to make the move, and soon Tyler's hand is weaving through my hair, the other on my waist, pulling me closer. I can feel his relief too in the way he kisses me, slow and deep, his hold on me tight, like he never wants to let me go. It's been a long wait for him too, and he's fought hard to earn my forgiveness through the power of honesty and a sincere apology, which I'm more than willing to accept. Sometimes people have to be selfish. Sometimes people have to put themselves first, and for that, I can never hate him.

Slowly, I feel him tear his lips from mine, but he doesn't move away, his mouth lingering only a mere inch from mine. His hand's still in my hair, his forehead against mine. "If you want to make this work," he murmurs, emerald eyes piercing mine, "then let's make it something. It's been too long."

Teasingly, I gently push his face back, my hand still cupping his jaw, and I dramatically widen my eyes at him. Inside, everything is somer-saulting at once. I'm surprised my heart hasn't lurched straight out of my chest yet. "Is Tyler Bruce asking me to be his girlfriend?"

Tyler can't suppress his grin. I don't think he wants to. It's as wide as ever, reaching straight to his eyes that are brightened with a certain glow that only comes from raw happiness. "He just might be," he says.

I direct his face back to mine, leaning in toward his lips. I'm never going to grow tired of admiring him up close, and I pause there with our gazes locked so that I can take a second to really appreciate the deep verdant green of his eyes that I truly am in love with. "Then I might just be saying yes."

I press my lips back to his and sink into that feeling of his mouth against mine, swift and fast and eager and entirely enthralling. I forget that we're in the middle of downtown Portland, but it isn't long until I hear some guy whistling at us. Another is cheering and whooping. Someone is saying *Aww*. And everything feels so perfect at that exact moment, like everything is finally falling into place. Everything feels so right, and I'm not even thinking about that fact that Tyler is my stepbrother because I don't care. It doesn't matter anymore. It's not wrong for us to feel the way we do. It's not wrong for us to be together. From day one, we have never, ever been wrong.

Maybe these past three years we've been fighting so hard to get everyone else to accept our relationship when the only two people who needed to accept it us was ourselves.

And after all this time, I think we finally have.

chapter

20

I don't wake until after 10:00 a.m. The past few days have been so crazy, and I'm exhausted, which explains the deep slumber I'm pulling myself out of. Through a crack in the blinds, there's a thin line of sunlight illuminating a tiny portion of the room. I'm in Tyler's room, not the living room, and I'm in his bed, not on the couch. I'm wrapped up in his comforter, feeling way too warm and slightly hazy. Releasing a yawn, I roll onto my opposite side, expecting to see him there, his green eyes gazing back at me. I'm expecting to see him smile at me when he realizes I'm finally awake.

But the other side of the bed is empty.

Immediately, I blink and sit up, wide awake. Even though I'm alone, I cling to the comforter, holding it against my bare chest.

I glance around the room. At first I don't even notice the words on the wall directly in front of me. When I do, I think maybe Tyler has taken some inspiration from the *KEEP PORTLAND WEIRD* mural last night. There waiting for me, scribbled in black Sharpie in large letters in the center of his bedroom wall, is a message:

Sorry had to go to work but
im missing you already and
im allowed to write on my
walls because im painting
them soon anyway. te amo

I'm smiling by the time I finish reading it, and I can't help but shake my head. Of course, he returns to work today, which explains why he's not here and why the house is dead silent. I run a hand through my hair, which is tangled and matted, and then I rub at my eyes, only to find that I've still got yesterday's makeup on. I feel so unattractive that I think I might just be relieved that Tyler isn't here to witness it.

I can't even remember what day it is. Tuesday, I think, and I sit there wondering what exactly I'm supposed to do today. I eventually decide that whatever I end up doing, the day has to at least begin with coffee. Specifically coffee made by Tyler.

Pushing the comforter away, I slide out of Tyler's bed—which is much comfier than his couch—and gather up my clothes that are scattered all over the hardwood floor. Then I make a dash from Tyler's bedroom to the spare room. I grab the first set of fresh clothes that I can find, before darting into the bathroom and finally the shower.

From what I can remember, I think Tyler's shift at the coffee shop ends at noon, so I need to get ready and find my way downtown before then. I spend only ten minutes in the shower, massaging my conditioner into my hair at super speed and being careful not to get too much water on my new tattoo that I keep forgetting about. I get dressed and then dry my hair in the bathroom because I've realized it's the only damn room in this apartment that has a mirror. *Guys are just typical.* I pull my flat iron through my hair while sitting on the lid of the toilet, and then I place my makeup bag inside the sink as I apply a natural look. Finally, I make my way back through to Tyler's room in search of my phone.

I find it underneath the pillows, and I have an entire list of new notifications, which is unusual for me. I know I haven't checked my phone since yesterday morning, too preoccupied with Tyler and every-thing else going on around me, but I never get this many messages in the space of twenty-four hours.

Sitting on the edge of Tyler's bed, I scroll all the way back to the earliest messages. The first is from Dad, received at 10:14 a.m. yesterday morning:

If you're planning on crawling home anytime soon, don't.

And then another, at 10:16:

In case it wasn't obvious, you're no longer welcome in this house. Go to your mom's.

Dad's contempt for me doesn't even bother me anymore. I'm just so used to it, and I can't say I didn't expect this reaction from him. I knew what decision I was making when I left Sacramento with Tyler. I knew the impact it would have. I knew I would make things worse.

There're some texts from Mom, and although I haven't told her that I'm in Portland, she has apparently figured it out herself. I was supposed to be home yesterday. The fact that I wasn't only shows that I did, in fact, make the choice to come to Portland. She says I made the right decision, and she asks me to call her when I get a chance.

I've even got a text from Ella yesterday afternoon, asking me if things are going okay.

But I don't reply to any of them because I'm more concerned about the texts I've received from Rachael and the alarming amount of Twitter notifications I seem to have.

The first text came through at 7:58 a.m.

umm wtf are u doing in portland?

Then another.

Can u tell me whats going on?? I thought u hated him

Then a third.

And u got that dumb tattoo again oh mY GOD is this even real

Then a fourth, all within a minute of each other.

If ur dad doesnt kill u then I will

I stare at her messages, reading them over and over again. I haven't told Rachael that I'm in Portland. I haven't told her about the tattoos either. In fact, I haven't told anyone, so I can't figure out how she can possibly know about them. That's until I check my Twitter.

I've been tagged in a tweet, and the only person who ever tags me in anything is Rachael, but for once, it's not her. I've been tagged by Tyler. For a few seconds, I'm actually too scared to even open his account, but I exhale and pull up the tweet because my curiosity is killing me.

It's Tyler's first update in over a year, since last June.

Portland ain't so bad with my girl

He posted this six hours ago, just after 5:00 a.m. Two photos are attached. The first is of our matching tattoos, with my arm held up against his chest in order to fit both into the picture. We took it last night once we got back to his apartment and removed our bandages. It was to send to Liam. The second photo is of me at Multnomah Falls. I'm not even looking at the camera, but I'm laughing.

So far, fifty-nine people have favorited it. I try to check the replies, but there are none. No mocking insults. No outbursts of disgust. Just nothing, like no one even cares. Either that or they're simply afraid to express their opinion in case Tyler will kick their ass. Because that's something the old Tyler would have done. But not the new one.

Rachael's texts make sense now. Of course she's confused. On Friday, I was whining relentlessly to her about having to spend the weekend with Tyler, and now suddenly we're in Portland together with matching tattoos and smiles on our faces. That sudden shift has taken me by surprise too. I didn't realize it would be *this* easy to fall back in love with Tyler.

To keep Rachael from bursting into flames, I shoot her a vague text back.

Things change and so do people :) will fill you in when I get back (and don't ask me when that will be because I have no idea)

My phone's battery is down to four percent, so I leap off Tyler's bed, fumble around in my suitcase in the spare room for my portable charger, and then I make for the door. Luckily, Tyler has taped the spare key to the wall, circling it with that same black permanent marker so that it's impossible for me to miss. I guess he figured I wouldn't want to spend the day here.

So I lock up and head out, pulling on my shades as the blinding sunlight shines down over the city yet again. I flag down a lady walking a pair of dogs and ask where the nearest MAX station is, sounding like a tourist who has found herself lost in a residential neighborhood, and she points south and gives me directions. It's a good fifteen-minute walk to the station, and then another twenty minutes to actually get downtown. I get off at Pioneer Square just after eleven thirty and make a beeline straight for Tyler's work.

The place is busy but not thronged when I get there. There's a small line of people dropping in for a late morning coffee just like I am, so I join the end and rest my eyes on the baristas. The guy from yesterday is here again. Mikey. So is the girl, but I don't know her name. And then there's Tyler, bright-eyed and smiling as though he's the happiest, most easygoing guy there is. The sleeves of his black shirt are rolled up to just below his elbows, so there's not a single tattoo of his to be seen. My lips part as I stare at the veins that run from his knuckles up his forearm, emboldened and tight as his muscles contract each time he pulls the lever to release coffee from the grinder and into the porta-filter. He hasn't spotted me yet, too focused on the cup of coffee he's making, but in a way, I'm glad. It allows me to stare lustfully at him without receiving a funny glance in return, and my eyes are smoldering with desire. *He's so effortlessly perfect.* All I can think about is the way his hands felt on my body last night, the way his lips had left their trace all over my skin, the way his sparkling eyes never left mine, even in the darkness of his room.

Mikey is the one taking orders, so when I reach him, he glances up at me and a hint of recognition crosses his face. I may not be a regular, but he certainly remembers me from yesterday. "Hi again," he says. His nose piercing shines each time he moves. "What can I get you, Eden?"

"Vanilla latte with two extra shots of caramel," I answer, the words rolling off the tip of my tongue without having to think about it. Mikey nods and starts to scribble my words down onto a small pad of sticky notes, but I'm already feeling guilty before he's even finished writing. I need to stop doing this. I need to stop complaining about gaining weight yet continuing to consume the most fattening things like ice cream and damn vanilla lattes. I need to adopt the same mind-set as Tyler. I need to actually make changes rather than just hoping for them. "Wait," I say, and the pen pauses on the paper as Mikey glances up. "Can I make it a skinny white Americano?" Nowhere near as good, but nowhere near as fattening.

"No problem." He scraps the first sticky note and then writes on another, tearing it from the pad and sticking it to the counter alongside the previous orders that have yet to be filled. He turns to the cash register, ringing me up, and it turns out to be extremely cheap. "Friends and family discount," he says with a wink. I hand him five bucks, and he passes me my change. The shop is abuzz with the sounds of conversation and constant steaming, the chirping of milk and the tamping of ground coffee.

"I wrote down that you're here," Mikey murmurs, lowering his voice. I can also see his tongue piercing as he talks. He subtly gives a pointed glance in Tyler's direction. Tyler has his back to us, shifting between machines, reaching for cups and syrups and milk. "Give him a second to realize."

I chuckle. Tyler's so oblivious sometimes that I doubt he even will. "Thanks," I tell Mikey, then move farther along the counter, making way for the next customer as I wait for my coffee. Tyler is the one making all the orders, so I'm looking forward to testing his skills when it comes to making the perfect cup of joe.

I watch him closely with a goofy smile plastered on my face as he picks up a sticky note, reads it, then makes the coffee with extreme concentration. The effort he puts in is adorable. The girl working alongside him passes the cup to the customer waiting in the corner, then Tyler picks up the next order and begins making it. Again the girl delivers it to the customer. And then he picks up the bright-orange sticky note that has my order, running his eyes over it. Quickly, his lifts his head and glances over his shoulder. He scours the shop before he spots me, and I have never, ever seen him grin so fast in my entire life.

He hands the girl the note with my order, and he must ask her if he can take a minute to talk to me because she nods and they switch positions. She falls into place behind the coffee machines, and Tyler makes his way toward me, playfully pushing the back of Mikey's head on the way over. So much for having Tyler make my coffee.

"I was hoping you'd come by," he admits when he reaches me. He presses his palms flat on the counter that separates us, leaning over to hear me better through all of the noise. "Sorry I wasn't there this morning. I left before six, so I didn't want to wake you."

"It's okay," I reassure him. "I got your message. It was kind of impossible not to."

A rosy hue tints his cheeks, and he lowers his head, tilting his face down to the counter. "I was going to write you a note, you know, like they do in the movies. But I couldn't find any paper."

"You're really painting the walls?"

"Yeah," he says. Glancing back up, he runs his eyes over me, his gaze eventually coming to rest on my arm. *No te rindas* still has a shiny gloss to it that only comes with fresh tattoos.

"I saw your tweet," I tell him, and his eyes meet mine. "I think you gave Rachael a heart attack."

He releases a laugh, shaking his head. "I wasn't going to post it," he says, "but then I remembered that we'd stopped caring what everyone thinks. At least now they've all heard it directly from me."

"Wait until Jamie sees it," I scoff. *Oh God.* I can already imagine him throwing his phone across the room in disbelief before scrambling to fetch it again so that he can run and show Dad. Being told via social media that Tyler and I are together isn't exactly the way I imagined our family finding out.

"He already has," Tyler says, and I draw my eyebrows together at how nonchalant he sounds. "He texted me a couple hours ago like *What the fuck?*" He chuckles just as the girl who's been filling his role of making the coffee appears with mine.

"Here you go," she says, leaning over the counter and passing me the to-go cup. It's so hot that it practically scalds me the moment I take it from her, but I quickly thank her, and Tyler lets her know that he'll be back over in a second.

When she leaves, he holds up his wrist and tilts his watch toward him, then he looks back at me. "Twenty minutes to go," he says. "I'll be heading over to the center after. How about you? What are you doing?"

"I'm not sure yet." I shrug and drop my gaze to my coffee, tracing the rim of the lid with an index finger. "But I'll definitely come by later."

"Good," he says. When I glance back up, he's grinning, but it quickly fades into an apologetic smile as he casts a look over his shoulder at the girl who's struggling to keep up with all of the new orders. "I should get back." Stretching over the counter, he plants the quickest of kisses against the corner of my mouth, and out of the corner of my eye, I catch Mikey puckering his lips teasingly at us.

I let Tyler get back to work, and to prevent myself from distracting him, I head straight out of the shop rather than sitting around.

Navigating downtown Portland is easy because I know it like the back of my hand, so I head to Pioneer Square and find myself a spot on the steps to sit down and drink my coffee. And honestly, it's shit. Not because it's been made badly, but because I would much rather be drinking a vanilla latte over a crappy Americano any day.

Pioneer Square is packed, which isn't unusual, because it's summer and the sun is being gracious to us, and it's the perfect spot to bask in the heat and watch the constant flow of people that passes through. But as I'm sitting there, blowing on my coffee to cool it down, I realize that although Portland is my home, I don't actually know anyone in this city. Half the friends I did have when I was sixteen and still lived here have moved out of town for college. Mom's side of the family are all in Roseburg, and so are Dad's. The only people I actually have in this city right now are Tyler and Emily. And Amelia.

I don't know why Amelia hasn't crossed my mind until now. She was my best friend. From the moment we met in the sixth grade, we did everything together, but we drifted apart a lot after I left. It's just the way things go. We lived in different states, and it grew difficult to keep in touch. But Amelia still lives here. She goes to school at Portland State.

I set my coffee on the ground beside me and pull my phone out of my pocket, scrolling through my limited contacts and finding her number. We send each other the occasional text to check in on how we're doing, but the last time I saw her was three years ago. We clung to each other on her porch, sixteen and in tears, wondering how we were supposed to live from then on without each other. When you're young, everything seems like the end of the world. Looking back, it wasn't.

Quickly, I call her number and press my phone to my ear, drumming my fingertips against my knees as I listen to the monotonous dialing tone. It's a long shot hoping she'll be around and available, but there's no harm in checking. Either way, I want to talk to her and let her know that I'm back in Portland.

She answers at the very last second, right before the call goes to her voice mail. "Eden?" There's surprise in her voice, most likely because I don't think we've actually called each other in a long time, so this is a little random.

"Guess what?" I reply. I want to cut to the chase about why I'm calling. Amelia is quiet for a second as she thinks, because unlike most people, she actually does like to make a reasonable guess. But today she can't seem to think of anything that would be logical, for all she answers is, "No idea, but please tell me."

"Well," I say, leaning back and reaching for my coffee, tilting my face up to the sky, "I'm sitting at Pioneer Square."

"*What?*" Amelia explodes, and I can do nothing but laugh. "You're here? You're in Portland?"

"Yes!" I take a long sip of my coffee, catch my breath, then add, "I've been here since Sunday night."

"Oh my God!" Her excitement radiates across the line, and her energy is contagious. I've missed her so much, more than I've even realized. "What are you doing here?!"

"It's a long story," I admit, "which I'll tell you when I see you. Where are you right now? Are you busy?"

"I'm on campus," she says, but she sounds sheepish. I think she knows that I'm about to ask what the hell she's doing at school during summer vacation because she provides me with an answer before I even open my mouth. "I've been taking some summer classes, so I'm just catching up on some studying that I've been slacking on. You should totally come by! I'm just sitting outside. Do you know where the library is?"

I'm rolling my eyes as I get to my feet. Amelia definitely has not changed. She does enough talking for both of us, but I was always grateful for that when I was younger. In my head, I begin mapping a route to Portland State University. It's just south of downtown, not too far from where I am now. It's perfectly walkable, and although the campus is huge and I don't know my way around it, I'm sure the library won't be hard to find. "I'm on my way right now."

"I can't believe you're here!"

"Me either," I say. It's true. "See you soon."

Ending the call, I pull my earphones out and hook them up to my phone, searching through all of my playlists for one with some upbeat songs that have the best summer vibes. It takes me a while to find one because for the past year my playlists have been pretty depressing.

Now that I have Hunter Hayes singing into my ears at full volume, it's a satisfying feeling. I'm in such a good mood, possibly even the best mood I've been in over the past twelve months.

I can't stop smiling as I head south, coffee in hand, sunglasses on, earphones in, fresh tattoo on my arm, like a true Portland native. I've never felt more at home in this city. Leaving for three years was the best thing I could have done, and honestly, I'm glad Tyler came here. None of this would be the same if we were in any other city.

It doesn't take long to reach the campus. I've drifted through it a couple of times when I was younger, tagging along behind fifteen-year-old Amelia because she liked to imagine what it would be like to be a college student. She had every intention to head to Oregon State in Corvallis, but Portland State eventually won her over when the time came to decide. Maybe it was those aimless strolls through the campus that changed her mind. Either way, she never planned to leave Oregon, whereas I always had. Although I did once take a guided tour of the campus when I was sixteen, but that was only to please Mom. She held on to the hope that there *might* have been a chance that I could be interested in sticking around, but I never was. I wanted to leave as soon as possible, and college was always that ticket out of Portland that Mom could never say no to.

It's ironic now that I'm back here three years later, meeting Amelia on campus, as if time has been rewound and we're fifteen again. The only difference is that this time, I'm not faking the smile on my face. This time around, things are better.

I follow the signs around the campus before I eventually have to ask a couple of guys which way the library is. They point me in the right direction, just around the corner. As I spot the building, I pull off my sunglasses and start scouring the people that are sitting outside, some on the grass in the shade offered by the endless array of trees, some on benches huddled over books. It's summer, so the campus is a lot quieter than it would be during the semester. It doesn't take me long to spot Amelia out of the handful of people here.

She's on the grass, legs crossed, a book balanced on her thighs. There's a half-eaten apple in her hand and her phone in the other, with the wires of her earphones tangled in her hair. She hasn't noticed me yet, so I creep around a set of trees, stealthily edging my way toward her from behind. Then I pounce, leaping toward her as I grab her shoulders, and she jolts in fear, releasing a scream in surprise. Her apple flies halfway across the lawn.

I'm shaking with laughter as I crawl around to face her, ignoring the fact that the attention of all of the surrounding students is now on us, and I grin back at her.

"Jesus, Eden!" she says, almost breathlessly, as though I've sent her heartbeat rocketing. She yanks her earphones out of her ears and presses a hand over her chest, then she cocks her head and seems to forgive me because she grins straight back at me. Tossing her book to the side, she reaches over and wraps her arms tightly around me, drawing me into the tightest hug I can recall having since that day on her porch. I squeeze her back twice as hard, and we remain like that, embraced and unwilling to let go, for a good long minute. Finally, we pull away from one another.

"Seriously, what the hell are you doing in Portland?" she asks, shaking her head as though she can't believe that I'm really sitting in front of her. She must be growing her hair out because it's a lot longer than I remember it ever being, and I think she may have lightened it a few shades. It's much blonder, I'm sure.

I know I've told her it's a long story why I'm here, but it really is quite simple. Still grinning, I pluck up the courage to just tell her, "My boyfriend lives here."

The word ignites something within me that sets my entire body on fire, and I can feel my skin heating up just from the joy of being able to use *that* word at last. I'm blushing and I know it, but there's nothing I can do to suppress it. I am just so happy to be sitting here, under the Portland sun next to Amelia and being able to bring Tyler into the conversation as my boyfriend. I never thought this could ever be possible.

"Whoa," Amelia says. Her eyes widen, and she holds up a hand, right before she leans toward me and echoes, "*Boyfriend?* You're dating someone from Portland?"

"Actually," I murmur, "I'm dating someone from Santa Monica who just so happens to now live here."

I think she may be on the verge of squealing. She's always been a sucker for love stories and happily ever afters. Desperately, she demands, "Who?"

The thought of saying it doesn't scare me anymore. Saying his name is as easy as saying anyone else's. However, it's going to take some getting used to before it really sinks in. "I'm dating Tyler," I tell her. My voice is firm and confident, my gaze never leaving hers. "Remember him? My stepbrother?" I'm never going to hide the fact that Tyler is my stepbrother. It's the truth, and I'm not ashamed to admit it.

Confusion flits across Amelia's freckled face. She seems to wait, as though she's expecting me to burst into laughter and say, "Just kidding!" But I maintain a loose smile and pick at the grass, pulling a handful straight out of the ground before feeling guilty and trying my best to stuff it back into place. The Portland air must be getting to me.

"Really?" is all Amelia says. Her tone is gentle, like she's afraid the issue is a sensitive one, and she continues to blink at me in such a way that it's clear she doesn't really know what's going on.

"Yeah," I reply, then casually add, "He moved here a year ago. I'm just visiting for a little while." I don't wait for Amelia to start asking questions, so I decide to change the subject as fast as I can. "How are things with you? How's school?" I motion around me to the surrounding area of the campus.

"Oh, Eden, it's amazing!" Amelia gushes as her entire face lights up with enthusiasm. She picks up the thick textbook she was studying earlier and places it back into her lap, running her fingers down the cover. It's something about chemistry, which I never understood but which Amelia always loved. "The program I'm in is fucking awesome, and the parties here are even better. Did I mention I got arrested?"

Now it's my turn to gauge whether or not she's being serious. Arrested? Amelia? Never. "You're kidding," I say.

"Nope," she says, then laughs sheepishly and pulls her bangs over her eyes. "People shouldn't let me try to walk home after a party when I've drank too much. I had to spend the night in a cell and then pay two hundred bucks for disorderly conduct." She rolls her eyes. "Apparently, yelling in the street is a criminal offense these days."

"You're crazy," I say, but I'm laughing. Amelia was always up for a good time, always up for fun. Nothing is ever too serious with her, and I miss hanging out with someone who lived their life that way.

"I know," she agrees. "I'm working on having more self-control so that my parents aren't forced to disown me."

She begins to laugh along with me, and it feels so good to be laughing with her again that I never want to take it for granted. Knowing that Amelia is here only adds to the growing number of reasons why I seem to be falling in love with Portland. Maybe it's selfish, but I want my life to be full of everything that I love. Like Tyler and Amelia, Portland and coffee, Rachael and Emily, college and adventures, Mom and Ella, reckless ideas and the chance to always feel as happy as I feel now. That's all I want, everything at once, perfectly intertwined.

My laughter subsides, and I blink a couple of times, snapping back to reality. My eyes find Amelia's, and I purse my lips innocently at her. "Do you really have to be here right now?"

"Not really," she says. "Why?"

I push myself up off the grass, getting to my feet and taking Amelia's book from her. I grab her backpack and stuff the book inside, then reach for her hand and pull her up. She's giving me a curious look, waiting for an explanation, so I pass her the bag and nod in the direction I came from. "There're some people I want you to meet."

♥

chapter

21

On the walk across downtown to the youth center, I have ample time to give Amelia the long story. I tell her that Tyler and I have been in love with each other for three years, but that we've only been official for approximately eighteen hours. I tell her about Dean and the real reason we broke up, which was most definitely not a mutual decision made on good terms like I'd once told Amelia before. I tell her about Dad, and that he's an even bigger moron than he ever was before, that he hates Tyler and me together. I tell her about Tyler leaving last summer and that I didn't see him for a year, that he'd been here the entire time setting up a youth group. I tell her that when he turned up again, I wanted him gone. But then I also tell her that I'm glad I gave him a second chance because now I've never been happier.

And Amelia nods the entire time, trying her best to absorb my overload of information, and I think that at first she may possibly believe I'm not the same person she used to know. The old Eden would never have taken risks like I've taken. The old Eden would never have come back to Portland. The old Eden would never blush at the mere thought of a guy.

"This is it," I state, coming to a halt outside the huge black door to the center. There's no sign, but I really think there should be. More people need to know what's behind this door.

I push it open, pressing my weight against it because it's unbelievably heavy, then hold it open for Amelia as she follows me inside. The entry-way is bright again, lighting up the stairs, and we steadily climb them. Amelia's already nervous about meeting Tyler and Emily, but I think she'll definitely approve of Tyler, and she's bound to get along with Emily. It's impossible not to love them, and I want all three of them to know each other.

I can hear the music before we've reached the top of the stairs, and it only gets louder when I pull open the second door. It's much busier than it was yesterday morning, perhaps because it's the afternoon, and the place is alive with the sound of voices, music, and laughter.

"Whoa," Amelia says. I glance sideways at her. She's taking in every-thing with wide eyes full of surprise, the same way I did yesterday. It really is amazing to see how big this place is, and how crowded. "Is that him?"

My eyes snap from Amelia to Tyler. He must have spotted us when we walked through the door because he's already making his way toward me with that grin of his. It's just after 1:00 p.m., so he'll have been here for an hour already.

"Yeah," I whisper, my eyes never leaving Tyler, a smile spreading across my face, "that's him."

"Mmm," Amelia murmurs. "You've got my approval already."

I tear my eyes away from Tyler simply so that I can roll them at Amelia. She's already adjusting her bangs, tucking them behind her ears and then running her fingers through the ends of her hair as Tyler reaches us.

"Nice to see you again," he tells me, smirking. It's been less than two hours since I dropped by his work to grab some coffee, and here I am again, showing up at his other workplace as though I can't possibly stay away from him. I can. I just don't necessarily want to. Glancing at Amelia, Tyler arches an eyebrow and then looks at me for an answer. "Who's this?"

"Amelia," I say. No further explanation required. Tyler knows exactly who Amelia is. I told him all about her years ago, my best friend from back home in Portland. My only *nice* best friend.

"Hi," Amelia says, blinking intensely, a sure sign of her nerves. There's this awkward moment where she almost holds out her hand but then seems to think it's too formal and ends up retracting it.

"Ah," Tyler offers. His teeth flash in a smile, his expression friendly and warm. "Great to finally meet you. I'm Tyler, Eden's…" He trails off, glancing at me before he says it, like he's worried I haven't told her yet.

But Amelia cuts in before I do, finishing, "Boyfriend and stepbrother?"

"Yeah, that," Tyler says with a laugh. He looks both relieved and pleased that I've told her. The two of us were never all that great at being honest before, but I like to think that we're getting better.

"Where's Emily?" I ask. Scanning the crowds of people drifting around, I try to pick her out among them, but I just can't spot her. I hope she hasn't left. I really want Amelia to meet her.

"She's in the back," Tyler responds, pointing to a door on the far wall. I didn't notice it yesterday. "Come on through."

As Tyler makes his way across the carpet, Amelia and I follow behind him. She nudges me in the ribs and widens her eyes with enthusiasm, mouthing, "He's hot," while dramatically fanning her face with her hand. Some things never change. We used to gush about the hot seniors back in high school, blushing with humiliation in the hallways whenever they overheard us. Playfully, I push her shoulder and bite down on my lip to stop myself from laughing. Tyler is completely oblivious to it all, and when we reach the door at the back, he types a sequence of digits into a keypad and the door clicks. He pushes it open, holding it for us as we enter what appears to be a storage room. Tyler hovers by the doorway, keeping an eye on everyone else back in the main hall, and immediately, Emily's face pops up from behind a stack of cardboard boxes.

"Hey!" She dumps the batch of water bottles she's holding on top of another unopened box, then skillfully maneuvers herself around the haphazardly stacked boxes that cover the floor, creating a path toward us.

"Emily?" I hear Amelia say in a tone of recognition, and my gaze snaps straight over to her in surprise.

"Oh my God, hey!" Emily exclaims. "What are you doing here?"

Both Tyler and I glance back and forth between them, trying to figure out what the hell is going on. "You guys know each other?" I ask, confused.

"Um, *yeah*," Emily says matter-of-factly in the best American accent she can attempt, although it comes out curiously Southern. Then she promptly switches back to normal and explains, "She gives me free popcorn every time I go to the cinema because she's trying to set me up with the guy she works with."

"It's shameless, I know," Amelia adds. Color floods her cheeks, and I'm trying to recall if she ever told me she worked at a movie theater. I can imagine her spilling popcorn all over the carpet hourly. "But Gregg is totally crushing on you and it's *so* adorable. I still think you should give him a chance."

"Nooooo," Emily says, but she's blushing now too as she tries to wave Amelia away. I'm still blinking at them both, stunned at how easy this is. "I've never gotten your name," Emily admits. "What is it?"

"Amelia." There's a slight hesitation where she seems to realize that Emily doesn't yet know why she's here, so she quickly adds, "I'm actually, like, Eden's childhood best friend."

Emily's lips part as she looks at me, clearly taken aback by the news. "No way!"

Next to me, Tyler clears his throat and says, "Do you guys mind if I borrow Eden for a second?" I fire him a questioning glance, but Amelia and Emily are reassuring us they'll be fine together, and Tyler is already directing me back through the door.

"Yes?" I ask once we're back in the main area and surrounded by teenagers. My expression has caution written all over it as I look up at him.

"My dad's here again," he states. His eyes study me, his features relaxed with a hesitant smile on his lips, like he's apologizing.

I know his dad is supposed to be this reformed guy who's trying to fix things with Tyler, but I can't shake the hatred I have for him. Even the thought of him is enough to make me grit my teeth. "Why?"

"He's just finishing up going through some stuff before he heads to the airport," Tyler explains, nodding to the office. The door is closed. "He wants to meet you. Like, officially. He thinks you guys got off on the wrong foot yesterday, which is partly my fault for not warning you that he was around again." That explains the apologetic smile.

"Hmm." Although I despise Tyler's dad, my contempt for him doesn't stop me from being utterly curious. Part of me does want to hear what he has to say. I've known about him for so long that it would be crazy of me to turn down a chance to talk to him. "Okay," I say. "I'll talk to him."

There's a flash of gratitude in Tyler's eyes before he takes my hand and leads me over to the office. It frustrates me that I feel nervous, and slowly, Tyler pushes open the door a little. He peers around the frame, and I hear him murmur, "Dad, Eden's dropped by." I don't hear what Peter replies, but suddenly, Tyler's swinging the door fully open and pulling me into the small room.

His dad is sitting there in that huge executive chair, comfortable and relaxed, sheets of paper spread out on the desk in front of him. He's wearing a pale blue shirt, buttoned straight to the collar, and there's a fountain pen between his thumb and index finger. The gold watch on his wrist is poking out from the cuff of his shirt, and I wonder how a man with such a disgusting past can present himself as being successful.

"Hello, Eden," he greets. Like yesterday, his soft-spoken nature takes me by surprise, the same way the warmth in his eyes does. He is Tyler but shorter, with green eyes that aren't as vibrant and a jaw that isn't as defined. Yet, the similarity is going to take some getting used to.

"Hi," I say. There's a silence in which I look at Tyler, perplexed to discover that he's already backing out of the room.

"I better get back to work," he says. He glances between his dad and me for a second or two, offering us a tight-lipped smile before he nods and disappears through the door, pulling it shut behind him.

We're left alone, Peter and I. It's unbearably awkward, no doubt because he can sense my hostility toward him. Plus, the fact that I'm lingering in front of this desk while he stares back at me from that chair makes the entire thing feel very authoritative. I'm grateful when he stands up and moves around the desk, coming to a stop a few feet in front of me.

"I understand that you don't like me," he begins, and it's so blunt and straightforward that I quickly swallow. "I don't blame you. I'm not a huge fan of myself either. But you're Tyler's...you're Tyler's girlfriend, I've been hearing?"

Uncomfortable, I shift my footing. "Yes."

"Then I'd like to be on good terms with you," he says.

I stare back at him, my expression blank. I don't know how I can ever be on good terms with someone who put Tyler through hell. I can never forgive him for that, and if I can't forgive him, then I most certainly can't like him. "What you did..." I mutter through stiff lips, but God, I can't even finish my sentence. It angers me so much that the muscles in my throat tighten and I grind my teeth together. Even looking at him is enough to make my blood boil, so I close my eyes and tilt my face to the floor. I'm starting to realize how difficult it must have been for Tyler to sit and talk to him because even I can't do it and I'm just a third party.

"What I did, I regret every day of my life."

Slowly, I raise my head and open my eyes. Peter is looking back at me with the saddest expression I think I've ever seen. I could swear that for a second, his eyes aren't even green, just two black voids, weary and wrinkled, the result of years of overwhelming regret. His deepening frown seems natural, as though his lips have been set that way for far too long.

"I lost everything, and I deserved to," he says quietly. "I lost my business and my career, my reputation and my freedom, my parents and myself. But the worst thing of all was that I lost my wife and my kids." He swallows the lump in his throat and shakes his head gently back and forth. "And you can dislike me, Eden, but you should know that I really am just trying my best to make things right with Tyler. I'm here because of him, because he deserves to have a father who is trying his damned hardest to show just how sorry he is."

I'm not sure why he's telling me this, but I'm glad that he is. Hearing it from his own lips is reassuring, even more so that each of his words are laced with sincerity, but I still want to get my own opinion across. I want to express myself too. "I get that you're trying," I tell him, "and honestly, you've gained some respect from me for coming up here and attending those sessions with Tyler. But you didn't get to see what he was like three years ago and how off the rails he used to be. Did you know that your son was only known for being an asshole? Someone no one wanted to get on the wrong side of because of how violent and aggressive he was? Someone who depended on alcohol and drugs to distract him from thinking about all of the shit *you* put him through? You may know that, but you didn't *see* that. You didn't see how completely broken he was, and I don't think you have any idea just how damn hard he's worked lately to become a better person than the one you made him into." I take one step back and fix Peter with a firm glare, my eyes ablaze with my contempt for him. "So you may have my respect, but you'll never have my forgiveness. And I swear to God…I swear…if you fuck this up, you won't only have Tyler to deal with, but you'll also have to deal with me. You aren't getting any more chances after this one."

Peter only nods. Maybe he's used to this, maybe he just accepts it. Turning to the desk, he picks up his phone, slips it into the pocket of his pants, then grabs that same folder he was carrying yesterday. He gathers the sheets of paper into a pile, then moves across the room to place them into one of the filing cabinets. The entire time, my eyes follow him, studying his mannerisms for any resemblance to Tyler's, but thankfully, there are none until he stops back in front of me and runs a hand through his dark hair exactly like he did yesterday, exactly like Tyler does. I have to suppress a groan.

"I'm heading off now," Peter tells me. "I'll be back again next month, so if you're still around, I'll see you then. It was nice to finally meet you, and please trust me when I say you have nothing to worry about. "

All I reply is, "Okay."

We're definitely not on good terms. It's going to take a lot more than talking for a couple of minutes for me to be able to tolerate him. I'm willing to try though, for Tyler's sake, and because I'm slowly taking the first steps toward making my own life better too. So although it's hard, the next time I see Peter, whenever that will be, I'm willing to make some effort with him.

Offering me a small smile, Peter turns for the office door and heads into the main hall. I wait a few seconds before making my way after him.

When I do, I spot him making a beeline for Tyler. I can't stop myself from watching them interact with one another because it creates such an unsettling, sickening feeling in my stomach that I'm trying to eradicate. *It's different now*, I have to remind myself. They're working together to fix things between them, and it's clearly still a work in progress because they don't seem to get too close to each other. They do, however, firmly shake hands. After that, Peter disappears through the main door, and he's gone.

Tyler returns to what he's doing, which is talking to a girl who looks rather sullen as she leans against the wall with her arms folded across her chest, so I make my way back to the storage room in search of Amelia. I have to knock a few times before Emily scrambles to let me in, and after a brief discussion, both Amelia and I decide to stick around at the center for a while. Neither of us has anything else to do today, and Tyler and Emily seem to enjoy our company.

We even lend a hand, with Amelia helping to restock the vending machines and with me offering to tidy up the mound of boxes in the storage room. It's such a great atmosphere, with loud music and a steady flow of kids coming and going while the four of us joke around with each other. It makes the afternoon fly by, and I'm so glad Amelia is getting along with Tyler and Emily because they're three people who matter immensely to me. Emily is having such a good time hanging with us that when it turns 5:00 p.m. and her day is officially over, she still decides to stick around, and it's worth it because we all end up ordering takeout later.

Even the teenagers that come here are all extremely friendly. I've been floating between groups and chatting to them all, laughing at their quick wit and sarcasm. I can understand why Tyler and Emily enjoy doing this each day. It's rather rewarding being here, surrounded by positivity, which is reflected in the good mood I'm in. But being this happy is almost starting to make me feel exhausted. I'm not used to it.

It's just after 9:00 p.m. when the last person leaves the building. Tyler's been talking to him for a while, the pair of them slouched down on some beanbags over in the corner. Emily left at 7:00 p.m., Amelia at 8:00 p.m. It's just Tyler and me now, and I've been patiently waiting for him, because not only do I refuse to ride the MAX at night, I also do not want to head home without him.

"So what do you think of Amelia?" I ask as I'm helping him roll down all the blinds. The music is off, and the center is silent. It feels strange without all the noise.

"She's nice," Tyler says over his shoulder. "It's great that you met up with her, and even better that she's still in Portland. Now you've got someone else here who you know."

"Yeah," I say. "Portland isn't turning out to be that bad, you know."

Tyler smirks at me, clearly holding back an "I told you so."

We finish closing up the center, shutting off the lights and locking all the doors before we head out. It's dusk, with the sun already hidden below the horizon and the darkening sky streaked with orange and pink. Tyler's pulled on a hoodie now, and I press my face against his back and wrap my arms around him as he locks the main entrance. Then he grasps my hands and removes himself from my grip so that he can swivel around to face me, grinning.

"How about a late-night trip to the hardware store for some paint?"

It took a lot of convincing on my part to persuade Tyler to opt for ivory paint over a vibrant red. The rule of sticking to neutral colors doesn't seem to register with him, but after an hour of debating, we're back at the apartment, eight buckets of ivory paint sitting in the center of the living room floor.

The walls are all currently white and in desperate need of touching up with a fresher color. Over the next few days, the plan is to paint the entire apartment. The idea seemed fun back in the car, but now that I'm standing here in an old pair of jeans and one of Tyler's oversize T-shirts, a paintbrush in one hand, my enthusiasm is starting to fade.

"I say we start with my room so that I can cover up that writing," Tyler says. He's pulled on a pair of gray sweats with a plain white T-shirt, and he's got that effortlessly hot thing going on again, yet I'm stuck looking like I'm homeless.

"Sure."

We each grab a bucket and move into Tyler's room. It takes only a few minutes to get set up because there's nothing in here to move besides his bed. He moves the mattress into the spare bedroom, then tilts the bedframe onto one side and eases it through the doorframe and into the other room, all while I cover the floor in the multiple shower curtains we bought from the store. It's also after 10:00 p.m. by now, and I'm thinking we maybe should have waited until tomorrow. It's getting late.

Tyler's writing from this morning is still scribbled across the wall, and I don't realize I'm smiling at his words until he walks back into the room and gives me a funny look.

"Time to get painting," he says. He crouches down and cracks open the lid of one of the paint cans, pours some into a tray, then starts dipping a roller brush into it. I've never really imagined Tyler as the DIY type, and I laugh as I watch him because he's so innocently adorable when he's trying to concentrate, with his gaze soft and his lips parted. "What?" he says, glancing up.

"Nothing."

Jokingly, he narrows his eyes at me and then turns to the wall. I know it's my designated role to be crawling on the floor, painting around the edges of the walls, but I'm too busy staring at him to realize that

I'm not even helping. He wants to cover up his words first, so he starts rolling the brush against his writing, and within a few seconds, the first line is already gone. But I'm not even watching the words as they disappear because the view of Tyler's body is a lot more appealing. Each time he stretches up, his T-shirt lifts slightly to reveal the tight elastic waistband of his black boxers peeking out from under his sweats.

"How's that?" I hear him ask, and when I snap out of the daze I'm in, I realize he's facing me with a small smirk toying at the corner of his lips. On the wall next to him, all of the words are gone, except just two. The final two.

te amo

I look back at Tyler, who now has his head tilted slightly and his emerald eyes smoldering back at me. There's a challenging glint to them, and I think he's waiting for me to kiss him. It's a challenge I'll gladly accept, although I do want to taunt him first. I take a large step forward and quickly plant a kiss on his lips, then step back again just as fast.

"Where's the marker?" I ask.

Tyler purses his lips at me, then says, "Kitchen. First drawer on the left."

I leave him with nothing but a secretive smile as I spin around and make my way through to the kitchen. I rummage through the drawer before grabbing the black Sharpie, popping the lid off as I head back into Tyler's room. He's returned to painting, starting at the far corner, but when he senses me next to him, he casts a glance at me from over his shoulder and then stops what he's doing.

"So," he says, giving me an inquisitive look, "what exactly do you need the marker for?" I don't know why he even needs to ask. Judging by the smile he's trying to bite back, it's clear he already knows exactly what I'm about to do.

As I'm grinning at him, I move closer to the wall. Careful not to touch the wet paint that's already there, I run the tips of my fingers over the remaining words. Then, underneath, I write: *je t'aime*.

"How's that?" I say, purposely mimicking him as I step back and nod to my addition to the wall. This painting thing isn't going all that well so far. We only seem to be making the walls worse.

Tyler's eyes brighten as he reads the words. Then he stares at me for the longest of seconds, and as each one passes, his smile continues to grow, wider and wider, until suddenly, he's in front of me, his hands on my jaw, his mouth against mine.

He's so full of energy that I'm knocked back a step or two, and tonight there's no time for slow, deep kisses because we're both far too eager and far too playful, the sexual attraction too hard to ignore. Our lips are moving in sync with the speed of our heartbeats as his tongue works against mine. I don't ever think I'll be able to get used to the exhilaration I get from kissing him. It gives me goose bumps, sends shivers down my spine, and makes my legs feel numb. It's the most amazing feeling in the world.

Tyler's hands work their way over my body, running down my waistline until they slide under my thighs and sweep me up off the floor. I wrap my legs tightly around his body, my arms looped around his neck, my lips pressing even harder against his. I can feel his hands on my ass as he holds me up, as he pushes me against the wall. Within a matter of seconds, I can feel the wet paint dampening my T-shirt.

I don't want to, but I have to tear my lips away from his so that I can glance over my shoulder. The back of the black T-shirt now has a thick layer of fresh paint over it. Of the entire wall, Tyler just *has* to press me against the one spot that's been painted.

"You did that on purpose!" I groan at him as I turn back around, his face only an inch from mine.

He's grinning at me, eyes sparkling with a glint of mischief. "Better take that shirt off," he mumbles, but he's already doing it for me. Still holding me up between his chest and the wall, he's tugging the hem of the T-shirt up and over my head, throwing it behind him.

The paint is cold and wet against the skin on my back now, but I don't bother to complain because Tyler's lips are on the soft spot behind my ear. I angle my head to the side and then tilt it back against the wall to give him better access, my fingers tangled in his hair, my eyes closed as I revel in the sensation of his mouth leaving a trail from my ear to my jaw to my neck, sucking on my flesh and planting slow, soft kisses. His thumbs are skimming the waistband of my jeans, his fingertips warm as they brush over my skin. One hand runs its way up my back to the clasp of my bra, and suddenly, it's tossed over Tyler's shoulder and lying on the floor.

His lips move to my breasts, and I'm desperate to see his own body, so I reach for his shirt at the same time and help him pull it off. As he continues to decorate my body in lustful kisses, I can only stare at his. I love his Hispanic roots because the tone to his skin is gorgeous, naturally tan. His abs aren't quite as defined as they used to be, but they're still there, still perfectly aligned into a neat six-pack. Every curve of his torso is sharp, from the roundness of his pecs where his new tattoo sits, to the deep v-lines that disappear into his boxers. As he holds me up, both hands squeezing my ass, his biceps are huge. The muscles are flexed, the veins running through them bold and electrified.

"So much for painting." He chuckles, lifting his head. He kisses my forehead, then my nose, then my cheeks, then the corner of my lips. He fixes his eyes on me, entirely consumed with admiration, lust, and love.

I can imagine mine are somewhat similar, because as I look back at him in that moment, I don't think I will ever fall out of love with him. It's impossible. He's too perfect, and he's perfect for me. "Were we ever really going to paint, anyway?"

"No," he admits. Then in a breathy laugh he whispers, "This was always the intention. Much better." His lips find mine again, and I tug playfully at his hair as he pulls me away from the wall. I don't know how he manages to carry me out of the room while kissing me at the same time, and I'm not sure why we don't end up colliding with something, but we end up safely through in the spare bedroom.

"Give me one second," Tyler says. Setting me down, he quickly runs a hand through his hair as he makes a start on piecing back together his dismantled bed, and I'm standing there in my jeans by the door, laughing at the desperation on his face as he tries to do it as quickly as he can.

My eyes drift to the room next door, between the two bedrooms. It's the bathroom, with the door already open and the shower in sight. Just the mere thought of it is enough to send waves of adrenaline coursing through my body, and all I can think about is that time in New York last summer, in the shower in Tyler's apartment on the Fourth of July. But the fun came to an end almost as soon as it began when Snake and Emily came back earlier than expected.

My eyes flicker back to Tyler, and before he can even pick up the mattress, I take a few steps closer to him and hook my hand over the waistband of his sweatpants. He blinks down at me, surprised when I begin to pull him out of the room. My smile has developed into a seductive smirk, as I bring him to a stop outside the bathroom door. I seem to gain an alarming amount of confidence whenever I get the slightest burst of adrenaline, so I quickly step in front of him before I have the chance to get nervous, widening my eyes innocently at him.

I reach up to kiss the edge of his jaw, then I run both my hands down his chest as I move my body closer to his. My breasts press against his chest, my hips against his, and I can feel how rigid and firm he is against me. I glance up, looping my arms back around his neck. "Did we ever finish what we started in New York?"

Tyler takes a moment to figure out what I'm referring to, and most importantly, what I'm suggesting. As soon as it hits him, his grin is back on his face. "No," he says, "I don't think we did."

We stumble inside the tiny dark bathroom together, the tiles cold beneath my feet. I steady myself on the sink as I wriggle out of my jeans, then I climb into the tub and squint through the darkness at the dials as I try to turn on the water. It sparks to life in one huge burst, soaking me entirely. The paint on my back chips off slowly, the pieces flowing down into the bottom of the tub, disappearing from my skin the same way Tyler's writing had last year.

As the water runs down my face and rolls off my chin, I find him in the dark, nothing but a silhouette as he steps out of his sweats, then his boxers. He lingers for a moment, his eyes watching me, and then ever so quietly, I hear him whisper, "Fuck."

Reaching out for him, I grasp his hand in mine and pull him toward me as our bodies intertwine beneath the flow of water once again. Only this time, there are no interruptions.

♥

chapter

22

On Thursday, Tyler has the morning off work from the coffee shop, so he and Emily switch shifts at the center, meaning she has the morning free for once to hang with me instead. It's nearing noon, and we've been strolling around downtown for thirty minutes already, drifting in and out of stores. The weather isn't as great today. It's still warm, but there's a thick layer of clouds preventing the sun from shining through, so the streets are dull.

"What do you think of this one?" Emily asks. She's modeling a black miniskirt and studying it intently before glancing at me, waiting for an answer.

I'm not sure why she's asking me because I don't exactly have the greatest fashion sense. "What for?"

"Say, for a party?" she says.

"Then it's cute," I tell her, and that must seal the deal because she decides to buy it. While she's changing and paying, I make my way back to the exit and wait for her there.

These past two days, I haven't been entirely focused. Physically, I'm here. Mentally, I'm not. There's too much going on inside my head right now, too many things to fix and work out, too many questions needing answers. Piecing my life together is turning out to be a lot harder than just introducing my friends to one another. Yesterday morning, it seemed to slowly dawn on me that although I love being in Portland, this is all just temporary. I need to go back to Chicago in two months, and when that happens, everything has the potential to fall apart. Now I just can't shake the thought that very soon, Tyler and I will be separated again, and it's making me feel nauseous.

"We should go visit Amelia," Emily suggests when she appears next to me again with her Forever 21 shopping bag in tow. "The cinema she works at is like four streets away."

"I think you mean it's four blocks away," I correct, my tone teasing. "But sure. Let's go."

Amelia had been invited on this casual-walk-turned-shopping-trip, but couldn't make it because she works at the theater on Thursdays. I'm sure she'll be grateful to see us because I can imagine it being pretty empty there at this time on a weekday. Emily leads the way, although I quickly figure out which movie theater we're headed for.

Yet even the thought of seeing Amelia isn't pulling me out of the disconnected mood I'm in. The truth is, I don't just hate the idea of having to leave; I'm terrified of it. Everything is finally the way I always dreamed of it being, and Tyler and I being apart may just damage the relationship we've fought so hard to have. Maybe we won't be able to handle it.

"Emily," I say, slowing my pace down a little. I have to swallow back the anxious lump that's growing in my throat. "Can I ask you something?"

She gives me a quick glance out of the corner of her eye. "You know you can."

And she's right. Emily's always great at giving advice. I love talking to her because I know she'll be honest and real with me no matter what. "Do you think Tyler and I would be able to do long distance?" *Ugh.* Long distance. Just the sound of it sucks.

Emily immediately frowns and stops walking, looking me straight in the eye. "Is this about uni?" she asks, but she already knows that it is. "Because, yeah, I do think you would be able to do it. You guys are used to spending time apart." She pauses when she sees the sadness that crosses my face. Even I can feel it, in every single inch of my body. "Eden, c'mon," she says soothingly. "Try not to think about it too much. Just enjoy your summer."

It's hard not to think about it, but I nod and start to walk again. She does have a point. I don't want to spend the limited time Tyler and I have together being upset.

We make our way along another two blocks to where the movie theater sits. There are a couple of people milling around when we walk through the doors, but there are no lines snaking all over the place like there are at theaters on Friday nights. It makes it much easier to spot Amelia, sitting behind the ticket counter and staring at her hands. As predicted, she looks as though she might just die of boredom. When she looks up as we're approaching the counter, her eyes spark with the sheer joy of having another human being to talk to.

Sliding off her chair, she pulls open the door to the small booth and steps out. "Hey!"

"Nice hat," I tell her, but I'm laughing already. She looks ridiculous in her uniform, and because she's a close friend of mine, I'm allowed to tease her about it. "I really love the pants," I comment, my laughter muffled as I try to hold it back.

"This job makes me feel like I'm burning in hell," Amelia says. Reaching up, she pulls the cap off her head, but it leaves her hair static and a little wild, so I end up laughing even harder. "What did I do to deserve this? I'm a good student. I'm taking freaking summer classes. I've never told my parents I've hated them. I've only ever hit my sister once. I've never cut someone off on the interstate. Yet one little time I yell in the street and get arrested, and God thinks I deserve all of *this*?"

This is what I've missed about Amelia. She's always so dramatic. I suspect it stems from the fact that she was a total theater freak back in high school, performing in each school show.

"When do you get off?" Emily asks her, I think mainly just to shut her up.

"Two," Amelia says. She looks at the huge clock on the far wall, then heaves a loud, long sigh when she realizes it's only 12:30 p.m. "Then I've got a lab from three to five. Seriously, Thursdays *suck*. Oh, and Gregg has clocked you."

She nods across the foyer to the short guy behind the concession stand. He's wearing a cap too, only his has a damn hot dog extending from it. He's already watching us, yet when we all glance over, he doesn't even make the effort to look away. He appears to be in his twenties. Seeing us, he smiles way too enthusiastically and waves, all directed at Emily.

She doesn't wave back, only presses a hand to her temple and turns her back on him, shaking her head. "Bloody hell. Amelia, *why* did you tell him I was interested?"

"Just look at him!" Amelia says, pouting sympathetically. At Gregg. Not Emily. "How was I supposed to tell that adorable face that you didn't want to go on a date with him?"

Emily says something in reply, but I've tuned out by then. A movie seems to have just ended because a small flow of people exit through a set of doors and into the foyer. There's a trio of guys, and Emily and Amelia will most probably think that I'm checking them out, but I'm not. I'm staring at their clothes, at the Portland State University apparel they all seem to be wearing. One, a green hoodie with *PORTLAND STATE* emblazoned across the front in white. Another, a PSU snapback. The third, a green *PSU VIKINGS* T-shirt.

Suddenly, that's the only thing running through my mind.

Portland State University.

The apparel. Amelia's classes there. The campus yesterday. Mom's years of relentless attempts to convince me to apply there.

The decision is instantly crystal clear. It's like everything clicks into place.

"Eden?"

"Huh?" I snap my eyes back to Emily, who seems genuinely concerned. I guess I've zoned out because both she and Amelia are looking at me questioningly.

"Amelia's asking if we want to see a movie," Emily explains, still looking at me funny. "I mean, we could. I don't have to be at the center until after two."

"Emily," I say, and the firm solemnity of my voice takes them both by surprise. "I'm really sorry, but there's something I need to do."

"What?"

I'm already backing away, my steps increasing with speed with each one I take. There's no time to explain it to them, because now that the idea is in my head, there's a sense of urgency to it. Turning for the door, I manage to quickly call over my shoulder, "There's a campus I need to take a second look at."

I've got a stack of notes in my hands as I make my way from the MAX station back to Tyler's apartment. It's just after 6:00 p.m., and it's a lot brighter now, as the sun has finally broken through the clouds. I know that Tyler will be at the apartment because he left the center at five. He texted me an hour ago wondering where I was, and I told him that I'd be home soon.

And I will be because I'm on my way now, consumed by excitement. Over and over again in my head, I practice what I'm going to tell him, trying to get it right. I can't wait to see his reaction. I've made a decision that makes so much sense, that feels so right to me. It's the vital step I need to take in order to live my life the way I intend to, with the people I love around me, in a city I once took for granted but have now learned to appreciate. The way I have felt this past week is the way I want to feel every single day.

By the time I reach the apartment courtyard, my throat feels dry. It's not necessarily because I'm nervous about making such a huge decision, but because I'm anxious about saying it out loud to Tyler. Once I say it, that makes it all feel real.

The door is unlocked when I reach it, and as soon as I swing it open, I'm hit with the overwhelming fumes of paint. They make me feel faint. There's music playing too, and the couch is gone. Instead, those ugly shower curtains are spread across the floor, and Tyler has already painted most of the room. He's shirtless, and I think it might just be the most amazing view in the world to come home to. The muscles in his back, the broadness of his shoulders, the curve of his spine…

He hasn't heard me walk through the door, so I keep my steps light as I skirt my way around the shower curtains toward him. Then silently I wrap my arms around his body, planting a soft kiss against his shoulder blade, against *guerrero*. He jolts at the sense of my touch, startled until he realizes that it's just me.

"Finally," he says, turning around. He sets the roller brush down into its tray and then straightens back up. The view from the front is even better, and I'm staring at his chest rather than his eyes as he says, "Emily told me that you randomly bailed this morning. Where'd you go?"

When I glance up, I'm grinning. I step closer to him and envelope him in a hug, absorbing the warmth of his skin. But suddenly, every single sentence I have rehearsed seems to disappear. I can't remember the dramatic speech I strung together, so the moment isn't as special as I'd planned it to be when the only words to leave my lips are, "I'm staying in Portland." It's blunt, but it's simple.

Immediately, Tyler looks perplexed. There are flecks of paint on his chest. "For the rest of the summer?"

"No," I say. My smile is small but warm, and very slowly, I tell him, "I'm staying in Portland for good."

"But…" He's unable to process what I'm saying because he draws his eyebrows together and shakes his head in confusion. "But you can't. You've got to go back to school."

"And I will be going back to school," I reply, my eyes drifting downward as I move a hand to his chest, tracing circles on his skin. "Only I'll be attending Portland State."

Silence ensues for what seems like forever as Tyler remains still beneath my touch. His only movement is his heavy breathing, his chest rising and falling, and when I look to see his expression, he's blinking at me with eyes full of panic and alarm rather than the delight I was hoping for. "What?" is all he says.

Disappointed by his reaction, I step back from him, breaking our embrace. My smile is gone, replaced instead by blank features. The moment is pretty lackluster. Nothing like I expected. Now I'm left standing here in front of Tyler with my shoulders sunk low and with nothing to do but to keep explaining myself. "I'm going to transfer," I state. Then to make it clear, I add, "Schools, Tyler. To here. To Portland State."

Again, silence. But this time, it's for only a few seconds until the moment he explodes with, "Are you crazy?" He throws his hands up in exasperation. I can tell by the hard edge in his voice that he's pissed at me, and I take another step back, surprised at his outburst. "I can't let you transfer fucking schools, Eden. We can do long distance. I'll fly out to Chicago to see you. Whatever happens, you can't transfer. You never used to shut up about that damn school, and you're just going to give it up? Where the hell did this even come from?"

This definitely isn't going as planned, and the only thing I can think to do is thrust my stack of notes at him. "I've been researching it all day at the library on campus. Amelia let me use her account," I say quickly, as though I have to defend myself and my decisions. Tyler glances between the notes and me as I begin to ramble off the speech I prepared earlier. All of this negativity seems to have cleared my head. "Sure, it's not as great as Chicago, but the psychology program is still one of their top degrees, and my credits can easily transfer. And you know I love Chicago, but it's so far away from everything else that I love. I have friends there but not *best* friends, whereas you're here, and Amelia's here, and Emily's here—for a little while, anyway—and Mom's only one state away. It'll mean that Dad will be permanently closer to me again, which is unfortunate, but I can live with that. And Portland State has a super high transfer acceptance rate. If I'm transferring from a school like Chicago, they're bound to accept me."

Tyler passes my notes back to me, although I don't think he's even glanced at them. They have everything taken into account, with everything that I need to know and do, all scribbled down hours ago in a rush of excitement. "How long have you been considering this?" he asks, tone sharp. "Why didn't you tell me before?"

"I only made the decision today," I admit. I know it must seem so rushed to him, like I haven't thought any of this through, but I have. I can't just ignore how right transferring seems. It's an all-consuming feeling, one that's been taking over every single one of my thoughts since this morning.

"Why are you even making such a decision?" he throws at me. Shaking his head again in disbelief, he walks around me and moves toward the window, pausing the music that's been playing from his phone and then leaning back against the glass. All of the walls are wet with paint. Folding his arms across his bare chest, he stares across the room at me, although his gaze is softer around the edges now.

"Don't you want me to stay in Portland?" Even the thought of it almost paralyzes me, but I can't pinpoint any other reason why Tyler is reacting so negatively to the idea of me living here permanently.

"Of course I do," he murmurs, exhaling a long breath of air. He glances at the floor, then back up again, his features gentle. The hardness is gone, both in his expression and in his voice. "But not on these terms," he says. "Not with you messing with your education. Because I swear, Eden, I fucking swear…if this is just because you don't want to be over in Chicago while I'm here, then don't do this. It's so damn irrational, and you're making me feel guilty for it, like I'm the reason you want to give up that school."

Ah, I think. *That's why he's acting like this.*

Slowly, I approach him again, my eyes locked with his as I make my way across the floor. I stop only a few inches in front of him and glance up, my gaze sincere. "When I ask myself which city is the hardest to leave…" I murmur. "It's Portland, Tyler. I'm not doing this for you. I'm doing this for myself. You made your changes, now it's time for me to make mine."

Tyler's eyes are already widening in surprise as relief fills his expression. "You promise?"

Nodding, I close the small gap between us and wrap my arms around him once more, my body fitting against his. "I swear. I'm happier here," I tell him. "That's why I want to stay. I want to live my life here."

He moves his hands to my face, gently cupping my jaw as his warm skin brushes against mine. Tilting his face closer to me, he studies my expression carefully, before he quietly asks, "Are you sure about this?"

"I don't think I've ever been more sure about anything in my life."

"Then move in with me," he whispers, skimming his lips over mine, so softly and so delicately that a shiver surges straight down my spine. "Move in with me," he says again, his face brightening with a smile as his words become more rushed. He continues to plant a series of sharp, eager kisses against my lips until *move in with me, move in with me, move in with me* is the only thing I can hear. "I may not have much furniture yet, but I do have freshly painted walls. Nice neighborhood. Lots of dogs. A short drive downtown." He's grinning by the time he pulls his mouth back from me. "What do you say? Surely this is much better than the student dorms."

"I say *hell yeah!*" We both laugh, then I press my lips back to his for a lingering moment. "But first things first," I say, leaning back from him, "I need to go back to Santa Monica as soon as possible. I'm going to book a flight back."

Tyler's perplexed again, as though he can't possibly see a reason why I would need to go back home. "Why?"

"Because there're so many things I need to fix," I admit, heaving a long sigh. The thought of going home to deal with my parents is daunting. "Before we all went to Sacramento, I was arguing with my mom, so I owe her an apology, but the main thing is that I need to set things straight with my dad. I need to tell him that we're together, but I also need to find out where he and I stand with each other, because right now, I have no idea."

"Okay," Tyler says, nodding. He gets it because he knows how damaged my relationship with my dad currently is. "We can leave on Saturday, drive down through the night, then take the Pacific Coast Highway back home on Sunday. What do you think? Nothing beats a summer road trip along the coast."

"Oh," I say, stepping back again. I would have gone on my own. It's too much to ask of Tyler to take more time off work. "I wasn't expecting you to come too."

"I know," he says, "but there's some things I have left to fix too. I need to tell my mom that Dad's back in my life, and I really need to talk to my brothers, especially Jamie. Besides, I think both of us should break the news to our parents that we're officially together, because this time around, you're not dealing with all of this on your own."

Knowing he's going to be with me is reassuring, and I like that feeling of us being in this together. "Then great," I say, "I'd love for you to be there. Now pass me a paintbrush and let's finish painting my living room."

Tyler releases a loud laugh, then sets his phone back down on the window ledge as he restarts the music. He kisses my cheek as he drifts past me in search of a paintbrush, then when he finds one, he dips it into the bucket of paint and hands it to me. We get started on the walls again, our walls, humming to the music and casting smiles over our shoulders to one another.

I know then that I've made the right decision, that Portland is the best place for me, and we are heading back to Santa Monica in two days to deal with our parents once and for all, to set things right, to tell the truth, to fix things. But unlike last time, we're not scared. This time, we are ready.

♥

chapter
23

The walk back to Tyler's apartment isn't that bad. It's Friday evening, just after 9:00 p.m., and the sun has only just disappeared beneath the horizon, leaving the air warm and the sky a deepening blue. Fridays, Tyler has informed me, are now our official date nights, which means that every Friday from now on, I get to dress up nice, as does he. Tonight, he has taken me out for dinner at a popular French restaurant in the downtown area, and now we are currently making the forty-minute walk back home, with my skirt swaying in the breeze.

"I still can't believe the waiter spilled that drink on you," I say, looking to Tyler. There's still a damp stain on his blue button-down shirt, and I'm giggling as soon as I spot it.

"That's why he only got half the tip," Tyler says, laughing alongside me. His hand is in mine, and although he should really be at the center right now, Emily has his shift covered, which means that tonight, he's all mine.

We're only a couple of blocks away from the apartment, but Tyler suddenly stops walking. "Jump up," he says, letting go of my hand. He nods over his shoulder toward his back then crouches down low.

"I'm wearing a skirt," I say.

"So?"

It doesn't take much for Tyler to convince me to do just about anything these days. I'm giving in already. Placing my hands on his shoulders, I pull myself onto his back. He slides his hands under my thighs as he stands back up again, straight and tall. He begins to walk rather effortlessly as I play with his hair, twirling the thick strands around my fingers.

"Can I ask you something?" Tyler says quietly, breaking the comfortable silence that had settled over us.

"Sure," I say. My cheek is resting on the top of his head, his hair soft against my skin.

"Were you really that mad on the Fourth of July?"

The question is so out of the blue that I have to lift my head and think about it for a second. I can't see his face, so I can't read his expression. "Well, yeah," I admit, shrugging against his body. Ella must have told him. "That's like *our* day. We've always been together on the Fourth, except the year you moved to New York, and I don't know, Tyler... don't you think it just feels special? The Fourth of July is kind of where everything started for us."

"Didn't everything start when you kissed me?" he teases, attempting to glance over his shoulder at me. I'm glad he can't see me because right now I'm so totally blushing.

"Can you blame me? I was sixteen and I hated you. Kissing you was the only way forward." We both burst into laughter, and as the apartment complex comes into view at the end of the street, Tyler sets me back down on the sidewalk. His hand immediately finds mine and our pace falls back into sync, side by side once more, strolling aimlessly toward the entrance of the courtyard.

"So you *were* really that mad, huh?" I hear Tyler murmur, and when I glance at him, he has a smirk on his lips and one eyebrow raised.

But before I can say anything, he places both his hands on my shoulders and spins me around, gently pushing me forward. In that instant, there's a collective yell of, "*Surprise!*"

290

The outburst startles me, and for a moment I'm frozen beneath Tyler's hold. I blink, trying to absorb the scene in front of me.

The place is entirely different to how we left it only hours ago. There's a string of mini U.S. flags tangled around the branches of the trio of trees that stand tall in the middle of the courtyard, with even larger flags poking into the grass, blowing very softly in the small breeze. Music immediately starts playing too, from a speaker that I can't quite spot. A collection of lanterns spreads out across the courtyard, creating a warm glow in the darkening sky.

But the thing that really takes me by surprise is the circle of deck chairs surrounding a makeshift fire pit on the center patch of grass and the people rising from them with wide grins on their faces.

Emily's here. Amelia too. Mikey from the coffee shop. Gregg from the movie theater.

And Rachael's here. And so is Snake.

I'm so shocked that I don't even react. I can only stare blankly at them all with my mouth slightly agape, trying to process what's going on.

Tyler's hands drop from my shoulders down to my hips. He latches firmly on to my body as he pulls me back against him. I feel him lean forward over my left shoulder, with his stubble tickling my cheek and his breath hot against my neck. He presses his lips to my jaw and then in a breathy whisper, he says, "Happy Fourth of July, baby."

I shake my head in disbelief, still staring at our small audience that is beginning to laugh at my expression. "But that…that was two weeks ago."

Tyler laughs too as he steps back and twirls me around to face him. He has that remarkable grin of his on his face, the same grin that was once so rare but is now so normal. His eyes are bright and glistening as they smolder down at me. "Yes," he answers, "but we're celebrating the Fourth *again*. Together this time."

It's then that I register what all of this is, and my shock and confusion is immediately replaced by joy and disbelief that Tyler has done all of this for me, because he knows he should have been with me the first time around. My expression immediately turns into an unbelievably wide grin as I stretch onto the very tips of my Converse and wrap my arms around him. No one has ever done something like this for me before.

Tyler hugs me back just as tight, and after I pull away from him, I turn back around to study our company.

Rachael is the first person I run to. I haven't seen her since the day I left for Sacramento, and there is so much that has happened since then that I really need to tell her about. She's wearing that American bandana in her hair again, the same one from the real Fourth of July. I seem to have accidentally nudged it out of place as I draw her into a tight hug because she quickly adjusts it once we pull away from one another. As always, she bears the overwhelming scent of her signature perfume. Her hair is in loose waves, her makeup noticeable but not too heavy.

"What are you doing here?" I question, because Rachael has never once stepped foot in the state of Oregon, let alone Portland, believing we're all nothing but tree huggers.

"Tyler's skilled when it comes to persuasion," she tells me, nodding in his direction. I've only just noticed that there's a drink in her hand. I wonder what it is. "He actually called me up a few days ago, but I kept refusing his calls, and so he called our fucking landline. Who the hell, in the twenty-first century, calls someone's *landline*? Talk about persistent." She shakes her head, and I'm smiling as I listen to her because this is all just so typically Rachael. I love the way she gets so worked up about the smallest of things, and I love the way she relays the information back to me even more. "So my dad walks into my room like, *Tyler Bruce is on the phone*, and I'm thinking to myself, *Are you kidding me?* So I take the call, only so I can tell him to leave me the fuck alone, but then he starts asking me to come all the way up to Portland for the weekend. We spoke for, like, twenty minutes. And I thought this whole idea was cute, so here I am. Ain't a party without your best friend by your side, right?" She bumps her hip against mine while winking, then thrusts the red cup she's holding into my hand. "Here. Keep it. I'll make myself another."

My eyes drift to the guy standing by her side, who is none other than Stephen Rivera. I haven't seen him since last summer in New York, where I know he's spent the past year finishing up his senior year at college. He looks exactly as I remember him, with his pale blue eyes that are almost gray and his short blond hair, with a crooked smile and an expression that is forever playful and mischievous. However, his skin is a lot tanner than I remember. He's also wearing a huge flag as a cape, tied in a knot around his neck.

"Stephen! You're here too?"

"Um, hell fucking yes I'm here," Snake says. His Boston accent is still as thick as ever. With a can of beer in one hand, he throws his other arm around my shoulders for a brief hug. When he moves a step back, he takes a quick sip of his beer and adds, "I'm here to celebrate the Fourth of July on July Eighteenth, like every other normal person does."

Over the sound of the music, I laugh and gently push his shoulder. Snake's always been a joker, and I'm in such a good mood I can't seem to stop smiling. "When did you guys get here?"

"This morning," Rachael answers. She and Snake exchange a glance as they beam at one another, then she links her arms through his and huddles closer to him. "Stephen drove to Santa Monica first, then we flew up together."

Curious, I give them a questioning look. Last summer, they went on a couple of dates in the limited time that Rachael had in New York, and they seemed to really like each other. "Together?"

"Yeah," Snake says. "I actually moved to Phoenix last month, after graduating and finding a job. That means"—he pauses, beaming to Rachael—"I'm only a five-hour drive from this beauty." That'll explain his tan. He slides his arm out from around Rachael's and throws it over her shoulders instead, ruffling her hair and sticking his tongue out at her.

Rachael's never once mentioned Snake in the past year. She's never told me that he was in Phoenix nor that they've been in contact, and the more I think about this, the more something becomes clear. "All those times you were visiting your grandparents…" I murmur, cocking my head at her with a suspicious yet teasing glint in my eyes. "Were you really just in Phoenix?"

Rachael's face immediately floods with color as she blushes, sheepish at the fact that she's kept it such a secret. Snake's a great guy. He's hilarious, and they're both so similar that I really do think they're a great match. There's nothing she needed to hide from me.

"Yes," she admits, covering her face with her hands, too embarrassed to look at me. "I didn't want to tell you because I didn't want to be that best friend that gushes about her boyfriend while you were so down about Tyler. I knew it would only make you feel worse, and don't say it wouldn't have, because you used to glare at every other couple you ever walked past."

She has a point, and as much as I want to defend myself and the shitty mood I was in constantly, I can't. My eyes widen as a pleased grin spreads across my face. "Boyfriend?" I throw Snake a glance. He looks smug as he holds Rachael even closer and tighter against him.

"Uh-huh," Rachael says, and the glow that radiates from her as she smiles tells me everything: she's happy, and she deserves to be. "And you and Tyler, huh?! Where the hell did that come from?"

"I guess we just stopped worrying," I tell her, but even my voice feels light and feathery, like the positive energy that's running through my veins is sinking into every fiber of my being.

"Aww," Snake coos. He pats my head the way he did a year ago when I first met him. "My roommates are growing up. Also, it's about fucking time this happened." The three of us laugh, and I think Rachael's shock and anger at Tyler and I being together has subsided, because right now, she seems to accept it.

"I'll go grab you a beer," Snake tells me, then strolls off after pressing a quick departing kiss to Rachael's temple.

As soon as he's gone, I flash my eyes back to Rachael, gaping at her. "I can't believe you guys are dating!"

She releases her excitement now, springing forward. "I know!"

"I'm so happy for you," I tell her, because honestly, I am. In the past, guys have tended to play her and mess with her head. Snake's not like that.

"Have you met Amelia yet?" I ask her then. Rachael's my best friend from Santa Monica, Amelia's my best friend from Portland, and Emily's my best friend from New York. The first time Rachael met Emily last summer, they got along well, so I'm hoping she'll like Amelia too. Having my best friends not get along is definitely not part of the perfect life I'm trying to build for myself.

"Yeah, Emily introduced us," Rachael says. She grabs her drink out of my hand and takes a long sip before she passes it straight back again. "She complains just as much as I do, so I love her already. Someone should set her up with the hot guy from the coffee shop. That one." She lifts an unsteady finger, and my eyes follow in the direction she's pointing, straight to Mikey.

It's different seeing him without his black shirt and apron on. He's wearing a tank top now, his fully tattooed arms on display, and his biceps are a lot more muscular than they seem at first glance. He's standing around the fire pit alongside Tyler and Snake, laughing about something as they crack open some more beers.

"You're right. He's super nice too," I say, looking back to Rachael. "And Amelia's been trying to set up Emily with Gregg. The short one."

"He's cute too," Rachael comments, nodding in approval.

I grin at her, glad that both she and Snake have made the journey here just for this yard party because it sure wouldn't be the same without them. I'm impressed by Tyler too. It was thoughtful of him to invite them, getting all the people I care most about to be here.

With Rachael by my side, we saunter over to the circle of deck chairs around the fire pit to join everyone else. Snake hands me a fresh beer, which I thank him for, and I exchange a wide smile of gratitude with Tyler over the glow of the fire, right before I sink down into a chair next to Emily. Amelia is next to her, then Gregg.

"Welcome back to the Fourth of July," Emily says. She leans forward, clinking her beer against mine and then chugging the remainder of it all at once.

I'm not sure how long everyone else has been waiting for Tyler and me to come home, but judging by the amount of empty beer cans and plastic cups stashed into a trash bag by the trees, it seems they've been here for a while. I run my eyes over Emily's outfit too. She's wearing that black skirt she picked out earlier in the week. It seems that *this* is the party she was talking about.

"Did you seriously not have any idea about this?" Amelia pipes up, pulling her bare legs up onto the deck chair and crossing them. She has a drink in each hand. "Tyler's been planning it all week. He told us all about it on Tuesday, so we've been keeping it a secret since then, but really? You didn't know?"

"No idea whatsoever. He's never once mentioned the Fourth of July until right before we got here," I admit, taking a sip of my beer. I have never been someone who loves parties, but this type of party is different. A small one, with only the people who really matter around you, and with nothing but good vibes in the air. This kind is the best.

Amelia pouts and says with a small hiccup, "Aww! Tyler's so sweet to do this for you, Eden!" I think she may be tipsy already. That's another thing she has in common with Rachael: not only are they both full-time complainers, but also lightweights.

I can't hide my smile. I feel so lucky to have Tyler, someone who goes to such lengths just to see me happy.

"Emily," I say, glancing over at her, "who's at the center?"

"No one," Emily answers, laughing. "We're closed for the night under special circumstances."

My gaze moves to Gregg. He's watching the three of us talk, a small smile on his lips, and I realize I've never actually spoken to him. I saw him briefly yesterday at the theater, but I'm not sure if he even knows my name yet. I look at Amelia and raise my eyebrows suggestively, throwing a pointed look in Gregg's direction.

"Oh," she says after the realization hits her. "Eden, this is Gregg. Gregg, this is Eden."

"Hey," I offer. Amelia has most likely insisted that he be here tonight, so that she has another opportunity to set him and Emily up. Right now, Emily doesn't seem to mind, otherwise she would be nowhere near him.

"What's up?" Gregg asks, and the deepness of his voice takes me aback. It doesn't match his appearance, and now I'm beginning to wonder if he's a lot older than I first thought. He's definitely cute, and with his eagerness aside, I'm starting to think that maybe Emily should just give the guy a chance.

"Alright," I hear Tyler say, and we all glance over to him. I don't know who's controlling the music, but whoever it is, they lower it. Rachael and Snake drop down into a pair of deck chairs, and Mikey sinks onto the grass, drawing his knees up to his chest as he continues to nurse his beer. The fire continues to crackle as it lights up our faces with a warm, orange glow.

"I was going to get fireworks," Tyler tells us, "but I didn't want to have the cops turning up. Those days are over. Sorry, Eden." He chuckles at me, then clears his throat. His can of beer is dangling from his fingertips by his thigh. "But we can party out here for as long as we want, as long as we turn the music down after midnight. I've spoken to all my neighbors and told them what this is for, and even though I can see Mrs. Adams watching us from her window right now, she's totally cool with this. Told them all that they can even come out and join us if they want. They've promised not to tell our landlord. And one last thing," he says, glancing at me once more, grinning as he holds up his beer. "Happy Fourth of July, everyone."

Emily dramatically applauds while Snake whoops, and we all hold up our drinks in unison, simultaneously cheering, "Happy Fourth of July!" The neighbors in this small complex may be cool with what we're doing tonight, but that doesn't mean they don't think we're idiots for it. We're celebrating our nation's independence two weeks late, as though it's perfectly normal. I love how spontaneous and unique this all feels, creating even more special moments for me to cherish and hold on to.

"Actually," I say loudly through the clash of voices as I get to my feet, "while you're all listening, there's something I need to tell you."

Tyler flashes me a look of concern, but it doesn't take him long to figure out for himself what I'm about to say. He knows exactly what it is, and he must approve of my decision to tell everyone at this moment because he gives me a single nod and a reassuring smile as he presses his can of beer to his lips, watching me intently from over the rim.

Everyone else, on the other hand, is staring at me with curiosity and intrigue. So I don't keep them waiting, and as I kick anxiously at the grass with my Converse, I bite down on my lip before glancing back at them. I run my eyes around the circle, and I realize that these people right here…these are the people who really matter to me.

"I'm transferring to Portland State," I announce, releasing the breath I'm holding. "I'm moving here to Portland."

There's a split second of silence until a deafening scream of excitement escapes Amelia's lips. She drops both drinks and leaps out of her chair, hurling her body into mine and almost knocking me off my feet. Now I can tell that she's definitely tipsy, because as she locks her arms around me, she can't stop squealing in my ear while jumping up and down, almost dislocating my shoulder. We'll be attending the same college, just like she always wanted us to. Her reaction has me grinning, until I open my eyes and look over her shoulder to find Rachael's expression faltering. Her face falls in disappointment as she watches Amelia and I together, and I'm not sure whether she's jealous of us or if she's just taking time to absorb the news I've shared.

Amelia finally lets go of me, and as the volume of the music increases again, everyone starts mingling with each other while throwing me remarks such as "That's so awesome!" and "No fucking way!"

Rachael, however, hasn't said anything. She's sitting still and alone in her chair, appearing out of place against the movement of everyone else. Her eyes stare blankly at the grass, her grasp tight around her drink. I navigate around the fire pit, weaving my way past Snake and Gregg, and then sit down in the deck chair next to her. I don't know what to say, but luckily I don't have to say anything at all, because

Rachael glances up from the ground with her eyes wide, quietly asking, "You're seriously moving?"

"Yeah," I say, shrugging. To Amelia and Emily, the idea of me moving to Portland seems great because it's where they are. To Rachael, however, it means I'll be leaving Santa Monica. I may already live in a completely different state, but we both always knew that Chicago was just temporary until I graduated. Moving to Portland is permanent.

"But you're still going to come back to Santa Monica to visit, right?" she queries, her words quick, almost panicked. "Just like you do now? For Thanksgiving and Christmas? For summer?"

"Duh," I say, trying to lighten the mood. I nudge my knee against hers and give her a small smile. "Besides, it looks like you'll be in Phoenix half the time anyway. You won't even miss me."

"True," she says, blushing again as her eyes latch on to Snake. I wonder if she even realizes that she smiles whenever she so much as glances at him. He's talking to Tyler, and I'm so thrilled to know that he lives much closer to us all now. Maybe we'll get to see him more often. "And by the way," Rachael murmurs, fixing her gaze back on me, "you were right. I was *so* wrong about him."

At first I think she's talking about Snake, but then she nods to Tyler. I've spent a long time trying to convince her that he has changed, that his head's in a better place now and that he's much happier, but I think it's one of those things where people can really only believe it if they see it for themselves firsthand. "He's different, isn't he?"

"Completely," Rachael agrees. Her eyes flicker to the drink she's holding, then she presses the cup to her lips and takes a sip. Suddenly, she shoots upright and dumps the drink on the grass, grabbing my arm and almost yanking me off the chair. She holds my forearm up in front of her face, only she's grasped my left, which has nothing but that awful dove on my wrist, so she lets go and reaches for my right instead. She studies *No te rindas*, rolling her eyes at the tattoo and shaking her head at me with a teasing smirk on her face. "Still stupid," she mutters under her breath, but I know she's just kidding. "Although when it comes to dating Tyler…not so stupid. I can see now why it was so easy for him to win you over, because he's won me over too, and I know you don't need anyone's approval, but you definitely have mine."

I can do nothing but grin at her, relieved that *finally* she has seen Tyler for who he really is.

As the music bounces around the courtyard, I get to my feet and pull her up with me. We danced on the first Fourth of July, so it's only right to dance on the second. My hand finds hers, and I twirl her around on the grass while whipping my hair around, dramatically nodding my head in sync with the music. Amelia rushes over to join us, dragging Emily with her, and as the music seems to increase in volume once again, the four of us dance together. There's some air guitars, some cartwheels. Some lousy footwork, some falls, but the entire time, we are laughing.

When I pause to catch my breath, I'm still grinning as I watch my best friends, perfectly wrapped around each other as they sway together like they've been friends for years. And I realize how lucky I am to finally have three incredible best friends, the kinds of friends who accept me for who I am no matter how crazy my decisions in life may seem, the kinds of friends who are willing to dance like fools with me in the courtyard of an apartment complex in Portland as we celebrate the Fourth of July on July Eighteenth.

Lately, everything just feels that way. Just *finally*, like I've waited my entire life for things to be this way. It's the only word that's running through my head, so heavy that it's pressing down on me.

Finally, finally, finally.

Finally, everything is starting to feel perfect. Finally, I'm truly happy.

As the night wears on and the sky shifts from blue to black, we all end up slumped around the fire pit, slouched in our deck chairs and playing Truth or Dare. Mikey has climbed a tree in nothing but his boxers. Amelia has confessed to getting arrested a second time, this time for skinny-dipping in the Willamette last summer. Rachael has downed a beer, only to throw it straight back up.

It's just after midnight, and although it's dark, the lanterns keep the courtyard lit and the fire keeps us warm. I have Emily on my left and Tyler sitting on the grass to my right. It's Snake's turn to spin the empty beer can we've been using, and it lands on me. His eyes glint with glee as he leans back in his chair, feigning deep consideration and rubbing his chin. Then he sits back up and smirks deviously at me. Loud and clear without offering me a choice between a truth or a dare, he says, "I dare you to kiss your stepbrother."

We all know he's just being playful and teasing as always, but everyone else decides to join in on the act too. Gregg is saying, "Whoa, dude, that's totally crossing the line," and Amelia is gasping in fake disbelief.

"Yeah, Stephen," Rachael says, clucking her tongue in mock disapproval. "Too far."

I glance at Tyler, who's shaking his head at the grass as he bites back laughter. For once, I think he's actually blushing, and when he looks up and his eyes meet mine, I decide to joke around too. Scrunching my face up in disgust and making my voice as high-pitched as possible, I simply say, "Ewww. That's *so* gross."

And then I promptly spring off my chair, straight into Tyler's embrace, throwing my body against him. Within a heartbeat, my lips have found his, and I'm kissing him there on the lawn, sitting in his lap with his hand on the small of my back, holding me close. I'm smiling against his mouth, my eyes squeezed tightly shut as I hold his jaw in my hands. The kiss is energetic and fast, fueled by the rush of excitement at kissing him with an audience.

When I hear Rachael start to cheer, I can't hold back my giggling, so I throw my head back and release a laugh into the air. My cheeks are flushed.

"That's all you've got?" Tyler challenges. When I tilt my face back down to his, he has a mischievous look on his face and his eyes are daring me to kiss him again.

I move my lips to his ear so that no one but him can hear me, and in a quiet whisper, I murmur, "That's all I've got until we head back inside."

Sharply, I press a kiss to the edge of his jaw and then roll off him. His expression is priceless as he stares at me, the seduction evident across my features, and he swallows hard.

Emily cracks a yawn then as the laughter dies down, and Mikey checks his watch. It's 12:30 a.m., and although it's still technically early when it comes to parties, we're all exhausted. We've enjoyed the night and we've enjoyed each other's company. It's been our own personal Fourth of July. It's been special. I think now is as good a moment as any to turn in, and everyone seems to think the same because they get to their feet and stretch their legs.

With there being only eight of us, everyone feels as though they have some responsibility to help clean up. We close up the deck chairs and stack them into a pile, and we tear down the flags from the trees and pull them out of the grass. We throw all the empty cans and cups into trash bags, and we turn off all of the lanterns, and then finally, we extinguish the fire until only a tiny flicker of a flame remains.

Mikey is the first to leave. His younger sister turns up to give him a ride, and he promises that the next time I drop by the shop for coffee, it's on the house. Amelia and Gregg catch a cab, and Emily ends up joining them. I think maybe Gregg is growing on her. Rachael and Snake are the final two left as they wait for their own cab to turn up to take them back to their hotel downtown.

"Are you only here for tonight?" I ask Rachael. We're leaning against the fence, watching the street as we wait for a cab's headlights to come into view.

"Yeah," she says, shrugging. "We fly home tomorrow. Stephen has to go back to work on Monday, so we couldn't exactly stick around to explore this lame old city. Your words, not mine."

Gently, I elbow her in the ribs. "It's not *that* lame," I say, although she's right. I did once think that about Portland. Not anymore. "By the way, we're going back home on Sunday to talk to our parents, so I'll drop by your place before we travel back up."

"Ah," she says, pulling a face, "your parents. Do they know yet?"

"No," I admit. "Not unless Jamie has told them."

"Well, good luck."

Just as the words leave her lips, their cab pulls up outside the apartment complex. We draw each other into one final farewell hug as Tyler and Snake approach us. I've loved having both Rachael and Snake here tonight, so I hug him too, and just before the two of them slip inside the cab, we promise to meet up again soon. Maybe like a double date.

The doors slam shut, and the cab accelerates off down the road, leaving Tyler and I alone for the first time in hours. The courtyard is in dark silence now, and it feels odd after it being so full of life only twenty minutes ago. The air is much cooler too, and I'm getting a slight chill, so I fold my arms tightly across my chest and hug my body as I drift toward the remnants of the fire. There's nothing but a glow of ashes as the flame burns out.

I feel Tyler following across the small lawn behind me, and I end up pausing at the fire pit, absorbing its dying warmth. Tyler lingers on the opposite side, staring back at me through the darkness of the night. It's almost 1:00 a.m.

"Thank you," I tell him, my voice quiet. My eyes never leave his. They're twinkling back at me, vivid and glossy. "Just…thank you for doing this, Tyler. It seriously means a lot."

Tyler gives me a solemn nod, then he kicks at the ashes of smoke. He looks so perfect right now, with his hands in his pockets and his features soft, his lips forming a small smile and his gaze full of love. "Anything for you," he murmurs.

The glow of the ashes dies out then, fading to black as Tyler captures my lips with his, as perfectly as always.

chapter
24

We left for Santa Monica late Saturday evening, drove through the night, and took turns in the driver's seat, switching every couple of hours to let each of us catch some sleep in between. By 8:00 a.m. the following morning, Tyler took over for the remainder of the journey, and I fell into a deep slumber, curled up against the passenger seat with the radio on low, Tyler's hand on my thigh, and a smile on my lips.

I don't wake again until just before noon. I must have a sixth sense because my eyes are fluttering open just as Tyler is following the exit road off the 405 and into the city we will no longer call home. The sudden brightness of the sun shining through the windshield dazzles me, and my eyes feel strained as I push myself up and pull the sun visor down.

"Oh," Tyler says once he notices I'm awake, casting his gaze quickly on me out the corner of his eye while trying to keep his attention on the road. "Morning. We're here."

I run a hand back through my hair and shift my gaze to my right, studying the city through the car window. I love Santa Monica. It's a great city, but for reasons that are so different than the reasons I love Portland. I love the pier and the beach, the surrounding cluster of amazing cities and neighborhoods to explore, the glamor of Hollywood and the occasional A-list celebrity who slips past you unnoticed. I graduated from high school here. I met Tyler here. My family is here.

I'll always have ties to this city, but Portland has always, always been my home.

I look to Tyler as he brakes for a stop sign. "Can we go to my mom's first?" I ask him. We don't exactly have a plan to follow. I think we're both just winging it. "I need to be fully awake before I try to deal with my dad."

Tyler nods and takes a sharp right, accelerating a little too roughly down the street. He seems on edge, more so than I am, and I know exactly why. He's terrified of telling Ella about his dad, the same way he was terrified of telling me. I think he's worried she's going to be furious at him for being in touch with his father again, and honestly, I'm not too sure how she's going to take the news. Shocked, yes. Pleased, no. I don't think she's ever forgiven Peter for everything he has done, and I doubt she's going to feel comfortable with him being around Tyler again. But Tyler knows what he's doing, and Ella's always been so understanding and caring, so I believe she'll trust him on this the same way I have.

I, on the other hand, have to deal with both my parents today. My mom first, then my dad. But it's my dad I'm dreading the most. I'm not nervous because I'm ready to stand up to him now after so long of sitting back. I have spent the past couple of days preparing exactly what I'm going to tell him. I have the words etched into my mind, ready to spill out as soon as I get the chance. I don't want to be aggressive with him. I just want to be honest because there is nothing more meaningful and raw than sincerity, and I hope Dad will appreciate that more than he would appreciate me yelling at him.

As we're approaching Mom's house, we inevitably have to pass Dean's. Every time I have passed his house this past year, I have experienced the most sickening feeling in my stomach as my throat dries. Usually, I can't bear to so much as glance at the house, but today, I'm staring.

Tyler releases a slow breath of air so softly that it's almost inaudible. I wonder if we'll ever forgive ourselves for the wrong we committed against Dean and if he'll ever forgive us. Tyler and I have made a lot of mistakes in the past, but we're learning from them.

A matter of minutes later, I can see my mom's place ahead. I'm relieved to find both her car and Jack's truck parked in the driveway.

"Is that my mom's car?" Tyler asks suddenly, squinting through the windshield. I follow the direction of his eyes until my gaze lands on the white Range Rover parked directly opposite my mom's house.

"It looks like it," I reply. My eyebrows knit together, perplexed, as I rack my brain for an explanation as to why Ella could possibly be parked there. "What's she doing here?"

Neither of us expected Ella to be here, and quite frankly, I don't know why she even is. She and my mom get along well, but they aren't close friends or anything. They stop and talk for a few minutes if they pass each other in the street, and they did get a little drunk together at my graduation party, but other than that, they haven't done much socializing, and they definitely don't drop by each other's houses for casual visits. Although Mom does like Ella, there will always be a hint of jealousy.

"No idea," Tyler says, shrugging. There's confusion on his face too as he pulls up behind Ella's car and shuts off the engine. He's been driving for a few hours now, and he heaves a sigh, relieved to have finally come to a stop. After rubbing at his bloodshot eyes, he steps out of the car.

I slide out after him, my body stiff and knotted from having slept in such an uncomfortable position. We exchange one final look of concern before we make our way up the small footpath to Mom's front door. Tyler's hand finds mine the way it always does, our fingers intertwining with unspoken reassurance and support.

Gucci must hear our footsteps as we approach because she starts barking before I've even touched the door handle. She's on the other side, her paws scratching against the wood. I know for a fact that she will tackle us both as soon as I swing the door open, so I knock instead, waiting patiently.

And now that I'm here at the front door, the nerves begin to hit me. I'm not sure how Mom's going to feel about me moving to Portland and transferring schools. Maybe she'll think I'm being totally ridiculous, or maybe she'll see it as a good thing. I have no idea. The only way to find out is to tell her.

The door creaks open a few inches, and Jack peers around the frame, holding Gucci back by her collar. When she sees me, she attempts to make a lunge, almost yanking Jack's arm straight out of its socket.

"Oh!" Jack exclaims, surprised. Last he and Mom knew, I was in Portland. "It's you. Come on in! This is great timing." He swings the door open fully and drags Gucci away from the threshold, allowing Tyler and me to step inside.

Gucci's tail is wagging so fast that I think it may just be hurting her, and she so desperately wants to come to me that she's even whining. I reach over and rub her ears playfully with my hands, then bend down to plant a kiss on the tip of her nose.

"Eden!" I hear Mom's voice say, and her tone is cheerful, obviously delighted to see me. I spin around to see her rushing across the living room toward me, a wide grin on her face, as though our argument before I left didn't even happen. With Mom, our forgiveness is always unspoken.

She throws her arms around me and hugs me tight, then steps back to examine me thoroughly. "How was Portland?" she asks teasingly. "I didn't expect you to be back so soon. I thought you'd stay there for at least a couple weeks. Did I pack enough clothes for you? I threw in your entire closet."

I laugh, thankful that there's no tension between us, and then my laughter subsides when I notice Ella getting to her feet from the couch. She's widening her eyes in surprise because neither Tyler nor I have told her that we were coming home today. Like Mom, I think she believes we would have stayed up in Portland for much longer than a week, but what they don't know is that we're going straight back tonight.

"What are you guys doing here?" Ella asks, blinking rapidly as she forces herself over to Tyler, hugging him briefly. She seems more worried than anything else.

"What are *you* doing here?" Tyler asks, giving her a questioning look. His gaze flickers between her and my mom. "What's going on?"

"We were just talking," Ella tells us quickly. For a moment, she looks unsettled, but then slowly, a smile spreads across her face as she exchanges a knowing glance with Mom. "And now I'm just passing on my congratulations," she adds.

"Congratulations?" I echo, firing Mom a look.

"Oh, Eden," Mom says, trying to suppress her grin, "I didn't want to tell you over the phone. I wanted to wait until you came home so that I could tell you in person."

"Tell me what, Mom?" I say very slowly, very firmly. I'm holding my breath.

She looks at Jack, beaming, and he smiles back at her from the doorway as he continues to hold Gucci. When Mom looks back at me, she jumps forward and thrusts her left hand at me. There's a dazzling ring on her finger, sparkling as the light hits it.

My mouth falls open, my jaw hanging low in disbelief. I hold her hand up to my face to study the silver and diamond ring, then I look over at Jack, staring at him in shock. He's grinning just as wide as Mom, and he gives me a nod as though to say, *Yes, I finally did it.*

I press both my hands over my mouth, absorbing the fact that my mother is *engaged*, and then I scream. Just like that, I release a squeal of excitement and drag her into a hug, tears cascading down my cheeks, dampening her shirt. Gucci even howls in sync with my screaming. I think Mom's crying too. I can't stop squeezing her. I'm so overwhelmed and so happy for her. I know how long she has waited for this and how badly she has wanted it. Jack treats her well, much better than Dad ever did, and they love each other immensely. It's about time Jack finally asked that all-important question.

I think Ella may start tearing up too as the excitement radiates across the room. She's fanning her eyes with her hands, like she's trying to stop herself from getting emotional, all the while smiling at us.

I run from Mom over to Jack, throwing myself against him too. Now I have a stepmom *and* a stepdad. Maybe having two sets of parents is being greedy, but I love it. I love Ella and I love Jack, and I couldn't have asked for two better people to become a part of my family.

With all the commotion that's going on, Gucci won't stop barking, and now that Jack has released her, she's running wild around the living room. Tyler has given my mom a brief hug and has shaken Jack's hand, congratulating them both.

"When?!" I ask Mom, wiping tears from my eyes, my grin never fading.

"Friday!"

I pull her back into another hug. This was definitely not what I expected to come home to, and I'm so distracted that I've forgotten why Tyler and I are even here. That is, of course, until Mom says, "Enough about me. I think Ella and I are desperate to know about *you* two." She wipes her eyes with the back of her hand and then narrows her curious gaze at Tyler and me.

Tyler glances up from ruffling Gucci's fur, his cheeks flushed. He attempts to suppress his sheepish smile, but he fails miserably at it as he straightens up, taking in Mom's and Ella's awaiting gazes. "Um," he begins. Anxiously, he scratches the back of his neck, and I'm trying not to laugh as I wait for him to just say it. I don't know why he's nervous because both our moms have already made it clear that they accept and support us. And besides, we've done this all before anyway. "So Eden and I are kind of…" He pauses, swallowing hard. I think it's from the pressure of having us all stare at him, impatiently waiting for those words to escape his lips. Taking a deep breath, he announces, "Eden and I are together."

"I knew it," Ella says, and her smile develops into a huge grin.

Mom's eyes never leave mine, and we can only smile back at each other, because for the first time in a long time, I think we are realizing that we are both happy. There appears to be pride in her expression, like she knows how hard it was for me to give Tyler a second chance, yet I still did it. Proud that I didn't follow in her footsteps of just giving up completely when things got tough. Proud that I took the time to hear Tyler out. Proud that we're now finally together without letting the fear of everybody else's opinion of us hold us back.

"Looks like our kids are dating each other," Mom tells Ella, and they both laugh, high on the joy and excitement that's already in the atmosphere.

I glance at Tyler, and he's already looking at me, appearing relieved. However, as our moms continue to crack jokes, he raises an eyebrow and nods to my mom, mouthing, "Portland." I'm glad he reminds me because I've been totally distracted. That's really the main reason why we're here: to tell my mom that I'm moving back to Portland for good, and that I'm going to continue school there.

I give Tyler a nod in return, and then I swallow and clear my throat. "Mom, there's something else."

Both Mom and Ella stop laughing, turning to look at me. This time, Mom's expression is full of concern. "Okay. What?" she asks, sitting down on the couch. Jack immediately joins her, placing an arm around her shoulders. Even Ella looks worried when Tyler nudges her down onto the opposite couch and he sits next to her, while I slide onto the rug in the center of the floor. I cross my legs, and Gucci pads over to me, demanding affection. Rubbing her soft ears helps to keep me calm.

"I've made a really big decision," I begin, staring into Gucci's big, round glossy eyes because I can't bring myself to look at Mom. I'm definitely nervous. "I've thought it all through, and it's what I want, so I'm not asking for your permission, I'm just letting you know what I'm doing." I glance up then, my eyes immediately latching on to Mom's, and I tell her, "I'm going to transfer to Portland State. I'm moving back to Portland." It's as simple and as straightforward as it sounds.

Mom sits forward, blinking at me. "You're leaving Chicago?"

"Yes," I say. "And I'm moving in with Tyler."

I catch Ella glance at him, and he gives her a small smile in return. Mom, on the other hand, has her eyes wide. She looks at Jack as though she's searching for some sort of reassurance from him, but I don't think he has an opinion on the matter because he just shrugs.

"Isn't this all just a little fast, Eden?" she asks when she glances back at me. Her lips have formed a frown, and I can see her shifting her position on the couch with unease as she thinks about the decision I've made. I know I'm taking a huge step, so she has every right to worry that I could be making a mistake, but I know in my heart that I'm not.

"I'm an adult," I remind her. "I know what I'm doing and I know what I want. Can you trust me on that?"

"Yes," Mom says. "I guess I can." She stands and then reaches for my hands, pulling me to my feet and ushering me into another hug. Yet this one is different. It's extremely tight and meaningful, conveying her support, which I seriously appreciate. I can never ask more of her. "If it's really what you want," she murmurs against my hair, "then you go for it, Eden."

I nod and pull away from her with a smile on my lips, full of gratitude and relief. I can tell that she doesn't believe my decision is the smartest, but she supports it, and that's enough.

"We're actually heading back to Portland today," I announce as I take a step back, careful not to trip over Gucci, who's circling my legs.

"Today?" Mom repeats.

"Yeah. We're taking the coastal route back. We're making it a road trip, stopping at each city along the way," Tyler explains, rising to his feet. He falls back into his permanent place by my side. "We're just here to make everything right."

I move closer to him, linking my arm with his. I may have planned at first to have come back on my own, but I'm glad he's here. Having him around only encourages me to make the changes I desperately need to make. "I'm going to talk to Dad," I say, glancing between Mom and Ella, and silence ensues.

After a few long moments, Ella stands and swallows. "We were actually just…just talking about you and him," she admits, and I furrow my eyebrows at her, waiting for her to explain further, but she only lets out a frustrated sigh. "He's been unbearable this week, Eden, ever since he found out that you both left for Portland. I don't know what to do anymore. I'm glad you've been gone because I don't want you to hear the things he's been saying." She seems almost guilty as she tells me this, like she's hurting my feelings. She's not, because it's nothing new. That's why I know there's something seriously wrong: no father should vocally express contempt for his daughter. "Are you sure you want to talk to him?" Ella asks gently. "Because I really don't think he's going to be all that nice."

"I'm talking to him," I state firmly, pressing my lips into a bold line.

No matter how much of a douche Dad has been this past week, I'm still going through with this. I'm going to stand up to him.

Ella and Mom both seem incredibly concerned. Maybe they think it's a bad idea for me to talk to Dad when he's already so furious at me, but I can't afford to wait around until he even remotely calms down because I could be waiting a very long time.

"Do you want me to come with you?" Mom offers hesitantly. I know she doesn't want to face Dad, but she's offering nonetheless, because she's my mom, and that's what moms do.

"No," I tell her, my voice clear. I can feel my courage building in my chest as my adrenaline starts to flow, and I just want to talk to him *now*. "I want to do it on my own. Is he at the house?"

"Yes," Ella says, albeit reluctantly.

"Great, then let's go." With a brave grin plastered on my face, I unhook my arm from around Tyler's and head back toward the front door, perfectly aware that each of their eyes are on me. I think even Tyler is surprised by how ready I am to do this.

"Let me get there first," Ella says quickly. Already, she's grabbing her purse from the couch and fumbling around inside it for the keys to her Range Rover. When she finds them, she comes rushing over to me. I don't think I've ever seen her look this distressed before, and she seems to have aged a decade within the space of a minute. "Let me warn him that you're both coming."

I think if I just spontaneously walked through the front door, Dad would most likely burst every single blood vessel in his head, so warning him that Tyler and I are coming isn't a bad thing. Maybe it'll give him time to release his anger before we get there. "Okay," I agree.

Ella offers me a weak smile then heads out the door while calling, "Congratulations again, Karen," over her shoulder. Then she almost breaks into a jog as she crosses the road and climbs into her car, the engine purring to life within seconds.

"Is he really that bad these days?" Tyler asks, turning to me once Ella has driven out of sight. He looks worried now too, mostly because neither of us has seen his mom so on edge before.

"He must be," I respond. Last week, he was such an asshole that I didn't think it was possible for him to get any worse, but apparently he has. I have no idea what to expect when I turn up at that house.

"I don't think he'll ever change," Mom remarks bitterly. She can't help herself. Every opportunity she gets to express her hatred for Dad, she'll take. "Eden, you are one brave human being."

I pull a face and shrug, but when I drop my eyes to the floor, the Converse on my feet grab my attention more than usual. Something's tugging at me, but I can't figure out what it is exactly, so I stare at my shoes in silence until finally it hits me. There's one last thing I need to do here before I say my good-byes to Mom, Jack, and Gucci, before we head over to Dad and Ella's place, before we head back to Portland. There's something I can't leave behind.

"Give me a second," I say.

Leaving Tyler with Mom and Jack, I dart toward the hall and through my bedroom door. It's much tidier than it was when I left it, so I figure Mom has cleaned up after me, and when I slide open the door to my closet, it's completely bare, nothing but a row of empty hangers. It looks like Mom really did pack my entire closet into that suitcase.

At the end of the summer, I will come home again to officially make my move to Portland, where I will stack the remainder of my belongings into cardboard boxes, which I will then pile into my car, ready for the long drive. So right now, I'm not thinking about grabbing the rest of my stuff. I'm only thinking about one thing and one thing only: the tattered old shoe box tucked away in the far corner of the shelf at the top of my closet.

Reaching up on my tiptoes, I stick my hand onto the shelf, searching through the pile of junk that has gathered here over the years, until finally, my hand hits the box. Skillfully, I manage to grab it and take it down. There's a thin layer of dust covering the lid, which I blow off before flipping it open.

Inside are my Converse, the pair Tyler gave me last summer in New York. The ones that have the original *No te rindas* scrawled along the rubber in Tyler's handwriting, with the ink still perfectly clear and bold.

Sitting on the corner of my bed, I slip off the red Chucks I'm already wearing and replace them with the white pair, Tyler's pair. They're coming home to Portland with me, and I'm never going to stop wearing them. I throw my red pair into the box and shove it back up onto the shelf, sliding my closet doors shut.

I once swore to myself that I would never wear them again, but yet I kept them, because deep down, I knew I still had some hope left. And I was right to have hope, and I was right to give Tyler another chance, and I was right to follow my heart, because sometimes, just sometimes, taking risks turns out to be worth it.

Dad's already waiting for us when we pull up to the house. He's standing at the front door, arms crossed, chest puffed out. His stance is threatening as he glares at us, and I think he may just be attempting to act as a barricade. With his eyes narrowing, his gaze follows Tyler's car. It is clear he doesn't want to have this discussion inside.

Tyler parks behind Jamie's car out on the street. He stares back at Dad through his window before he swallows hard and removes his seat belt, angling his body around to face me. He presses a hand to my headrest, then frowns. "And the plan is…?"

"You tell your mom the truth about your dad while I deal with the raging bull over there," I say, nodding over his shoulder. Dad's still watching us, *waiting*. Maybe he believes that if he looks menacing enough, it'll scare us off. Maybe he thinks his pathetic glower is enough to get us to give up and drive off.

"Sounds a hell of a lot easier than it actually is," Tyler murmurs. His nerves are rattling him, and it's evident in his features. He looks like he might just throw up.

"Tell her exactly what you told me," I say, reaching for his hand. I squeeze my fingers reassuringly around his, smiling gently. I think he definitely has it harder than me. Dealing with Dad is going to be tense and uncomfortable, but Tyler telling Ella the truth about his therapy and his father is going to be overwhelming and emotional, and I know just how difficult it is for Tyler to open up about these things. "She's your mom, Tyler. She'll understand. She always does."

"I know," he says, exhaling. He takes a deep breath and glances at our hands. Raising them, he rests his jaw against the back of my hand, his breath warm against my skin. "Are you sure you can handle your dad? He looks so pissed. I can talk to him with you."

I grind my teeth together and fix Tyler with a look that says I don't need his help. "Why don't any of you believe that I can deal with him on my own?" I ask, but my voice is soft. I'm not annoyed at him for offering, but I'm disappointed that both he and Mom have felt as though I'm not strong enough to defend myself against Dad. "I'm the one who needs to talk to him, and only me, because it's our relationship that's in turmoil. No one else can fix it for us."

Tyler drops our hands so that he can take in my expression fully, like he's searching for signs of weakness. But I'm not lying to myself: I *know* I can handle it. I *want* to handle it.

Right then, there's a thundering rap against the passenger window, startling us. I pull my hand away from Tyler's and spin toward the window. In response, Dad raps his knuckles so harshly against the glass that I'm surprised it doesn't shatter.

"If you're so eager to come talk to me, then get out of the damn car!" he orders, bending down to glower at us. Up close, there's a fire in his eyes that is sparked by hatred and fueled by contempt.

"What a jerk," I hear Tyler mutter. He would never say it to Dad's face these days, but that doesn't mean he can't still think it. And he's right because Dad *is* a jerk. A jerk who is pounding relentlessly on the windows of Tyler's car, as though he's a kid. It's sad, really. He's supposed to be the parent, yet he's the most childish. Slowly, Tyler pushes open his car door and steps out onto the sidewalk.

I follow suit, swinging the door wide and almost hitting Dad with it. "Damn it, Eden!" he growls.

It's an accident because he's the one in the way, but nonetheless, he is adamant in believing that I've done it on purpose.

"Are you trying to break my hip?" he hisses at me. I'm starting to forget what his regular voice sounds like because his gruff tone is the only one I've heard for so long.

"No," I say, fixing him with a hard look as I shut the door and move around to join Tyler. "I'm trying to be civil with you. Can you at least do the same?"

"Civil," Dad barks. He even rolls his eyes, as though it's a bizarre request when really, it's the least I could possibly ask of him. Is it really too much for a father to just be calm? To just quit with the aggravation for once and hear his daughter out? Apparently, it is.

"Yes. Civil," Tyler says, and I shoot him an alarmed look, warning him not to step in for me. *Please*, I'm thinking. *Please don't start an argument.* And thankfully, he doesn't. "Just for Eden."

"Oh, look," Dad says, folding his arms across his chest and taking some thundering steps toward Tyler, "it's the drugged-up kid who dragged my daughter off to Portland."

Anger ripples through me, but I remind myself to keep it together, to continue breathing deeply. Showing aggression toward him today will not help, and although Dad's words are tainted by judgment and scorn, Tyler doesn't react. It's remarkable to not see him so much as clench his jaw.

Instead, he presses his lips together and takes a step away from Dad. "I'm not here to talk to you, Dave," he tells him calmly, but firmly. "I've already said what I needed to say to you, and you completely shut me down, so I'm not going to waste my breath trying to fight for you to like me. I'm a good guy, and if you can't see that, then that's your problem. I'm only here to talk to my mom and Jamie."

Dad's a little taken aback by his attitude, and as Tyler gives me a tight, reassuring smile before he leaves us and heads across the lawn to the front door, I can swear there's a flash of disappointment in Dad's expression. It's almost like he was *hoping* for Tyler to lash out so that his contempt for him could be justified. But the truth is, there aren't any reasons for Dad to loathe him anymore because Tyler has changed. The only thing he has done lately that is even remotely wrong is tell Dad that there was nothing going on between him and me anymore. That was a lie, but we were lying to ourselves too, so I'm not sure if it counts.

There's silence between Dad and me as we watch Tyler make his way toward the house. I know his anxiety will be killing him now, and I spot Ella at the living room window, peeking through the blinds at the scene outside. Upstairs, Jamie and Chase peer out my bedroom window but dart out of sight when they realize I've noticed them. Then Tyler is at the open door, quickly drifting over the threshold and disappearing inside.

"Dad," I voice, returning my gaze to the man standing opposite me. When I look at him, I feel nothing but a pain in my chest. He's my father. I should feel love, but I don't. "We need to talk," I say. "Really, really talk."

"I have nothing to say to you."

"Too bad, because I have *everything* to say to you." I turn toward the house and make a move for the front door. Behind me, Dad groans. Then, very reluctantly, his footsteps stomp across the lawn after me. I think he knows he's going to have to talk to me whether he wants to or not.

He follows me into the house, saying nothing. The house is silent too, and I glance into the living room as we pass, only to find Chase sitting on the edge of the couch, anxiously playing with his hands.

"Hey," I say, stepping into the room. He looks up. "Where's your mom and Tyler?"

"The office," Chase says, shrugging.

"And Jamie?"

"He's there too." Chase looks almost sad, like he's desperate to have some involvement in everything that's going on rather than constantly being left out of the important conversations that happen within this house, but the reality is that there's just too much he doesn't know about his family's past and too much for him to learn. Ella has always made it clear that the truth would hurt him more than the lies do. "Are you going to have a fight?" he asks, frowning at Dad and me. "Because I don't think you should fight. I'm bored of the fighting. Can we all go to Florida instead?"

"We're not going to have a fight," I reassure him, although maybe I'm lying. My intentions are to remain calm and confident, but I may just explode in a fit of rage if Dad pushes me enough. "We're just going to talk and sort some things out."

"And your mom and I will take you and Jamie to Florida," Dad adds gently, and the sudden change in his tone is infuriating. When I cast a glance over my shoulder at him, he's giving Chase a smile, and I will never understand the way he can be so great with Jamie and Chase but not with Tyler and me. The boys aren't even his own kids. I am.

Chase almost falls off the couch with excitement. Ever since Christmas, he hasn't shut up about the damn Sunshine State, so his face lights up with joy. "Really?"

"Really," Dad confirms with a nod. "But only if you stay here and let me talk to Eden. Alright, buddy?"

Chase nods back with enthusiasm, scrambling across the room to grab the TV remote. He turns it on and quickly flicks through the channels, finding something to watch as he settles into the couch, attempting to look busy and distracted.

Oh, Chase, I think. He will never know the truth about his family's past. Maybe in a few years Ella will decide to tell him the truth about his real father. But for right now, my dad is his dad.

I retreat out of the living room, pulling the door shut after me. Then I look at Dad. Of course, his smile is gone and his scowl has returned. "The kitchen?" I suggest. I don't want to go upstairs because that will distract Tyler from his own task, so I lead the way down the hall and into the kitchen. It may be Sunday, but there is nothing peaceful about this house right now.

Dad stands at the opposite side of the island in the center of the kitchen, his hands pressed against the countertop as he impatiently drums his fingers. Not impressed, he stares at me, waiting.

"Sit down," I tell him. I want to be in control, and having him tower over me doesn't exactly put me at ease. He looks more threatening that way, and I'm not here to challenge him. I'm here to be honest with him.

"I'm not sitting down," he argues.

"Sit. Down."

The firmness to my voice continues to surprise him, and I'm so relieved that today he isn't putting up much of a fight. I'm driven by determination, and I think he must see this in my expression because he's giving up much quicker than he usually does. I'm so adamant on talking to him that he's not even attempting to stop me.

Heaving another sigh of defeat, he pulls out a chair from the table and sits down, leaning back and crossing his arms again. "Alright, Eden," he says. "What is it?"

I run my eyes over him, really studying his expression. He doesn't seem so furious now that Tyler isn't here, but his eyes are still narrowed, conveying his annoyance. I don't know why we have allowed our relationship to get so strained. Once upon a time, we were close. I used to adore him the way a daughter always should. When I was younger,

I counted down the days until the weekend when Dad would get off work because I knew he'd have something cool lined up for us to do together. But it's all so different now. *We're* different now. The whole point of me coming to Santa Monica three years ago was to improve my relationship with him, but it seems to have done nothing but the opposite. All I can say to him is, "Why are we like this?"

There's an awkward silence that passes because neither of us can muster up an answer. I think we're broken because of multiple reasons that have built up over the years. It's hard to find the root cause of it all, although Dad isn't putting much thought into it, because he only shrugs and says, "You know why."

"No, actually, I don't," I say, leaning back against the island. "Can you tell me?"

Dad is silent again. He unfolds his arms and rubs his jaw, his eyes fixed on the floor. I've learned that Dad isn't great at being truthful, and as he contemplates whether or not he's actually going to give me an answer, he purses his lips. Then he meets my eyes and exhales. "Eden, why are you here?"

"I'm here because I have a dad that I don't have a relationship with," I answer immediately. Unlike him, I have actually spent a lot of time thinking all of this through in the past few days. I have prepared my words and the points I want to make, and finally, I can express myself. "I don't want to keep going on like this, arguing and fighting every single time we so much as walk into the same room as each other. I *want* to have a relationship with you, but I can't if you're going to treat me the way you do. I'm your *daughter*. You're supposed to support me, not tear me down and criticize my decisions even if they're stupid ones. You're supposed to be on my side, not against me."

"Eden," he starts.

"No," I cut in, my voice firm. "*Listen* to me. This family is a mess, and you know it. We all do, and you're so persistent on placing the blame on Tyler and me, but the truth, Dad? The truth is that we're not the problem at all. You are. *You* caused this. This is *your* mess. Your anger is tearing us all apart when you have nothing to even be angry about. We were honest with you and Ella, and do you have any idea how terrifying that was to have to come in here and tell you both that secret? Because it was the hardest thing I've done in my entire life, and you threw it back in our faces by reacting the way you did. We never expected you to agree with what we were doing, but we did want you to accept it. Maybe not at first, but eventually, yet you never have. *Why* have you been so against us? Why is there so much hatred for us? Where is that coming from?" I'm out of breath by the time I stop, my words tumbling from my lips in one huge rush. My pulse is racing because I desperately need answers. Finding out the truth from Dad is the only way we are going to be able to make progress, to move on from this.

"Alright," he says, sitting forward. "Forget the fact that you're stepsiblings. I can live with that, but what I can't live with is my daughter being involved with someone who's so unstable. I liked Dean. He was a nice kid. He treated you good. But Tyler?" He shakes his head, almost in disgust. "Tyler is just a kid who's only good at avoiding all of his problems."

"The same way you're only good at avoiding all of yours, right?" I shoot back at him, growing defensive. "Like the way you avoided Mom because you didn't just want to *try* and fix things with her? Like the way you've avoided me because it's easier to hate me than to accept me?" Now I'm becoming exasperated, and I straighten and throw my hands up. "How many times do you want me to tell you that Tyler is not the same person he was when he was seventeen? I couldn't stand him when I first met him. I hated everything he was doing. So trust me when I say that if he was seriously still like that, I wouldn't be in love with him."

"Huh," Dad says after a moment. "So now you're in love with him again, even though you've told me repeatedly that you aren't."

"Because I wasn't," I tell him, and there's a weight in my chest that seems to grow heavier. "He left me, Dad. He just walked out and never came back. You *know* how angry I was, but I've…I've heard everything Tyler has to say, and leaving really was the best thing for him. I can't continue to be mad at him for it, and I forgive him." I pause because I know there's still something more I need to tell Dad, and now feels like the right time to say it. "I don't know if Ella has already told you," I mumble, fiddling with my hands, unable to meet Dad's glare, "but Tyler and I are together now. We're a couple, and I'm moving to Portland. I'm transferring to Portland State. My decision is made."

"Well," Dad says with an air of sarcasm, "isn't that just great?"

"It *is* great," I answer, "because I'm happy, and shouldn't that be what you want for me? Happy and content and living my life the way I want to live it?"

"I do want you to be happy," Dad admits, his voice softer and quieter. "I just don't think you can be happy with Tyler."

"How would you know that, Dad? Only I can know what makes me happy, and that's Tyler."

I take a deep breath as I gather my thoughts, pulling out another chair and sitting down too, directly in front of Dad. The tension in the air seems to have dispersed, and I think remaining calm is definitely the best approach I could have taken. There is no room for anger here. Only honesty.

"Please just hear what I'm saying," I say gently. I look back at Dad with pleading, sad eyes, begging for him to actually absorb the words I'm saying. "Tyler has changed, okay? People do that sometimes. They change for the better. And Tyler…he's off the drugs for good. There's no anger in him. His temper is under control. He's happier and more easygoing. He's caring and he's thoughtful. He has his own place. He has a job. He runs a damn youth center voluntarily. He's even been to therapy and been in contact with his dad, which is actually what he's telling Ella right now." I can see Dad's eyes widening as I tell him this information because I know it doesn't sound anything like the Tyler he knows. "And, Dad," I say, "he cares about me. He really does. He would never do anything to hurt me."

"A youth center?" Dad repeats.

"Yes, and it's amazing. He's trying to help other teenagers who might be going through the same shit he was," I explain, and I find myself smiling as I talk about it because I'm still so proud of him. "Now don't try and tell me that he's just some guy who doesn't know what the hell he's doing, because he does, and he's completely turned his life around."

Dad falls very silent and very still. He looks all around the kitchen, his eyes flickering everywhere but me. "If this is true..." he eventually says, "then the guy can have a chance."

Progress, I'm thinking, but that's all this is. Just progress. Tyler may be getting a second chance from Dad, but that doesn't mean that I am. Our relationship is still nonexistent, and until we find out why *we* can't seem to get along, none of this matters. Having Dad tolerate Tyler from now on will help, but it's still not enough.

"Why didn't you seem to like me even before you found out about Tyler and me? I know we were trying, and things were slowly getting better, but I still felt like you didn't want to have me as your daughter. Like you'd be happier if I wasn't around. I *still* feel that way. How come you're a great dad to Jamie and Chase but not to me?" My voice is growing more brittle with each word that leaves my mouth, because now that I'm actually saying it aloud to him, it's starting to hurt a lot more than I originally thought it would. "Do you *want* to hate me?"

Dad releases another sigh as though each time he does, he's

letting go of more of his anger. The fire in his eyes has burned out. Instead, remarkably, he's listening to the way he has made me feel, his expression ridden with guilt. "I don't hate you. I don't want you to think that."

"Then what is this, Dad?" I ask, but I think I'm going to cry at any moment. I didn't expect Dad to actually hear me out today, but now that he's reacting to what I'm telling him, I'm realizing how long overdue this is. We should have done this a long time ago, because things can never be fixed unless words are exchanged. "Because it's certainly not love."

"I don't know," Dad says, tilting his head down, facing the floor. He seems ashamed, like he *knows* he's been treating me wrong and is now having to face up to his mistakes.

"Tell me why," I order, although my voice isn't as sharp as I'd like it to be. I'm starting to sound weak. "Just tell me why, Dad. Just give me a damn reason why you have always been so hostile with me."

"Because you took your mom's side, alright, Eden?" he snaps, firing straight out of his chair and onto his feet, exploding under the pressure. He's breathing heavily as his cheeks grow red, and he squeezes his eyes shut and pinches the bridge of his nose between his thumb and forefinger.

I blink at him, confused. "What?"

"With your mom and me," Dad says slowly, opening his eyes, "you took her side. You made me the bad guy even though I was a good father to you. Your mom and I...we fought because we were incompatible with different views and different opinions on just about everything. We didn't fight because I was a jackass, and I know she made it sound like that, but it wasn't fair for me to get the blame when neither of us was at fault. And I know you were only young, but every single time there was an argument, you would sit with your mom and glare at me when it hadn't even been me who'd started the fight in the first place. I was going through hell too, Eden. Not just your mom."

Having Dad finally open up and hearing him give me a damn explanation for once is enough to make me speechless. I never knew he felt that way. I never knew *I* made him feel that way. I have always grown up believing that Dad is the reason behind the divorce, even though I've always known it was down to the simple fact that Mom and Dad just didn't click anymore. It was always easier to just blame Dad for it.

"I know I left without saying good-bye," he continues, pacing in front of me. "I know I fucked up on that part, but I left because I knew all of the fighting wasn't good for you. I left for you, Eden, because you deserved more than two parents who were constantly at each other's throats."

"But," I choke, getting to my feet despite the fact that my legs feel numb. "But you never called."

"Because I thought you wouldn't want me to call," he admits. "That's why I left you both alone, and if you're so desperate to know why it's hard for me to cope with you, it's because I know you *still* think the divorce is my fault."

I don't say sorry, but I'm crying. The tears have escaped, rolling down my cheeks as the past few minutes overwhelm me entirely. *Even more progress.* Maybe, just maybe, we will eventually have a real relationship one day. Not now, not yet. It's going to take a long time to rebuild our trust and forgiveness, but this is a start. Uncovering the truth is only the beginning. Now the hard work starts.

"Don't," Dad says, stepping toward me. He looks as though he wants to wipe away my tears, but he also doesn't want to touch me, so he quickly steps back and rubs anxiously at the back of his neck. "Look, I...I know I've made mistakes. And I know you have too. We both have. We all do. And I don't want to fight with you, Eden. I really don't. But I'm going to need some time to take all of this in, and I'm willing to make an effort if you are because you're right. I'm putting a strain on this entire family."

"Especially on you and Ella," I murmur, dabbing at my eyes. I fan my face and exhale, and then, because I'm being entirely honest with him, I add, "She's beginning to look at you the same way Mom did right before the divorce. Please don't ruin this."

"I know," Dad says, frowning. He runs a hand back through his graying hair, glancing at the clock on the wall. "I'm not going to hug you or anything," he mumbles, "because I'm still pissed at you for running off last week. Waking up to discover that your daughter has run off in the night with a former troublemaker isn't exactly what I wanted to hear." So instead of hugging, we decide to shake hands under the agreement that we are going to try harder from now on.

Just as I'm dropping my hand from Dad's, I hear footsteps on the staircase. It's Ella, with Tyler and Jamie close behind. They spot us in the kitchen and make their way to join us.

As soon as Ella enters the room, I know she's been crying. Her eyes are red and swollen, and her makeup is smeared. She doesn't try to hide it, only sniffs and throws me a questioning glance. I know what she's trying to ask. She wants to know if Dad and I have made any progress. And I give her a small nod that says, *I've done it.*

Tyler follows behind her, slightly pale. He has his hands in his pockets, his bottom lip between his teeth, his eyes finding mine. We exchange smiles of relief and satisfaction, of pride and joy. It feels as though we have climbed a mountain to get to this point.

Behind Tyler, Jamie's eyes are devoid of any emotion. His face is blank, and he hovers by the archway into the kitchen, staring straight ahead. I'm not sure how he feels right now, but I can imagine the news that Tyler is talking with their father again has hit him hard.

Dad clears his throat and takes a step toward Tyler. "Congratulations," he says, and Tyler raises an eyebrow suspiciously, perplexed as to what Dad is even talking about. "On the youth center," he explains.

"Oh," Tyler answers. "Thanks." He extends his arm and finally, *finally*, the two of them shake hands, their grips firm. It's such a significant step, and Ella looks so relieved and thrilled that I think she might just faint.

Chase must hear all of the commotion in the kitchen because he creeps through from the living room and falls into place by the door alongside Jamie. His eyes are curious as he glances at us, trying to gauge whether or not the atmosphere is toxic. It's not. Only hopeful.

"We should get going," Tyler says, glancing at me as he holds up his car keys. Ella sniffs, and Chase starts to complain that we only *just* got back. Neither Jamie nor Dad say anything, mostly because I think they don't mind that Tyler and I are leaving.

"We should come and visit sometime," Ella suggests. With eyes brimming with hope, she looks to Dad. "David?"

Dad studies Tyler and me, and I know it's way too soon for him and Ella and the boys to be making trips to Portland to visit us, but he contemplates it nonetheless. All he says is, "Maybe in the future." And then he gives me a tight-lipped smile that says a thousand words before he turns for the patio doors and heads outside. This is hard for him, but I appreciate the fact that he has listened to me. I don't think he can deal with anything more today, so he has removed himself from the situation.

"I hope Portland is good to you both," Ella tells us, and although she is smiling, she is also tearing up again. She pulls Tyler into a hug first, and it's a long, tight one as she presses a kiss to his cheek. Then she comes to me, wrapping her arms around my body and squeezing me tight.

"Thank you," I murmur against her shoulder, "for everything." When she steps back, she only nods. Ella has supported us this entire time, and I will forever be grateful for that. She means a lot to me.

I turn to Jamie, but he's refusing to look at Tyler and me. Tyler does place a hand on his shoulder and squeezes it firmly, but I think it's going to take a long time for Jamie to accept our relationship. But if Dad can come around, then anyone can. I have a strong belief that eventually, whether it's three months or three years from now, he will stop being so against us.

Chase hugs us both though, because he's Chase, and Chase likes everyone no matter what they say or do. "Doesn't Portland suck though?" he asks me, cocking his head to one side and eyeballing me suspiciously with those blue eyes of his.

"No," I say, smiling. "I was just lying."

Tyler laughs as his hand slips into mine, and as we head through the hall toward the front door, Ella and Chase both follow. Jamie doesn't. Like Dad, I think he's had enough for the day. Some people need more time than others when it comes to accepting certain information.

"Please remember to call every once in a while," Ella reminds us, tears streaming down her face. Whenever Tyler has to leave this city, she gets emotional. Their bond is precious. "Or every day. I won't mind."

Tyler gives her one more final hug, and then we make our move, stepping through the front door of the house that was once both our home but is no longer. Portland is our new home, our new adventure, our new risk.

With it being Sunday, the street feels quiet and lazy as the early afternoon heat beats down over the neighborhood. Tyler is grinning at me as we head over the lawn, his green eyes smoldering at me, our fingers laced and our hands swinging between us.

"How was it?" he asks me, but all I can think about is how happy he seems.

"Good," I tell him. "I think we're finally getting somewhere. How about with you?"

Although he shrugs, he's still smiling, almost like he's satisfied and proud of himself to be getting everything off his chest. No more secrets now. "It's going to take some time before Mom accepts it all," he says, "but it went as good as it could have."

"And Jamie?"

"He just doesn't get it," Tyler says with a sigh, "but eventually, he'll understand that people deserve second chances. Like Dad, and me, and us."

I grin at him, so proud of everything he has achieved this past year and so proud of the person he has become. I'm proud to stand next to him, right by his side, knowing that he's finally mine and that I can show him off to the world. It's all I've ever wanted, and I lean in closer to him, squeezing our hands tighter.

Out of the corner of my eye, I spot Rachael's car parked in her drive-way across the street. I know I can't leave without saying good-bye to her. I tell Tyler to wait for me, and then I let go of his hand and run across the street, straight to her front door, ringing the doorbell over and over again. We're in no rush, but there's so much energy flowing through my veins that I just can't stop myself. Luckily, Rachael answers the door rather than her parents, and before she even has the chance to say anything, I'm already throwing myself into her arms.

I hug her tight, and when I pull back from her, she's giving me one of those sad smiles that I hate so much. "So you're really leaving, huh?" she asks, pouting.

I nod. "I'll be back again at the end of the summer but for just now, yes."

"Then you better hurry," she says, smirking, "because Prince Charming is waiting for you."

I follow her gaze over my shoulder to Tyler. He's watching us with a smile toying at his lips and with his arms folded over his chest as he leans back against his car, waiting patiently for me, ready to leave Santa Monica and head off on our road trip back to Portland. He looks so, so gorgeous. It's so effortless.

I'm blushing by the time I tear my eyes away from him and back to Rachael. "Good luck with Snake," I tell her.

"Good luck with your stepbrother," she replies, and we can do nothing but laugh, which is something I will never take for granted. How funny it is that the fact that Tyler and I are stepsiblings doesn't even matter anymore, that it's now just a casual remark used to crack a joke. I never thought that one day I'd be able to laugh about it, but here I am, and I think that reflects just how far we have come.

Blowing Rachael a kiss, I turn around and set my eyes on Tyler, and a glorious smile spreads across my face just from looking at him. I have so much love for him. I sprint across Rachael's lawn and onto the road, running to the person that always has and always will own my heart.

When I reach him, my lips are against his within a heartbeat, and there is just so much passion as his mouth moves in sync against mine that every single fiber of my being is on fire. There're shivers running down my spine, goose bumps on my arms, tingling sensations in my hands. I'm smiling against his lips because my happiness in that moment is so overwhelming that I just can't control it anymore, and when my eyes flutter open to look at him, his emerald eyes are sparkling back. In the background, I notice Ella covering Chase's eyes, but she's grinning. I can hear Rachael wolf-whistling from across the street.

When I shift my gaze back to Tyler, I cup his face in my hands, biting down on my lower lip. "Look down," I whisper.

Slowly, he drops his eyes to the ground, and I tilt my foot onto its side so that he can see exactly which pair of Chucks I'm now wearing.

His handwriting from last summer is facing us, and when he meets my eyes again, his expression is radiant.

After all these years, after all of the hurdles we have had to overcome, we are finally happy. Things aren't perfect. We're still figuring everything out, still fixing our mistakes and making our changes, but the main thing is that we are trying. We have grown and we have learned, but most importantly, we have finally accepted ourselves.

Finally, I think. *Just finally.*

Acknowledgments

As always, thank you to my readers from the very beginning, who have followed this story with dedication and love. I couldn't have done this without you, and for that, I am forever grateful. Thank you to my family, especially my parents, Fenella and Stuart, for their patience and support over the past five years while I've worked on this trilogy. Thank you to my best friends for keeping me sane. Thank you to my editors, Karyn, Kristen, and Janne, for their expertise and guidance and for their enthusiasm and care for Tyler and Eden's story. Thank you to everyone at Black & White Publishing for all of the hard work each of you put into this trilogy. I think you're all amazing, and thank you for making me feel so at home in the office in the final few weeks of writing this book. I couldn't have asked for a better group of people to work with, and I'm so, so proud to be one of your authors. You made my dream come true. Thank you.

READ THEM ALL!

DID I MENTION I LOVE YOU?

One forbidden kiss
was all it took.

DID I MENTION I NEED YOU?

What if your love
broke all the rules?

About the Author

Estelle Maskame started writing at the age of thirteen and completed the *Did I Mention I Love You?* trilogy when she was sixteen. She has built an extensive fan base for her writing by serializing her work on Wattpad. Fitting book writing between her schoolwork and part-time job, Estelle has amassed followers from all over the world. She lives in Scotland. For more, visit estellemaskame.com.